'It's a noir thriller in the best tradition of noir writing . . . a cracking good read. It's creepy and atmospheric, richly evocative of 1950s Dublin . . . The story is involving and intriguing . . . we might well see this series shortlisted for the most prestigious of prizes. You know the one. He's already got it once'

Northern Ireland Newsletter

'Scrupulously researched and carefully characterised . . . the prose is beautiful' *Literary Review*

'John Banville is not the first writer of literary novels to adopt a pseudonym to produce crime fiction, but he is certainly one of the more distinguished . . . The creeping sense of menace, corruption and existential despair is pure Banville and gives this tale of sexual obsession and betrayal its edge' *The Times*

'The novel is absorbing, atmospheric and moving, with all the characters, from major to minor, superbly drawn, and the writing is just lovely. More please' *Guardian*

'At its heart, this is a novel about sex, desire and lust for success. These are potent themes . . . Banville lushly evokes a tangle of sexual awakening, amateur pornography and deceit. It's a giddy combination, made dangerously toxic when mixed with drugs, embezzlement and extortion . . . The writing is of a standard rare in the genre, and the mood as rich and redolent as the oiled depths of an old master' *Herald*

'Even more skilful than its predecessor, *Christine Falls* . . . a dark and brooding mystery' *Good Book Guide*

THE SILVER SWAN

Benjamin Black

THE SILVER SWAN

A Quirke Dublin Mystery

PICADOR

First published 2007 by Picador

First published in paperback 2007 by Picador

This edition published 2011 by Picador
an imprint of Pan Macmillan, a division of Macmillan Publishers Limited
Pan Macmillan, 20 New Wharf Road, London N1 9RR
Basingstoke and Oxford
Associated companies throughout the world
www.panmacmillan.com

ISBN 978-1-447-26400-2

1 3 5 7 9 8 6 4 2

A CIP catalogue record for this book is available from
the British Library.

Typeset by SetSystems Ltd, Saffron Walden, Essex
Printed in the UK by CPI Group (UK) Ltd, Croydon, CR0 4YY

I

1

QUIRKE DID NOT recognise the name. It seemed familiar but he could not put a face to it. Occasionally it happened that way: someone would float up without warning out of his past, his drinking past, someone he had forgotten, asking for a loan or offering to let him in on a sure thing or just wanting to make contact, out of loneliness, or only to know that he was still alive and that the drink had not done for him. Mostly he put them off, mumbling about pressure of work and the like. This one should have been easy, since it was just a name and a telephone number left with the hospital receptionist, and he could have conveniently lost the piece of paper or simply thrown it away. Something caught his attention, however. He had an impression of urgency, of unease, which he could not account for and which troubled him.

Billy Hunt.

What was it the name sparked in him? Was it a lost memory or, more worryingly, a premonition?

He put the scrap of paper on a corner of his desk and tried to ignore it. At the dead centre of summer the day was hot and muggy, and in the streets the barely breathable air was laden with a thin pall of mauve smoke, and he was glad of the cool and quiet of his windowless basement office in the Pathology Department. He hung his suit jacket on the back of his chair and pulled off his tie without undoing the knot and opened two buttons of his shirt and sat down at the cluttered metal desk. He liked the familiar smell here, a combination of old cigarette smoke, tea leaves, paper, formaldehyde, and something else, musky, fleshly, that was his particular contribution.

He lit a cigarette and his eye drifted again to the paper with Billy Hunt's message on it. Just the name and the number that the operator had scribbled down in pencil, and the words 'Please call'. The sense of urgent imploring was stronger than ever. *Please call.*

For no reason he could think of he found himself remembering the moment in McGonagle's pub half a year ago when, dizzily drunk amid the din of Christmas revelling, he had caught sight of his own face, flushed and bulbous and bleary, reflected in the bottom of his empty whiskey glass and had realised with unaccountable certitude that he had just taken his last drink. Since then he had been sober. He was as amazed by this as was anyone who knew him. He felt that it was not he who had made the decision, but that somehow it had been made for him. Despite all his training and his years in the dissecting room he had a secret conviction that the body has a conscious-ness of its own, and knows itself and its needs as well as or better than the mind imagines it does. The decree deliv-ered to him that night by his gut and his swollen liver and the ventricles of his heart was absolute and incontestable. For nearly two years he had been falling steadily into the abyss of drink, falling almost as far as he had in the time, two decades before, after his wife had died, and now the fall was broken.

Squinting at the scrap of paper on the corner of the desk, he lifted the telephone receiver and dialled. The bell jangled afar down the line.

Afterwards, out of curiosity, he had upended another whiskey glass, this time one he had not emptied, to find if it was really possible to see himself in the bottom of it, but no reflection had appeared there.

The sound of Billy Hunt's voice was no help; he did not recognise it any more readily than he had the name. The accent was at once flat and singsong, with broad vowels and dulled consonants. A countryman. There was a slight flutter in the tone, a slight wobble, as if the speaker might be about to burst into laughter, or into something else. Some words he slurred, hurrying over them. Maybe he was tipsy?

'Ah, you don't remember me,' he said. 'Do you?'

'Of course I do,' Quirke lied.

'Billy Hunt. You used to say it sounded like rhyming slang. We were in college together. I was in first year when you were in your last. I didn't really expect you to remember me. We went with different crowds. I was mad into the sports—hurling, football, all that—while you were with the arty lot, with your nose stuck in a book or over at the Abbey or the Gate every night of the week. I dropped out of the medicine—didn't have the stomach for it.'

Quirke let a beat of silence pass, then asked: 'What are you doing now?'

Billy Hunt gave a heavy, unsteady sigh. 'Never mind that,' he said, sounding more weary than impatient. 'It's *your* job that's the point here.'

At last a face began to assemble itself in Quirke's labouring memory. Big broad forehead, definitively broken nose, a thatch of wiry red hair, freckles. Grocer's son from somewhere down south, Wicklow, Wexford, Waterford, one of the W counties. Easy-going but prone to scrap when provoked, hence the smashed septum. Billy Hunt. Yes.

'My job?' Quirke said. 'How's that?'

There was another pause.

'It's the wife,' Billy Hunt said. Quirke heard a sharply indrawn breath whistling in those crushed nasal cavities. 'She's after doing away with herself.'

They met in Bewley's Café in Grafton Street. It was lunchtime and the place was busy. The rich, fat smell of coffee beans roasting in the big vat just inside the door made Quirke's stomach briefly heave. Odd, the things he found nauseating now; he had expected giving up drink would dull his senses and reconcile him to the world and its savours, but the opposite had been the case, so that at times he seemed to be a walking tangle of nerve-ends assailed from every side by outrageous smells, tastes, touches. The interior of the café was dark to his eyes after the glare outside. A girl going out passed him by; she wore a white dress and carried a broad-brimmed straw hat; he caught the warm waft of her perfumed skin that trailed behind her. He imagined himself turning on his heel and following after her and taking her by the elbow and walking with her out into the heat of the summer day. He did not relish the prospect of Billy Hunt and his dead wife.

He spotted him straight away, sitting in one of the side

booths, unnaturally erect on the red plush banquette, with a cup of milky coffee untouched before him on the grey marble table. He did not see Quirke at first, and Quirke hung back a moment, studying him, the drained pale face with the freckles standing out on it, the glazed, desolate stare, the big turnip-shaped hand fiddling with the sugar spoon. He had changed remarkably little in the more than two decades since Quirke had known him. Not that he could say he had known him, really. In Quirke's not very clear recollections of him Billy was a sort of overgrown schoolboy, by turns cheery or truculent and sometimes both at once, loping out to the sports grounds in wide-legged knicks and a striped football jersey, with a football or a bundle of hurley sticks under his arm, his knobbly, pale-pink knees bare and his boyish cheeks aflame and blood-spotted from the still unaccustomed morning shave. Loud, of course, roaring raucous jokes at his fellow sportsmen and throwing a surly glance from under colourless lashes in the direction of Quirke and *the arty lot*. Now he was thickened by the years, with a bald patch on the crown of his head, like a tonsure, and a fat red neck overflowing the collar of his baggy tweed jacket.

He had that smell, hot and raw and salty, that Quirke recognised at once, the smell of the recently bereaved. He sat there at the table, propping himself upright, a bulging sack of grief and misery and pent-up rage, and said to Quirke helplessly:

'I don't know why she did it.'

Quirke nodded. 'Did she leave anything?' Billy peered at him, uncomprehending. 'A letter, I mean. A note.'

'No, no, nothing like that.' He gave a crooked, almost sheepish, smile. 'I wish she had.'

That morning a party of Gardai had gone out in a launch and lifted poor Deirdre Hunt's naked body off the rocks on the landward shore of Dalkey Island.

'They called me in to identify her,' Billy said, that strange, pained smile that was not a smile still on his lips, his eyes seeming to gaze again in wild dismay at what they had seen on the hospital slab, Quirke grimly thought, and would probably never stop seeing, for as long as he lived. 'They brought her to St Vincent's. She looked completely different. I think I wouldn't have known her except for the hair. She was very proud of it, her hair.' He shrugged apologetically, twitching one shoulder.

Quirke was recalling a very fat woman who had thrown herself into the Liffey, from whose chest cavity, when he had cut it open and was clipping away at the rib-cage, there had clambered forth, with the torpor of the truly well-fed, a nest of translucent, many-legged, shrimp-like creatures.

A waitress in her black-and-white uniform and maid's mob-cap came to take Quirke's order. The aroma of fried and boiled lunches assailed him. He asked for tea. Billy Hunt had drifted away into himself and was delving absently with his spoon among the cubes in the sugar bowl, making them rattle.

'It's hard,' Quirke said, when the waitress had gone. 'Identifying the body, I mean. That's always hard.'

Billy looked down, and his lower lip began to tremble and he clamped it babyishly between his teeth.

'Have you children, Billy?' Quirke asked.

Billy, still looking down, shook his head. 'No,' he muttered, 'no children. Deirdre wasn't keen.'

'And what do you do? I mean, what do you work at?'

'Commercial traveller. Pharmaceuticals. The job takes me away a lot, around the country, abroad, too, the odd occasion, to Switzerland, when there's to be a meeting at head office. I suppose that was part of the trouble, me being away so much—that, and her not wanting kids.' Here it comes, Quirke thought, *the trouble*. But Billy only said, 'I suppose she was lonely. She never complained, though.' He looked up at Quirke suddenly and as if challengingly. 'She never complained—never!'

He went on talking about her then, what she was like, what she did. The haunted look in his face grew more intense, and his eyes darted this way and that with an odd, hindered urgency, as if he wanted them to light on something that kept on not being there. The waitress brought Quirke's tea. He drank it black, scalding his tongue. He produced his cigarette case. 'So tell me,' he said, 'what was it you wanted to see me about?'

Once more Billy lowered those pale lashes and gazed at the sugar bowl. A mottled tide of colour swelled upwards from his collar and slowly suffused his face to the hairline and beyond; he was, Quirke realised, blushing. He nodded mutely, sucking in a deep breath.

'I wanted to ask you a favour.'

Quirke waited. The room was steadily filling with the lunchtime crowd and the noise had risen to a medleyed roar. Waitresses skimmed among the tables bearing brown trays piled with plates of food—sausage and mash, fish and chips, steaming mugs of tea and glasses of orange crush. Quirke offered the cigarette case open on his palm, and Billy took a cigarette, seeming hardly to notice what he was doing. Quirke's lighter clicked and flared. Billy hunched forward holding the cigarette between his lips with fingers that shook. Then he leaned back on the banquette as if exhausted.

'I'm reading about you all the time in the papers,' he said. 'About cases you're involved in.' Quirke shifted uneasily on his chair. 'That thing with the girl that died and the woman that was murdered—what were their names?'

'Which ones?' Quirke asked, expressionless.

'The woman in Stoney Batter. Last year, or the year before, was it? Dolly somebody.' He frowned, trying to remember. 'What happened to that story? It was all over the papers and then it was gone, not another word.'

'The papers don't take long to lose interest,' Quirke said.

A thought struck Billy. 'Jesus,' he said softly, staring away, 'I suppose they'll put a story in about Deirdre, too.'

'I could have a word with the coroner,' Quirke said, making it sound doubtful.

But it was not stories in the newspapers that was on Billy's mind. He leaned forward again, suddenly intent, and reached out a hand urgently as if he might grasp Quirke by the wrist or the lapel. 'I don't want her cut up,' he said, in a hoarse undertone.

'Cut up?'

'An autopsy, a post-mortem, whatever you call it—I don't want that done.'

Quirke waited a moment and then said: 'It's a formality, Billy. The law requires it.'

Billy was shaking his head with his eyes shut and his mouth set in a pained grimace. 'I don't want it done. I don't want her sliced up like some sort of a, like a—like some sort of carcass.' He put a hand over his eyes. The cigarette, forgotten, was burning itself out in the fingers of his other hand. 'I can't bear to think of it. Seeing her this morning was bad enough'—he took his hand away and gazed before him in what seemed a stupor of amazement—'but the thought of her on a table, under the lights, with the knife . . . If you'd known her, the way she was, before, how—how alive she was.' He cast about again as if in search of something on which to concentrate, a bullet of commonplace reality on which he might bite. 'I can't bear it, Quirke,' he said hoarsely, his voice hardly more than a whisper. 'I swear to God, I can't bear it.'

Quirke sipped his by now tepid tea, the tannin acrid against his scalded tongue. He did not know what he should say. He rarely came in direct contact with the relatives of the dead, but occasionally they sought him out, as Billy had, to request a favour. Some only wanted him to save them a keepsake, a wedding ring, or a lock of hair; there was a Republican widow once who had asked him to retrieve a fragment of a Civil War bullet that her late husband had carried next to his heart for thirty years. Others had more serious and far shadier requests—that the bruises on a dead infant's body be plausibly accounted for, that the sudden demise of an aged, sick parent be explained away, or just that a suicide might be covered up. But no one had ever asked what Billy was asking.

'All right, Billy,' he said. 'I'll see what I can do.'

Now Billy's hand did touch his, the barest touch, with the tips of fingers through which a strong, fizzing current seemed to race. 'You won't let me down, Quirke,' he said, a statement rather than an entreaty, his voice quavering. 'For old times' sake. For'—he made a low sound that was half sob half laugh—'for Deirdre's sake.'

Quirke stood up. He fished a half-crown from his pocket and laid it on the table beside his saucer. Billy was looking about again, distractedly, as a man would while patting his pockets in search of something he had misplaced. He had taken out a Zippo lighter and was distractedly flicking the lid open and shut. On the bald spot and through the strands of his scant pale hair could be seen glistening beads of sweat. 'That's not her name, by the way,' he said. Quirke did not understand. 'I mean, it is her name, only she called herself something else. Laura—Laura Swan. It was sort of her professional name. She ran a beauty parlour, the Silver Swan. That's where she got the name—Laura Swan.'

Quirke waited, but Billy had nothing more to say, and he turned and walked away.

In the afternoon, on Quirke's instructions, they brought the body from St Vincent's to the city-centre Hospital of the Holy Family, where Quirke was waiting to receive it. A recent round of imposed economies at the Holy Family, hotly contested but in vain, had left Quirke with one assistant only where before there had been two. His had been the task of choosing between young Wilkins the horse-Protestant and the Jew Sinclair. He had plumped for Sinclair, without any clear reason, for the two young men were equally matched in skill or, in some areas, lack of it. But he liked Sinclair, liked his independence and sly humour and the faint surliness of his manner; when Quirke had asked him once where his people hailed from Sinclair had looked him in the eye without expression and said blankly, 'Cork.' He had offered not a word of thanks to Quirke for choosing him, and Quirke admired that, too.

He wondered how far he should take Sinclair into his confidence in the matter of Deirdre Hunt and her husband's plea that her corpse should be left intact. Sinclair, however, was not a man to make trouble. When Quirke said he would do the post-mortem alone—a visual examination would suffice—and that Sinclair might as well take himself off to the canteen for a cup of tea and a cigarette, the young man hesitated for no more than a second, and removed his green gown and rubber boots and sauntered out of the morgue with his hands in his pockets, whistling softly. Quirke turned back and lifted the plastic sheet.

Deirdre Hunt or Laura Swan, or whatever name she went under, must have been, he judged, a good-looking young woman, perhaps even a beautiful one. She was—had been—quite a lot younger than Billy Hunt. Her body, which had not been in the water long enough for serious deterioration to have taken place, was short and shapely; a strong body, strongly muscled, but delicate in its curves and the sheer planes at flank and calf. Her face was not as fine-boned as it might have been—her maiden name, Quirke noted, had been Ward, suggesting tinker blood—but her forehead was clear and high, and the swathe of copper-coloured hair falling back from it must have been magnificent when she was alive. He had a picture in his mind of her sprawled on the wet rocks, a long swatch of that hair coiled round her neck like a thick frond of gleaming seaweed. What, he wondered, had driven this handsome, healthy young woman to fling herself on a summer midnight off Sandycove harbour into the black waters of Dublin Bay, with no witness to the deed save the glittering stars and the louring bulk of the Martello tower above her? Her clothes, so Billy Hunt had said, had been placed in a neat pile on the pier beside the wall; that was the only trace she had left of her going—that, and her motor-car, which Quirke was certain was another thing she would have been proud of, and which yet she had abandoned, neatly parked under a lilac tree on Sandycove Avenue. Her car and her hair: twin sources of vanity. But what was it that had pulled that vanity down?

Then he spotted the tiny puncture mark on the chalk-white inner side of her left arm.

2

AT SCHOOL THEY used to call her Carrots, of course. She did not mind; she knew they were just jealous, the lot of them, except the ones that were too stupid to be jealous and on that account not worth bothering about. Her hair was not really red, not rusty-red like that of some other girls in school—especially the ones whose parents were originally from the country and not genuine Dubliners like hers were—but a shining reddish-gold, like a million strands of soft, supple metal, catching the light from all angles and glowing even in the half-dark. She could not think where it had come from, certainly not direct from either of her parents, and she took no notice when she overheard her Auntie Irene saying something one day about 'tinker hair' and giving that nasty laugh of hers. From the start her mother would not let her hair be cut, even though she always said she took after her Da's side of the family, the fair-haired and blue-eyed Wards, and Ma had no time for 'that crowd', as she always called them, when Da was not around to hear her. To amuse themselves her brothers pulled her hair, grabbing long, thick ropes of it and wrapping them around their fists and yanking on them to make her squeal. That was preferable, though, to the way her father would smooth his hand down the length of it, pressing his fingers through it and caressing the bones of her back. She wore emerald-green for preference, knowing even as a child that this was the shade that best suited her colouring and set it off. Red hair like that and brilliant blue eyes, or a bluey sort of violet, more like, that was unusual, certainly, even among the Wards. Everyone admired her skin, too: it was translucent, like that stone, alabaster she thought it was called, so you felt you could see down into it, into its creamy depths.

Though she was perfectly well aware how lovely she was she had never been standoffish. She knew, of course, that she was too good for the Flats, and had only bided her time there until she could get out and start her real life. The Flats . . . They must have been new, once, but she could not imagine it. What joker in the city Corporation had thought to give them the name of Mansions? The walls and floors were thin as cardboard—you could hear the people upstairs and even next door going to the lavatory—and there were always prams and broken-down bicycles in the bare hallways, where the little kids ran around like wild things and stray cats roamed and courting couples fumbled at each other in dark corners. There were no controls of any kind—who would have enforced them, even if there had been?—and the tenants did anything they wanted. The Goggins on the fourth floor kept a horse in their living room, a big piebald thing; at night and in the early morning its hoofs could be heard on the cement stairs when Tommy Goggin and his snot-nosed sisters led the brute down to do its business and ride it around on the bit of waste ground behind the biscuit factory. Worst of all, though, worse even than the cold in the low rooms and the plumbing that was always breaking down and the dirt everywhere, was the smell that hung on the stairs and in the corridors, summer and winter, the brownish, tired, hopeless stink of peed-on mattresses and stewed tea and blocked-up lavatories—the smell, the very smell, of what it was to be poor, which she never got used to, never.

She played with the other children of her own age in the gritted square in front of the Flats, where there were broken swings and a seesaw with filthy things written all over it and a wire-mesh fence that was supposed to keep their ball from flying out on to the road. The boys pinched her and pulled at her, and the older ones tried to feel under her skirt, while the girls talked about her behind her back and ganged up against her. She did not care about any of this. Her father came home half-cut one Christmas with a present for her of a red bike—probably robbed, her brother Mikey said with a laugh—and she rode around the playground on it all day long for a week, even in the rain, until at New Year's someone stole it and she never saw it again. In a rage because of losing the bike she got into a fight with Tommy Goggin and knocked out one of his front teeth. 'Oh, she's a Tartar, that one', her Auntie Irene said, with her arms folded across her big sagging bosom and nodding grimly. There were moments, though, on summer evenings, when she would stand at the open window in the parlour, so-called—in fact it was the only room in the flat, apart from two stuffy little bedrooms, one of which she had to share with her parents—savouring the lovely warm smell from the biscuit factory and listening to a blackbird singing its heart out on a wire that was as black as the bird itself and seemed drawn in ink with a fine nib against the red glow dying slowly in the sky beyond the Gaelic football park, and something would swell in her, something secret and mysterious that seemed to contain all of the rich, vague promise of the future.

When she was sixteen she went to work in a chemist's shop. She liked it there among the neatly packaged medicines and bottles of scent and fancy soaps. The chemist, Mr Plunkett, was a married man, but still he tried to persuade her to go with him. She refused, of course, but sometimes, to get him to let her alone for a while and because she thought he might give her the sack if she did not co-operate, she would trail unwillingly behind him into the room at the back where the drugs were kept, and he would lock the door and she would let him put his hands under her clothes. He was old, forty or maybe even more, and his breath smelled of cigarettes and bad teeth, but he was not the worst, she reflected, gazing dreamily over his shoulder at the stacked shelves as he palmed and kneaded her belly under the waistband of her skirt and pressed his thumb to the stubbornly unresponsive tips of her breasts. Afterwards she would catch Mrs Plunkett, who did the books, studying her out of a narrowed, speculative eye. If old Plunkett should ever think of trying to get rid of her she would waste no time in letting him know that she had a thing or two she could tell his missus, and that would put manners on him.

Then one day Billy Hunt came in with his suitcase of samples, and although he was not her type—his colouring was something like her own, and she knew for a fact that a woman should never go with a man of the same skin type as herself—she smiled at him and let him know that she was paying attention as he did his salesman's pitch to Mr

Plunkett. Afterwards, when he came to talk to her, she listened to him with a concentrated look, and pretended to laugh at his silly, schoolboy jokes, even managing to make herself blush at the risky ones. On his next time round he had asked her out to the pictures, and she had said yes loud enough for Mr Plunkett to hear, making him scowl.

Billy was a lot older than she was, nearly sixteen years older, in fact—was there something about her, she wondered ruefully, that was especially attractive to older men?—and he was not good-looking or clever, but he had a clumsy charm that she liked despite herself and that in time allowed her to convince herself she was in love with him. They had been going together only a few months when one night as he was walking her home—she had a little room of her own now, over a butcher's shop in Kevin Street—he started to stammer and all of a sudden grabbed her hand and pressed a little square box into it. She was so surprised she did not realise what the box was until she opened it.

That was the first time she let him come up to her room. They sat side by side on the bed and he kissed her all over her face—he was still stammering and laughing, unable to believe she had said yes—and talked about all the plans he had for the future, and she almost believed him, holding her hand out in front of her with the fingers bent back and admiring the thin gold band with its tiny, flashing diamond. He was from Waterford, where his family kept a pub that his Da would probably leave to him, but he said he would not go back, though she noticed that when he spoke of Waterford city he called it 'home'. He told her about Geneva, where he was summoned twice a year for a meeting at Head Office, as he called it, of all the top bosses worldwide, hundreds of them. He was so proud to be brought all that way, him, who was only a salesman! He described the lake, and the mountains, and the city—'so clean, you wouldn't believe it!'—and said he would take her there, one day. Poor Billy, with his big ideas, his grand schemes.

So the years went on, and so it seemed they would go on forever, until the day the Doctor walked into the shop. Although his name was Kreutz, which sounded German, she thought he must be an Indian—an Indian from India, that is. He was tall and thin, so thin it was hard to know where there would be room inside his body for his vital organs, and he had a wonderfully long, narrow face, the face, she thought immediately, of a saint in one of those books they had in school about the foreign missions. He wore a very beautiful suit of dark blue material, silk it might be except that it had a weight that made it hang really elegantly from his sloped, bony shoulders and his practically non-existent hips. She had never been this close to a coloured man before and she had to stop herself staring at him, especially his hands, so slender and dark with a darker, velvety line along the edges where the pale, dusty-pink skin of the palms began. He had a smell that also was dark, she thought, spicy and dark—she caught it distinctly when he came in; she was sure it was not cologne or shaving lotion but a perfume produced by his skin itself. She found herself wanting to touch that skin, to run her fingertips along it, just to feel the texture of it. And his hair, very straight and smooth and black, black with a purplish sheen, and combed back from his forehead in smooth waves, she wanted to touch that, too.

He had come in to ask for some herbal-medicine stuff

that Mr Plunkett had never heard of. His voice was soft and light, yet deep, too, and he might almost have been singing rather than speaking. 'Ah, this is most strange,' he said, when Mr Plunkett told him he did not have the particular thing he wanted, 'most most strange.' Yet he did not seem put out at all. He said he had been to a number of chemist's shops but no one could help him. Mr Plunkett nodded sympathetically, but obviously could think of nothing else to say, yet the man went on standing there, frowning not in annoyance but only what seemed to be polite puzzlement, as if waiting for something more that he was sure was coming. Even when the chemist turned away pointedly the man still made no move to depart. This was something about him she would come to know well, this curious way he had of lingering in places or with people when there seemed nothing more that could happen; his manner was always relaxed and calm yet quietly expectant, as though he thought there must surely be something more and he was waiting to see if it might occur after all. She never heard him laugh, in all the time she knew him, nor did he smile, not what you would call a smile, but still he gave the impression of being quietly, benignly amused at something—or everything, more like.

That first time he did not look at her once, not directly, but she could feel him taking her in: that was how it felt to her, that he was somehow *absorbing* her. Most of the men who came into the shop were too timid to look at her, and would stand turned away a little from her, fidgeting, and grinning like fools with a tongue-tip showing between their teeth. But Dr Kreutz was not timid, oh, no—she had never before encountered a person of such self-confidence, such assurance. Contented, that was the word she thought of to describe him, quite contented—or *quite quite* contented, for that was another of his habits, the way he had of saying words twice over, so rapidly he made a single word of them, *mostmost*, *quitequite*, in his soft, amused, sing-song voice.

He took out a little leather-bound notepad from the inside pocket of his jacket and tore a page out of it and insisted on writing down his address for Mr Plunkett, in case the stuff he wanted should come in—it was only aloe vera, although she thought that day it was '*allo*' he was saying, like a Frenchman in a cartoon trying to say 'hello'— and then left at last, ducking his dusky, narrow head as he went through the door, like a pilgrim, she thought, or one of those holy men, bowing devoutly on the threshold of a temple. He had such beautiful manners. When he had gone, Mr Plunkett muttered something under his breath about darkies, and dropped the slip of paper with the address on it into the waste basket. She waited a while and then, when the chemist was not looking, retrieved the paper, and kept it.

Dr Kreutz had his consulting room—that was what he called it—in an old house on Adelaide Road, in the basement flat there. When she saw it first she was disappointed. She was not sure what she had expected, but it was not this poky, dingy place with a single window, the top half of which looked out on a narrow strip of fusty grass and a bit of black iron railing. On the day after he had come into the shop, a Wednesday, which was early closing and therefore she had the afternoon off, she told Billy she was going to visit her mother, and took the bus to Leeson Street bridge and walked down Adelaide Road, keeping to the opposite side, under the trees in front of the Eye and Ear Hospital. She passed by the house once and made herself go all the way to the top of Harcourt Street before turning round and coming back, this time on the right-hand side. She glanced at the house as she went past, and read the brass plate mounted on a wooden board on the railings.

DR HAKEEM KREUTZ
SPIRITUAL HEALER

There was nothing to be seen in Dr Kreutz's window, the panes of which gave her back briefly an indistinct, watery reflection of her head and shoulders. She told herself she was being stupid, creeping about the streets like this on an October afternoon, using up her half-day. What if he should come out of the house and see her there, and maybe remember her? And just as she was thinking it, there he was all of a sudden, walking towards her from the Leeson Street direction. He was dressed today in a sort of shirt-length tunic, gold-brown, with a high, round collar, and loose silk trousers and sandals that were just cut-out leather soles held on with a couple of lengths of thong wound round up to his ankles; his feet, she could see, were another version of his hands, long and narrow and golden brown like the stuff of his tunic. He was carrying a string bag with three red apples in it and a loaf of Procea bread—how strange, she thought, that even in her agitation she should notice these details. She considered turning and walking rapidly away, pretending to have remembered something, but instead she kept going, though her knees were trembling so much she could hardly walk in a straight line. *Will you get a grip, for God's sake!* she told herself, but it was no good, she could feel the blood rising to her face, that alabaster-white face of hers that registered even the faintest of embarrassments with a show of pink. He had seen her—he had recognised her. She wondered, with crazy inconsequence, how old he was—as old as Mr Plunkett, she guessed, but how differently he carried his age. Her steps led her on. What a lovely loose way he had of walking, leaning down a little way to one side and then the other at each long, loping stride he took, his shoulders dipping in rhythm with his steps and his head sliding backwards and forwards gently on its tall stalk of neck, like the head of some marvellous, exotic wading bird.

She was so flustered at the time that afterwards she could not remember exactly how he had got her to stop and talk. There was a raw wind, she recalled, swooping down in gusts from the sky and making the fallen sycamore leaves scuttle along the pavements like big, withered hands. He did not seem to mind the cold, even in his thin kaftan and his practically bare feet. A purple-faced old fellow going by in a motor-car slowed down and goggled at them, the pale young woman and the dark man standing there together, she grinning like a lunatic and he as calm as if they had known each other for ever.

Yes, forty, she thought, he must be forty if he's a day, older than Billy, even. But what did it matter what age he was?

He was asking her name. 'Deirdre,' she said, her voice hardly more than a breath, and he repeated it, trying it out, as if it were the first two syllables of a song, or of a hymn, even. *Deirdre.*

3

QUIRKE HAD LONG ago lost what little faith he might once have had in the Catholic pieties that the Brothers at the workhouse, officially known as Carricklea Industrial School, where he had endured his early childhood, had tried for so long to beat into him. Yet even now, when he was well into middle age, he still had his household gods, his not-to-be-toppled totems, one of which was the giant remnant of the man whom for most of his life he had unquestioningly taken to be good, even great. Garret Griffin, or the Judge, as everyone called him, even though it was some time since he had been in a position to deliver judgment on anything, had been felled the previous year, his seventy-third, by a stroke that had paralysed him entirely, except for the muscles of his mouth and eyes and the tendons of his neck. He was confined, mute but in some way sentient, to a large white room on the third floor of the Presentation Convent of St Louis in Rathfarnham, a far suburb of the city, where two windows, one in each of the adjoining corner walls of the room, looked out on two contrasting aspects of the Dublin Mountains, one rocky and barren, the other green and strewn with gorse. It was to these soft hills that his eyes turned constantly, with an expression of desperation, grief and rage. Quirke marvelled at how much of the man, how much of what was left of the living being, was concentrated now in his eyes; it was as if all the power of his personality had come crowding into these last, twin points of fierce and desperate fire.

Quirke visited the old man on Mondays and Thursdays; Quirke's daughter, Phoebe, came on Tuesdays and Fridays; on Sundays it was the turn of the Judge's son, Malachy. On Wednesdays and Saturdays the Judge was left to contemplate alone the day-long play of light and shadow on the mountains and to endure with speechless and, if the expression in his eyes was to be credited, furious resentment the ministrations of the octogenarian nun, Sister Agatha, who had been assigned to care for him. In his former life, his life in the world, he had done many quiet favours for the Presentation nuns, and it was they who had been the first to offer to take him in when the catastrophe befell him. It had been expected that after such a devastating stroke he would live no more than a week or two, but the weeks had passed, and then the months, and still his will to endure showed no sign of flagging. There was a school for girls on the first two floors of the building, and at fixed times of the day—mid-morning, lunchtime, the four o'clock end of lessons—the pupils' voices in raucous medley rose up as far as the third floor. At that sound a tense and concentrated look would come into the Judge's eyes, hard to interpret; was it indignation, nostalgia, sorrowful remembrance—or just puzzlement? Perhaps the old man did not know where he was or what he was hearing; perhaps his mind—and those eyes left little doubt that there was a mind at some kind of work behind them—was trapped in a state of continuous bewilderment, helpless doubt. Quirke did not know quite what to think of this. Part of him, the disappointed, embittered part, wanted the old man to suffer, while another part, the part that was still the child he had once been, wished that the stroke might have killed him outright, and saved him from these final humiliations.

Quirke passed these visits in reading aloud to the old man from the *Irish Independent*. Today was a Monday in midsummer and there was little of interest in the news pages. Eighty priests had been ordained in ceremonies at Maynooth and All Hallows—More clerics, Quirke thought, that's all we need. Here was a picture of Mr Tom Bent, manager of the Talbot Garage in Wexford, presenting the keys of a new fire engine to the town's mayor. The summer sale was on in Macy's of George's Street. He turned to the foreign page. Dozy old Ike was harrying the Russians, as usual. 'The German people cannot wait eternally for their sovereignty,' according to Chancellor Adenauer, addressing a North Rhine-Westphalia State election rally in Düsseldorf the previous night. Then Quirke's eye fell on a paragraph on the front page, under the headline *Girl's Body Found*.

> The body of Mary Ellen Quigley (16), shirt factory worker, who had been missing from her home in Derry since June 17th, was recovered yesterday from the River Foyle by a fisherman pulling in his net. An inquest will be held today.

He put the paper aside. He needed a cigarette. Sister Agatha, however, did not allow smoking in the sickroom.

For Quirke this was an added annoyance, but on the other hand it did give him the excuse to escape at least twice in every hour to pace the echoing, rubber-tiled corridor outside, tensely dragging on a cigarette like an expectant father in a comedy.

Why did he persist in coming here like this? Surely no one would blame him if he stayed away altogether and left the dying man to his angry solitude. The Judge had been a great and secret sinner, and it was Quirke who had exposed his sins. A young woman had died, another woman had been murdered, and these things had been the old man's fault. What impressed Quirke most was the cloak of silence that had been drawn over the affair, leaving him standing alone in his indignation, exposed, improbable, ignored, like a crackpot shouting on a street corner. So why did he keep coming dutifully each week to this barren room below the mountains? He had his own sins to account for, as his daughter could attest, the daughter whom he had for so long denied. It was a small atonement to come here twice a week and read out the court cases and the death notices for this dying old man.

His thoughts turned again to Deirdre Hunt. There had been no question of not performing a post-mortem, after he had chanced on that needle mark in the woman's arm. He had his professional duty to carry out, but that was not what had made him take up the knife. He had been, as always, simply curious, though Quirke knew there was nothing simple about his curiosity. He had cut open the cadaver, palped the organs, measured the blood, and now, with the Judge for silent witness, he had it all out for himself again and viewed it from all the angles he could think of. Still it made no sense.

He turned. 'What do you think, Garret?' he asked. 'Just another lost girl?'

The Judge, propped against pillows, his mouth awry, glared at him. Quirke sighed. The room was hot and airless, and even though he had taken off his jacket he was sweating and could feel the damp patches on his shirt under the armpits and between his shoulder blades. He wondered, as he often did, if the Judge registered these things: heat, cold, the commonplace vagaries of the day. Was he in pain? Imagine that—imagine being in unrelenting pain and not even able to cry out to be released from it or just to plead for sympathy.

He sighed again. He recalled the premonitory twinge of unease he had felt when the woman at the hospital reception desk had handed him the note from Billy Hunt asking him to phone him. How had he known that something was amiss? What intuition, what sixth sense, had forewarned him? And what was this dread he was feeling now? It was a postmortem he had performed on the body of another young woman that had led to the unravelling of the Judge's web of secrets; did he want to become involved in another version of all that? Should he not just let the death of Deirdre Hunt alone, and leave her husband in merciful ignorance? What did it matter that a woman had drowned herself? Her troubles were over now, why should her husband's be added to? Yet even as he asked himself these questions Quirke was aware of the old itch to cut into the quick of things, to delve into the dark of what was hidden—to *know*.

Sister Agatha came bustling back into the room, plainly irritated that he was still there, when at other times he so patently could not wait to be away. And why *was* he tarrying like this? Did he expect some silent revelation from the old man, some grand sign of guidance or admonition? Did he expect *help*? The nun was a little, wizened, bearded woman with an eye as sharp as a robin's. No matter in what part of the room she was she contrived always to seem planted protectively between him and her helpless, bedridden charge. She disapproved of Quirke and made no attempt to hide the fact.

'Isn't it grand,' she said, without looking at him, 'to see the sun shining still, and it so late?'

It was not late, it was six o'clock; she was telling him she wanted him gone. He watched as she tended the old man, adjusting his pillows and smoothing the thin blanket and the turned-back top of the sheet that lay across the middle of his chest like a broad, restraining band. The Judge had never seemed so huge as he did here, bound helpless in his narrow metal bed; Quirke recalled from long ago a day of fierce storm at Carricklea when he had witnessed a giant beech tree brought down by the wind, its fall making the ground quake and the crash of it rattling the panes of the window at the sill of which he was eagerly watching. The old man's lapsing was like that, an end of something that had been there for so long it had seemed immovable. How much of this destruction was Quirke's doing? And was he now about to start another storm that would topple from its pedestal the monument Billy Hunt wanted to erect to his dead wife?

He took up his jacket from where he had draped it on

the back of a chair beside the bed. 'Goodbye, Sister,' he said. 'I'll see you on Thursday.'

Still she would not look at him and said nothing, only made a little breathy sound down her nostrils that might have been a snicker of disdain. From the Judge too there was no response, and his eyes were turned away, as if in bleak disdain, towards the hills.

In Baggot Street Quirke ate a vile dinner in a Chinese restaurant, and afterwards walked back to his flat trying to strip a scum of grease from his front teeth with his tongue. Nowadays, without the anaesthetic of alcohol, he found the evenings the most difficult, especially in this midsummer season with its lingering white nights. His friends, or at least the few acquaintances he used to have, were pub people, and on the rare occasions when he met them now it was plain that he made them nervous in his new-found sober state. He thought of going to the pictures, but then saw himself sitting alone in the flickering dark among scores of courting couples, and even the deserted silence of his flat on a sun-washed summer evening seemed preferable. Arrived at the shabby Georgian house in Upper Mount Street where he lived, he closed the front door soundlessly behind him and went softly along the hall and up the stairs. He always felt somehow an intruder here, among these hanging shadows and this silence.

And in his flat on the third floor there was the usual atmosphere of tight-lipped stealth, as if something vaguely nefarious had been going on that had ceased instantly at the sound of his key in the door. He stood for a moment in the middle of the living room, the key still in his hand, looking about at his things: the characterless furniture, the obsessively neat bookshelves, the artist's wooden manikin on a little table by the window with its arms melodramatically upflung. On the mantelpiece there was a vase of roses. The flowers had been given to him, somewhat improbably, he thought, by a woman—married, bored, blonde—whom he had seen for a not very exciting week or two, and he had not had the heart to throw them out, although by now they were withered, and their parched petals gave off a faint, stale-sweet smell that reminded him disquietingly of his workplace. He turned on the wireless and tried tuning it to the BBC Third Programme, but the reception was hopelessly weak, as for some reason it always was in fine weather. He lit a cigarette and stood by the window, looking down into the broad, empty street with its raked and faintly sinister-seeming shadows. It was still too early for the whores who had their patch here—oh, well-named Mount Street!—though even the ugliest and most elderly of whom did a brisk trade on sultry nights such as this. He could feel the first fizzings of the desperation that often assailed him in these summer twilights. A soft small sound behind him made him turn, startled: a heavy petal had detached itself from one of the withered roses and had fallen, like a scrap of dusty, dark-red velvet crimped around its edges, into the grate. Muttering, he snatched up his jacket and made for the door.

Malachy Griffin, looked after by an ancient maid, was still hanging on in the big house in Rathgar that Sarah and he had lived in for fifteen years. He had thought of selling it, now that Sarah was gone, and would sell it, some day, but he could not yet face the prospect of estate agents, and having to consider offers, and arranging for the movers to come in, and then, at last, the move itself. He tried to imagine it, the final shutting of the front door as the movers' lorry drove away, the walk down the narrow pathway between the lawns on either side to the old gate knobbled with a century and more of coats of heavy black paint, the last smell of the privet, the last stepping on to the pavement, the last turning away in the direction of the canal and an inconceivable future. No, better stay put for now, bide in quietness, watching the calendar's leaf-fall of days. Nothing for it but to get up in the mornings, go to work, come back, sleep: exist. No, nothing for it.

The dog heard the footsteps approaching the front door and was already snarling and whining before the bell rang. Mal had been dozing in an armchair in the drawing room and the sound jerked him awake. Who could it be, at this hour? The french windows stood open on the wide back garden where the silver-green dusk was gathering. He listened for Maggie, the maid, but nowadays she kept stubbornly to her quarters below stairs, refusing to answer the doorbell. He thought of not answering either—was there anyone he would want to see?—but at last stood up with a sigh and put aside his newspaper and padded out to the hall. The dog scuttled behind him and crouched down on its front legs with its hindquarters lifted, growling deep in its throat.

'Quirke,' Mal said, with not much surprise and less enthusiasm. 'You're out late.'

Quirke said nothing, and Mal stood back and held open the door. The dog retreated backwards, watching Quirke with beady hostility, sliding along on its outstretched paws and making a noise in its gullet like a rattlesnake.

Mal led the way into the drawing room, and when Quirke had passed through he shut the door on the dog. Quirke went and stood in the open windows with his hands in his pockets and contemplated the garden, his wedge-shaped bulk almost filling the window-frame. He looked incongruous there in his black suit, a harbinger of night. Mal always thought of him as a huge, dangerous, baffled baby, needful and destructive. Quirke said: 'I hate this time of year, these endless evenings.' He was eyeing the peonies and the roses and the lavishly mournful weeping willow that Sarah had planted when she and Mal had first come to live here. The place had grown unkempt; Sarah had been the gardener.

The dog was scratching feebly with its claws at the door and whining.

'Want a drink?' Mal asked, and added quickly, 'Tea, or . . .' and faltered.

'Thanks—no.'

They had made a sort of truce, the two of them, since Sarah's going. Occasionally they dined together at the St Stephen's Green Club, where Mal had taken over his father's membership, and once they had gone to the races at Leopardstown, but that had not been a success: Quirke had lost twenty pounds and was resentful of Mal, who, though he had little knowledge of horse-flesh, had confined himself to betting a few shillings but still had managed to come away five pounds the better.

Mal was wondering now, uneasily, what the purpose of Quirke's visit might be. Quirke did not come to the house unless invited, and Mal rarely invited him. He sighed inwardly; he hoped Quirke was not going to tackle him again about budgets—Mal was head of obstetrics at the Hospital of the Holy Family and chairman of the Board of Management—but suddenly Quirke startled him by asking if he would care to come for a walk. Mal did not think of Quirke as a man who went for walks. But he said yes, that he had been about to take the dog out for its evening run anyway, and went off to change his slippers for outdoor shoes.

Left alone before the humming silence of the twilit garden, Quirke had an uncanny notion that the things out there, the roses and the heavy-headed peonies and the luxuriantly drooping tree, were discussing him, quietly, sceptically, among themselves. In his mind he saw Sarah there, in her big-brimmed Mediterranean straw hat, tweed-skirted, garden-gloved, walking towards him across the grass, smiling, and lifting a wrist to push a strand of hair back from her forehead.

The day's newspaper lay on the table where Mal had thrown it, the newsprint gleaming eerily, like tarnished white metal, in the evening light from the garden. Quirke saw the headline again:

GIRL'S BODY FOUND

Mal came back, in his cracked brogues and his crumpled grey linen jacket. He no longer dressed as he used to: the old sartorial care was gone; he had let himself go, like the garden. Physically, too, he had faded, his features become indistinct, as if a fine sifting of dust had settled uniformly over him. His hair was dry—it looked almost brittle—and was going noticeably grey at the temples. Only the lenses of his wire-framed spectacles were as glossy and intent as ever, though the eyes behind them seemed vague, as if worn and wearied by the strain of constant peering through those unrelentingly shiny rounds of glass.

'Well,' he said, 'shall we go?'

They strolled by the canal in the hush of evening. Few people were about, and fewer cars. They went as far as Leeson Street and then all the way down to Huband Bridge. Here, once, long ago, Quirke had walked with Sarah Griffin on a Sunday morning in misty autumn. He thought of telling Mal now about that walk, and what was said, how Sarah had begged him to help Mal—'He's a good man, Quirke'—and how Quirke had misunderstood what it was she was asking of him, what it was she could not bring herself to tell him outright.

Mal was humming tunelessly under his breath; it was another of the habits he had developed since Sarah's death.

'How are you managing?' Quirke asked.

'What?'

'In the house, on your own—how are you getting on?'

'Oh, all right, you know. Maggie looks after me.'

'I meant, how are you, in yourself?'

Mal considered. 'Well, it gets better in some ways and worse in others. The nights are hard, but the days pass. And I have Brandy.' Quirke stared, and Mal smiled wanly and pointed to the dog. 'Him, I mean.'

'Oh. That's its name, is it?'

Quirke looked at the beast as it pattered hurriedly here and there in the soft greyness of dusk with its curious, busy, stiff-legged gait, like a mechanical toy, bad-temperedly sniffing at the grass. It was a stunted, wire-haired thing the colour of wet sacking. Phoebe had got it for him, this man whom until two years ago she had thought was her father, to be company for him. It was plain that dog and master disliked each other, the dog barely tolerating the man and the man seeming helpless before the dog's unbiddably doggy insistences. It was odd, but ownership of the dog made Mal seem even more aged, more careworn, more irritably despondent. As if reading Quirke's thoughts, he said defensively: 'He is company. Of a sort.'

Quirke longed suddenly for a drink, just the one: short, quick, burning, disastrous. For, of course, it would not be just the one. When had it ever been just the one, in the old days? He felt the rage starting up, the dry-drinker's whining, impotent, self-lacerating rage.

The street-lamps shone among the barely stirring leaves of the trees that lined the towpath, throwing out a seething, harsh white radiance that deepened the surrounding darkness. The two men stopped and sat down on a black-painted iron bench. Leaf-shadows stirred on the path at their feet. The dog, displeased, ran back and forth fretfully. Quirke lit a cigarette, the flame of the lighter making a red globe that was cupped for a second in the protective hollow of his hands.

'A fellow called me this morning,' he said. 'Fellow that was at college when we were there. Billy Hunt—do you remember him? Big, red-haired. Played football, or hurling, I can't remember which. Left after First Meds.' Mal, watching the dog, said nothing; was he even listening? 'His wife was drowned. Threw herself off the jetty out in Sandycove. They found her yesterday washed up on the rocks on Dalkey Island. Young, in her twenties.' He paused, smoking, and then went on: 'Billy asked me to make sure there'd be no post-mortem. Couldn't bear to think of her being cut up, he said.'

He stopped and glanced sideways at Mal's long, angled profile beside him in the lamp-lit gloom. The canal smelled of dead water and rotting vegetation. The dog came and put its front paws on the bench and caught hold of the lead with its teeth and tried to tug it out of Mal's hands. Mal pushed the creature away with weary distaste.

'What did you say his name was?' he asked.

'Hunt. Billy Hunt.'

Mal shook his head. 'No, don't remember him. What happened to the wife—I mean, why did she do it?'

'Well, that's the question.'

'Oh?' Quirke said nothing and now it was Mal's turn to glance at him. 'Is it a case of—what do the Guards say?— "suspicious circumstances"?'

Quirke still did not answer, but after a moment said: 'Her name was Deirdre, Deirdre Hunt. She called herself Laura Swan. Very fancy.'

'Was she an actress?'

'No—a beautician, I think is what she would have said.' He dropped the end of his cigarette on the path and trod it under his heel.

The dog was worrying the lead again and whimpering. 'Better get on,' Mal said, and stood up. He attached the lead to the dog's collar and they went up through the gap in the railings on to Herbert Place and turned back in the direction in which they had come. The tall terrace of houses on the other side of the road loomed in the glistening darkness. Humans build square, Quirke thought, nature in the round.

'Laura Swan,' Mal said. 'Sounds vaguely familiar, I don't know why.'

'She had a place in Anne Street, over a shop. It was a success, it seems. Rich ladies from Foxrock came to her to have their legs shaved, their moustaches dyed, that kind of thing. Fake tans, creams to smooth away the wrinkles. Billy, the husband, travels for a pharmaceuticals firm, probably supplied her with materials at cost price or for nothing. Harmless people, you would think.'

'But?'

Quirke, his hands in his pockets, rolled his great bowling-ball shoulders. He was developing, Mal noticed, a definite paunch; they were both ageing. Under the brim of his black slouch hat Quirke's expression was unreadable.

'Something wrong,' he said. 'Something fishy.'

'You suspect he might have pushed her?'

'No. No one pushed her, I think. But she didn't drown, either.'

They did not speak again until they came to the house on Rathgar Road. They paused at the gate. All the windows were dark. The garden's mingled fragrances seemed for a second a breath out of the past, a past that was not theirs, exactly, but rather one where their younger selves still lived somehow in a long-gone and yet unageing present. Mal released the dog and it scampered up the path and on to the stone steps and began scratching frantically at the front door, its paws going in a circular blur that made Quirke think of a squirrel on a wheel. The two men followed slowly, their heels crunching on the dusty gravel. The walk was over yet they were not sure how to make an end.

'How was my father?' Mal asked. 'Did you see him today?'

'Same as usual. He doesn't know how to die. Pure will. You have to admire it.'

'And do you?'

'What?'

'Admire it.'

They came to the foot of the granite steps and paused again. A bat flittered above the garden in the lamplight; Quirke fancied he could hear the tiny, rapid, clockwork beating of its wings.

'He hates me,' he said. 'It's there in his eyes, that glare.'

'You tried to destroy him,' Mal said mildly.

'He destroyed himself.'

To that Mal answered nothing. The dog was still scratching at the door. 'Oh, that animal,' Mal said. 'When he's inside he howls to be let out and when he's out he can't wait to get back in.' They stood, Mal gloomily watching the dog and Quirke looking about for the elusive bat. Mal said: 'This young woman, this Deirdre Hunt—are you going to get yourself in trouble again, Quirke?'

Quirke sighed, rueful, and scuffed the gravel with the tip of his shoe.

'I wouldn't be surprised if it comes to that,' he said. 'Trouble, I mean.'

4

HE FOUND IT IMPOSSIBLE to sleep in these nights that seemed no more than the briefest of intervals between the glow of evening and the glare of morning. By four o'clock the daylight was already curling insidious fingers round the edges of the curtains in his bedroom. He had tried wearing a sleep-mask but found the blackness disorienting, while the elastic loops that held it in place left angry lateral V-shaped prints along his temples that lasted for hours. So he lay there, desperate as a beetle fallen on its back, trying not to think of all the things he did not want to think of, as the dawn sifted into the room like a radiant grey dust. This morning, as on every other recent morning, he was pondering the puzzle of Billy Hunt and his young wife's death, although this was probably one of those very things he should not be pondering.

If he was wise he would have nothing more to do with Billy Hunt and his troubles. He should have had nothing to do with him from the start. His first mistake had been to return his call, his second had been to agree to meet him. Was it that he felt a sympathy for Billy, an empathy with him, since they had both lost young wives? It seemed to Quirke unlikely. Delia had died a long time ago and, anyway, had he not been secretly and shamefacedly relieved at her death? Though Delia was the one he had married, it was not Delia he had wanted, but her sister Sarah, and he had lost her, through carelessness, and to Malachy Griffin, of all people. Yet there was something about Billy Hunt, something about his distress and sweaty desolation, that had stung Quirke, somehow, and that was stinging yet. 'Something fishy,' he had said to Mal, and he knew that it was indeed a whiff out of the deeps that he had caught. It was not the same as the stench that had come up out of the dead young woman's bloated innards; it was at once fainter and more pungent than that.

He did not know what to do next, even supposing there was a next thing and, if there was, that he should do it. He might talk to Billy Hunt again, find out more of what he knew about his wife's demise and, more significantly, perhaps, what he did not know. But what would he ask him? How would he frame the questions? *Who stuck the needle in her arm, Billy? Who pumped her full of dope—was it you, by any chance?* He did not believe Billy was the killer. He was too hapless, too inept. Killers were surely of a different breed from poor, shambling, freckled, sorrowing Billy Hunt.

Under the covers his knee began to ache, his left knee, the cap of which had been smashed when he had been set upon by a pair of assailants and flung down the area steps of a deserted house in Mount Street one wet night a couple of years previously. That, he reflected now, was just the kind of thing that happened to you when you poked at things better left unpoked.

He turned on his side with a hand under his cheek on the hot pillow and gazed at the heavy, floor-length curtains standing above him in the half-light like a massive fluted slab of dark stone. What should he do? The waters into which Deirdre Hunt's corpse had plunged were deep and turbid. The autopsy he had done on that other young woman two years ago had raised a wave of mud and filth in the lees of which he was still wading. Was he not now in danger of another foul drenching? Do nothing, his better judgement told him: stay on dry land. But he knew he would dive, head first, into the depths. Something in him yearned after the darkness down there.

At half past eight that same morning he was at Pearse Street Garda Station, asking for Detective Inspector Hackett. The day was hot already, with shafts of sunlight reflecting like brandished swords off the roofs of motor-cars passing by outside in the smoky, petrol-blue air. Inside, the day room was all umber shadow and floating dust motes, and there was a smell of pencil shavings and documents left to bake in the sun that reminded Quirke of his schooldays at Carricklea. Policemen in uniform and some in plainclothes came and went, slow-moving, watchful, deliberate. One or two gave him a sharp look that told him they knew who he was; he could see them wondering what he was doing there, Quirke, the hot-shot pathologist from the Hospital of the Holy Family, scuffing his fancy shoe-leather in these fusty surroundings; by now he was wondering the same thing himself.

Hackett came down to greet him. He was in shirt sleeves and broad braces; Quirke recognised the voluminous blue trousers, shined to a high polish at seat and knee, that were one half of what must still be the only suit he owned. His big square face, with its slash of mouth and watchful eyes, was shiny too, especially about the jowls and chin. His brilliantined black hair was brushed back fiercely from his forehead in a raptor's crest. Quirke was not sure that he had ever seen Hackett before without his hat. It was two years since he and Hackett had last spoken, and he was faintly surprised to discover how pleased he was to see the wily old brute, box-head and carp's mouth and shiny serge and all.

'Mr Quirke!' the detective said expansively, but kept his thumbs hooked in his braces and offered no handshake. 'Is it yourself?'

'Inspector.'

'What has you about at this hour of the morning?'

'I remembered you were an early riser.'

'Oh, as ever—up with the lark.'

The duty officer at the desk, a pin-headed giant with jug ears, was watching them with unconcealed interest. 'Come up,' Hackett said. 'Come up to the office and tell me all your news.' He lifted the wooden counter flap for Quirke and at the same time reached back with his foot and pushed open the frosted-glass door behind him that led to the stairs inside. The walls of the stairwell were painted a shade of grey-green, and the brown varnish on the banister rail was tacky to the touch. All institutional buildings made Quirke, the orphan, shiver.

The inspector's office was as Quirke remembered it, wedge-shaped and cluttered, with a grimy window at the narrow end where Hackett's big desk was planted, solid and square as a butcher's block. The space was so tiny it seemed Quirke's entry there, with his bullish shoulders and big blond head, must make the walls bulge outwards. 'Sit down, sit down, Mr Quirke,' the inspector said, laughing. 'You're making me nervous standing there like the Man in Black.' The hot air reeked of sweat and mildew, and the walls and ceiling were stained a bilious shade of Woodbine-brown from years of cigarette smoke. The inspector had to squeeze in sideways to get behind his desk. He sat down with a grunt, and offered Quirke an open packet of Players, the cigarettes ranked like a miniature set of organ pipes. 'Have a smoke.' Through the window behind him, which was hazed with grime and old cobwebs, Quirke could see a vague jumble of roofs and chimney-pots sweltering in the summer sun. 'How are you, at all?' the policeman said. 'Have you put on a few pounds?'

'I don't drink any more.'

'Do you tell me?' The inspector pursed his lips and whistled silently. 'Well,' he said, 'the booze is a great man for keeping the weight down, right enough.'

Quirke took a silver propelling pencil from his pocket and began to fiddle with it. Hackett leaned back on his groaning chair, directing a stream of smoke towards the ceiling, and regarded him down the side of his nose with a fond twinkle, though his little dark-brown eyes were as piercing as ever. The last time they had encountered each other had been on a morning two years previously when Quirke had come to this office with evidence of the Judge's guilty secrets and a list of the names of those who shared his guilt. Later, on the telephone, Hackett had said, 'They've circled the wagons, Mr Quirke, and us misfortunate pair of injuns can fire off all the arrows that we like.' Both knew well there would be no mention today of that business; what was there left to say? It was history, done with and gone, and the bodies were all buried—or, Quirke reflected, almost all.

'A grand day,' Hackett said. 'With that rain last week I thought we weren't going to get a summer at all.' The twinkle grew brighter still. 'I suppose you'll be off to the seaside, master of your own time that you are. Or the races—you have an eye for the gee-gees, I seem to remember, or am I thinking of someone else?'

'Someone else,' Quirke said grimly, recalling his disastrous day at Leopardstown with Mal.

They smoked in silence for a while, and at length the inspector enquired pleasantly, 'Tell me, Mr Quirke, would this be in the nature of a social call, or have you business on your mind?'

Quirke, sitting at an angle to the desk with one knee crossed on the other, considered the dusty black toe of his shoe. He cleared his throat. 'I wanted to ask—' He hesitated. 'I wanted to ask your advice.'

Hackett's expression of amiable, mild interest did not alter. 'Oh?'

Once more Quirke hesitated. 'There's a woman . . .'

The inspector's heavy black eyebrows travelled upwards an enquiring half an inch. 'Oh?' he said again, without inflection.

Quirke clipped the pencil back in his pocket and leaned forward heavily and stubbed out his half-smoked cigarette in the already overflowing Bakelite ashtray that stood on a corner of the desk.

'Her name,' he said, 'is Deirdre Hunt. Was.'

The inspector, his brows still lifted, now raised his eyes

along with them and studied the ceiling for a moment, making a show of thinking hard. 'Would that be the same Deirdre Hunt that we fished out of the water out at Dalkey Island the other day?' And then suddenly, before Quirke could answer, the policeman began to laugh his familiar, smoker's laugh, softly at first, then with increasing force and helplessness. He kicked himself forward in his chair, wheezing and whistling, and smacked a palm down on the desk in delight. Quirke waited, and at length the detective sat back, panting. He gazed at Quirke almost lovingly. 'God, Mr Quirke,' he said, 'but you're a terrible man for the dead young ones.'

'She was also known,' Quirke said, his voice gone gruff, 'as Laura Swan.'

This provoked a renewed bout of happy wheezing.

'Was she, now?'

'She kept a beauty parlour, in Anne Street.'

'That's right. My missus took herself there last Christmas for a treat.'

Quirke paused in faint consternation. It had never occurred to him that there might be a Mrs Hackett. He tried to picture her, large and square like her husband, with mottled arms and mighty ankles and a bust like the bust on a ship's figurehead. An unlikely client, surely, for the beautifying skills of a Laura Swan. And if Hackett had a wife, good heavens, did he have children too, a brood of little Hacketts, miniaturely hatted, blue-suited and in broad braces like their daddy?

The inspector, recovered from his mirth and having wiped his eyes, scrabbled among the disorderly papers on his desk and lifted out a page and set himself soberly to studying it. 'You seem to know an awful lot about this unfortunate woman,' he said. 'How is that?'

'I know her husband—knew him. We were at college together. I mean, he was there when I was there, but in a different year. He's younger than me.'

'Doctor, is he?'

'No. He gave up medicine.'

'Right.' Hackett was still studying the page, holding it up close to his eyes and squinting, pretending to read with deep attention what was written there. He glanced over the top of it at Quirke. 'Sorry,' he said, 'forgot my specs.' He let the paper fall on to the pile of its fellows and once again leaned back in his chair. Quirke, looking down, saw that the document was nothing more than a roster sheet. 'Well, then, Mr Quirke, what is it you think I can tell you about the late Mrs Hunt—or is there something *you* have to tell *me*?'

Quirke looked past him to the window and the hazy view beyond. Under the unaccustomed sunshine the roof-tops and the smoke-blackened chimneys appeared flat and unreal, like a skyline in a movie musical.

'I did a post-mortem on her.'

'I thought you might have. And?'

'Her husband had phoned me, out of the blue.'

'What for?'

'To ask that there *wouldn't* be a post-mortem.'

'Why was that?'

'He said he couldn't bear the thought of her body being cut up.'

'An odd thing to ask, surely?'

'It's the kind of thing that preys on people's minds, when

someone dear to them has died violently. I'm told it's a displacement for grief, or guilt.'

'Guilt?' the inspector said.

Quirke gave him a level look. 'The one that survives always feels guilty in some way.'

'So you're told.'

'Yes, so I'm told.'

Hackett's flat, square face had the look, in its wooden imperturbability, of a primitive mask.

'Well, you're probably right,' he said. He crushed his spent cigarette in the ashtray; one side of it kept burning, sending a busy thin stream of smoke wavering upwards. 'So what did you say to him, the grieving widower?'

'I said I'd see what I could do.'

'But you went ahead—you did the post-mortem?'

'As I said. Of course.'

'Oh, of course,' the detective murmured drily. 'And what did you find?'

'Nothing,' Quirke said. 'She drowned.'

The inspector was watching him out of a deep and, so it seemed, unrufflable calm. 'Drowned,' he said.

'Yes,' Quirke said. 'I wondered if'—he had to clear his throat again—'I wondered if you might drop a word to the coroner.' He got out his cigarette case and offered it across the desk.

'The coroner?' Hackett said, in a tone of mild and innocent surprise. 'Why would you want me to talk to the coroner?' Quirke did not answer. The detective took a cigarette and bent with it to the flame of Quirke's lighter. He had assumed an absent look now, as if he had suddenly somehow lost the thread of what they had been talking about. Quirke knew that look. 'Would you not, Mr Quirke'—the inspector leaned back again at his ease, emitting twin trumpets of smoke from flared nostrils—'would you not have a word with him yourself?'

'Well, in a case like this—'

The inspector pounced. 'A case like what?'

'Suicide, I mean.'

'And that's what it was, was it?'

'Yes. I won't say so, of course. To the coroner, I mean.'

'Yet he'll know.'

'Probably. But he'll keep it to himself—'

'—if someone drops a word to him.'

Quirke looked down. 'The fact that he came to me,' he said, 'the husband, Billy Hunt—I feel a responsibility.'

'To spare his feelings.'

'Yes. Something like that.'

'*Something* like that?'

'It's not the way I'd put it.'

There was a silence. The detective was watching Quirke with an expression of infantile curiosity, his gaze wide and shinily intense. 'It *was*, though, you say, a suicide?' he asked, as if to clear a faint and unimportant doubt.

'I assume it was.'

'And you would know—having done the post-mortem, I mean.'

Quirke would not meet his eye. After a moment he said: 'It's not much to ask. The majority of suicides are covered up, you know that as well as I.'

'All the same, Mr Quirke, I'm sure it's not the usual run of things that a husband will come to a pathologist and ask him not to perform a post-mortem. Might it be that Mr what's-his-name—Swan? no, Hunt—that he might have been worried what you would find if you *did* slice up his missus?'

Again Quirke offered no answer, and Hackett let his gaze go blurred once more. He pushed his chair away from the desk until the back of it struck the window-sill, and heaved up his feet in their heavy black hobnailed boots and set them down on the pile of papers on the desk, lacing his stubby fingers together and placing them on his paunch. Quirke noticed, not for the first time, his thick, blunt hands, a countryman's hands, made for spade work, for deep and tireless digging; he thought of Billy Hunt at the table in Bewley's, sorrowful and distracted, delving a spoon in the sugar bowl. 'I'm sorry,' Quirke said, gathering up his cigarette case and his lighter, 'I'm wasting your time. You're right—I'll talk to the coroner myself.'

'Or you'll wait for the inquest and tell a little white lie,' the inspector said, smiling happily.

Quirke rose. 'Or I'll tell a lie, yes.'

'To spare your friend's feelings.'

'Yes.'

'Since you couldn't see your way to doing what he asked you to do—what he asked you *not* to do, that is.'

'Yes,' Quirke said again, stonily.

The inspector regarded him with what might be the merest fag-end of interest, like a visitor to the zoo standing before the cage of a not very interesting specimen that had once, a long time ago, been a fierce and sleekly fearless creature of the wild.

'So long, then, Mr Quirke,' he said. 'I won't get up— you'll find your own way out?'

By Trinity College a ragged paper-boy in an outsized tweed cap was hawking copies of the *Independent*. Quirke bought one and scanned the pages as he walked along. He was looking for something on that shirt-factory worker drowned in the Foyle, but there was no news of her, today.

He went from Pearse Street to his subterranean office at the hospital and sat at his desk for five minutes tapping his fingers on the blotter. At last he picked up the phone. Billy Hunt answered on the first ring. 'Hello, Billy,' Quirke said. 'I've fixed that, you needn't worry. There'll be no post-mortem.' Billy's voice was thick and slurred, as if he had been weeping, as perhaps he had. He thanked Quirke and said he owed him one, and that maybe one of these days Quirke would let him buy him a drink. 'I don't drink, Billy,' Quirke said, and Billy, not listening, said, 'Right, right,' and hung up.

Quirke put down the receiver and sat a moment holding his breath, then released it in a long, weary sigh. He closed his eyes and pinched the skin at the bridge of his nose between a finger and thumb. What did it matter what had happened the night that Deirdre Hunt died? What did it matter if Billy came home and found his wife dead from an overdose and drove her naked body out to Sandycove and let it slip into the midnight waters. What did it matter? She was dead by then and, as Quirke knew, better than most, a corpse is only a corpse.

But it did matter, and Quirke knew that, too.

5

ON TUESDAYS, after her visit to her grandfather at the convent, it was Quirke's habit to treat his daughter to dinner in the restaurant of the Russell Hotel on St Stephen's Green. Phoebe professed to like it there; it was shabby-genteel and at the same time, as she said with a disparaging, steely little laugh, quite ritzy. The food was fine, although Phoebe hardly noticed it, and the wine was better—this was the one occasion in the week when Quirke allowed himself to roll gently and briefly off the wagon on to which he would calmly climb again next day. This was puzzling, since at other times he was convinced that even one sip would set him back on the old road to perdition, or at least a ruined liver. Somehow his daughter's presence was protection, a magical cordon, against ruinous excess. Tonight they were drinking a rusty claret that Quirke had first drunk on a weekend trip to Bordeaux years before, with a woman, the taste of whose mouth he fancied he could still detect in its grape-dark depths; that was what Quirke remembered of his women, their savours, their smells, the hot touch of their skin under his hand, when their names and even their faces had been long forgotten.

Phoebe wore a narrow black dress with a collar of white

lace. To Quirke's eye she looked alarmingly thin, and seemed more so each time they met. Her dark hair was cut short and permed into tight, metallic waves, her one concession to fashion. She favoured flat shoes and wore almost no makeup. The nuns who had given shelter to her grandfather would approve of Phoebe. Over the past two years she had fashioned a personality for herself that was cool, brittle, ironical; she was twenty-three and might have been forty. Under her wry and sceptical regard Quirke felt discomfited. Phoebe had grown up thinking she was Mal and Sarah's daughter, not Quirke and his wife Delia's, and all her life he had let her go on thinking it until the crises of two years ago had forced him to reveal the truth to her. When she was born it had seemed best, or at least easiest, with Delia dead, to let Sarah take the infant—the Judge had arranged it all—since Sarah and Mal could have no child of their own making, and since Quirke did not want the one he had been so tragically presented with. The trouble, the trouble upon trouble, was that he had gone along with the pretence to Sarah, that he thought Delia's baby had died and that he believed Phoebe was indeed Sarah's own. And now Phoebe knew, and Sarah was gone, and Mal was alone, and Quirke was as Quirke had always been. And he was afraid of his daughter.

Only a few of the tables in the restaurant were occupied, and the two waiters on duty were standing motionless like caryatids on either side of the door that led to the kitchen. The room was lit dimly from above, like a boxing-ring, and the off-pink walls lent a rosy, tired tinge to the heavy air.

'I saw Mal the other evening,' Quirke said.

Phoebe did not look at him. 'Oh, yes? And how is he, my erstwhile pa?'

'Rather sad.'

'You mean sad sad or in a sad condition?'

'Both. That dog was a mistake.'

'Brandy? I thought he was fond of the poor thing—he said he was.'

'I don't think your—' He stopped himself; he had been about to say 'your father', out of old habit. 'I don't think Mal is a dog person, somehow.' He poured an inch of wine into her glass and his own; the bottle would have to last through dinner, that was the rule.

'He should remarry,' Phoebe said.

Quirke glanced at her. To Quirke, Mal seemed to have arrived at the condition that was most natural to him, as if he had been born to be a widower.

Quirke said: 'And what about you?'

'What about me?'

'Any romantic prospects on your horizon?'

She looked at him with one eyebrow arched, unsmiling, pursing her pale mouth. 'Is that supposed to be a joke?'

He blenched before her steeliness; she was Delia's daughter, after all, and grew more like her every day. Delia had been the hardest woman he had ever known; Delia had been steel all the way through. It was what he had most loved in her, this exquisite, tormented and tormenting woman.

'No,' he said, 'I'm not joking.'

'I'm wedded to my job,' Phoebe said, with mock-solemnity, 'don't you realise that?'

She had taken a job in a hat shop on Grafton Street, wasting her talents, but Quirke had made no protest, knowing she would just set her jaw, that straight and lovely jaw which was another thing she had of Delia's, and pretend not to hear him.

Now she laid her knife and fork side by side across her plate—she had hardly touched her steak—and brought out a slim gold cigarette case and a cylindrical gold lighter, not much fatter than a pencil, that Quirke had not seen before. He felt a pang. She must have bought these things herself, for who else would have done so? He pictured her in the shop, poring over the glass cases, the shop assistant watching her with spiteful sympathy, a girl buying presents for herself. He looked at her wrists, at her sharp cheekbones, at the hollow of her throat: everything about her seemed deliberately thinned out, as if she were bent on refining herself steadily until at last there should be nothing of her left but a hair's-breadth outline sketched from a few black and silver lines.

'I had a funny experience today,' she said. 'Well, not funny, not funny at all, in fact, but strange. I can't stop thinking about it.' She frowned, while she selected a cigarette; Passing Cloud, he noticed, was still her brand. He went on studying her sidelong, covertly. The more he saw of her the more he saw her old, sitting in some shabby hotel dining room like this one, in her black dress, poised, wearied, desiccated, incurably solitary. She lit the cigarette and blew a thin stream of smoke and leaned on her elbows on the table, turning the lighter end over end in her fingers. 'I called up someone in a place round the corner from the shop, who had ordered something for me from America—

Kiehl's rose water, you can't get it here. She wasn't there
and so I telephoned her home number—she had given me
her number, and said to call her any time I needed something. I'd been waiting for the thing and was surprised it
hadn't come and I wondered what had happened to it. Her
husband answered—at least, I assume it was her husband.
He sounded very odd. He said she wasn't available. That's
the way he said it: "She's not available." Then he hung up.
I thought maybe he was drunk or something. By now I was
intrigued, so I called her business partner, the man who
runs the place with her. He wasn't at home either, but I got
his wife. I said how I had been trying to get in touch with
this person, and had spoken to her husband or whoever it
was, and how he had said in that peculiar way about her
being not available. At that the woman gave a laugh—not a
happy laugh, more a sort of angry snigger—and said, "Well,
it must be the first time in a long time that that bitch isn't
available," and by the way she said "available" I knew what
she meant. It gave me a start, I can tell you. "Sorry," I said,
"I've obviously called at a bad time," and tried to hang up.
But she must have been waiting for someone to come on
the telephone so she could have a rant about "that rat",
which was how she described her husband. She proceeded
to tell me the most amazing things. I think she was a bit
hysterical—well, more than a bit, in fact. She said she had
found a hoard of dirty pictures—I don't know what that
meant, exactly—and letters from this woman to her husband, which apparently were pretty filthy too. It was obvious, she said, they'd been having an affair under her nose,
the rat and this woman. She went on about it for ages.
Some of the time I think she was crying, but as much in

rage as anything else. Yes, definitely hysterical. But who wouldn't be, I suppose, after making that kind of a discovery?'

While she spoke Quirke had felt something stretching in him and gathering force, like a bowstring being drawn back slowly, quivering and humming. Phoebe was still turning the lighter in her fingers. 'This woman,' he asked, 'what's her name?'

She looked at him. 'Which one?'

'The one who wasn't available.'

He knew what she would say before she said it.

'Deirdre somebody, but her professional name is Laura Swan—why?'

They left the hotel and crossed the road to the Green and strolled along by the railings in the direction of Grafton Street. Dusk was thickening in the air but the sky above them was still light, a clear dome of whitish blue with one star palely burning low above the rooftops. 'What do you do in the evenings,' Phoebe asked, 'now that you don't go boozing any more?' He did not answer. But what *did* he do nowadays with his time? He feared becoming a nightwalker, one of those solitaries who paced the city's streets at evening, keeping close by the walls, or stood in shop doorways or sat in their cars with the engines running, blurred, faceless fellows glimpsed in the flare of a match or by the light from a dashboard, nursing their obscure sorrows. Phoebe said, 'You're the one who should be looking for romance.'

They went to the Shelbourne, their old haunt, and sat in the lounge and drank coffee. When she was a schoolgirl he used to take her there of an afternoon and give her tea with little sandwiches and chocolate éclairs and scones with jam and cream. It seemed an age ago—it *was* an age ago. Tonight the place was empty save for a trio of blue-suited politicians from nearby Government Buildings who were conspiring together in a corner beside the empty fireplace. The light at nightfall in this large room was always strange, more a grainy shadowiness than a radiance, drifting down from two enormous, eerily motionless chandeliers. Quirke for his part was wondering what Phoebe did with *her* evenings. She lived alone in a three-roomed flat in Harcourt Street. She had no boyfriend, of that he was sure, but did she have friends, people she saw? Did people invite her out, call round to visit her? She would tell him nothing of her life.

She was smoking again, sitting upright on a little gilt chair with one knee crossed on the other. There was lace at the cuffs of her dress as well as at the throat. It gave her a faintly antique aspect: she might have been a governess, he idly thought, in the olden days, or a rich lady's paid companion. She asked: 'Why are you so interested in Laura Swan?'

He lifted an eyebrow. 'Am I?'

'I saw how you looked when I mentioned her name. Do you know her?'

'No. No, I don't. I knew her husband, a little, a long time ago.'

'What's he like? He sounded a bit mad on the phone.'

Quirke hesitated. 'He's had a loss,' he said. He let another momentary silence pass. 'The fact is, his wife is dead.'

She stared at him, the cigarette lifted half-way to her mouth. 'Who?'

'His wife. Deirdre—Deirdre Hunt. The one calling herself Laura Swan.'

Something flickered in her eyes, a childlike uncertainty, and a flash almost of fear. For some time she did not speak, then she asked: 'How? I mean, what happened?'

'They found her body one morning last week, on Dalkey Island, washed up on the rocks. I'm sorry—did you know her well? Was she a friend of yours?' She sat frowning now, staring before her blankly. 'I'm sorry,' he said again, and she gave herself a rapid shake, or it might have been a shiver.

'I knew her,' she said, 'but I wouldn't say I knew her well. She stopped to chat sometimes when she was passing by, and I bought cosmetics at the place she has in Anne Street. The Silver Swan, she calls it.' She paused. 'Drowned. The poor thing.' A thought struck her and she looked at him quickly. 'Was it suicide?'

'That will be the coroner's verdict,' Quirke said carefully.

She caught his measured tone. She said: 'But you think otherwise?' He did not answer, only lifted one shoulder and let it fall again. She persisted. 'Did you deal with the body—did you do the post-mortem?' He nodded. 'And what did you find?'

He looked in the direction of the three politicos in the corner, not seeing them. He asked: 'What was she like?'

Phoebe considered. 'I don't know. She was just ... ordinary. Pretty, but ordinary. I mean, there was nothing special about her that I could see. Very serious, hardly ever smiled. But always polite, always helpful. I had the impression there was something going on between her and the fellow she runs the place with.'

'Who is he?'

'Leslie White. English, I think. Tall, skinny, really pale—colourless, even—with the most extraordinary silvery-white hair. Well named I suppose you could say: White. Wears a silver cravat, too.' She wrinkled her nose.

He was watching her closely as he asked: 'How do you know him?'

'He gave me his card one day when I was in the shop.' With a finger she sketched a legend on the air. '"Leslie White—Business Director—The Silver Swan." He's always in and out. Creepy type. I wouldn't put it past him to push a woman into the sea.' She looked hard at Quirke. '*Was* she pushed?'

He turned his gaze from her again. The fact of her knowing them, knowing Deirdre Hunt and this fellow White, was disturbing. It was as if something he had thought safely distant had suddenly brushed against him, touching him with its tentacle. The clock on the mantelpiece at the far end of the room began to chime, a whispery, sinister sound, and at its signal the three politicians rose and hurried together out of the room, still in a huddle, like a skulk of villains in a melodrama.

'I don't know,' Quirke said. 'I don't know what happened to her. But I know she didn't drown.'

He lied to the Coroner's Court, as he and Inspector Hackett had known he would. He did not try to fool himself that he was sparing Billy Hunt's feelings or shielding his wife's reputation. He was, as it were, sealing off the scene, as Hackett would seal off the scene of a crime, for further investigation. That was all.

When the court convened at mid-morning the air in the room was already soupy and stale. There was the usual headache-inducing bustle, with clerks ferrying documents here and there and the jury settling down grumpily and the newshounds swapping jokes in their kennel off to one side of the court. Quirke noted that the reporters were mostly juniors—it seemed their news editors did not expect much of a story. If it was a suicide it would not be reported; that was the unofficial rule the newspapers observed. The public gallery had its accustomed sprinkling of gawpers and ghouls. Billy Hunt sat at one side of the front row, flanked by two women, one old and one young, and held his face in his hands throughout the proceedings. At the other side of the row sat a couple who, Quirke guessed, must be Deirdre Hunt's parents, a washed-out, sick-looking woman in her fifties with peroxided hair, and a short, grizzled, angry-eyed fellow in a brown suit, the jacket of which was buttoned tightly over a keg-shaped torso.

Sheedy, the coroner, was in his habitual dust-grey suit and blue pullover and narrow, striped tie. He listened to the evidence of the Garda sergeant whose men had lifted Deirdre Hunt's naked corpse off the rocks at Dalkey, then turned his long, pale head towards Quirke and enquired in his chilly way if in the examination he had made of the deceased's remains he had arrived at a conclusion as to the cause of death. 'I have,' Quirke said, too loudly, too stoutly, and thought he saw the tip of Sheedy's pale nose twitch;

Sheedy had been City Coroner for twenty years and had a
keen sense of the hesitations and evasions that slithered like
fish through the evidence of even the most blameless wit-
nesses who came before him. Quirke hastened on. He had
performed an external examination of the body, he said, and
as a result had come to the conclusion that the woman had
died by simple drowning.

In fact, he had cut Deirdre Hunt open, and had not
found the foam in her lungs that would have been there had
she drowned; what he did find were strong traces of alcohol
in her blood and the residue of a mighty and surely fatal
dose of morphine.

Sheedy listened to him in silence, one hand placed over
the other on his desk, and then, after a brief but, so it
seemed to Quirke, sceptical pause, directed the jury to return
a verdict of death by accidental drowning. Billy Hunt took
his hands from his stricken face and rose and strode out of
the court, scurried after by the two women accompanying
him, who Quirke surmised, from the family likeness in their
looks, must be his mother and his sister. Quirke, too, made
to get away, but Sheedy called him over and, not looking at
him but concentrating on squaring a sheaf of documents on
his desk, asked quietly, 'There isn't something you're not
telling me, is there, Mr Quirke?' Quirke set his shoulders
and his jaw and said nothing, and Sheedy sniffed, and
Quirke could see him deciding to let it go. After all, no one
was innocent here. Sheedy himself most likely suspected
suicide but had made no mention of it. Suicide was trouble-
some, involving tedious amounts of paperwork, and besides,
a verdict of *felo de se* only caused heartache to the relatives,
who would have to think of their departed loved one even

now roasting in what the priests assured them was a special pit in deepest Hell reserved for the souls of those who had done away with themselves.

When Quirke turned from the desk he saw for the first time—had he been there all along?—Inspector Hackett, standing in the aisle with his hat in his hands, breasting the surge of the crowd of onlookers and pressmen making for the exit. He smiled and winked at Quirke and flapped the hat against his chest in a droll greeting, like Stan Laurel flapping the end of his tie, at once bashful and knowing. Then he turned and sauntered out in the wake of the others.

Once outside, Quirke walked down to the river in the noonday heat, regretting his black suit and his black hat. He stopped to smoke a cigarette, leaning on the granite wall of the embankment. It was low tide and the blue mud of the riverbed stank and the seagulls wheeled and shrieked about him. He was glad the inquest was over, yet he still felt burdened, a peculiar sensation: it was as if he had emptied something out only to find that the container that had held it was as heavy as before. He still wanted to know how and why Deirdre Hunt had died. He had assumed she had overdosed by accident—although there were no signs to suggest she had been an addict—and that someone had driven her corpse out to Sandycove and slipped it into the sea. But if it was Billy Hunt who had thus disposed of his inconveniently dead wife, why had he imagined that suicide by drowning would seem less of a disgrace than death from an inadvertent overdose of morphine? For even if he had thought Quirke would not notice that puncture mark, he could not have known that Quirke and the coroner would collude in ignoring the obvious likelihood that his wife had drowned herself. Had Billy hoped the body would sink and never be recovered? Or had he thought that if it was found it would be unrecognisable? Was that why he had undressed her, if it was he who had done so? People were amazingly ignorant of the intricacies of forensic medicine, and of police procedures, for that matter. When the body was found, with such shocking promptness, how had Billy imagined that Quirke, even if he had not performed a post-mortem, would fail to uncover what it was she had died of? But maybe Billy did not care. Quirke knew how it felt to lose a wife, knew that confused blend of grief and rage and bafflement and strange, shameful elation.

He flicked the stub of his cigarette over the embankment wall. A gull, deceived, dived after it. Nothing is what it seems.

6

IT FELT AS natural as anything, that windy Wednesday afternoon, when Dr Kreutz invited her to come into the house, yet she could hardly believe it when she found herself, a married woman, following him through the little gate in the black iron railings that made a sound on its hinges like a gasp of surprise, or a sharp, warning cry. He brought out his key and opened the basement door and stood back and held it wide, nodding for her to go ahead of him. There was a short, dim passageway and then the room, the consulting room, low-ceilinged and also dim. The air was pleasantly perfumed with some herb or spice; it was a nice smell, woody yet sharp and not at all like the cheap, cloying scents that Mr Plunkett sold, Coty and Ponds and Evening in Paris. The fragrance made her think of deserts and tents and camels, though she knew these were things that would not be in India—not that she knew much about India, except from the pictures, and she supposed that stuff was all made up, anyway, and nothing like the real-life place. There was a low, deep sofa draped with a red blanket, and a little low table and four brightly coloured cushions on the floor around it, for sitting on, it must be, instead of chairs, or maybe they were for kneeling on. There was no carpet and the floorboards were painted with shiny, dark-red varnish.

'Welcome welcome,' the Doctor said, and urged her towards the sofa with a gesture of one long, slender hand the colour of melted chocolate. But she would not let herself sit, not yet.

On the table there was a bowl made of hammered copper, and into this the Doctor emptied the three bright red apples from the string bag—she thought of Snow White and the Witch—and then went out through a doorless archway into another room, from where she heard him filling a kettle with water. She stood in the silence, feeling the slow, dull beating of her heart. She was not thinking anything, or not in words, anyway. It was the strangest thing she had experienced in her life so far, just being there, in that room, with that exotic perfume in the air, and the look of everything somehow different from anything she was accustomed to. If Billy had walked in the door this minute she would hardly have known who he was. She felt no touch of worry or alarm. In fact, she had never felt so far from danger. In the street outside the wind soughed, and vague shadows of leaves moved before her on the far wall. She was trembling, she realised, trembling with excitement and a strange sort of expectant happiness that somehow had something to do with the deep-red colour of the rug on the sofa and the cushions on the dark-red floor and those three unreally perfect, glossy apples in the copper dish, each one reflecting on its cheek an identical gleaming spot of light from the window.

The room beyond the arch was a little kitchen, with badly painted cupboards and an old stone sink and a Baby

Belling stove, on which the Doctor boiled the kettle and made herbal tea in a green metal pot that was not round but boat-shaped, a bit like Sinbad's lamp, with a long, curving spout and swirling designs cut into the metal all over. This time she accepted his invitation to sit, and arranged herself carefully on the sofa with her knees pressed tight together and her hands clasped in her lap. The Doctor, with marvellous grace and effortlessness, folded himself rapidly downwards, like a corkscrew going into a cork, until he was sitting tailor-fashion on one of the cushions by the table. He poured the almost colourless tea into two dainty little painted cups. She waited for him to offer milk and sugar but then realised that of course this was not that kind of tea, and even though she had not said anything to show up her ignorance she blushed anyway, and hoped he would not notice.

They began to talk, and before she knew it she was telling him all sorts of things about herself, things she would never have told anyone else. First she talked about her family and her life in the Flats, or a version of it—she was careful not to say what the Flats were called or where they were, exactly, in case he might know what they were like, for they had an awful reputation that people who had never had to live there made jokes about all the time—and managed to give the impression that they were old and quite grand, grand as the ones on Mespil Road that she often passed by when she went for walks on her own at the weekends. She told him, too, about the stolen bicycle when she was little and how she had broken Tommy Goggin's tooth, and that was certainly not the sort of thing that would happen on Mespil Road. She was even going to tell him what her father used to do to her when she was a little girl, what he had made her promise would be 'our own little secret', but stopped just in time, shocked at herself. How could she talk like this to a total stranger? Thinking of her Da and all that, she got a wobbly feeling in the pit of her stomach, and despite the spicy perfume in the air and the fragrance of the tea she was sure she smelled distinctly for a second the very smell Da always used to have, of coal dust and fags and sweat, and she had to stop herself from giving a shiver. But what was she doing here, anyway, she asked herself, as she sipped the bittersweet tea, what did she think she was at, sitting on this red rug in this strange man's room on an ordinary autumn afternoon? Only the afternoon was not ordinary, she knew that. She knew, in fact, that she would think of this for ever after as one of the most momentous days of her life, more momentous even than the day she was married.

She stopped talking then, thinking she had said quite enough about herself for the moment, and waited to see what he in return would reveal about himself and his life. But he told her little, or little that she could get a real grasp of, anyway, it sounded so strange. He had been born in Austria, he said, the son of an Austrian psychoanalyst and a maharajah's daughter who had been sent from India to be the psychoanalyst's pupil but had fallen in love with him. As she listened to this she felt, despite herself, a small qualm of doubt; though he spoke matter-of-factly, seeming not to be concerned whether she believed him or not, there was something in his tone that did not sound to her entirely, well, natural. She caught him watching her, too, with what looked to her like a speculative gleam in those black-brown eyes of his, and she wondered if he was testing her gullibility or, indeed, if he might be laughing at her. But she could not believe that he would lie, and she did not mind even if he was making fun of her, which was strange, for if there was one thing that usually she would not stand for it was being made a mockery of. Later, she would come to see that this was how he was with everyone and everything, that for him there was nothing that did not have its playful side, and he taught her, or at least he tried to teach her—she had never been good at getting jokes—that being solemn was the same as being sad, and that God wanted us only to be happy.

He explained to her that he was a Sufi. She did not know what that was, or even how to spell it. She assumed at first it was the name of the tribe or—what was the word?—the caste that he came from, or at least that his mother came from, in India. But no, it was a religion, it seemed, or a kind of religion. He explained that the name was a version of the Arab word *saaf*, meaning pure. Sufism was based on the secret teachings of the Prophet Muhammad—at that name he bowed his head and muttered something, a prayer, she assumed, in a guttural language that sounded as if he was clearing his throat—who had lived almost fourteen hundred years ago, and who was as great a teacher as Jesus. The Prophet had been sent by God as 'a mercy to all the world', he explained, and always talked to people in a way they could understand. Since most people are simple, he had put his teachings into simple words, but he had other doctrines, too, mystical and difficult, that were meant for only the wisest ones, the initiates. It was on these teachings that the Sufis had founded their religion. The

Sufis had started out in Baghdad—she had seen that picture, *The Thief of Baghdad*, but thought she should not mention it—and their teachings had spread throughout the world, and today there were Sufis everywhere, he said, in all countries.

He talked for a long time, quietly, gravely, not looking at her but gazing dreamily before him, and from the way he spoke—chanting, it was more like—he might have been thinking aloud, or repeating something he had said many times before, in many other places. She was reminded of a priest giving a sermon, but he was not like a priest, or not like the priests she was used to, at any rate, with their smelly black clothes and badly shaved chins and haunted, resentful eyes. The Doctor was, quite simply, beautiful. It was a word she would never have thought of applying to a man, until now. He told her so many things, and said so many names—Ali somebody Talib, and El-Ghazali, and Omar Khayyám whom at least she had heard of, and ones that were almost funny, like Al Biruni, and Rumi, and Saadi of Shiraz—that soon her head was spinning. He instructed her that Sufis believe that all people must try to cleanse them-selves of low human instincts and approach God through stages, *maqaam*, and states of mind, *haal*. He pronounced these and other exotic words very clearly and carefully, so that she would remember them, but most of them she immediately forgot. However, there were two words that she knew she would remember, and these were *shaykh*, which is the sage, and *murid*, the student or apprentice who places himself under the guidance and care of the *shaykh*. As she listened to him talk about the love that must exist between these two, the teacher and his pupil, that feeling she had felt when she had first entered the room glowed in her more strongly than ever. It was a sort of—she did not know how to describe it to herself—a sort of calm excitement, if such a thing was possible; excitement, and heat, and a sense of happy yearning. Yes, yearning—but for what?

It was only afterwards that she came fully to realise just how extraordinary had been that hour she had spent with him—how extraordinary, that is, that she had gone there at all, and had sat there all that time, listening to him. She had always been impulsive—everyone said it about her, even her Auntie Irene, though she managed to make it sound like a big fault—but this was something different. She had been drawn to Dr Kreutz out of need. What that need was, or how she had known that he was the one who could fulfil it, she could not say. Only she was aware, when he had shown her out and she was walking again along Adelaide Road towards the bus stop in the windy twilight—it must have been more than an hour she had spent with him, if it was this late—of having been set apart somehow from everything around her. She felt like the people in the advertisement for Horlicks, or maybe it was Bovril, who are shown walking along through driving winter rain but smiling cheerfully, each one enclosed in a protective aura of light and warmth.

She went over in her mind what she could recall of the tales and parables he had recounted. The story that had made the strongest impression on her was that of the girl who had been brought back from the dead. This girl had three suitors and could not choose between them. Then one day she fell ill and was dead within the hour. The suitors were heartbroken, and each mourned in his own way. The first would not leave the graveyard, day or night, and ate and slept beside the grave; the second went wandering and became a fakir, or wise man, while the third gave over all of his time to comforting the girl's grieving father. One day on his travels the second suitor, the fakir, learned from another wise man the secret magic charm that would bring the dead back to life. He hurried home, and went to the cemetery and said the magic formula to summon the girl out of her grave, and in a moment she appeared, as beautiful as she had ever been. The girl returned to her father's house, and the suitors began to argue among themselves as to who should have her hand. Eventually they went to the girl and each put his case to her. The first said he had not left the graveside for an instant, therefore his grieving had been of the purest. The second, the fakir, pointed out that it was he who had acquired the knowledge to bring her back from the land of the dead. The third spoke of the consolation and comfort he had brought to her father after she had died. The girl listened to each in turn, and then said to them, 'You who discovered the spell to restore my life, you were a humanitarian. You who took care of my father and comforted him, you acted like a son. But you, who lay in grief beside my grave, you were a true lover—and you I will marry.'

It was, she knew, only a story, and even a silly story, at that, yet something in it moved her. She felt that of all that the Doctor had said, this was the one thing meant especially for her. The shape of the fable seemed the shape of a life that would one day be hers. The future, she believed, the future in the unlikely form of Dr Kreutz, had sent her a message, a prophecy, of survival and of love.

•

7

QUIRKE WAS NOT surprised when he heard who it was that was asking to see him. Since the day of the inquest he had been expecting a visit from the inspector. He put down the phone and lit a cigarette and sat thinking—let Hackett cool his heels for five minutes, it would do him good. It was morning, and Quirke was in his office at the hospital. Through the glass panel in the door he could see into the unnatural glare of the dissecting room where Sinclair, his assistant, dourly handsome with black curls and thin, down-turned mouth, was at work on the corpse of a little boy who had been run over by a coal lorry in the Coombe that morning. Thinking of the policeman, Quirke experienced a twinge of unease. The years at Carricklea had left him with a lurking fear of all appointed figures of authority that no subsequent accumulation of authority of his own could rid him of.

He crushed out the cigarette and took off his green surgical gown and went out of the office. He paused a moment to watch Sinclair cut into the child's exposed rib-cage with the bone-cutter that always made Quirke think, incongruously, of silver secateurs. Sinclair was deft and quick; someday, when Quirke was gone, this young man would be in charge of the department. The thought had not occurred to Quirke before. Where, exactly, would he be gone to when that day came?

Inspector Hackett was standing by the reception desk with his hat in his hands. He was in his accustomed outfit of shiny suit and slightly soiled white shirt and nondescript tie; the knot of the tie, sealed tight and also shiny, looked as if it had not been undone in a long time, only pulled loose at night-time and tightened again in the morning. Quirke pictured the detective at end of day sitting wearily on the side of a big bed in angled lamplight, his shoes off and his hair on end, absently widening the loop of the tie with both hands and lifting it over his head, like a would-be suicide having second thoughts.

'I hope I'm not taking you away from your important work,' Hackett said, in his flat, Midlands accent, smiling. He had a way of making even the most bland of pleasantries sound laden with scepticism and sly amusement.

'My work can always wait,' Quirke answered.

The inspector chuckled. 'I suppose so—your clients are not going anywhere.'

They left the hospital and walked out into the morning's smoky sunlight. Hackett ran a hand over his oiled, blue-black hair and set his hat in place, giving the brim an expert downwards brush with an index finger. They turned in the direction of the river, which announced itself with its usual greenish stench. An urchin in rags scampered by, almost colliding with them, and Quirke thought again of the child's corpse on the slab, the pinched, bloodless face and the rickety legs stretched out.

'That was a decent thing to do,' the inspector said,

'sparing the feelings of the relatives of that young woman—what was her name?'

'Hunt,' Quirke said. 'Deirdre Hunt.'

'That's right—Hunt.' As if he would have forgotten. He pulled at an earlobe with a finger and thumb, screwing his face into a thoughtful grimace. 'Why, do you think, would she do a thing like that, fine young woman as she was?'

'A thing like what?'

'Why, do away with herself.'

They came to the river and crossed to the embankment and strolled in the direction of the Park. The smoke of the streets did not reach over the water and the high air there shone bluely. An unladen Post Office delivery wagon thundered past, the big Clydesdale high-stepping haughtily, its mane flying, its huge, fringed hoofs ringing on the roadway as if they were made of heavy, hollow steel.

'The coroner's verdict,' Quirke said measuredly, 'was accidental drowning.'

'Oh, I know, I know—I know what the verdict was. Wasn't I there to hear it?' He chuckled again. ' "A verdict in accordance with the evidence", isn't that what the papers say?'

'Do you doubt it?'

'Well, now, Mr Quirke, I do. I mean to say, it's hard to think that a young woman would drive out to Sandycove at dead of night and take off every stitch of her clothes and leave them folded on the ground and then let herself fall by accident into the sea.'

'A midnight swim,' Quirke said. 'It's summer. It was a warm night.'

'The only ones that swim out there are men, at the Forty Foot—no women allowed.'

'Maybe she did it for a lark. It was night-time, there would be no one to see. Women do that kind of thing, when the moon is full.'

'Oh, aye,' the policeman said, 'a midnight lark.'

'People are odd, Inspector. They get up to the oddest things—no doubt you've noticed that, in your line of work.'

Hackett nodded and closed his eyes briefly, acknowledging the irony.

They came level with Ryan's pub on Parkgate Street. The policeman gestured towards it. 'You must miss the company,' he said, 'of an evening.'

Quirke chose not to understand. 'The company?'

'Being strict teetotal now, as you tell me. What do you do with yourself after dark?'

It was Phoebe's question again. He had no answer. Instead he asked, in a tone almost of impatience: 'Are you investigating Deirdre Hunt's death?'

The inspector stopped short with exaggerated surprise. 'Investigating? Oh, no. No, not at all. I'm just curious, like. It's an occupational hazard that I think we both share.' He glanced quickly sideways at Quirke with a sort of leer. They walked on. It was noon and the sunshine was very hot now, and the policeman took off his jacket and carried it slung over his shoulder. 'I had a nose around to find out where she came from, Deirdre Hunt. Lourdes Mansions, no less. The Wards—that was her maiden name—are a tough crowd. Father worked on the coal boats, retired now—emphysema. Hasn't stopped him boozing and throwing his weight around. The mother I surmise might have been on the game, in her younger days. There's a brother, Mikey Ward, well known to the local constabulary—breaking and entering, that kind of thing. Another brother ran away to sea when he was fourteen, hasn't been heard of since. Oh, a tough lot.'

'I suppose that's why she went into the beauty business,' Quirke said.

'No doubt. Intent on bettering herself.' The policeman sighed. 'Aye—it's a shame.' They crossed again and walked up the steep slope to the gates of the park. Before them, the trees on either side of the avenue stood throbbing against a hot, bleached sky. 'Do you know the fellow she was running it with?'

'What?'

'The beauty shop.'

'No.'

'Fellow by the name of White. Bit of a wide boy, I'm reliably informed. Had a hairdresser's in the premises in Anne Street before they opened the shop.'

'Why is he a wide boy?'

'Takes risks—financial. The wife had to step in a couple of years back to keep his name out of Stubbs's. Then the hairdresser's failed.'

'She has money?'

'The wife? Must have. She's in business herself, runs a sweatshop on Capel Street, high-class fashion work at tuppence an hour.'

Now it was Quirke's turn to chuckle. 'I must say, Inspector, for a man who isn't conducting an investigation you seem to know a great deal about these people.'

The inspector treated this as a compliment, and pretended to be embarrassed. 'Arragh,' he said, 'that's the kind of stuff you'd pick up by standing on a street corner listening to the wind.' Off to their left a herd of deer stood in the long grass amid a shimmer of heat; a stag lifted its elaborately horned head and eyed them sideways with truculent suspicion. 'Look, Inspector,' Quirke said, 'what does it matter, any of this? The woman is dead.'

The inspector nodded but might as well have been shaking his head. 'But that's just when it does matter, to me—when someone is dead, and it's not clear how they came to be that way. Do you see what I mean, Mr Quirke? And by the way,' he added, smiling, 'it was you that brought poor Deirdre Hunt to my attention in the first place—have you forgotten that?'

Quirke had no answer.

They turned back then, and boarded a bus outside the Park gates and stood on the open platform at the back, clinging to the handrail and swaying in awkward unison as the bus plunged and wallowed its way along the quays. The Inspector took off his hat and held it over his breast in the attitude of a mourner at a funeral. Quirke studied the man's flat, peasant's profile. He knew nothing of Hackett, he realised, other than what he saw, and what he saw was what Hackett chose to let him see. At times the policeman gave off a whiff of something, it was as tangible as a smell, chalky and grey, that hinted of institutions. Was there perhaps a Carricklea in his far past, too? Were they both borstal boys? Quirke did not care to ask.

He got off at the Four Courts, stepping down from the platform while the bus was still moving. A wild-haired drunk was sprawled on the pavement by the court gates, unconscious but holding tight to his bottle of sherry. Quirke sometimes pictured himself like this, lost to the world, ragged and sodden, slumped in some litter-strewn corner, his only possession a bottle in a brown-paper bag.

As the bus swept away in a miasma of dirty-grey exhaust smoke the inspector looked after him, smiling his fish-smile, and did that Stan Laurel gesture with his hat again, flapping it on his chest in a mock-mournful, comic gesture that seemed both a farewell and—was it?—a caution.

8

PHOEBE GRIFFIN—it had not occurred to her to change her name to Quirke, and if it had she would not have done it—was unaccustomed to taking an interest in other people's lives. It was not that she considered other people entirely uninteresting, of course; she was not so detached as that. Only she was free of the prurience that seemed to be, that, indeed, must be, so she supposed, what drove gossips and journalists and, yes, policemen to delve into the dark crevices where actions tried to hide away their motives. She thought of her life now as a careful stepping along a thin strand of thrumming wire above a dark abyss. Balanced so, she knew she would do well not to look too often or too searchingly from side to side, or down—she should not look down at all. Up here, where she trod her fine line, the air was lighted and cool, a heady yet sustaining air. And this high, illumined place, sparse though it was, was sufficient for her, who had known enough of depths, and darkness. Why should she speculate about the crowd that she was aware of below her, gazing up in envy, awe and hopeful, spiteful, anticipation?

She trusted no one.

Yet she found herself thinking, again and again, of

Deirdre Hunt, or Laura Swan, and the manner of her death. The woman had been pleasant enough, in a brittle sort of way. Perhaps it was that very brittleness that had attracted Phoebe's sympathetic interest. But here she checked herself—sympathetic? Why sympathetic? Laura Swan, or Deirdre Hunt, had never given her reason to think she was in need of anyone's sympathy. But she must have been in need of something, and in great need, helplessly so, to have ended as she had. She could not imagine what would have brought her to do such a thing, for even in her lowest times Phoebe had never for a moment entertained the possibility of suicide. Not that she did not think it would be good, on the whole, to be gone from this world, but to go in that fashion would be, simply, absurd.

Suicide. The word sounded in her mind now with the ring of a hammer falling on a dull lump of steel. Perhaps the fascination of it, for her, was merely that she had never known anyone personally, or in the flesh, at least—and certainly she had not known Laura Swan in anything other than appearance—who had vanished so comprehensively, who had become non-flesh, as it were, by one sudden, impulsive dive into darkness. Phoebe thought she knew how it would have been for the other woman, knifing through the gleaming black surface with lights sliding on it and plunging deep down, deeper and deeper, into cold and suffocation and oblivion. The diver would have felt impatience, surely, impatience for it all to be over and her to be done with; that, and a strange, desolate sort of joyfulness and satisfaction, the satisfaction of having been, in some paradoxical way, avenged. For Phoebe could not conceive of that young woman going to her death unless someone had driven her to it, wittingly or unwittingly, someone who now was surely suffering the cruel pangs of remorse. Surely.

It was five thirty and the summer afternoon was turning tawny. Although her pride would not have allowed her to admit it, even to herself, this was, for Phoebe, the bleakest moment of the day, made bleaker by the sense of quickening all around her in the other shops up and down the street, where a multitude of other sales assistants were already eagerly pulling down blinds and shutters and turning the signs in the glass doors from 'Open' to 'Closed'. Now Mrs Cuffe-Wilkes, the owner of the Maison des Chapeaux, came bustlingly from the back in a somehow pulsing cloud of the peach-scented perfume that she wore, fluttering her eyelashes like sticky-winged butterflies and making little *mmm mmm* noises under her breath. She was going to a gallery opening, where a *terribly* talented young man was showing his latest drawings, and before that to the Hibernian Hotel for drinks and afterwards to dinner at Jammet's with Eddie and Christine Longford, among others. Mrs Cuffe-Wilkes was a figure in society, and only the best people wore her hats. Phoebe found her amusing, and valiant in her way, and not entirely ridiculous.

'Aren't you going to close up, dear?' Mrs Cuffe-Wilkes said. Her frock was a gauzy concoction of lemon-yellow chiffon, and above her right ear was perilously perched one of her own creations, a tiny pillbox in white and gold, with a spindly wire filament rising from it tipped with a tuft of silk shaped like an orchid, and pierced through by a long, pearl-headed pin. 'That young chap of yours will be getting impatient.' It was one of Mrs Cuffe-Wilkes's fancies to insist that Phoebe must have a young man whose identity she was withholding, and, indeed, whose very existence she denied, out of an incurable shyness.

Phoebe said: 'I was waiting for you to go before I locked up.'

'Well, I'm off now so you're free to put him out of his misery.'

She smiled teasingly—thirty years fell from her face with that smile—and shimmered forth into Grafton Street.

Phoebe lingered in the sudden desertedness of the shop. She put away some toques she had been showing earlier to an elderly, vague woman who obviously had no intention of making a purchase and had come in merely to while away a little part of another long and lonely day. Phoebe was always patient with such non-customers, the 'afternoon callers', as Mrs Cuffe-Wilkes witheringly dubbed them, the aged ones, the solitaries, the dotty, the bereft. Now she stood for a long moment looking vacantly out at the street of slanted shadows. There were times, such as this, when it was as though she had lost herself, had misplaced the self that she was and become a thing without substance, a mote adrift in motionless light. Now she blinked, and shook her head, and sighed at herself impatiently. Things would have to change; she would have to change. Yes—but how?

When she had locked the shop, making sure the deadbolt was in place, she turned in the direction of Anne Street. The old flower-seller at the corner by Brown Thomas's was dismantling her stall. She greeted Phoebe, as she did every evening, and presented her with a leftover bunch of violets. As she walked on Phoebe held the flowers to her nostrils. They had begun to fade already and only the faintest trace of their scent remained, but she did not really mind since flowers, to her, always smelled disturbingly of cats.

She stopped opposite the optician's shop and looked up at the window on the first floor and the sign painted there in metallic lettering:

The Silver Swan
Beauty and Body Care

The window had a blank, deserted look, but she supposed that was only because she knew whom it had been deserted by, and in what manner. Strange, she thought again, this business of people dying. It happened all the time, of course, it was as commonplace as people being born, but death was surely a far deeper mystery than birth. To not be here and then to be here was one thing, but to have been here, and made a life in all its variousness and complexity, and then suddenly to be gone, that was what was truly uncanny. When she thought of her own mother—of Sarah, that is, whom she still regarded as her mother, just as, with somewhat less conviction, she considered Mal to be her father—she felt, along with the constant ache of loss and grief, a kind of angry puzzlement. The world for her had seemed so much larger and emptier after Sarah died, like an enormous auditorium from which the audience had departed and where she was left to wander lost and, yes, bereft.

The narrow door beside the optician's shop opened and Leslie White came out, walking backwards with a large cardboard box in his arms. It struck her again how well his colourless, androgynous name suited him. He was very tall and very thin—*willowy* was the word that came to her—

and his large, hooked nose had a way of seeming always to be detecting a faint, displeasing smell. He had on a pale-blue striped blazer and white duck trousers and two-tone shoes and, of course, his silver cravat; his gleaming hair—in sunlight it had the quality, she thought, of burning magnesium—was Bohemianly long, falling foppishly to his collar. She supposed he would be considered handsome, in a pale, jaded sort of way. He pulled the door shut with his foot; he was gripping a set of keys in his teeth. He put the box down on the step and locked the door, then dropped the keys into his jacket pocket and had picked up the box again and was turning to go when he caught sight of her regarding him from the other side of the street. He frowned, then bethought himself and quickly smiled, even though, as she could plainly see, he did not remember her; Leslie White, she felt sure, would always have a ready smile for the girls.

She was crossing the road. *What are you doing?* she asked herself, but she knew very well it was in hope of seeing him that she had come to loiter here. The man hesitated, his smile faltering; girls, smiled at or not, would be, she supposed, as often a source of trouble as of promise for the Leslie Whites of this world. 'Hello there,' he said brightly, rapidly scanning her face for a clue to her identity. What should she say? Her mind was a blank—but then he rescued her. 'Listen,' he said, 'will you do me a favour?' He turned sideways to her, hefting the box higher against his midriff. 'The keys are in my pocket, the car is round the corner. Would you—?'

She fished for the keys—what a shivery sensation, delving in someone else's pocket!—while he smiled down at her, confident now that even though he could not place her he must know her, or confident at any rate that he soon would. She saw him noticing the flowers she was still clutching— she could not think how to get rid of them—though he made no comment. They walked to the corner and turned into Duke Lane. She was aware that she had not yet spoken a word to him, but he seemed not to mind it or think it odd. He was one of those people, she guessed, who could maintain a perfectly easy silence in any situation, no matter how awkward or delicate. His car was an apple-green Riley, rakish and compact, absurdly low to the ground, and fetchingly a little battered about the bumpers. The hood was down. He tumbled the box into the passenger seat, saying, '*Ouf!*', and turned to her with a hand out for the keys. 'Very kind of you,' he said. 'Don't know what I'd have done.' She smiled. What help she was supposed to have been to him she did not know, since the car had not needed to be unlocked. He held her gaze with his. He had the way that all attractive men have, with their crooked, half-apologetic smiles, of seeming at once brazen and bashful. 'Let me buy you a drink,' he said, and before she could reply went on, 'We'll go in here, where I can keep a watch on the car.'

The interior of the pub was dark and the atmosphere as close as in a cave. They approached the narrow bar and she sat on a high stool. When she asked for a gin and tonic he beamed and said, 'That's my girl,' as if she had passed a test, one that he had prepared especially for her. He offered her a cigarette from a gunmetal case and beamed more broadly when she took one; the test had multiple parts, it seemed. He held his lighter for her. 'The name is White, by the way. Leslie White.' He spoke the name as if he were imparting to her something of great and intimate value. His plummy accent was put on, she could detect clearly the hint of Cockney behind it.

'Yes,' she said, turning her head and blowing the cigarette smoke sideways, 'I know.'

He raised his eyebrows. His skin really was extraordinarily pale, silver, almost, like his hair. 'Now, I'm sure I should know,' he said, laughing apologetically, 'but you are . . . ?'

'Phoebe Griffin. I was a customer, in the shop.'

'Ah.' His look darkened. 'You'll have known Laura, then.'

'Yes. You gave me your card, once.'

'Of course I did, I remember now.' He was lying, of course. He took a sip of his gin. The evening sunlight in the doorway was a wedge of solid gold. 'Did you know what happened to her—Laura, I mean?'

'Yes.' She felt ridiculously giddy, as if she had already consumed half a dozen drinks.

'How did you hear?'

'Someone told me.'

'Ah. I was afraid there might have been a story in the papers. I'm glad there wasn't. It would have been unbearable, seeing it in cold print.' He looked at his shoes. 'Christ. Poor Laura.' He knocked back the last of his drink and caught the barman's eye and waggled his empty glass. He looked at hers, and said, 'You're not drinking.'

'I don't, really.'

He gazed at her for a moment in silence, smiling, then asked suddenly, 'What age are you?'

'Twenty-five,' she said, and was surprised at herself: why had she lied, adding two years to her age? 'And you?'

'Oh, now,' he said. 'A girl doesn't ask a gentleman his age.'

She smiled back at him, then looked into her glass.

The barman brought the second drink and Leslie turned the tumbler this way and that in his hand, making the ice cubes chuckle. For the first time since he had spoken to her he seemed momentarily at a loss. She asked: 'Are you closing up?'

'Closing up . . . ?'

'The Silver Swan. I thought, when I saw you with the cardboard box . . .'

'No, I was just taking away some of—some of Laura's things.' He paused, with an exaggeratedly mournful expression. 'I don't know what I'll do with the place, really. It's com-plicated. There are a number of interests involved. And the finances are a little—well, tangled, shall we say?'

Phoebe waited, then said, 'Her husband, is he one of the "interests"?'

For a second he was struck silent. 'Do you know him, the husband?' he asked, a hint suspiciously.

'No. Someone I know knows him—used to know him.'

He shook his head ruefully. 'This city,' he said. 'It's a village, really.'

'Yes. Everyone knows everyone else's business.'

At that he gave her a sharp look from under his eyebrows. 'It's true, I'm sure,' he said, letting his voice trail off.

A couple came into the pub then and greeted him. The man was dressed in a remarkable ginger-coloured suit made of a coarse, hairy material. The woman with him had dyed shiny black hair that was gathered in a top-knot and tied tightly with a ribbon, which gave her a look of wide-eyed,

fixed astonishment. Leslie White excused himself and sauntered over to them. She watched him as he talked to them,
in his languidly animated way. If Laura Swan had been
more than his business partner, as Phoebe had suspected,
it was clear that her death had not broken his heart. All
at once she saw in her mind with unnerving clarity Laura
Swan's—Deirdre Hunt's—broad face with its slightly flawed
features, the saddle of faint freckles on the bridge of her
nose, her purplish-blue eyes and the look in them, eager,
anxious, excited, and she felt a stab of pity—was it?—so
piercing that it made her catch her breath. She was surprised
at herself, and even a little shocked. She had thought she
had grown out of the way of such feelings.

Leslie White came back looking apologetic again, and
urged her to have another drink, but she said no. She
stepped down from the stool. She was uncomfortable. It
was so hot and airless in here and the stuff of her thin dress
clung briefly to the backs of her thighs and she had to reach
a hand down quickly and peel the material from her skin.
Leslie—was she really thinking of him already by his first
name?—laid two long, slender fingers on her wrist to detain
her. She fancied she could feel the faint rustle of his blood
beneath the pads of his fingertips. Life consists, she reflected
with matter-of-fact clarity, in a long series of misjudgements.
The man in the hairy suit and his top-knotted companion—
she looked, in fact, as if she were suspended from the ceiling
by an invisible cord attached to her hair—were examining
her from across the room with unmasked speculation.

'I must go,' she said. 'There's someone waiting.'

She could see him not believing her. 'You have my card,'
he said. 'Will you ring me?'

She tipped her head to one side and looked at him, allowing herself a faint smile. 'I very much doubt it.'

She realised she was still clutching the bunch of violets in her damp and not quite steady hand; they looked like some small, many-headed creature that had been accidentally strangled.

Quirke, too, had been brooding on that place over the optician's shop in Anne Street, and he, too, had found himself being led there after he had finished work for the day, so that when Phoebe left the pub in Duke Lane he was standing at the very spot, although he did not know it, where she had stood a half-hour earlier watching Leslie White come out of the doorway with the cardboard box in his arms. She did not see Quirke now, but he saw her. He did not hail her, and let her go on, and watched as she turned into a now near-deserted Grafton Street and disappeared from his view. He frowned. He did not like coincidences; they made him uneasy. Again he felt the touch of a cold tentacle of unease. A few seconds later, as he was about to move off, he saw another figure duck out of the pub, and knew at once who it must be—there was only one person who could have hair like that. Quirke was familiar with the type: long and gangly, with a stooping, sinuous, flat-footed gait, his long pale hands swinging at the ends of his arms as if they were connected to his wrists not by bone but skin alone. A hollow man: if he were to be rapped on there would come back only a dull, flat echo. The fellow climbed into his little car, not bothering to open the door but throwing one long leg and then the other over it and plumping down in the seat beside the cardboard box and starting up the engine and making it roar. What was his name—White? Someone White, yes. The car shot out of the lane and turned in the direction of Dawson Street, sweeping past Quirke where he stood with his back to the window of a draper's shop. The man, his fine hair flying, did not look at him. Leslie, that was the name. Leslie White.

9

QUIRKE FELT LIKE a man who has been making his way safely along beside a tropic and treacherous sea and suddenly feels the sand begin to shift and suck at his bare, defenceless and all at once unsteady feet. The possibility that Phoebe, too, might be somehow involved in the business of Deirdre Hunt's death, that was a thing he could not have anticipated, and it shook him. It was Phoebe who had told him about Leslie White in the first place. Did she know him better than she had pretended to? And if so, what kind of knowing was it?

He walked slowly up Dawson Street and across the Green in the direction of Harcourt Street. Couples sat on benches self-consciously holding hands, and white-skinned young men with their shirts open to the waist lay sprawled on the grass in the last of the day's sunshine. He felt acutely, as so often, the unwieldy bulk of himself, his squat neck and rolling shoulders and thick upper arms and the vast, solid cage of his chest. He was too big, too barrelsome, all disproportionate to the world. His brow was wet under the band of his hat. He needed a drink. Odd, how that need waxed and waned. Days might go by without a serious thought of alcohol; at other times he shivered through endless hours clenched on himself, every parched nerve crying out to be slaked. There was another self inside him, one who hectored and wheedled, demanding to know by what right he had imposed this cruel abstinence, or whispering that he had been good, oh, so good, for so long, for months and months and months, and surely by now had earned one drink, one miserable little drink?

In Harcourt Street he rang the bell of Phoebe's flat and heard faintly its electric buzzing from high above him on the fourth floor. He waited, looking down the broad sweep of the street to the corner of the Green and the glimpse afforded there of crowding, dejected leafage. A hot breeze blew against his face, bearing a dusty mix of smells, the exhausted breath of summer. He remembered the trams in the old days trundling along here, clanging and sparking. He had lived in this city for most of his life and yet felt a stranger still.

Phoebe did not try to hide her surprise; it was a part of the unspoken understanding between them, the father-daughter contract—treacherous father, injured daughter—that he would not call on her unannounced. Her hair was held back with a band, and she was wearing black velvet pointed-toed slippers and a peignoir of watered silk with an elaborate design of dragons and birds that had once belonged, he realised, to Sarah. 'I was about to take a bath,' she said. 'Everything feels so filthy in this weather.' Side by side they plodded up the long flights of stairs. The house was shabby and dim and in the stairwell there hung the same greyish smell as in the house that he lived in, on Mount Street. He imagined other, similar houses all over the city, each one a warren of vast, high-ceilinged rooms turned into flats and bed-sitters for the likes of him and his daughter, the homeless ones, the chronically unhoused.

Once inside the door of the flat she asked him for a shilling for the gas meter. 'Lucky you came,' she said. 'Hot and horrible as it is I don't fancy a cold bath.'

She made tea and brought it into the living room. They sat, with their cups on their knees, facing each other on the bench seat under the great sash window the lower half of which was opened fully on to the stillness of the evening. The workers in the offices round about had all gone home by now and the street below was empty save for the odd motor-car or a green double-decker bus, braying and smoking and spilling its straggle of passengers on to the pavement. Behind them the room stood in dumb stillness; the light from the window reflected in the mirror of a sideboard at the back wall seemed a huge, arrested exclamation. 'I'm keeping you from your bath,' Quirke said. She continued gazing into the street as if she had not heard. The old-gold light falling from above lit the angle of her jaw and he caught his dead wife's very image.

'A detective came to see me,' he said. A faint frown tightened the pale triangle between her eyebrows but still she did not look at him. 'He was asking about Deirdre Hunt—or Laura Swan, whichever.'

'Why?'

'Why?'

'I mean, why was he asking *you*?'

'I did a post-mortem on her.'

'That's right. You said.'

She picked at a thread in the rough covering of the window-seat. In her silk gown she had the look of one of the fragile figures in a faded Oriental print. He wondered if she would be considered pretty. He could not judge. She was his daughter.

'Tell me,' he said, 'how well did you know this woman?'

'I told you already—I bought some stuff from her, hand lotion, that sort of thing.'

'And the fellow who was in business with her, Leslie White—did you know him?'

'I told you that, too. He gave me his card one day. I have it somewhere.'

He studied her. So it was true: she had been with Leslie White before he saw the two of them in Duke Lane going their separate ways. He turned his head and looked about the room. She had impressed herself hardly at all on the place. The few oversized pieces of furniture had probably been there for a century or more, relics of an oppressively solid, commodious world that was long gone. The mantelpiece bore a few knick-knacks—a Meissen ballerina, a brass piggy-bank, two miniature china dogs facing each other from either end—and in a corner of the horsehair sofa a one-eyed teddy bear was wedged at a drunken angle. The only photograph to be seen, in a tortoiseshell frame on the sideboard, was of Mal and Sarah on their wedding day; there was no image of her mother, or of him. Where was the Evie Hone pencil-study of Delia that he had given her when she came back from America? She had pared her life to its essentials. A bunch of wilted violets lay on the table.

He had been in Dublin on the day that Sarah died, in Boston, in the same hospital where he had first met her nearly twenty years before. The brain tumour, the signs of which none of the medical men around her had recognised, had in the end done its work quickly. After he had got the news from Boston, Quirke had spoken long-distance to Phoebe on the telephone. She was staying in Scituate, south of the city, with Rose Crawford, her grandfather's widow. The connection on the transatlantic line had an eerie, hollow quality that brought him back instantly to the big old gaunt house in Scituate that Josh Crawford had left to his wife. He had pictured Phoebe standing in the echoing entrance hall with the receiver in her hand, gazing at the arabesques of light in the stained-glass panels on either side of the front door. She had listened for a while to his halting attempts to find something to say to her, some word of condolence and apology, but then had interrupted him. 'Quirke,' she said, 'listen. I'm an orphan. My mother is dead, now Sarah is dead, and you're dead to me, too. Don't phone again.' Then she had hung up.

When she came home from America he had expected her to refuse to see him, but it had been a time of truces, and she had joined up, however unenthusiastically, to the general amnesty. He wondered, as he so frequently wondered, what she thought of him now—did she resent, despise, hate him? All he knew was how much easier it had been between them in all the years before she had found out that he was her father. He would have liked to have them back, those years; he would have liked that ease, that dispensation, back again.

She rose and carried the tea tray into the kitchen and came back with her cigarette case and her lighter. She stood by the mantelpiece and lit a cigarette and swivelled her mouth to blow a line of smoke down at the fireplace, and there was Delia again, his hard-eyed, dark, dead wife.

'Let me see that card,' he said.

'What card?'

'The one Leslie White gave you.'

She looked at him levelly with a faint, brittle smile. 'You're starting to meddle again, Quirke, aren't you?' she said.

He was never sure, now, what to call her, how to address her. Somehow just her name was not enough, and yet at the same time it was too much. 'The world,' he said, 'is not what it seems.'

Her smile turned steelier still.

'Oh, Quirke,' she said, 'don't try to sound philosophical, it doesn't convince. Besides, I know you. You can't leave anything alone.' She took another, long, draw at her cigarette, flaring her nostrils. When she leaned her head back to breathe out the smoke her eyes narrowed and she looked more Oriental than ever. Behind him, down in the street, a bicycle bell tinged sharply. 'You think there's some mystery to Laura Swan's death, don't you?' she said. 'I can hear the little grey cells working.'

She was mocking him; he did not mind. He turned his face away from her to look down into the street again. At the far pavement a clerical student, sombre-suited, had dismounted from his bike and was leaning down to remove his cycle clips. Even yet the sight of that glossy, raven-black suiting made something tighten in Quirke's gut.

'There are dangerous people about,' he said. 'They might not seem dangerous, but they are.'

'Who are you thinking of, specifically?'

'No one, specifically.'

She gazed at him for a long moment. 'I'm not going to give you Leslie White's number.'

'I'll get it anyway.'

She rose and walked into the shadowed depths of the room and sat down on the sofa, crossing one leg on the other and smoothing the silk stuff of the gown over her knee. In the dimness there her pale face shone paler still, a Noh mask. 'What are you doing, Quirke? I mean, really.'

'Really? I don't know—and that's the truth.'

'Then if you don't know, shouldn't you not be doing it?'

'I'm not even sure what "it" is. But, yes, you're right, I should stay out of it.'

'Yet you won't.'

He did not answer. He was recalling his first glimpse of Billy Hunt that day in Bewley's, sitting at the little marble table before his untouched cup of coffee, erect on the plush banquette the red of which was the colour of an open wound, lost in his misery. It was, Quirke reflected now, so easy to pity the pitiable.

There was a distant rumble of thunder, and a breeze brought the tinny smell of coming rain.

'You're such an innocent, Quirke,' his daughter said, almost fondly.

10

THE WEATHER BROKE, and there was a day of wild wind and driving showers of tepid rain. First the streets steamed, then streamed. The river's surface became pocked steel, and the seagulls whirled and plummeted, riding the billowing gales. An inside-out umbrella skittered across O'Connell Bridge and was run over, crunchingly, by a bus. Quirke sat with his assistant, Sinclair, in a café at a corner by the bridge. They drank dishwater coffee, and Sinclair ate a currant bun. They came down here sometimes from the hospital at lunchtime, though neither of them could remember how they had settled on this particular place, or why; it was a dismal establishment, especially in this weather, the windows fogged over and the air heavy with cigarette smoke and the stink of wet clothing. Quirke had taken out his cigarette case and was preparing to contribute his share to the general fug. His knee ached, as it always did when the weather turned wet.

He had found Leslie White's number in the telephone book—it was as simple as that—but still he hesitated to call him. What was he to say? He had no business approaching him or anyone else who had known Deirdre Hunt. He was a pathologist, not a policeman.

'Tell me, Sinclair,' he said, 'do you ever consider the ethics of our business?'

'The ethics?' Sinclair said. He looked as if he were about to laugh.

'Yes, ethics,' Quirke said. There were moments, and they were always a surprise, when Sinclair's studied, deadpan obtuseness irritated him intensely. 'There must be some. We swear the Hippocratic Oath, but what does that mean when all the people we treat, if that's the word for what we do, are dead? We're not like physicians.'

'No, we just slice 'em and bag 'em.'

Sinclair was fond of making cracks like this, delivered in a Hollywood drawl. This also irritated Quirke. He suspected they were intended as a challenge to him, but he could not think what it might be he was being challenged about.

'But that's my point,' he said. 'Have we a responsibility to the dead?' Sinclair looked into his coffee cup. They had never spoken of their trade like this before, if indeed, Quirke reflected, they were speaking of it now. He sat back from the table, drawing on his cigarette. 'Did you want to be a pathologist?' he asked. 'I mean, did you know that was what you were going to be, or did you switch, like the rest of us?' Sinclair said nothing, and he went on, 'I did. I had intended to be a surgeon.'

'And what happened?'

He looked up at the icy-seeming wet on the window and the vague, blurred shapes of people and cars and buses beyond. 'I suppose I must have preferred the dead over the living. "No trouble there," as someone once said to me.' He laughed briefly.

Sinclair considered this.

'I think,' he said slowly, 'I think we do the best we can by them—the dead, that is. Not that it matters to a corpse whether we treat it with respect or not. It's what the relatives expect of us. And in the end I suppose it's the relatives that count.' He looked at Quirke. 'The living.'

Quirke nodded. This was the longest sustained speech he had ever heard Sinclair deliver. Was he being challenged again? He would have found it hard to like this unnervingly self-contained young man, if liking was what was required, and happily it was not. He stubbed out his cigarette in the tin ashtray on the table. Did he do his best by the dead? He was not sure what that would entail. For Quirke a corpse was a vessel containing a conundrum, the conundrum being the cause of death. Ethics? It was precisely to avoid such weighty questions that he had gone in for pathology. He *did* prefer the dead over the living. *That* was what had happened. *No trouble there.*

When he parted from Sinclair in the street—it struck him that he did not even know in what part of the city Sinclair lived—he waited for him to be lost in the afternoon crowd before going in search of a telephone kiosk. Inside, there was the usual mingled smell of sweat and urine and fag-ends. He flipped through the mauled and tattered book that was tethered to its stand by a length of chain and checked that he had remembered the number correctly. This time he noted also the address. Castle Avenue, Clontarf—an oddly sedate place of abode for someone as louche as Leslie White. He put in the pennies and dialled the number. Gusts of wind made the door behind him squeal on its hinges. After half a dozen rings, and as he was about to hang up, suddenly a woman's voice answered. The pennies clattered one by one down the chute. He thought of dropping the receiver and fleeing. Instead he asked for Leslie White.

'He's not here,' the woman said brusquely; she had a light, strong voice; a tall woman's voice. There was a definite accent—English? 'Who is this?' she asked.

'I was a friend of Deirdre Hunt,' Quirke said, unable to think of a better lie. 'Mr White's partner.'

The woman gave a cold laugh. 'His partner? That's a good one.' Clearly this was the wife to whom Phoebe had already spoken on the phone. 'Anyway, he's not here. And he's not likely to be here. I threw him out. Who did you say you were?'

'The name is Quirke,' he said, and then, with a sensation of being about to tip headlong down a staircase, he heard his voice ask, 'Could I come round and have a word with you?'

There was a silence. He could not decide whether the faint surgings on the line were the sound of her breathing or of the wind in the telephone wires. 'Quirke, did you say?' she said at last. 'Do I know you?'

'No, we haven't met.'

Again there was a pause, then, 'Oh, what the hell.'

His guess had been right: she was a tall woman, broad-shouldered and long-hipped, with black eyes and very black hair cut in a dramatic, straight style like that of a pharaoh's daughter, and her eyes, too, were pharaonic, painted round the lids with heavy black lines. She wore a complicated crimson silk wrap and sandals with narrow gold straps.

When she opened the front door of the house on Castle Avenue she held her head back and looked at Quirke sceptically down her fine, narrow-winged nose. She lifted one hand and set it against the edge of the door and the loose sleeve of her wrap fell away to reveal the milky underside of a long, slim, shapely arm—Quirke had a weakness for the inner sides of women's arms, always so pale, so soft, so vulnerable. In her other hand she was holding a wine glass at a slight tilt. Her name she said was Kate—'Kate for Kathryn, with a *k* and a *y*.' She was, he estimated, at the latter end of her thirties. 'Come in,' she said. 'You may as well.'

The house was a big, ugly, red-brick affair, three storeys over a windowed basement, with black railings at the front and a garden where lilac trees and roses grew. Inside, however, the place had been entirely dismantled and remodelled in the most up-to-date severe, chunky, steel-and-glass style. Kate White led the way into what she called the den, walking ahead of him with a lazy, lounging swing. In the room there were numerous items of angular white furniture and a scattering of rugs and small square glass tables, on one of which stood a white telephone, and on another a recently opened bottle of white wine misted down its sides. All this, Quirke saw at once, had been laid on in his honour, the painted eyes, the silk wrap and the gold sandals, the chilled bottle of Chablis, perhaps even the white phone, set just so on its little pedestal. In the far wall and taking up most of it was an immense picture window. Kate White went to it and, with a dramatic gesture, seized the cord and jerked up the Venetian blind to reveal an elaborate back garden of trees and flowerbeds and lily ponds and meandering, crazy-paved pathways. She waved her wine glass at it all and said drily, 'My needs are modest, as you see.' She came back to the little table and took up the wine bottle. 'Fancy a splash?'

'No, thanks.'

She looked at him. 'Oh? I'd have taken you for a drinking man.'

'I used to be.'

'Well, sorry, but I feel the need of a pick-me-up at this hour of the afternoon.'

She refilled her glass and invited him to sit, and draped herself across one end of the big white sofa with her back to the garden. She crossed her legs, affording him a glimpse of a smooth length of thigh clad in taut nylon, and the start of a stocking-top. Outside the window the sun had broken through big-bellied clouds and the drenched trees sparkled.

'So,' she said. 'You were a friend of what's-her-name's.'

'No, not really.'

She took this with seeming indifference.

'Glad to hear it,' she said. He brought out his cigarettes. She leaned down to the low table and pushed forward a square, cut-glass ashtray. 'So who *are* you?'

'I'm a pathologist.'

She laughed incredulously. 'You're a *what*?'

'I knew—that is, I used to know—her husband, Deirdre Hunt's.'

She gave him a long look, then sipped her wine. 'And what exactly is it that you want from me, Mr . . . ? Sorry, I've forgotten.'

'Quirke.' He paused, looking at his hands. 'Frankly, Mrs White—'

'Call me Kate.'

'Frankly, I don't know what I want.'

She gave another soft snort of laughter. 'That makes a change, for a man.' Her glass was almost empty again.

'Did *you* know her,' Quirke asked, 'Deirdre Hunt?'

'She was called Laura in this house. Laura Swan.' Again a snort. 'The former ugly duckling.'

'Your husband was in business with her.'

'That's what he called it. Some business. Unlike you, *he* knew what he wanted.' She frowned. 'By the way, how did you know where he lived—used to live?

'I looked him up in the phone book.'

Her frown deepened and turned suspicious. 'The husband, the Swan woman's husband, did he send you?'

'No. Why would he?'

She poured yet another go of wine into her glass; the bottle was two-thirds empty by now. She said: 'I don't know—you tell me.' In the garden a gust of wind shook the trees, scattering handfuls of diamond drops. She was studying him again over the rim of her glass. 'A pathologist,' she said. 'Are you with the police?' He shook his head. 'But you're some kind of investigator or something, are you?'

'No. I'm a consultant pathologist. I work at the Hospital of the Holy Family. Deirdre Hunt's husband called me. That was how I knew about her death.'

She suddenly smiled. It was a startlingly candid, accommodating smile, and it transformed her for a moment from the hard-eyed virago she was pretending to be into something else. 'I'm thinking, Mr Quirke, that I'm sitting here, alone in my house in the middle of the afternoon with a complete stranger, drinking too much wine—shouldn't I be worried?'

'Worried?'

'Well, that you might try to take advantage of me, for instance.' She gave him that ambiguous smile again. It made her eyes go moist and puckered the skin round them so that it seemed she might be about to cry, even as she was smiling. 'Happens all the time, I'm told,' she went on. 'Gullible housewives let in people who say they're travelling salesmen or insurance brokers and the next thing they're on their backs battling for their honour.' She laughed, making a gurgling sound deep in her throat, and leaned forward and grasped the neck of the bottle and filled her glass again. She spilled a few drops of wine on the white cushion where she sat—'Oops! Clumsy me'—and wiped at the stains and then put her fingers to her mouth and licked the tips of them, one by one, watching him from under her eyelashes. She drank, sat back, sighed. 'I probably drove the little slut to it, you know,' she said complacently. She waited for him to react and pouted when he did not. 'I phoned her. I'd discovered some things, incriminating things—letters, photographs. I rang her up and told her what I'd found. I'm afraid'—again that movie vamp's fluttering glance from under black-caked lashes—'I'm afraid I gave her a piece of my mind. As you can imagine. It's quite upsetting, you know, when a woman suddenly finds out that someone is having an affair with her husband.' She stopped, and looked into her glass again, pursing her lips and slowly blinking. He could hear her breathing. 'I think I must be a little drunk,' she murmured, in a tone of vague surprise.

She put the glass down carefully on the low table and pulled herself up from the sofa and walked to the window and stood there with her back to him, her hands on her hips.

'I'm glad the trollop is dead,' she said. She let her arms drop to her sides and turned her head and looked at him. 'I suppose you think I'm a prize bitch, Mr . . . What was your name again? Quirke, yes, sorry. And I suppose I am—a bitch, I mean. But she was no better than a whore, and, frankly, I'm happy she's gone.'

She frowned then, and tilted her head as if she were listening to something inside herself, then excused herself and brushed past him quickly and left the room. He heard her hurrying upstairs, and a door slamming. He was sitting on a square white chair with his hands on his knees. Slowly the silence congealed around him. The house was like an overgrown doll's house, with its pale walls and paler furniture, its dainty tables and cubic chairs. The air smelled of nothing. It was like a house that had not been lived in yet. He gazed out at the wet, wind-tossed garden where the afternoon sunlight dazzled. Upstairs a lavatory flushed, and water gurgled along a grid of pipes. He crept into the hall and was heading for the front door when she appeared above him at the top of the stairs. She had changed into a black polo-necked sweater and black slacks. He stopped, and she came down to him. She had removed her makeup, and her face now had a raw, chalky texture. 'Making a break for it, were you?' she asked, with an attempt at brightness, then looked aside. 'I'm sorry,' she said. 'I'm not much of a drinker.'

She brought him into the kitchen. Here, too, all was white

plastic and glass and matt-grey steel. He sat on a high stool, leaning an elbow on the tiled work-top while she spooned coffee into a metal percolator with a glass dome and put it on a ring of the gas stove to brew. She had managed somehow to sober up, and in her severe black outfit, which threw her features into sharp relief, she was a different person from the one who had sat draped on the sofa taunting him with her big-boned beauty and almost bragging of the deluge of dirt that had overwhelmed her life.

The water in the percolator came to the boil and began to splutter into the little glass dome. Kate stood with her arms folded, leaning her hip against the stove and studying the toes of the black pumps she had put on in place of the Egyptian sandals. He offered her a cigarette but she did not take it.

'Have you ever been jealous, Mr Quirke?' she asked. 'I mean really jealous? Jealous not just of something you suspect but of a definite, identifiable person, a face, a body that you know as real, that you can picture, on a bed, doing things. It makes you feel sick, that kind of jealousy, I mean physically sick, all the time, sick like with the worst hang-over you ever had. Have you had the misfortune ever to find yourself in that state?'

He had a sudden image of his wife, Delia, before they were married, walking away from him wearing only high-heeled slippers and a pearl necklace and turning to look at him over her shoulder with that cat-smile of hers, the barest tip of a pink tongue showing between her scarlet-painted lips.

'No,' he said. He noticed he had taken out his propelling pencil and was fiddling with it. 'Not like that.'

'What they don't warn you about, the books and so on, is the loneliness. Jealousy makes you feel you're the only person suffering in the entire world, the only person suffering like this, like having a red-hot knife-blade lodged in your side, the side where your heart used to be.' She smiled that wet-eyed, weepy smile at him again. He pictured himself reaching out and pressing his fingers to her temples and drawing her head slowly towards him and kissing her eyelids, first one, then the other. In the harsh light reflected from the gleaming walls he could see the countless tiny grains of her skin and the faint down on her upper lip.

She turned off the gas and fetched two cups from a cupboard above the stove and set them on the work-top and poured the coffee. 'I shouldn't have telephoned her, I suppose,' she said. 'She was nothing, just another poor bitch on the make, absolutely common, dragged up from the slums.' She lifted the cup to her lips and narrowed her eyes against the coffee's heat. 'That's another thing they don't tell you, how the other woman—the other woman!—even when you know her, becomes a sort of evil, scheming, irresistible serpent coiled round your life, putting its slime on everything, squeezing the goodness out of everything. In your heart you know she's just a person like any other—like yourself, even—maybe a bit more selfish than most, a bit more ruthless, wanting to have her way, wanting the man she's put her eye on even though he's someone else's husband, but still, just a human being. But you can't allow yourself to admit that. Not if you're to preserve any shred of self-respect.' She drank the coffee, sip by sip, grimacing at the scalding heat of it, punishing herself. Quirke watched her. 'No,' she said, 'she has to be a—what do you call it?—

a gorgon, something not human, more than human. A devil.'

She carried her cup to the plastic-topped table in the middle of the floor and sat down. Quirke looked about. Everything was too clean; the shining cleanliness of these surfaces made something in him cringe. Even the air, the very light in the room, seemed drained of all impurities. Kate saw him looking and read his mind. 'Yes, I do a lot of cleaning,' she said. 'It seems to help.'

He went and sat opposite her at the table.

'I'm sorry,' he said, not knowing what exactly he was apologising for.

'I'm too old for this kind of thing, really, I am,' she said. She leaned forward, hunching over the coffee cup as if she were suddenly cold. 'In two years' time I'll be forty. What man will look at me after that?' She gave a low, mock-mournful laugh, and then, surfacing to another level of sobriety, focused on him suddenly. 'Why are you involved in this,' she asked, 'this grimy little suburban melodrama?'

He lifted one shoulder. 'I suffer from an incurable curiosity.'

She nodded, as if she considered this a sufficient answer. Another thought struck her. 'Are you married?'

'I was. A long time ago. She died.'

'Sorry.' She did not look it; she looked, with that tightened mouth and narrowed eyes, as if she envied him, having a spouse who was dead. 'What happened to her?'

'Childbirth. A fluke, one in ten thousand.'

'And the child?'

'She survived.'

'A daughter.'

'She's twenty-two now. Twenty-three.'

'Does she live with you?'

'No.'

'Well, at least she doesn't remember. Losing her mother, I mean.' Idly she dabbled a fingertip in the ash from his cigarette in the ashtray between them on the table. 'I have no child,' she said. 'Leslie couldn't have any. That was fine by him. He was pleased as Punch when he found out. Handy, I suppose, for'—she made a crooked mouth—'"getting round the girls", as he would put it, I've no doubt.' She was silent again, but after a moment stirred herself. 'What can I tell you, Mr Quirke? I've no idea what you want to know. And nor have you, so you say. Is there something suspicious about Deirdre Hunt's death? Do you think she was pushed? I'd have done it myself, if . . .' She stopped, and sat back hard on her chair, making the legs squeal on the floor's rubber tiles. 'You don't think Leslie— you don't think Leslie was somehow involved, do you? I mean, you don't think he—?' She laughed. 'Believe me, Leslie wouldn't hurt a fly, he'd be afraid it would bite him. Oh, he could be dangerous, if cornered, I know that. But I can't see him pushing a woman into the sea. Leslie, Mr Quirke'—she reached out and seemed about to touch his hand but then withdrew her fingers—'my poor Leslie has about as much backbone as a sea-slug. Sorry—I love him dearly, or used to, God help us, but it's the truth.'

He stayed another hour. She prepared plates of smoked salmon and salad and they ate without speaking, facing each other across the table in the gleaming light and silence of the unreal room. The refrigerator jolted into life and hummed away grumpily under its breath for a while, then abruptly switched itself off again with another, seemingly rancorous, jolt. A bubble of trapped air in a waterpipe somewhere made a pinging sound. Their knives and forks rang sharply against their plates, their water glasses made joggling noises when they set them down on the Formica table-top.

'I'm sorry,' Kate White said, 'about earlier.'

'Earlier?'

'You know what I mean. Guzzling wine and throwing myself about. That's not me, really, or at least I hope it's not. I've been struck a blow and I don't know how to deal with it. I keep trying out other personalities, to see if I can find one that will work better, be more plausible, more persuasive, than the one I'm stuck with.' She smiled, her somehow bruised-looking, beautiful black eyes glistening in the teary way that they did. 'No luck, so far.'

She rose and collected their plates and cutlery and carried them to the sink.

'Don't imagine,' she said, 'that I've forgotten the fact that I have no idea who you are or why you're here. I'm not in the habit of letting strange men into the house and treating them to smoked salmon and intimate revelations.'

He put down his napkin. 'I should be on my way.'

'Oh, I didn't mean that, necessarily. I've quite enjoyed having you here. Not much company about, these days. Leslie and I never went in for friends and all that.' She smiled again. 'He's English. So am I. Did you know?'

'Yes. Your accent . . .'

'I thought I'd lost it. It's reassuring that I haven't. I

wonder why? I mean, why reassuring.' She ran the tap and stood pensive, waiting for the water to turn hot. Above the sink a square window gave on to a side garden with stands of African grass. The day was failing, growing shadowed. 'Maybe I should go back,' Kate said. 'My mother had Irish blood, but I think I'm a London girl at heart. Bow Bells and all that. Winkles, skittles, the Pearly King and Queen.' She gave a brittle little laugh. She began to wash the dishes, rinsing and stacking them on a plastic rack. He stood up and went to her side. 'Is there a tea-towel?'

'Oh, let them drain,' she said. A pale, greenish radiance from the window touched her face. 'Just stand about and look handsome, that will do.'

He lit a cigarette. 'You have a workshop, have you?' he said. 'A design workshop?'

'Yes. I call it a factory—may as well be honest. We cut for the top designers. Irish girls make wonderful seam-stresses. It's the training they get from the nuns.' She smiled, not looking at him. 'And yes, if you're wondering: I'm the breadwinner in the family, or was, when there was still a family. Leslie used to run a hairdressing business, until he ran it into the ground. That's why he went in with little Miss Swansdown. He thought he was her Svengali, but I bet she was the one doing the hypnotising.' She stopped, and raised her face to the window again. 'I wonder what he'll do now, old Leslie. Too late for him to become a gigolo. He used to be quite decorative, too—different type from you, of course, but dishy, all the same, in his languid way. Lately the rot has set in. I suppose that's the main reason he took up with that poor little tart: she was young enough for him to feel flattered.'

She went off to the den and came back after a moment with her wine glass and the remains of the wine from earlier. She put the almost empty bottle into the fridge and plunged the glass into the dishwater in the sink and shook it vigorously in the suds.

'We were quite well off, in London,' she said. 'My father made a lot of money out of the war—' She glanced at him sidelong. 'Are you shocked? I think you should be. He was a bit of a crook, more than a bit, in fact—the Black Market, you know. So naturally he got on with Leslie. Then Leslie and I decided to come over here, much against Father's wishes—he wasn't very hot on the Irish, I'm afraid, despite Mother's Tipperary roots—and after that the Daddy Warbucks fund dried up. Leslie was terribly disappointed, and blamed me, of course, though he tried not to show it, bless him. Then I opened the factory and the moolah started rolling in again and all seemed well. Until the Black Swan swam into our lives.'

'How did they meet, your husband and Deirdre—Laura Swan?'

She turned her head slowly and gave him a smilingly quizzical, long look. 'Are you sure you're not with the police? You have the tone of an interrogator.' There was a muffled sound down in the dishwater—*tok!*—and she looked up quickly and gave a tiny gasp. 'Oh, Christ, I think I've cut myself.' She lifted her hand out of the suds. There was a deep gash, unnaturally clean and straight, on the underside of her right thumb close to the knuckle. The dilute blood raced with impossible swiftness down her wrist and along her arm. She stared aghast at the wound. Her face was paper-white. 'The glass,' she said tonelessly. 'It broke.'

He put a hand under her elbow.

'Come,' he said, 'come and sit down.'

He led her to the table. She walked as in a trance. The blood had reached her elbow and was soaking into the rucked sleeve of her black sweater. She sat. He told her to hold her hand upright and made her grasp the ball of her sliced thumb with her other hand and squeeze hard to reduce the flow of blood.

'Have you a bandage?' he said. She gazed at him in frowning incomprehension. 'A bandage,' he said. 'Or something I can cut up and use for one?'

'I don't know. In the bathroom?'

He took out his handkerchief and tried to rip it but the seam would not give. He asked if there was a scissors. She pointed to a drawer under the work-top by the sink. 'There.' She gave a brief, faintly hysterical laugh. He found the scissors and cut a strip of cotton and set to binding the cut. As he worked he felt her breath on the backs of his hands and the heat of her face beating softly against his cheek. He tried to keep his hands from shaking, marvelling at how quickly, how copiously, the blood insisted on flowing. A dull crimson stain had appeared already in the improvised bandage. 'Will it need to be stitched?' she asked.

'No. It will stop soon.' Or so he hoped; he did not know what to do with living flesh, with freely running blood.

She said: 'Do me a favour, will you? Look in my handbag, there are some aspirin.' He went into the hall as she directed and took her black handbag from where it hung by its strap on the coat rack behind the front door and brought it to her. 'You look,' she said. 'Don't worry, you won't find anything incriminating.'

He rummaged in the bag. The lipstick-face-powder-perfume smell that came up from its recesses reminded him of all the women he had ever known. He found the aspirin bottle, shook out two tablets, and brought a tumbler to the sink and filled it and carried it back to the table. Kate White's good hand trembled as she lifted the glass to her lips. She was still holding her bandaged thumb aloft in a parody of jaunty affirmation. 'Will I have to stay like this all day?' she asked, making her voice shake with comic pathos. He said the cut would seal and then the bleeding would stop. She glanced about the room. 'Christ,' she murmured, with vague inconsequence, 'how I hate this house.'

She asked him to turn the gas on under the coffee pot, and when it was hot she poured a cup for herself, and tasted it, and grimaced. They went back to the den and she sat on the sofa with her legs tucked under her and looked at him over the rim of the coffee cup. 'You're quite the Good Samaritan, aren't you?' she said. 'Have you had a lot of practice?' He did not answer. He went and stood by the window, where she had stood earlier, and put his hands in his pockets and contemplated the garden. The evening would soon turn into night. Above the trees small puffs of pink cloud sailed against a band of tender, greenish sky. 'Tell me,' she said, 'what's your interest in the Swan woman? The truth, now.'

'I told you—her husband telephoned me.'

'You said.'

'He asked me not to do a post-mortem.'

'Why?'

He went on studying the garden. In the dimming air the trees, glistening yet from the long-ceased rain, were ragged globes of radiance. 'He didn't like the idea of it, he said.'

'But you didn't believe him. I mean, you didn't believe that was why he was asking you not to do it.'

'I had no reason to doubt him.'

'Then why are you here?'

He turned to her at last, still with his hands in his pockets. 'As I say, I was curious.'

'Curious to do what? To get a look at the betrayed wife?' She smiled.

'I really must be going,' he said. 'Thank you for seeing me, Mrs White.'

'Kate. And thank you for binding my wounds. You did it expertly, like a real doctor.' She set the coffee cup beside the telephone on the glass table and stood up. When she was on her feet she swayed a little, and put a hand, the unbandaged one, weakly to her forehead. 'Oh dear,' she said. 'I feel quite woozy.'

In the hall she lifted his hat from the peg where she had hung it and handed it to him. He was at the door but she put a hand on his arm, and as he turned back she stepped up to him swiftly and kissed him full on the mouth, digging urgent fingers into his wrist through the stuff of his jacket. He tasted a trace of lipstick. On her breath behind the smell of coffee there persisted a faint sourness from the wine. The tips of her breasts lightly brushed against his shirt-front. She released him, and drew away. 'Sorry,' she said again. 'As I say, I'm not myself.' Then she stepped swiftly back and shut the door.

11

SHE DID NOT know what she wanted from Dr Kreutz, or what she expected from him; she was not sure that there was anything for her to expect. At first she was pleased—she was thrilled—simply to have been noticed by him. It was true, plenty of people noticed her, men especially, but the Doctor's was a unique kind of noticing, in her experience. He did not seem to be interested in her because of her looks or of what he might think he could persuade her to do for him. It was a long time before he even touched her, and when he did, his touch was special, too. And it was strange, but she was never wary of him, as she had learned to be wary of other men. In a curious way she did not think of him as a man at all. Oh, he was attractive—he was the most attractive, the most exquisite, human being she had ever encountered in her life—but when she thought about him she did not imagine him kissing her or holding her in his arms or anything like that. It was not that kind of attraction he had for her. The nearest thing she could think of was the way, when she was a little girl, she used to feel sometimes about an actor in the pictures. She would sit at matinées in the sixpenny seats with her hands joined palm to palm and pressed between her knees—an upside-down attitude of prayer, it struck her, though it was certainly not God she was praying to here—and her face lifted to the flickering silver-and-black images of John Gilbert or Leslie Howard or the fellow who played Zorro in the follyeruppers, as if one of them might suddenly lean down from the screen and kiss her softly, quickly, gaily, on the lips, before turning back to join in the action again. This was how it would be with Dr Kreutz, she was convinced, this magical, this luminous, this infinitely tender leaning down, when he would eventually judge the time was right to show her how he really felt about her.

Of course, he did not try anything with her, nor even made a suggestive remark, as men always did, sooner or later. No, there was nothing like that, with Dr Kreutz.

He tried to teach her more about Sufism, and gave her books and pamphlets to read, but she found it hard to learn. There were so many names, for a start, most of which she could hardly get her tongue round, and which confused her—half of them were called Ibn-this or Ibn-that, though he told her it only meant 'son of', but still. And the teachings of these wise men did not seem to her all that wise. They were so sure of themselves and sure that they were dispensing the greatest wisdom, but most of the things they said seemed to her obvious or even silly. *I have never seen a man lost who was on a straight path*, or *If you cannot stand a sting do not put your finger in a scorpion's nest*, or *What may appear to you a clump of bushes may well be a place where a leopard is lurking*—what was so clever or deep in such pronouncements? They were not much different from the kinds of thing her father and his cronies said to each other in the pub on a Saturday afternoon, hunched over their pints at the bar with the wireless muttering in the background and someone doing a crossword puzzle in the paper—*It's a wise child that knows its father*, or *There's more than one way to skin a cat*, or *It's a long road that has no turning*.

However, there was a saying by one of those Ibns that was uncontradictable, as she could ruefully attest after all those dizzying lectures from Dr Kreutz, and that was a definition of Sufism itself as 'truth without form'. But to be fair, that was what Dr Kreutz kept telling her over and over: that, or versions of it. 'My dear dear girl,' he said to her one day early in their acquaintance, 'you must ask for no answers, no facts, no dogmas, like the ones your priests tell you that you must believe in. To be a sufi is to be on the way always, without expectation of arrival. The journeying is all.' Well, it was certainly true that there was a lot of moving about the place involved in this religion, if it was a religion: the Sufis never seemed to stop in one spot for more than a day or two but then were off again on their travels. She supposed it was because it all happened in hot countries and desert places where there were nomads—that was a new word she had learned—who had to keep on the move in search of water and food and places where their camels and their donkeys could graze. She could not get over her amazement at being a part of this world that was so different from everything she had known up to now. And she *was* a part of it, even if she was not the totally convinced convert Dr Kreutz thought she was.

She came to him most Wednesday afternoons and sometimes at the weekends, too, if Billy was away travelling. When he had a client with him—he never called the ones that he treated patients—he would move the copper bowl from the low table to the window-sill as a signal for her that someone was there. Then she would have to pass the time strolling aimlessly up and down Adelaide Road until she saw the client leaving. As the winter went on she got friendly with the man who tended the gates of the Eye and Ear Hospital, and when it rained or was very cold he would invite her into his cabin, which was made of creosoted wood that smelled like Jeyes' Fluid. His name, Mr Tubridy, sounded funny to her, she was not sure why, except that he was a tubby little man, with a round, shiny face and a bald head across which were carefully combed a few long strands of oiled lank hair. He had a paraffin stove, and smoked Woodbine cigarettes, and read the English papers, the *People* or the *Daily Mail*, out of which he would recount to her the juicier stories. He made tea for her, and sometimes she would try one of his cigarettes, though she was not a smoker. She felt, there in that little cabin, sitting at the stove with her coat pulled tight round her, as if she was back in childhood, not her real childhood, in the Flats, but a time of cosiness and safety she had never known that was yet somehow familiar to her—a dream childhood. Then she would go out and walk up the road and look to see if the copper bowl was moved from the window-sill, and if it was she would open the iron gate and tap on the basement door and step into that other world, as exotic as the one in the cabin was ordinary.

Dr Kreutz never spoke about his clients. They were all women, so far as she could see. That did not surprise her—what man would consult a Spiritual Healer? She longed to know something about these women, but she did not dare to ask. She supposed they must be rich, or well-off, anyway; more than once after a client had left she came in while Dr Kreutz was still putting money away in the strong-box he kept in a locked filing cabinet in the hallway, and she saw many a five- and ten- and even twenty-pound note going on top of the thick wads that were already in the box.

Sometimes the clients left traces of themselves behind, a forgotten glove or a scarf, or even just a hint of expensive perfume. Oh, how she longed to meet one of them.

And then one day when she came out of Mr Tubridy's cabin she was in time to see a client leaving, and before she knew what she was doing she was following her. The client was a slimly built, dark-haired woman in her forties, expensively dressed in a midnight-blue costume with a fitted jacket and calf-length pencil skirt; she had a fox-fur round her shoulders and wore a little black hat with a half-veil. She walked rapidly in the direction of Leeson Street, her high heels tap-tapping along the pavement. There was something about the way she hurried along, with her head down, that made it seem as if she was nervous of being spotted by someone. Her car, a big shiny black Rover, was parked by the canal. The day was bright, with sharp sunlight glinting on the water, and swoops of wind shaking the trees along the towpaths. The woman opened the car door but did not get in, and instead took a fur coat from the back seat and put it on and rewound the fox-fur round her throat and locked the car again and turned and set off walking towards Baggot Street. Deirdre continued to follow her.

The woman stopped at Parson's bookshop on Baggot Street Bridge and went inside. Deirdre stood at the window pretending to look at the books on display there. Inside, through the confusingly reflecting glass, dimly, she saw the woman examining the stacks of books set out on tables, but it was obvious that she, too, was only pretending. Plainly she was nervous, and kept glancing towards the door. Then a man approached over the bridge from the direction of Baggot Street, a tall, slim man in a camel-hair overcoat with a belt loosely knotted. He was good-looking, though his eyes were set a little too close together and his hooked nose was too big. His hair was long and of a silvery shade that she had never seen before, in man or woman, though it was not dyed, she was sure of that. He stopped at the door of the bookshop and, having glanced carefully over one shoulder and then the other, slipped inside. Somehow she knew what was going to happen. She saw the woman registering his entrance but delaying for a moment before acknowledging him, and when she did she put on a show of being oh-so-surprised to see him there. Smiling down at her, he leaned sideways easily with a hip against the table of books where she was standing and undid the knotted belt of his overcoat. It was that gesture, the careless flick of his hand and the belt loosening and the coat falling open, that somehow told Deirdre just what the situation was, and she turned quickly and walked away.

There was a little green sports car parked outside a newsagent's in Baggot Street, and when she spotted it she knew, she just knew, that it belonged to the silver-haired man.

What she had seen in the shop, the two of them there together and the woman trying to keep up the pretence of being surprised, gave her a shaky, slightly sick feeling. But why? It was only a man and a woman meeting by arrangement, after all. All the same, the woman was a good bit older than the man, and from the nervous way she put on a show of being surprised to see him it was obvious that they were not married—not married to each other, that is. But that was not what had sickened her. What was sickening was the connection with Dr Kreutz. She knew she was being silly. A woman who had been to see the Doctor had gone from there to meet her boyfriend, that was all. It did not mean the Doctor was involved in whatever was going on between those two—she had no reason whatever to think he even knew about them meeting up the way they did. And yet somehow a taint had crept into the fantasy she had worked up round the figure of Dr Kreutz, a taint of reality: commonplace, underhand, soiled reality.

That was the first time it occurred to her to wonder what exactly Spiritual Healing might be. Up to then it had not mattered; suddenly now it did. She had assumed, when she had speculated about it, which was seldom, that these women brought him their troubles—a marriage on the rocks, problem children, the change of life, nerves—and that he talked to them much as he talked to her, about how they should try to put aside worldly things and concentrate on the spirit, which was the way to God and God's peace, as he was forever declaring in his soft, unsmiling but amused and kindly way. Rich women had time on their hands and the money to find the means of making it pass. She was sure there was nothing wrong with most of them, that they were just indulging themselves by paying for an hour or two a week in the care of this beautiful, tranquil, exotic man. And thinking this, she realised that she was, of course, jealous. She pictured them together, Dr Kreutz and the woman in the blue suit, she kneeling on a cushion on the floor, barefoot, with her eyes closed and her head back, and he standing behind her, caressing her temples, the warm pads of his fingertips barely touching the skin and yet making it tingle, as her own skin had tingled on the couple of occasions when he had massaged her like that, speaking to her in his purring voice about the wisdom of the ancient Sufi masters, who a thousand years ago, so he said, had written of things that the world was only now discovering and thinking it was for the first time.

But why had her jealousy been stirred by seeing the woman with the silver-haired man? It should have been the opposite, she should have been glad to know that the woman was in love with someone else and not with the Doctor. It was confusing.

She wished she had someone to talk to about all this. She could not mention any of it to Billy—she could just imagine what Billy would say. She had not told him about Dr Kreutz. He would not understand, and besides, it was her secret.

12

LESLIE WHITE HAD given Phoebe a phone number where she could contact him, which he hoped—*sincerely*, as he said—that she would do, soon. And, to her surprise, she did. She knew she could expect nothing from him but trouble. But perhaps trouble was precisely what she wanted. When he answered the phone and she said her name he seemed not at all surprised. She supposed it had never crossed his mind that she would not call, that any girl would not call him, the silver-haired Leslie White. He was staying in temporary digs, he told her, 'due to a contretemps on the domestic front'. He said that his wife had thrown him out of the house, for reasons that he did not specify. She liked his frankness. She supposed it was due to the fact of his being English. No Irishman, she knew, would admit so lightly, so gaily, almost, to having been kicked out of the family home by his wife. When she said this to him he pretended to be surprised and fascinated, as if it were some piece of anthropological lore she had imparted. It was one of the tricks he had, to put on a show of astonished interest at the most mundane of observations—'Gosh, that's amazing!'—and even though she knew it was a trick, still it pleased her. She was taken by his boyishness, or his pretence of it. He had a repertoire of exclamations—*gosh, crikey, crumbs*—that she supposed he had got from Billy Bunter books or the like, for these words and his way of tossing them about so casually were the stuff of public-school life, and Leslie White, she felt sure, had never seen the inside, or possibly even the outside, of such an institution.

He took her for tea to the Grafton Café, above the cinema. They had a table by the window looking down on Grafton Street. It was Saturday and the street was busy with shoppers. After the thunderstorms of the previous day the fine weather had returned, and below them the sun was making inky shadows from the awnings above the shops. Leslie wore a light-brown corduroy suit today, and suede shoes, and sported a silver kerchief in his top pocket to match his silver cravat and, of course, his silver hair. How he admires himself, she thought, with faint amusement. It's almost lovable, his self-love. She was surprised to be here with him. He was, she very well knew, what the nuns at her convent school used to warn against, a 'bad companion', and his company was certainly an 'occasion of sin'. The truth was, she was not sure why she had called him in the first place. She was not in the habit of phoning men she barely knew; but then, she was not in the habit of phoning men, known or not, and men did not phone her, at least not the kind of man that Leslie White so obviously was.

She smoked a cigarette and gazed into the street. She could feel him studying her. He asked: 'Do you always wear black?'

'I don't know. Do I? It's required, at the shop, and I suppose I've got into the habit.'

He laughed. '"Habit" is about right.'

She raised an eyebrow. 'You think I look like a nun?'

'I didn't say that, did I?'

'I haven't much interest in clothes, I'm afraid.'

He smiled to himself as at a private joke.

'I hope you don't mind my saying,' he said, 'but you don't really look or sound like a shop girl, either.'

'Oh? What do I look and sound like?'

'Hmm. Let me think.' He put his head on one side and narrowed his eyes and considered her from brow to foot. She suffered his scrutiny with unruffled calm. She was wearing a black skirt and a black jumper and cardigan; her only adornment was a loop of pearls, which had been her mother's, that is, Sarah's. She had no doubt that Leslie White would be interested to know—'Golly, I should say so!'—that the pearls were genuine, and quite valuable. He was still looking her up and down and rubbing a hand judiciously back and forth on the side of his chin. 'I would guess you were,' he said, 'a well brought-up and very proper young lady.'

'Can't girls who serve in shops be proper?'

'Not the ones of my acquaintance, darling. Why are you slumming?'

From anyone else this would have been offensive, and she knew he was trying to provoke, but she could not take him seriously enough to be provoked, or offended, by anything he might say. She turned her head and looked him full in the face and in her turn asked: 'Why is your wife so angry with you?'

He stared for a second and then laughed. 'I'm afraid I did give her cause.'

'Was Laura Swan part of the cause?'

He straightened slowly on the chair, uncoiling his long, skinny frame, and she thought he was about to get up and leave. Instead, he cleared his throat and reached for her cigarette case on the table and opened it and helped himself to a cigarette, which he lit with her lighter. He was frowning. She noted how he held the cigarette affectedly between the second and third fingers of his left hand.

'You're quite a girl, aren't you?' he said.

'You mean, quite a shop girl?'

He flinched in pretend pain, smiling wryly. '*Touché.*'

The waitress was hovering. Leslie asked of Phoebe if she wanted anything more but she said no, and leaned down and delved in her handbag in search of her purse.

'Let me,' he said, bringing out his wallet.

'No!' It had come out too sharply, and made him blink. 'No,' she said again, more gently, 'I'd like to, really. I want to.'

'Well, thank you.'

She passed a coin to the girl and told her she need not bring back the change. They stood up from the table. She was aware of that awkward moment when a decision must be made. If they parted now, she knew she would never see him again, not because she did not want to, not because she was indifferent to him, but in obedience to an unformulated and yet iron-clad convention. She did not look at him, but busied herself in putting away her purse. 'Would you like,' she asked, 'to go for a walk with me?'

They strolled along St Stephen's Green. They caught the fragrance from the flowerbeds inside and, from closer by, the sharp, almost animal scent of privet with the sun strong on it. The tiny leaves of bushes thronging behind the railings were of an intense bottle-green, and each leaf looked as if it had been individually and lovingly polished. Sometimes the beauty of things, ordinary things—those unseen flowers, this burnished foliage, the honeyed sunlight on the pavement at her feet—pressed in upon her urgently while at the same time the things themselves seemed to hold back, at one remove, as if there were an invisible barrier between her and the world. She could see and smell and touch and hear, but somehow she could hardly feel at all.

Leslie, who must have been brooding on it for some time, said, 'Yes, I'm afraid Laura was indeed the trouble, or a largish part of it.' He sucked in his breath sharply between his teeth as if he had felt a blast of icy wind. He walked with his hands in his pockets. He had the way of walking of so many tall, thin men, his shoulders drooping back and his pelvis thrust out; she liked this boneless, sinuous gait. 'That wasn't her real name, you know,' he said, seeming faintly aggrieved and eager to expose a petty piece of fraudulence. 'That was just an invention. Deirdre Hunt, she was called.'

'Yes.'

'Oh—you knew?' She nodded. 'Yes, of course,' he went on, sounding more aggrieved than ever, 'and you knew she was married, too, I remember. To a fellow by the name of Billy. Poor chump.'

'Why Laura Swan?'

'The name, you mean? Oh, it was just silliness. I told her she looked like a Laura, God knows why—even Lauras don't look like a Laura—and she decided that's what she'd be.'

'And Swan?'

He made a sound that might have been a giggle. '*She* said *I* looked like a swan. Something to do with my hair, I don't know what.'

'Ah,' she said, 'I see: the Silver Swan.'

'As I say, the most awful silliness.' They came to the corner and crossed over into Harcourt Street. 'I still blush to think of it.'

They were at the steps of the house, and she stopped. He looked at her enquiringly. 'I live here,' she said.

He put on a crestfallen look. 'Well, that wasn't much of a walk.'

She hastened on so as not to lose her nerve. 'Will you come in?' *He has a wife who has kicked him out,* she told herself, in some wonderment, *and a mistress who killed herself, and I am inviting him to step into my life.* She pointed upwards. 'My flat is there.' *But which of us is the spider, and which the fly?*

They had climbed the stairs and she was shutting the door behind them when he put an arm round her waist and drew her against him and kissed her. She felt the breath from his nostrils feathery on her cheek. She thought, We must both smell of Passing Cloud. He was at once diffident and insistent; he held her so lightly that his arm might have been a delicately balanced spring that would release her at the slightest pressure of resistance, but that yet was made of steel. His way of kissing her was dreamy, almost absent-minded. She thought he might be humming at the back of his throat. The embrace lasted no more than a second or two and then he turned from her with a sort of sweep, like a dancer whirling languidly away to indulge in a figure or two on his own. He strolled ahead of her into the flat, definitely humming now, and stopped in the middle of the living room and looked about. 'This is nice,' he said. 'A trifle spartan, but nice.' He turned and smiled at her, throwing back his head. The kiss might not have happened at all—had she imagined it?

She offered him a drink. She had a bottle of gin, somewhere, she said, but there was no tonic, or ice— 'Haven't got a fridge.' He said gin on its own would be fine. She stood a moment, looking at the floor—something was wobbling in the pit of her stomach—then turned and marched herself into the kitchen. Alone there, she touched her fingers gingerly to her lips. She could hear her heart, a dull *thud-thud*, *thud-thud*, like the sound of some dolt clomping along a muddy footpath in big wet boots. Foolish, she was being so foolish! The gin was at the back of the cupboard high on the wall, she had to stand on a chair to reach it, and thought she might fall off, she felt so giddy. She could hear him in the living room, singing softly to himself: '*Enjoy yourself, it's later than you think . . .*'

She took down two tumblers and polished them with a tea-towel. 'What if he did it?' she whispered aloud to herself. 'What if he pushed her?' Her insides had stopped wobbling and burned now with a sullen, low fire. Shakily she poured two accidentally mighty measures of gin and carried the glasses into the living room.

He was standing at the sideboard, bent forward with his hands in his trouser pockets, peering at the photograph in its tortoiseshell frame of Mal and Sarah on their wedding day. 'Your mum and dad?' he asked. She nodded. She set down his glass on the sideboard beside the photo and walked away from him and stood by the window, looking out at the street and seeing nothing. She heard him take up the glass and drink, then gasp. 'Crikey,' he said, 'it's strong, when it comes straight like this, isn't it?'

He moved, and in a second was standing beside her. How silently he moved, how softly. In the street the Saturday quiet was strung between the houses like a gauze net. He was again singing very low under his breath. '*Enjoy yourself, while you're still in the pink . . .*' He sniffed. 'I'm guessing,' he said, 'that they're no longer with us. Your pater and mater.'

'Sarah is dead. Mal is alive.' She spoke without emphasis.

'Sarah and Mal. Mal and Sarah. Funny, isn't it, how two names can sound right together, I mean natural, like a formula, when really they're just . . . names? Romeo and Juliet. Fortnum and Mason. Mutt and Jeff.' He hardly paused. 'Do you miss her?'

'Do I miss who?'

'Sarah. Your mum.'

'Do you miss Laura Swan?'

She did not know why she had said it, and why so harshly. Was it somehow because he had kissed her? Perhaps it was because he had not kissed her again, or because he was behaving as if he had not kissed her at all. Her head was in a whirl. She was not accustomed to such situations, she did not know what to do, how to behave. Someone should have taught her, someone should have advised her. But who was there? Who, really, had there ever been?

He was considering her question. For a moment she forgot what it was she had asked him—about Laura Swan, yes. He seemed not at all put out. 'I haven't really had time to think about it,' he said. 'Oh, I mean, I miss her, of course.' He took a long drink of his gin and smacked his lips and grimaced. 'No doubt any night now I'll wake up shedding buckets of tears, but so far, not a tinkle. Is it shock, do you think?' He was looking at her sidelong, almost merrily, the tip of his hooked nose seeming to quiver.

'Yes,' she said, as drily as she could manage. 'It's shock, no doubt.'

He ignored her sarcasm. 'That's what I think.' He put his glass down on the bench seat under the window and clasped his hands behind his back and turned to her, putting on a face as grave and unctuous as that of a Victorian swain about to request a daughter's hand in marriage, and asked, 'Will you go to bed with me?'

She sat on the bench seat by the open window again in the dragon gown that had belonged to Sarah. The summer evening was at an end and what sunlight remained was a dark-gold glow against the tops of the houses opposite. Before, she had not known what to do, what to think, and now, afterwards, she still did not know. She had been brought to a standstill in mid-air on her tightrope, and she was unable for the moment to go forward or back. Leslie White's empty gin glass was beside her on the seat. She stared at it, frowning. This was only the second time in her life that a man had thrust himself into her. The first time it had been against her will, in violence, with a knife at her throat. Leslie White had been violent with her too, but in a different way. What had struck her was the seeming help-lessness of his need; she might have been nursing at her breast a grotesquely elongated, greedy infant. Was this how it was supposed to be? She had no way of knowing. When it was over he was as he had been before, light and playful in his slightly menacing way, as if nothing at all had happened between them, or nothing of much importance, anyway. For her, everything was changed, changed beyond recognition. She looked out at the evening sky and the light on the faces of the houses as if she had never seen such things before, as if the world had become unrecognisable.

She took up his glass and put it to her lips, touching the place where his lips had touched.

What started her out of her reverie was the sudden feeling that someone was watching her. She looked sharply down into the street. There was an old man with a little dog on a lead; a couple strolled past arm in arm; an old tramp was picking through the contents of a litter bin at the bus stop. Yet she was convinced someone had been there, a second ago, standing on the pavement, looking up at her framed in the window. She even thought she had seen him, out of the corner of her eye, without seeing him, or without registering him, at least not while he was there, a man in a—in a what? What had he been wearing? She did not know. It had been only the merest presence, the shadow of a shadow. And where had he gone to, if he had ever been there? How had he slipped away so quickly? She told herself she had imagined him, that she was seeing things. The light at dusk played tricks like that, conjuring phantoms. She stood up from the seat, though, and drew the window shut, and went into the bedroom to dress.

In the days that followed she had the feeling again of being watched, of being followed. It was always unexpected, always vague, yet she could not rid herself of the ever-strengthening conviction that she was the object of someone's intense interest. Once in the shop she thought there was a person outside looking in at her and when she turned to the window seemed to glimpse a figure darting away. However, when she went to the door and looked up and down the street there was no one to be seen, or no one that resembled the figure she thought she had caught looking in at the window. She was walking in the Green one lunchtime when she suddenly had the strong sense that among the people strolling by the flowerbeds or lying on the grass there was one who was secretly observing her. She stopped by the bandstand where the Army Band was playing and scanned the faces in the audience to see if she could catch an eye covertly fixed on her, but could not. Again she tried to make herself believe she was deluded. Who would be watching her, and why? Then there came the night when she arrived home after being at the pictures and saw the body slumped on the steps outside the house, and her knees went weak and her heart seemed to drop for a second and rise again sickeningly, as if on the end of an elastic string.

13

INSPECTOR HACKETT WOULD not have claimed to be the most relentless of investigators. He preferred a quiet life, and did not pretend otherwise. He had his garden, where he grew vegetables, mostly, though Mrs Hackett, whose name was May, a dainty little bird of a woman, was forever nagging him to plant more flowers; she particularly favoured dahlias, and he put some in, to keep her quiet, though he secretly considered them to be little more than a haven for earwigs. He was a fisherman, too, and went down to Greystones whenever he could manage a weekend off from his domestic duties, and usually brought back a clutch of bass for the table, though Mrs H. complained bitterly of having to clean them, for she was of a delicate disposition when it came to gutting fish. The house, too, kept him busy. There seemed always to be something in need of fixing, of nailing down or tearing up, of repainting, of refurbishing. His two big lumps of sons—this was how he thought of them—were of little help to him, and seemed to be forever out at football matches or going to the pictures. So all in all his was a crowded life, his time was precious, and he was careful to avoid taking on things that could safely be left alone, or to others.

However, the death of Deirdre Hunt niggled at him. He suspected that every policeman, or every policeman of his rank, anyway, had a private way of knowing when something was just not right in a case that was supposed to be straightforward on the surface. With him it was not anything specific; his nose did not twitch or his insides constrict, as was the way with the sleuths in detective yarns. What he felt, when his suspicions were roused, was a general sense of being ill at ease. It was a bit like having a mild hangover, the kind you get up with and wonder what is wrong with you, until you remember those two or was it three balls of malt downed hurriedly the night before as closing time approached. And that was how he felt when he thought of Deirdre Hunt, hot and headachy and fizzing slightly all over.

He was a loner, too, was the inspector. He had no plodding sidekick to whom he could confide his doubts and his suspicions and on whom he could try out his theories as to who had done what and why and how. He preferred his own judgements, and, if the truth were told, his own company, too. That was how he had always been, even as a boy, always by himself, stravaiging the fields or the backstreets of the Midlands town where he was born, looking for something and never knowing what, hoping to chance on something, anything at all, that would interest or amuse him.

He caught up with Billy Hunt one evening at the Clontarf Rovers' football club. He had consulted his sons, wondering if they might know of him. At the name, the two lads had looked at each other and laughed. 'Oh, aye,' one of them said. 'We know the brave Billy Hunt. A hard man. I wouldn't like to tell you his nickname, but it has a rhyme in it.' And they laughed again. Hackett sighed. He had long ago acknowledged that his boys were not going to be exactly what he would have wanted in the way of sons and heirs, but they loved their mother and respected him—or at least they showed him respect, which was not necessarily the same thing—and he supposed that was the most a man could reasonably ask for, nowadays.

Billy, the young Hacketts informed their father, was a full-forward for the Rovers, and that very evening, as chance would have it, they were playing a match against a team from Ringsend, a useless crowd, as the lads declared, and as the Inspector saw for himself within a minute or two of his arrival at the pitch. The game was in the last quarter. The lads had been right: Billy was a hard case, and a rough, not to say a dirty, player. The backs were obviously wary of him and he scored two easy goals and three or four points in the short while that the inspector was there. After the full-time whistle the teams went off to the clubhouse, and as the last of the few spectators left the detective loitered at the gate to the pitch, leaning against the cement gatepost and smoking a cigarette. The evening was overcast but mild, and looking down the street before him to the front he could see people strolling by, and a few sailboats out on the water and, farther off again, on the horizon, the mailboat from Dun Laoghaire setting off on its way to Holyhead. Why, he wondered, with that vague, warm sense of contentedness that always welled up in him when he considered the foolishness and perfidy of his fellow-men, why would anybody who was not mortally ill want to do away with themselves and leave this world? For Inspector Hackett enjoyed being alive, however modest and ill-rewarded his own life might be. And stranger still, why would a man want to do away with his wife, no matter how difficult she was or how badly she treated him? There were times, it was true, when his May had driven him to the brink of violence, especially in their early years together, but that was a brink he would never, no, never, have allowed himself to blunder over.

Billy Hunt smelled of sweat and liniment. He looked at the inspector with his mouth half open, the blood sweeping up from his throat until his freckled face was fairly aflame. The two players he had been walking with went on a little way and stopped and looked back, curious. Billy was, the detective noted, older than he had seemed at a distance, and quite a bit older, too—he was forty if he was a day. That would go some way to accounting for his truculence on the field. Would he have had to prove himself to the wife, too, who must have been not two-thirds his age? Interesting. That kind of age difference was hardly likely to have been conducive to domestic bliss, Hackett felt sure.

'Only a few questions,' he said easily, 'just routine.' He employed this formula deliberately: it made people uneasy, for it was the kind of thing they would have heard police-men in the pictures saying when what they really meant was that what was going to follow would be anything but routine. 'You could drop into the station tomorrow morn-ing, if you happened to have a spare minute or two.'

Billy Hunt, still goggling, his face turning pale now as the blush subsided, did not ask what it was he was to be questioned about. This, the inspector cautioned himself, was probably not as significant as it might otherwise have been.

Hunt's wife, after all, had died in questionable circumstances, so why would the police not want to talk to him? All the same, should he not have been puzzled, at least, at being approached only now, considering the time that had elapsed since her death? Billy mumbled that yes, all right, he would come to the station, he would be there, yes. 'Grand,' the inspector said, beaming, and sauntered off down the street in the direction of the front, passing by Billy Hunt's two pals and winking at them both in friendly fashion.

Billy turned up at the station next morning at nine o'clock sharp. He was dressed in a dark suit and dark tie and a white shirt. The inspector supposed these were his work clothes—the suit was rubbed in places and the collar of the shirt looked as if it might have been turned. Slim times, nowadays, for a travelling salesman, he supposed. He tried to think what it was the fellow travelled in, and then remembered that it was chemist-shop stuff, pills and potions and the like, expensive cures for imaginary illnesses. There was always call for that kind of thing, of course, but he had a notion that Billy Hunt was not the greatest salesman the world had ever known. There was something about him that did not inspire confidence, an itchy something, as if he was not entirely comfortable in his skin, and he had a way of running a finger under his shirt collar and at the same time thrusting out his lower jaw that reminded the inspector of a chicken with the gape. Though the sun was shining it was still early and the air was cool down here in the dayroom, yet Billy's face glistened with a fine sheen of sweat and his forehead and the tips of his ears were flushed. Fair-skinned people were always the hardest to measure, the inspector found, tending as they did to blush even when there was nothing to blush about.

They climbed to the inspector's cluttered office, which was wedged under a mansard roof. Unlike downstairs, it was hot up here already, as it always was in summer, while in winter, of course, the bloody place froze. The inspector pointed Billy to a straight-backed chair and sat down himself behind his desk and offered cigarettes, and lit up and leaned back comfortably and blew smoke and regarded the young man opposite him benignly. 'Thanks for coming in,' he said. 'Isn't the weather holding up lovely?' Billy Hunt blinked, swallowing with a gulp loud enough for them both to hear, and put his hands together and plunged them between his knees. He had declined a cigarette, but brought out a Zippo lighter and began to flick it open and closed. 'Do you not smoke?' Hackett enquired with a show of interest.

'Not when I'm in training.' He put the lighter back in his pocket.

'Ah,' the inspector said. 'Training. You're big on the sport, are you?'

Billy looked down, as if it were a question that required serious consideration. 'It takes my mind off things,' he said at length.

The inspector let another moment's silence pass and then said, mildly, that he supposed it would, indeed. He leaned forward, making the chair grunt under him, and dashed his cigarette in the direction of the ashtray on the corner of his desk, tapping off the ash. 'It's a hard thing,' the inspector said, 'to lose a wife so young, and in those kind of circumstances.' Billy nodded mutely, still with eyes downcast. On the crown of his head there was a neat round patch of premature baldness, the skin there a touching shade of baby-pink. 'Was she a swimmer, your wife?'

Billy looked up quickly, startled. 'A swimmer? I don't know. I never saw her in the water.'

The inspector marvelled, as he so often had cause to do these days, at how little the younger generation knew about each other, if Billy Hunt could be said to be a member of that younger crowd. But imagine not being able to say whether your missus could swim or not! The inspector looked more closely into Billy Hunt's eyes; was he pretending ignorance, or was it genuine? Billy seemed to read his thought, and said, with a touch of sullenness: 'She was a city girl. She didn't like the seaside, or the country—nature, any of that kind of thing. She used to say it gave her hives.' He smiled, which only made him look all the more dismayed. 'She always made a joke of saying how surprised she was to have married a culchie.'

'Where are you from?'

'Waterford.'

'The town or the county?'

'The city.'

'The *city*, yes, of course. The grand city of Waterford. Have you people there still?'

'My mother and father, and a married sister.'

'Do you go down often to see them?'

'Now and then.'

'Where were you on the night your wife died?'

Billy Hunt's brow furrowed, and he gave his head a shake, as if he was not sure that he had heard aright. 'What?' he said.

'I was just wondering where you were when your wife drowned, that night.'

'I was . . .' Billy looked away, suddenly more dazed and helpless than ever. 'I suppose I was at home. I don't go out much—I get enough of that when I'm on the road.'

'So you're a homebody, are you?'

Billy Hunt turned his eyes and gazed at him for a moment carefully, but the Inspector's look was as bland and amiable as ever. Billy said: 'We were fine together, Deirdre and me. That's the God's truth. Maybe I didn't give her enough of—maybe I didn't—I mean, maybe there wasn't enough of—of whatever it was she needed. But I did my best. I tried to make her happy.'

'And did you succeed?'

'What?'

'Did you succeed in making her happy, would you say?' Billy did not answer, but again looked to the side, his jaw set in a glower of babyish resistance. The Inspector waited, and then asked: 'What do you think happened that night?'

'I don't know,' a muffled mutter.

The policeman crushed his cigarette end in the ashtray and leaned back again in his chair and clasped his hands behind his large, squarish head. His shirt collar was unbuttoned and his tie was loosened; the leather hooks of his braces looked like two pairs of splayed fingers. He let his gaze wander idly over the ceiling. 'The thing is,' he said, 'I've been wondering at the strange way it must have happened, the accident. She drove all the way out to Dalkey—'

'Sandycove,' Billy Hunt said.

'—Sandycove, along those lonely roads, at night, and

parked her car, and walked in the dark to the end of the jetty there, and stripped off all her clothes and dived into the sea—'

Billy interrupted again, saying something the inspector did not catch, and he had to ask him to repeat it. Billy cleared his throat, coughing into a fist.

'It wouldn't have been so dark,' he said thickly, 'even that late, at this time of year.'

'Dark enough, though, surely, to give a person the heebie-jeebies, especially a female on her own, out there by the sea in the middle of the night. She must have been some brave woman.'

'There weren't many things Deirdre was afraid of,' he said. 'Where she came from, they build them tough.'

An extended, vague silence followed this. Billy squeezed his hands between his knees again and rocked himself back and forth a little, while the policeman vacantly inspected a corner of the ceiling. At last he said, in a slow, deliberately absent-minded fashion, 'You don't think it was an accident, do you?'

This time the look Billy Hunt gave him was hard to measure. There was surprise in it, certainly, but calculation, too, and something else, something surly and resistant, and the inspector recalled how on the football pitch the previous evening Hunt had hurled himself like some kind of animal through the line of defenders again and again to get to the goal, impervious to everything, shoulder tackles, kicks, under-hand punches, the referee's whistle. It was a far different figure he had cut there from the helpless sad poor galoot sitting slumped here now. The inspector had known fellows like this at home, when he was young, in school and later in the Garda training college at Tullamore, gawky, slow-seeming ones with lopsided John Wayne grins and gorilla arms who at a word would turn from good-humoured tolerance to amazing, bloodshot, fist-flailing rage.

The expression on Billy's face lasted only a second, then he sat back on his chair and said: 'How do you mean?'

'What I say: you don't think it was an accident.'

Billy sighed as if suddenly weary. 'No, I suppose I don't.'

The Inspector lit another cigarette. He smoked for a moment in silence, then roused himself. 'Awful stuffy in here,' he muttered, and stood up, turning awkwardly in the cramped space behind his desk, and pulled up, not without difficulty, the lower half of the small window, the fag dangling from a corner of his mouth. His blue suit trousers, attached to broad braces, were hitched up higher at the back than at the front. He sat down again, and leaned forward with his elbows on the desk and his fingers clasped in a dome in front of his face. 'What was it, then, do you think, if not an accident?' Billy Hunt shrugged. Now that the topic of how precisely Deirdre had died was out in the open he seemed all at once to have lost interest in it. The Inspector watched him closely. 'Tell me, Mr Hunt—Billy—why would your wife have wanted to do away with herself?'

At that Hunt lowered his head and put up a hand and in a curiously dainty, almost feminine gesture wrapped it round his eyes, and when he spoke his voice was a despairing, teary gurgle. 'I don't know—how would I know?'

'Well,' the inspector said, and his voice was suddenly sharp as a knife, 'how would anyone else?'

Billy dropped his hand from his eyes. He had gone slack all over, as if a skeletal support inside him had collapsed.

'Don't you think,' he said, with angry imploring, 'that's the question I've been asking myself every minute of every day since it happened? Who would know, if not me? But I don't.' He stared with stricken eyes past the inspector's big head to the window and the sunlit rooftops beyond. Through the open window could be heard, faintly but distinctly, the sounds of heavy hoofs and the metal grind of cartwheels; a Guinness dray, the inspector guessed, going along the quays. 'I thought she was all right,' Billy said, seeming weary now, suddenly. He was, the inspector thought, a mass of changes, abrupt shifts, switches of temper; how, he wondered, had his wife coped with him? 'I thought she was happy, or content, anyway,' Billy said. 'We had our ups and downs, like everyone does. We had rows— she was a terrible fighter when she got going, like a wildcat. I'd say to her, I'd say, "You can take the woman away from Lourdes Mansions, but you can't take Lourdes Mansions away from the woman." That would really set her off.' He smiled, remembering. 'And then she'd end up crying, sobbing on my shoulder, shaking all over, saying how sorry she was and begging me to forgive her.' He came back from the past and focused on Inspector Hackett's large flat face and his unfailingly amused and seemingly friendly brown eyes. 'Maybe she wasn't happy. I don't know. Do people fight and scream like that and then sob their hearts out if they're happy?' He lunged forward suddenly and took a cigarette from the inspector's pack where it lay on the desk. He fumbled in his pocket for a lighter but the inspector had already struck a match, and held it out to him. Billy was a nervous smoker, pulling in quick mouthfuls of smoke with a hiss and breathing them out again at once as if in exasperation. 'I don't know,' he said, 'I just don't know what to think, I swear to Christ I don't.'

The inspector leaned back again and put his feet up on the desk and folded his hands on his paunch. 'Tell me about her,' he said.

'Tell you what?' Billy Hunt snapped petulantly. 'Haven't I told you?'

The Inspector seemed unperturbed. 'But tell me what way her life was. I mean, what sort of friends had she?'

'Friends?' He almost laughed. 'Deirdre didn't go in for friends.'

'No? There must have been women of her own age, women she'd talk to, confide in. I haven't come across the woman yet who didn't need someone to tell her secrets to.'

Although he had hardly started on it Billy Hunt now screwed the cigarette savagely into the ashtray. 'Deirdre wasn't like that. She was a loner, like me. I suppose that's what we saw in each other.'

'She seldom went out, you tell me. Neither of you did. Is that so?'

Billy Hunt gave a sardonic nod and turned aside as if he might be about to spit. 'Oh, she went out, all right.' He stopped, as if realising he had already said too much.

The inspector, seeing the other's sudden caution, decided to wait. He said, 'But she was a homebody, so you said.'

'No, I didn't—that's what *you* said *I* was.'

'Did I? Ah, I'm getting very forgetful. It must be old age creeping up.' He inserted a little finger delicately into his right ear and waggled it up and down, then extracted it again and peered to see what had lodged under the nail. 'So where would she go, when she went out?'

Billy would not meet his eye. 'I don't know.'

'Was this when you were away?'

'Was what when I was away?'

'That she went out.'

'I don't know what she did when I was working, travelling.' He winced, as if at a stab of pain. 'And now I don't want to know.'

'And who would she see, do you think, when she went out?'

'She wouldn't say.'

'And did you not press her to say?'

'You didn't press Deirdre. She wasn't the kind of person that you press. All you'd get is a wall of silence, or be told what to do with yourself. She was her own woman.'

'But you must have wondered—I mean, who she saw, when she did go out. I take it it was at night? That she went out?'

'Not always. Sometimes she'd disappear for whole afternoons. There was some doctor fellow she would go to see.'

'Oh?'

'A foreigner. Indian, I think.'

'An Indian doctor.'

'And there was that other long streak of mischief, of course. Her "partner".' He spoke that last word with venom.

The inspector had begun to hum softly under his breath, it sounded as if there were a bee trapped somewhere in the room, inside a cupboard or a drawer. 'And who,' he said, 'was this partner?' Quirke had told him the name but he had forgotten, and anyway, he wanted to hear Billy say it.

'Fellow called White. Some kind of an Englishman. Used to have a hairdressing place until it went bust. It was him that got Deirdre going in the beauty parlour. He had the premises and helped her to get set up. Then something happened there, too. The money ran out, I suppose.'

'What sort of help did he give Deirdre?'

'What?'

'You said he helped her to get set up. Did he put up the funds?'

'I don't know. I'm not sure. He must have had money from somewhere, to get the thing going. Maybe his wife kicked in—she has a business of her own. But Deirdre wouldn't have needed much assistance. She had a good head on her shoulders, Deirdre did.'

'Had she money too, like this fellow's wife?'

'Not what you'd call real money. But we were doing all right, between us.' He ruminated, a muscle working in his jaw. 'I thought I might have gone in with her on something, give up the travelling and start a business together, but then White came along. I suppose she was a bit taken with him, what with the fancy accent and all.'

'Were you jealous?'

He considered. 'I suppose so. But he was such a—such a drip, you know. I always thought he was a bit of a pansy. But you can never tell, with women.'

'True enough.'

Billy Hunt looked at the policeman sharply again, as if suspecting he was being mocked; the inspector gazed back at him with unwavering blandness.

'If I thought,' Billy Hunt said, in a strangely dull, distant tone, 'if I thought it was him that drove her to do what she did, I'd . . .' He let his voice drift off, his imagination failing him.

The inspector, his head cocked to one side—*to do what she did*—studied him thoughtfully. 'Was she in love with him, maybe, would you say?'

Billy Hunt put that hand over his eyes again, more in exhaustion than distress, it seemed, and slowly shook his head from side to side. 'I don't know that Deirdre loved anyone. It's a harsh thing to say, but I've thought about it a lot over the past couple of weeks and I think it's true. I don't hold it against her. It just wasn't in her nature. Or maybe it was, to start with, and got knocked out of her. If you knew her father you'd know what I mean.'

'Aye,' the inspector said. 'Life is hard, and harder for some than others.' Abruptly he rose and extended a hand. 'I won't take any more of your time, I'm sure you've things to do. Good day to you, Mr Hunt.'

Billy Hunt, taken by surprise, rose slowly, and slowly took the offered hand and slowly shook it. He mumbled something, and turned to the door. The inspector remained standing behind his desk, expressionless, but when Billy had the door open he said, 'By the way, this doctor that Deirdre used to see—what's his name, do you know?'

'Kreutz,' Billy said. He spelled it.

'Doesn't sound Indian to me.'

Billy looked as if this had not occurred to him. But he answered nothing, only nodded once, and went out, shutting the door softly behind him. For a long moment the inspector stood motionless, then slowly he sat down. He took a pencil from a cracked mug on the desk and in the looping, rounded handwriting that had not changed since he was in fourth class he wrote out the name on the back of a manila envelope: *Kreutz*.

14

PHOEBE HAD NOT seen Leslie White again after that afternoon in her flat when they had gone to bed together, nor had she telephoned him. Yet the thought of him haunted her. She had only to close her eyes to see his long, pale body suspended above her in the velvet dimness of her mind. Half a dozen times at least she had picked up the telephone and begun to dial his number but had made herself put the receiver down again. Was she in love with him? The notion was preposterous, it almost made her laugh. She cursed herself for her foolishness, yet there he was, the memory of him, the image of him, trailing her everywhere like that other phantom watcher she was convinced was following her in the streets. This was the state of mind she was in—on edge, bewildered, caught up in a tangle of half-memories and weird fancies—when she stopped that night on the pavement in the greyish dark of eleven o'clock and peered at the crumpled figure on the steps.

Her first thought was to turn and flee. Then she saw who it was. She hesitated. She was sure he was dead, lying there like that, like something broken. *Why did you come here?* she wanted to ask him. And what was she to do? The

Garda station was not far: should she go there now, straight away, summon help? The street was deserted. For a moment she was back again in the car on the headland with the steel blade against the vein that was beating in her throat and that maddened creature gasping foul endearments in her ear. Her hands were shaking. *Why did you come to my door, why?* She held her breath and forced herself to take a step forward. She knew instinctively he would not want her to call the Guards. She reached out a hand and touched his shoulder. He flinched, then groaned. Not dead, then; she was conscious of a fleeting pang of regret. Her fright was abating. Perhaps he was only drunk.

'Leslie,' she said softly—how strange it felt to say his name! 'Leslie, what is it, what happened to you?' With another, long-drawn groan he lifted his head and tried to focus on her, licking his swollen lips. She drew back with a gasp. 'My God—have you been in an accident?'

His face was so badly battered she would hardly have recognised it. The narrow gleam of his eyes between the puffed-out lids seemed to her devilish, as if there were someone else crouched inside him, someone different, peering furiously out. 'Get me inside,' he muttered hoarsely. '*Get me inside.*'

It was a grim coincidence that in the film she had been to see, a violent tale about the French Resistance, there had been a scene in which a young woman, a member of the Maquis, had helped a wounded English soldier out of a burning building. Draping his arm over her shoulders, the dauntless girl, scornful of falling rafters and blazing floors, had walked the Tommy with unlikely ease and dispatch out into the night where a band of her comrades was waiting to receive them both with cheers. Now Phoebe learned just how heavy a weight an injured man could be. By the time she got to the fourth floor, with him clinging to her and her arm supporting him about his waist, she had an agonising ache across her back and her face was dripping sweat. In the flat she kicked the door shut behind them and they hobbled to the sofa and fell down on it together in a scramble, and his right knee bashed her left knee and they both cried out in pain simultaneously.

When she was able to stand upright at last she limped into the kitchen and found the gin bottle in the cupboard and poured a quarter of a tumblerful and brought it back to him. He took a greedy swig, wincing as the liquor hit his broken lips. She busied herself finding a cushion for his head and helping him to stretch his legs out on the sofa, not only in an effort to make him comfortable but also to avoid having to look directly at his bashed and bleeding face. When she bent over him she could feel the heat from his bruises. He finished the gin and let the glass fall to the carpet where it rolled in a half-circle, drunkenly. She felt that she was about to cry, but stopped herself. Leslie put his head back against the cushion and closed his eyes and lay there breathing with his mouth open. She hoped he would not go to sleep, for she did not want to be alone in the room with him, and for a moment she even considered slapping his face to keep him awake, but she could not bear the thought of even touching those terrible bruises. All sorts of things crowded together in her mind, a jumble of random thoughts, jagged and senseless. She must get control of herself, she must. She rose and went to her handbag for her cigarettes, lit two and fitted one between Leslie's lips. He mumbled something from the side of his mouth, blowing a bubble of bloodied spittle, but did not open his eyes. She stood over him, smoking nervously, an elbow clutched in a palm.

After a while he began to speak, with his head thrown back against the cushion and his eyes still closed, and slurring his words. There had been a gang of them, he said, three at least. They had set on him in a laneway beside the College of Surgeons. They must have been following him since he left the Stag's Head, where he had been drinking with a pal. One of them had stuck a solid rubber ball into his mouth to gag him; then he had been hustled into a doorway down the lane and they had gone to work on him with fists, and some kind of sticks, or bats. Not a word had been spoken. He did not know who they were, or why they were beating him. But they had known who he was.

They had known who he was. And at once she thought: *Quirke.*

She wanted to ask why he had come to her, and he read her mind and said hers was the nearest place he could think of, and anyway he had been on the way here when his attackers caught up with him. He closed his swollen eyelids. 'Christ,' he said, 'I'm tired,' and fell asleep at once.

She did not believe he had been on his way here. She believed very few of the things he said. But what did it matter, truth or lies? He was so hurt, so hurt.

She went and sat in an armchair by the fireplace, and for a long time kept a silent vigil there. She recalled the night two years previously when she had been brought to see Quirke in the Mater Hospital; he, too, had been beaten up by people he did not know and for reasons that were, so he claimed, beyond him. He had tried to convince her he had fallen down a set of steps but she had known he was lying. Now she was certain it was he who had set those fellows on to Leslie. Why? To warn him to keep away from her? And it was Quirke, too, who had been watching her, and following her, snooping into her life, she was convinced of it. She looked at her knuckles: they were white. Would that man—she did not permit herself to call Quirke her father, even, or especially, in her own mind—would he never leave her be, would he continue to interfere in her life and what she did, ruining things, blackening things, soiling all he touched? She hated him with passion, and loved him, too, bitterly.

She must have fallen asleep, for when Leslie spoke—how much time had passed?—she started up in the chair in fright. He said her name, weakly. She went to him and, before she knew what she was doing—was she still thinking of Quirke?—she had fallen to her knees beside the sofa and taken his hand in both of hers. The knuckles were horribly grazed, two of the nails were broken and bleeding. His eyes were open and he was looking at her. He licked his dry and swollen lips. 'Listen, Phoebe,' he said, 'I want you to do something for me.' He tried to pull himself up against the cushion and grimaced in pain. 'There's a man, a doctor. I want you to go to him. He'll give you something for me, some medicine. I need it.'

'Who is he?'

'His name is Kreutz.' He spelled it for her. 'He has a place in Adelaide Road, opposite the hospital. There's a plaque on the railing, with his name.'

'Do you want me to go *now*?'

'Yes. Now.'

'But it's—I don't know—it's the middle of the night.'

'He'll be there. He lives on the premises.' He made a rattling sound in his chest that it took her a moment to recognise as laughter. 'He doesn't sleep much, the Doctor. You can take a taxi. Tell him you need the medicine for Leslie. He'll know.' His fingers squeezed one of her hands. 'Will you do that? Will you do that for me? Leslie's medicine—that's all you need to say. Tell him I said it's the least he can do, that he owes it to me.'

From the other end of the sofa her one-eyed teddy bear regarded them both with a glassy, outraged stare.

Away beyond the Green, in his flat in Mount Street, Quirke, too, had been called out of sleep. He stood in the darkness of the living room, in his drawers, barefoot, holding the receiver to his ear and gazing bleakly before him. He had not bothered to switch on a light. The street-lamp below threw a ghostly image of the window high into the room, half on the wall and half on the ceiling, a crazy, broken, vertiginous shape.

'It's the Judge,' Mal said, his voice down the distance of the line sounding exhausted. 'He's gone.'

And so it was that at the junction of Harcourt Street and Adelaide Road the two taxis, Quirke's and Phoebe's, passed in their separate directions, though neither of them saw the other, lost as they were in their own troubled and disordered thoughts.

II

1

A SAGGING PALL of cloud hung low over the airport and a steady summer drizzle was drifting slantways down. For a time it seemed the plane would be diverted because of the poor visibility but in the end it was allowed to land, though more than an hour late. Quirke stood with Phoebe at the observation window and watched the machine come nosing in from the runway, its four big propellers churning in the rain and dragging undulant tunnels of wet air behind them. Two sets of steps were wheeled out by men in yellow sou'westers and the doors were opened from inside and the passengers began disembarking, looking groggy and rumpled even at this distance. Rose Crawford was among the first to appear. She wore a close-fitting black suit and a black hat with a veil—'Mourning becomes her,' Quirke observed drily—and carried a black patent-leather valise. She paused at the top of the steps and looked at the rain, then turned back to the cabin and said something, and a moment later one of the stewardesses appeared, opening an umbrella, and under this protective dome Rose descended, stepping with care on to this alien soil.

'Really, I can't think what they expected to find in my bags,' she said, exaggerating her Southern drawl, when she came striding out of the Customs hall at last. 'Six-shooters, I suppose, seeing I'm a Yank. Quirke, you look ruined—have you been waiting long for me? And I see you still have a limp. But, Phoebe, my dear, you—you're positively radiant. Are you in love?'

She permitted her cheek to be kissed by both of them in turn. Quirke caught her remembered scent. He took her suitcases, and the three of them walked through the throng of arriving passengers. The taxi rank was busy already. Rose was surprised to learn that Quirke did not drive—'Somehow I saw you behind the wheel of something big and powerful'—and wrinkled her nose at the smell in the taxi of cigarette smoke and sweated-on leather. The rain was heavier now. 'My,' she said, with honeyed insincerity, 'Ireland is just as I expected it would be.'

Soon they were on the road into Dublin. In the rain the trees shone, a darker than dark green.

'It's almost gruesome, isn't it?' Rose said to Quirke, who was sitting in the front seat beside the driver. 'The first time we met, you were arriving in America for what would turn out to be a funeral—my poor Josh—and now here I am, come to see his great friend Garret buried in his turn. Death does seem to follow you about.'

'An occupational hazard,' Quirke said.

'Of course—I always forget what it is you do.' She turned to Phoebe. 'But you must tell me everything, my dear, all your news and secrets. Have you been misbehaving since I saw you last? I hope so. And I bet you're wishing you had stayed with me in North Scituate and not come back to this damp little corner of the globe.'

Rose was the third wife, now widow, of Phoebe's late

grandfather Josh Crawford. It was at Rose's house, on the day of the old man's funeral, that Phoebe had found out from Quirke at last the facts of her true parentage. Ever since then Quirke had gone in fear of his daughter, a subdued, constant and hardly explicable fear.

'Oh, I'm happy here,' Phoebe said. 'I have a life.'

Rose, smiling, patted her hand. 'I'm sure you have, my dear.' She sat back against the upholstery and looked out at the grey, rained-on outskirts passing by and sighed. 'Who wouldn't be happy, here?'

From the front seat Quirke said over his shoulder: 'Are you tired?'

'I slept on the flight.' She turned her eyes from the window and looked at his profile before her. 'How is Mal?'

'Mal? Oh, Mal is Mal. Surviving, you know.'

'He must be sad, losing his father.' She glanced from him to Phoebe, who sat gazing stonily before her at the back of the taxi driver's stubbled neck. Rose smiled faintly; the subject of lost fathers, she noted, was obviously still a delicate one.

'Yes,' Quirke said, tonelessly. 'We're all sad.'

Again she studied his Roman-emperor's profile and smiled her feline smile. 'I'm sure.'

At the Shelbourne the doorman in grey top hat and tails came to meet them with his vast black umbrella, beaming. Rose gave him a cold glance and swept on through the revolving glass door. Quirke was about to say something to Phoebe but she turned from him brusquely and followed quickly after Rose into the hotel lobby. What was the matter with her? She had spoken hardly a word to him since he had picked her up that morning on the way to the airport. She had not even invited him into the flat, but had left him standing in the drizzle under the front doorway while she finished getting ready upstairs. She was upset over her Grandfather Griffin's death—she and the old man had been close—but she seemed more angry than sorrowful. But why, Quirke wondered, was it him she was angry at? What had he done? What had he done, that is, that he had not been already punished for, many times over? He tipped the doorman and gave directions for the luggage to be brought in. He was weary of being the object of everyone's blame. The past was tied to him like a tin can to a cat's tail, and even the smallest effort he made to advance produced a shaming din behind him. He sighed, and walked on into the hotel, shaking a fine dew of raindrops from his hat.

While Rose was unpacking they waited uneasily together, man and daughter, in the tea lounge on the ground floor. Phoebe sat on a sofa, curled into herself, smoking her Passing Clouds and watching the rain that whispered against the panes of the three big windows giving on to the street. The massed trees opposite lent a faint greenish luminance to the room. Quirke sat fingering his propelling pencil, trying to think of something to say, and failing. Presently Rose came down. She had changed into a red skirt and a red bolero jacket—'I thought I'd add a little colour to this grim occasion'—and Quirke noted how these bright things, despite her perfect makeup and gleaming black hair, only showed more starkly how she had aged in the couple of years since he had seen her last. Yet she was still a handsome woman, in her burnished, metallic fashion. She had asked him to stay with her in Boston after her husband died, him and Phoebe both. He smiled to himself, thinking how that would have been, the three of them there in Moss Manor, Josh's big old mausoleum, lapped about by dollars, Mrs Rose Crawford and her new husband, the pampered Mr Rose Crawford, and his at last acknowledged and ever unforgiving daughter. Now Rose said to him: 'I thought you'd be in the bar.'

'Quirke has given up bars,' Phoebe said, in a tone at once haughty and spiteful.

Rose lifted an eyebrow at him. 'What—you don't drink any more?'

Quirke shrugged and Phoebe answered for him again. 'He takes a glass of wine with me once a week. I'm his alibi.'

'So you're not an alcoholic, then.'

'Did you think I was?'

'Well, I did wonder. You could certainly put away the whiskey.'

'We say here "he was a great man for the bottle",' Phoebe said. Throughout this exchange she had not once looked at Quirke directly.

'Yes,' Rose murmured. She held Quirke's gaze and her black eyes gleamed with mirthful mischief. 'Just like a baby.'

The waitress came and they ordered tea. Quirke asked Rose if her room was satisfactory and to her liking and Rose said it was fine, 'Very quaint and shabby and old-world, as you would expect.' Quirke brought out his cigarette case. Rose took a cigarette, and he held the lighter for her and she leaned forward, touching her fingertips to the back of his hand. When she lifted the cigarette from her lips it was stained with lipstick. He thought how often this little scene had been repeated: the leaning forward, the quick, wry, upward glance, the touch of her fingers on his skin, the white paper suddenly, vividly stained. She had asked him to love her, to stay with her. Sarah was still alive then, Sarah who—

'For God's sake stop fiddling with that!' Phoebe said sharply, startling him. He looked dumbly at the propelling pencil in his hand; he had forgotten he was holding it. 'Here,' she said, for a moment all matronly impatience, 'give it to me,' and snatched it from him and dropped it into her handbag.

A brief, tight silence followed. Rose broke it with a sigh. 'So many deaths,' she said. 'First Josh, then Sarah, now poor Garret.' She was watching Quirke. 'You sort of feel the Reaper out there with his scythe, don't you'—she made a circling motion with a crimson-nailed finger—'getting closer all the time?' Phoebe was looking to the windows again. Rose turned to her. 'But my dear, this is far too gloomy for you, I can see.' She laid a hand on the young woman's wrist. 'Tell me what you've been doing. I hear you're working—in a store, is it?'

'A hat shop,' Quirke said, and shifted heavily on his chair.

Rose laughed. 'What's wrong with that? I worked in stores—or shops, if you like—when I was young. My daddy kept a grocery store, until it went bust, just like so many others. That was in the hard times.'

'And look at you now,' Quirke said.

She waited a moment, and then, 'Yes,' she answered softly, 'look at me now.'

He shifted his gaze. Rose was always most unsettling when she was at her softest.

Phoebe murmured something and stood up and walked away from them across the room and out. Rose looked after her thoughtfully and then turned to Quirke again. 'Does she have to be so deeply in mourning? It seems a little much.'

'You mean the black? That's how she always dresses.'

'Why do you let her?'

'No one *lets* Phoebe do anything. She's a woman, now.'

'No, she's not.' She crushed her cigarette in the glass ashtray on the table. 'You still don't know a thing about people, do you, Quirke? Women especially.' She took a sip of her tea and grimaced: the tea had gone cold. She put the cup back in its saucer. 'There's something about her, though,' she said, 'something different. *Has* she got a beau?'

'As you say, I don't know anything.'

'You should make it your business to know,' she said sharply. 'You owe it to her, God knows.'

'What do I owe?'

'Interest. Care.' She smiled almost pityingly. 'Love.'

Phoebe came back. Quirke watched her as she approached across the room. Yes, Rose was right, he had to acknowledge it, there was something different about his daughter. She was paler than ever, ice-pale, and yet seemed somehow on fire, inwardly. She sat down and reached for her cigarettes. Perhaps it was not him she was angry at. Perhaps she was not angry at all. Perhaps it was only that Rose's arrival had stirred memories in her of things she would rather have forgotten.

Mal appeared. He hesitated in the archway that led in from the lobby and scanned the room with the tentativeness that was his way now, his spectacles owlishly flashing. He saw them and came forward, picking his way among the tables as if he could not see properly. He wore one of his grey suits with a grey pullover underneath, and a dark-blue bow-tie. His hair, brushed stiffly back, stuck out in sharp points at the back of his high, narrow head, and on each cheekbone there was a livid patch of broken veins. Every time Quirke saw Mal nowadays his brother-in-law seemed a little more dry and dusty, as if an essential fluid were leaking out of him, steadily, invisibly. He leaned down and awkwardly shook Rose's hand. One could weep, Quirke thought, for that pullover.

They left the lounge and crossed, the four of them, into the dining room, and took their places at the table Quirke had reserved. When the flurry of napkins and menus had subsided a heavy silence settled. Only Rose seemed at ease, glancing between the other three and smiling, like a person in a gallery admiring the likenesses between a set of family portraits. Quirke saw how Mal's face, when he looked at Phoebe, who for so long the world had thought his daughter, took on a blurred, pained expression. Phoebe, for her part, kept her eyes downcast. Quirke looked at her thin white clawlike hands clutching the menu. How unhappy she seemed, unhappy, and yet—what was it? Avid? Excited?

'Well,' Rose said mock-brightly, narrowing her eyes, 'isn't this lovely?'

On a cool grey summer morning Judge Garret Griffin was laid to rest beside his wife in the family plot in Glasnevin. There was an Army guard of honour, and the many relatives were joined by scores of the public for Judge Griffin, as he was known to all, had been a popular figure in the city. Eulogies were delivered by politicians and prelates. As the first handfuls of clay fell on the coffin a fine rain began to fall. No one, however, wept. The Judge's life had been, the Archbishop said in his homily at the funeral Mass in the overflowing cemetery chapel, a life to be celebrated, a full and fulfilled life, a life of service to the nation, devotion to the family, commitment to the Faith. Afterwards the mourners mingled among the graves, the women talking together in low voices while the men smoked, shielding their cigarettes surreptitiously in cupped fists. Then the black cars began to roll away, their wheels crunching on the gravel.

Inspector Hackett was among the attendance, standing well back at the edge of the crowd in his blue suit and black coat. He had caught Quirke's eye and tipped a finger to his hat-brim in a covert salute. Later they walked together along a pathway among the headstones. The rain had stopped but the trees were dripping still. On a child's grave there were plaster roses under a glass dome mottled with lichen on its inner sides.

'End of an era,' the detective said, and glanced sideways at Quirke. 'We won't see his likes again.'

'No,' Quirke said flatly. 'We won't.'

The Archbishop's Bentley glided through the gate, the Archbishop sitting erect in the back seat like a religious effigy being borne on display in its glass case. The inspector brought out a packet of Players and offered it open to Quirke. They stopped to light up. Then they walked on again.

'I had a word with that fellow,' the inspector said.

'Which fellow is that?'

'Your friend Mr Hunt. The one whose wife died—remember?'

Now the hearse followed where the Archbishop's car had gone; the long bare space in the back, where the coffin had been, was lugubrious in its emptiness.

'Yes,' Quirke said. 'I remember. And?'

'Ah, God help the poor fellow, he's in an awful state.'

'I imagine he is.'

The policeman glanced at him again. 'I sometimes suspect, Mr Quirke,' he said, 'that you have a hard heart.'

To this Quirke made no response. Instead he asked: 'What did Billy Hunt say?'

'About what?'

They came in sight of Rose Crawford and Phoebe, walking ahead of them along the cinder path, Rose linking the younger woman's arm in her own.

'About his wife's death,' Quirke said patiently.

'Oh, not much. Doesn't know why she did it, if she did it.'

'If?'

'Ah, now, Mr Quirke, don't play the innocent. You have your doubts as much as I have in this case.'

They had gone half a dozen paces before Quirke spoke again. 'Do you think Billy Hunt is not innocent, either?'

The inspector chuckled. 'In my experience, no one is completely innocent. But then, you'd expect me to say that, wouldn't you?'

They caught up now with Rose and Phoebe. When Phoebe saw it was Quirke behind her she murmured something and disengaged her arm from Rose's and walked off briskly along the path. Rose looked after her and shook her head. 'So abrupt, the young,' she said. Quirke introduced her to the policeman. 'How do you do, Officer?' she said, offering a slender, black-gloved hand to Hackett, who smiled shyly, the corners of his fish-mouth stretching up almost to his earlobes. 'So glad to meet a friend of Mr Quirke's. You're one of a select and tiny band, so far as we can see.'

Quirke was gazing after Phoebe, who had met up with Mal and stood with him now under the arched gateway that led on to Glasnevin Road. They looked more like father and daughter, Quirke knew, than Quirke and she would ever look.

'And you must have known the Judge, too, of course,' Rose was saying to the policeman.

His grin grew wider still. 'Oh, I did, ma'am,' he said, putting on his Midlands drawl to match her Southern twang. 'A grand person he was, too, and a great upholder of justice and the law. Isn't that so, Mr Quirke?'

Quirke looked at him. Did he imagine it, or did the policeman's left eyelid momentarily flicker?

2

SHE MET THE silver-haired man one Wednesday afternoon when she arrived at the house in Adelaide Road and he was there, sitting on the sofa in Dr Kreutz's room and looking as if he owned the place. She had thought the Doctor was alone because the copper bowl, his signal to her, was not on the window-sill, but it was only that he had forgotten to put it there, which just showed how agitated he must have been. When he opened the door to her he gave her such a strange, wild look, the meaning of which she could not understand until she went in ahead of him and there was the man sitting sprawled on the sofa in his camel-hair coat. He had one arm draped on the back of the sofa and his feet with his ankles crossed were on the low table. He was smoking a cigarette, holding it in an affected way, between the second and third fingers of his left hand. He gave her a lazy smile and looked her up and down and said, 'Well well, who have we here?' It was the camel-hair coat again, the wings of it flung wide open on either side of him, that made him seem to be displaying himself to her in a way that was almost, she thought, indecent. Dr Kreutz stood to one side, glancing from one of them to the other with a bemused, helpless expression. She felt awkward, and did not know where to look. The man took his feet from the table and stood up languidly and offered her a slender, almost colour-less hand.

'The name is White,' he said. 'Leslie White.'

She took his hand, which was soft as a girl's and coolly damp, but forgot to say her name, so mesmerised was she by that crooked smile, that lock of hair flopping on his forehead—it was platinum, really, more than silver—and those eyes in which were mixed amusement, curiosity, brazenness, but which also had a rueful, mock-apologetic gleam, as if he were saying to her, *Yes, I know, I'm a rogue, but I'm such fun, too, you'll see.* Dr Kreutz roused himself then and introduced her, as 'Mrs Hunt', but she, lifting her chin, looked straight into Leslie White's face and said: 'Deirdre.' She was surprised how steady her voice sounded.

Dr Kreutz mentioned tea, but it was plain to see his heart was not in the offer. She had never seen him so unsure of himself. He still had that wild, mute look with which he had greeted her at the door, like that of a character in the pictures trying to let the heroine know there is a man with a gun hiding behind the curtains, and he kept lifting his two hands, palm upwards in a peculiar gesture, almost as if he was praying, and letting them fall back again, defeatedly, to his sides. Leslie White ignored him, did not even glance in his direction. 'I must be going,' he said now, in that soft, sleepy voice that he had, still smiling down at her. As if he knew how uneasy she felt about that coat of his he drew it now slowly, caressingly, round himself, watching her all the time, and knotted the belt loosely, disdaining the buckle. 'Goodbye, Deirdre,' he said. He pronounced it *Deardree.* He went to the door, followed hurriedly by Dr Kreutz, and turned once more before going out and gave her a last, faint, mischievous smile.

She heard them in the hall, Dr Kreutz speaking in an urgent undertone and Leslie White saying dismissively, 'Yes, yes, yes, keep your hair on, for heaven's sake.' She heard the front door open and shut again, and a moment later she glimpsed that shining head of his, like a silver helmet, ducking past the window.

What seemed a long time went by before Dr Kreutz came back into the room. She had not realised that a person that colour could turn pale, but his brown skin had taken on a definite greyish tinge. He would not look at her. She said she was sorry to have interrupted but when she saw that the copper pot was not in the window . . . He nodded distractedly. She felt sorry for him, but she was burning with curiosity, too.

She did not stay long, that day. She could see Dr Kreutz was relieved when she lied and said that she had arranged to meet Billy, and that she would have to go. At the door he made that ineffectual, pleading gesture again, lifting only one hand this time, and letting it fall back, helplessly.

It was Christmas time and the weather was raw, with flurries of wet snow and showers of sleet as sharp as needles. Although it was the middle of the afternoon it was almost dark, and what light remained was the colour of dishwater. Outside the gate she paused and glanced in both directions along the road, then turned right and walked towards Leeson Street, pulling up the collar of her coat against the cold.

He was standing in the shelter of the newspaper kiosk at the bridge. She was not surprised; something in her had told her he would wait for her. He crossed the road, rubbing his hands together and smiling reproachfully. 'Crumbs,' he said, 'I thought you were never going to get away.'

She considered telling him what she thought of his presumption, but before she could say anything he took her arm and turned and drew her with him across the road to the corner of Fitzwilliam Street.

'And where,' she said, with a disbelieving laugh, 'do you think we're going?'

'We're going, my dear, to a pub, where I shall order a hot whiskey for each of us, to warm us up.'

She stopped and unhooked her arm from his and faced him squarely. 'Oh, is that so, now?'

He laughed, looking down at his feet and shaking his head, then reached out and grasped her firmly by the upper arms. 'Listen,' he said, 'we could stand here exchanging pleasantries if you like, telling each other about our past lives and what we had for breakfast this morning, but since we've already been introduced, and since it's bloody cold, can we just go to the pub, where you can stand on your dignity, if you must, but I, at least, can have a drink?'

She had been hoping he would have his car, she would have liked a go in it, but he said Old Mother Riley, as he called it, was sick, and in the car hospital. So they walked down the long avenue, under the tall windows of the houses where already the electric lights were coming on, past the square with its leafless, dripping trees, and into Baggot Street. Grainy drifts of sleet had gathered in the corners of the tiled porch of the pub, but inside there was a coke fire burning and the lamps on the bar shed a warm yellow glow. They were the only customers. There were tables with low chairs, but they chose to sit on two stools at the bar. 'It's friendlier, don't you think?' Leslie White said, moving his stool nearer to hers. 'Besides, if I sit in one of those chairs my knees will be jammed under my chin.'

As she was climbing on to the stool she had seen him trying to look up her skirt, but he had seen her seeing, and only grinned into her face; he had done it, glancing down and up, not in the dirty way that fellows often did in pubs, leering and licking their lips, but openly, unashamedly, and with a kind of invisible twirl, somehow, like one of those singers in an opera gaily twirling a straw hat or the waxed ends of a moustache. He called the barman and gave his order, telling him exactly how the drinks should be made— 'Hot water, mind, not boiling, and no more than three cloves in each glass'—and then offered her a cigarette, which she was going to take but then thought better of it, afraid she would cough and splutter and make a show of herself, for she did not smoke and had only ever in her life taken a couple of puffs. The stool was high and when she crossed her legs she felt herself teetering for a second, and it almost seemed she might fall forward, swooningly, so that he would have to hold her up, in his arms. When the steaming whiskeys came her head was already spinning.

He asked her how she had come to know Dr Kreutz. She made up a story about Mr Plunkett sending her to Adelaide Road to deliver something that the Doctor had ordered, but it was plain from his half-suppressed smirk that he did not believe her.

'Want to watch him, old Kreutzer,' he said, getting rid of the ash on his cigarette by rolling it on the edge of the ashtray until the smouldering tip was pointed like a pencil. 'They call him the Wog with the Wandering Hands, you know.'

She wondered who *they* were, or were they really only Leslie White? She wanted to ask him how *he* had got to know him, but she supposed he would only lie, as, of course, she had done herself. It was strange, but she had to admit there was something about the Doctor that would make a person wary of being completely frank in talking about him. Why was that? Anyway, there were things about Leslie White, she was sure, more and murkier things, that would make frankness seem entirely out of the question.

They stayed in the pub for the best part of two hours— it was a good thing Billy was on the road and not waiting for her at home, to smell the whiskey on her breath. Later, she had only the haziest recollection of what they had talked about, she and Leslie. It was not the alcohol that had affected her memory—though, goodness knows, she was not used to drinking whiskey in the afternoon, or at any other time of day, or night, for that matter—but she had felt so giddy that she had not been able to concentrate properly. She thought of the hoop she had one summer when she was a child—it was only a rusty old bicycle wheel with no tyre and half the spokes broken or missing—which she used to bowl with a bit of stick along the pathway that ran all the way round the yard outside the Flats, and which, when she grew too tired to run along with it any more, would roll off by itself for a little way, upright and really fast at first, then more slowly, until at last it began to wobble before falling over. That was just how she felt now, as if she was slowing down and wobbling, unable to control herself. It was not at the end of something that she was, though, but at the start.

After the third drink she held up a hand and told him not to order another, that she would have to go home, and lied and said that her husband would be expecting her. She was not sure why she had mentioned her husband—was it to put this fellow in his place, because he was so cocksure of himself, or was it, as she dimly suspected, some kind of challenge to him? But what would she be challenging him to do? He was watching her, his eyes roving all over her so that she could almost feel them on her skin, like a blind man's fingertips. She saw herself lying back on Dr Kreutz's sofa with not Dr Kreutz but this silvery, slender-limbed man leaning over her, lifting away layer after layer of some gauzy stuff that was all that was covering her, lifting and softly lifting, pushing aside her ever more feeble protests, until she lay naked before him, naked and trembling and damp. The picture was so strong in her mind that this time she really did lose her balance briefly, and had to close her eyes for a moment and concentrate hard to keep from toppling off the stool.

Afterwards she could not stop thinking about him. He haunted her mind, a sort of debonair, cheerful and all too real ghost. In the shop the next morning she found herself more than once being glared at by Mr Plunkett, having drifted off into a dream while she was in the middle of serving a customer. Her head was still buzzing from the lingering effects of those three unaccustomed whiskeys, but that was not the real cause of her inattention, and she knew it.

She liked the neat way he did things, Leslie White: little, inconsequential things that he seemed not to notice himself doing, like sharpening the ashy tip of his cigarette that way on the side of the ashtray, or making little lattices out of spent matches, or stacking his change in separate piles on the bar, ha'pennies, pennies, threepenny bits, the edges all perfectly lined up. He could do that thing with a coin, too, rolling it over and over along the knuckles of his hand, so fast that the one coin seemed multiplied into three or four, spinning and flashing. And he dressed well. She was not sure if the shades he favoured, white and off-white and metallic grey, were right for his colouring, but the cut of the things he wore was good, she could see, for she had an eye for fine tailoring. Maybe he would take her advice if she offered it. He would look grand in blue, or even better black, a good black suit, maybe double-breasted, that would show off his slim figure, or even a three-piece, with a gold watch chain across the waistcoat. She saw herself on his arm, him all silver and jet and she in something pale and flowing ... 'Deirdre!' Mr Plunkett muttered furiously, making her jump, and she had difficulty focusing on the old biddy in front of the cash register holding out her trembling shilling.

She felt guilty, not towards Billy, of course, but—and this was very strange—because she felt as if she was betraying Dr Kreutz. She told herself she was stupid to think this way—what had she done, after all, except go for a drink with a man, and not even at night, at that, but in the afternoon? But try as she would to make little of what had happened, even she was not convinced. For something *had* happened, and something more would happen, and soon, she was sure of it.

But first there was another and altogether unexpected thing, a thing that made her see Dr Kreutz in an entirely new, lurid light.

3

WHEN PHOEBE WAS a little girl, her parents, or the couple who at the time she thought of as her parents, used to take her in July each year for a two-week stay in a house in Rosslare Strand that was lent to them by friends of Sarah's, theatre people, as she recalled. This holiday by the sea was made out to be a great thing, but the truth was that none of the three of them really enjoyed it, down there in what was called the Sunny South-east. Mal fretted at being away from his work, and Sarah had nothing to do and, although she tried not to show it, was bored most of the time. As for Phoebe herself, she did not care for the seaside. She hated showing herself half naked on the beach—she was skinny and knock-kneed, and her pale skin refused to tan no matter how long she spent in the sun—and she had no talent for making friends. Besides, she was afraid of the sea. One year, when she was nine, or ten, she was walking by herself on the broad strip of thorns and tough grass that ran between the village and the beach, known for some reason as the Burrow, when she stumbled, literally stumbled, on a hare's nest with two baby hares in it. She had never seen such a thing before. It appeared that the mother hare had fashioned the nest by turning and turning herself around in the grass to form a smooth, tightly braided hollow, in which now the leverets lay coiled against one another head to tail, each a mirror image of the other, so that they looked, she thought, like an emblem on a flag, or on a coin. They were very young, for their eyes were hardly open, and they seemed not so much to breathe as throb, faintly and fast, as if they were already exhausted at the very prospect of all the desperate running they would have to do in their lives. She decided immediately, although she knew in her heart it was not true, that they had been abandoned, and that therefore it was up to her to save them. So she picked them up—how soft they were, and so hot!—and made a pouch of her cardigan at the front and carried them home that way, and lodged them in the long grass in the corner by the rain barrel behind the house, where no one would see them. She knew, though she would not admit it, that she should not have taken them, and when she came down next morning and they were gone she experienced a surge of panic and shameful guilt that almost made her be sick there on the spot. She tried to tell herself that the mother hare had somehow been able to follow the babies' scent and had come and taken them away again in the night, but she could not make herself believe it. She ran down to the Burrow again, to see if they might be there, but she could not even find the nest, though she searched all morning until it was time to go home for lunch.

She had never told anyone of the incident, and whenever she thought of it, as she did with surprising frequency, even all these years later, she was still a little ashamed, yet she recalled, too, recalled so sharply that she as good as experienced it again, the warm thrill of carrying them, these frail, helpless yet miraculously living creatures, in the pouch of her cardigan, up Station Road, in the silence of the summer afternoon.

Having Leslie White in her flat gave her something of that same thrill. She knew it was wrong, and probably dangerous, to be sheltering him. He was from a world of which she knew little, a disreputable world of sports cars and drinks in the afternoon and shady business deals, a violent world in which one was liable to be set upon in dark alleyways by silent, hard-breathing men with cudgels. He would tell her nothing of the assault other than what he had told her that first night. He insisted he did not know the three toughs or why they had attacked him. She did not believe this. From the way his eyes slid away from hers when she questioned him she saw there were things that he was hiding from her. And she was glad that he hid them. She was sure it was better not to know very much about Leslie White's doings.

Phoebe had gone that night to Dr Kreutz, as he had asked her to do. The place was not at all what she had expected—it was not a surgery, for a start. When the taxi dropped her at the address in Adelaide Road she had an immediate sense of something indefinably sinister, which was due, she felt sure, to something more than the lateness of the hour and the deserted streets. Although it was past midnight there was a ghostly glow in the sky, but whether it was the last of the day's radiance or the light of an as yet unrisen moon she could not tell. She was not often abroad at such an hour, and the world in the darkness seemed tentative and without definite shape, as if everything were in the process of being dismantled for the night. Above the trees the street-lamps shone, and giant shadows of leaves trembled on the pavements. On the far side of the road, near the gate of the hospital, a pair of prostitutes loitered, the tips of their cigarettes making angular weavings in the shadows, like fireflies; seeing her hesitate at the black-painted iron gate of the house they said something to each other and laughed, and one of them called out softly to her what seemed to be a question, or an invitation, the words of which she was not able to catch, which, she thought, was probably just as well.

There was no sign of life in the basement flat, no sounds from within and no light in the window, but she had hardly taken her finger off the bell when the door suddenly swung open, as if under its own power. Dr Kreutz had not switched on the light in the hall, and at first all she saw of him was the glint of the whites of his eyes, which were like the eyes of the snake-charmer in that jungle painting by the Douanier Rousseau. Kreutz must have known somehow that she was there, even before she rang the bell. When she said Leslie White's name it seemed for a moment that he would shut the door in her face, but instead he came out on to the step, pulling the door to behind him and holding it ajar with his hand. This was the strangest doctor she had ever encountered.

'He's had—he's had an accident,' she stammered. 'He said to ask you to give me his medicine for him. He said you'd understand.'

He was tall and thin, and his face was darker than the night. He was wearing some kind of tunic without a collar, and when she glanced down she saw that he was barefoot. He gave off a faint odour, too, spicy and sweet.

'An accident,' he said, without emphasis. His voice was deep and unexpectedly soft and almost musical.

'Yes.' She was conscious of the two whores still watching from the other side of the road; she could feel their eyes boring into her back. 'He's quite badly hurt.'

'Ah.' Dr Kreutz pondered for a moment in silence, measuring the import of what she had said. 'This is most most distressing.'

Why did he not ask her what kind of an accident it had been?

'I don't know what the medicine is,' she said. 'I mean, Mr White didn't say, he just asked me to come and tell you that he needed it.' She was babbling. She could not stop. 'I'm not sure if there's a chemist's open at this time of night, but maybe if you give me a prescription I could get it filled somewhere, maybe over there at the hospital.' She half turned, to indicate where she meant, and saw the prostitutes out of the corner of her eye, craning in curiosity. Dr Kreutz was shaking his head slowly from side to side.

'There is no medicine,' he said. 'You must tell him that—no medicine, no medicine any more.'

'But he's hurt,' she said. She felt suddenly close to tears. Every word she uttered dropped like a stone into the bottomless depths of his calm and seemingly unbridgeable remoteness. 'Can't you help?'

'I am sorry, Miss,' he said, 'very very sorry,' although he did not sound it, not at all. A moment passed, in which she could think of nothing more to say, and then he stepped back soundlessly into the dark hallway, and again there was that flash of the glistening whites of his eyes, before he shut the door.

It was only on the way out that she saw the plaque on the railings with his name on it. 'Spiritual Healing'—what was that, exactly, she wondered.

Leslie was lying on the sofa where she had left him, dozing, his head set crookedly against the cushions. In the light from the electric lamp on the sideboard his battered face seemed more swollen than it had been before, with shiny, purplish-red bruises; it looked like something in a butcher's-shop window. When she told him what Dr Kreutz had said, that there would be no more medicine, he put a hand over his eyes and turned away from her, and his shoulders began to shake, and she realised that he was weeping. Whatever she had expected, it was not tears. She put out a hand to touch him but held back. Suddenly there was a gulf between them, a distance not broad but immensely, immeasurably, deep. She thought again of the baby hares. It was with him as it had been with them: she was of a different species. She turned away and went into the bedroom and left him there, crying desolate tears into a corduroy-covered cushion.

In the days that followed, that feeling of difference and distance never quite left her. All the same she nursed him as best she could, with tenderness and diligence. She supposed this was how a real, a trained, nurse—when she was little she had intended to be a nurse when she grew up—would do her work, caring and yet impersonal. In the mornings she tried to make him take breakfast, a bowl of cereal or a slice of toast with tea, but he would eat nothing. At lunchtimes she came back to check on him, and in the evenings she would run up the stairs, preparing her smile for him before she burst through the door, expecting him to be gone.

'Why, Miss Nightingale,' he would croak, 'it's you.'

She could see he was suffering not just from his injuries but that there was some additional, deeper anguish. She did not know what kind of medicine it was he had hoped for from Dr Kreutz. Nor did she ask, partly because an admonitory voice inside her told her it was better that she should not know. She thought at first he might be diabetic, and that it was insulin he needed, but as the days went on it became evident that this was not the case. He suffered violent bouts of fever, and would lie shaking for hours, glaring at the ceiling, with his teeth clenched and a film of sweat on his forehead and on his upper lip. He had shed his soiled and torn suit, and wore her—or Sarah's—silk dressing-gown with the dragons and birds on it, loosely closed over his concave and palely glimmering chest. She took his things, his shirt and underclothes, and washed them in the sink in the bathroom, averting her eyes from who knew what variety of stains. She had never before been called on to do someone else's laundry.

It was remarkable, though, how little difficulty she had adjusting to this unwonted male presence in her hitherto solitary domain. She did not stop being aware of the strangeness of him, of what he was, how different from her, yet even the difference and the strangeness she got used to. It really was as if some exquisite, half-wild injured creature had attached itself to her, and given itself into her care. She felt like one of those brocaded ladies in a tapestry, with a unicorn at her feet. She could hardly remember how it had been when they were together in bed that afternoon, and what details she could recall seemed more dreamlike than real.

She tried to get him to allow her to call a doctor, a real doctor, this time, but he made a sound that was half groan half laugh and flapped a long, pale hand bonelessly at her. 'No quacks!' he cried, in a tone of exaggerated comic distress. 'No quacks, for pity's sake!' He said he knew there was nothing broken; his ribs ached, but they were sound, he was sure of it. When she helped him to the bathroom she felt as if she were supporting a sack of sticks. Yet, to her puzzlement and mild consternation, it was his very frailty, his insubstantiality, that she found most arousing. What did that mean? This was, she reminded herself, a new landscape into which she had ventured. She had never lived in close contact before with a man who was not a relative. *Propinquity*, that was the word, sounding as it did like the name of a reserved sin out of the Catechism: she had until now not lived in propinquity with a man. She smiled to herself, and made a faint, involuntary, feline sound deep in her throat. Yes, this was sin, the real thing at last, and all unexpectedly. One hot and airless night when she had lain for what seemed hours sleepless on her bed with the sheet thrown aside she rose with the dawn's first grey glimmer and went into the living room and lay down in her damp slip beside him on the sofa, and he woke and murmured something and turned, groaning a little, and took her in his arms, and she felt the heat of his bruised flesh burning against hers, and she closed her eyes and opened her lips and heard herself cry out, as if she were the one who was in pain.

Still she could not get him to eat properly. He subsisted mostly on Garibaldi biscuits—they reminded her of fly-papers—and Gordon's gin, four bottles of which he had drunk in as many days. After the first one, which she had got in the pub at the end of the street, she had to go farther and still farther afield to buy replacements, afraid that if she went to the same pub she might be reported to the Guards as a dangerous drunkard. He had a craving for sweet things of all kinds, cake, chocolate, sugar-coated bon-bons. He sent her out to buy Yorkshire Toffees and sucked away at them all day, like a schoolboy.

Was she afraid of him? Yes, she was. Even as she held him, burning, against her, with his hands in her hair and his mouth on hers and beads of sweat trickling down between her breasts, she could feel her fear, she could almost hear it, a sort of high-pitched whirring inside her. He was not physically strong, she knew, and the beating had left him weaker, but were not the weak ones often the most dangerous of all? She thought of Laura Swan, and saw her floating dead under murky, bile-green water, her long, thick hair swaying about her featureless face like fronds of russet seaweed.

She went to see Rose Crawford at the Shelbourne. She knew she could not tell her about Leslie White—no one could be told about that—but just to be in her presence was somehow a comfort, and soothed for a while the confused racings of her mind. Rose, she felt, would not judge her, if she were to reveal her secret; Rose in her casually amoral way would understand about Leslie.

They had lunch together in the hotel grill room. 'All I seem to do is sit here and eat,' Rose said, with a jaded sigh.

'I no sooner finish breakfast than it seems time for lunch, then there's afternoon tea, and then'—she tucked in her chin and mimicked a head waiter's booming bass—'*dinner, Madame!*' She smiled. 'Oh, my dear, never get old.'

'You're not old,' Phoebe said.

'But I'm not young, either, which seems almost worse, in a way. You see that man over there, the one having lunch with his rich aunt?'

Phoebe looked. The man, pinstriped and shod in hand-made brogues, was large and florid-faced with hair parted in the middle and brushed back in two floppy wings at either side of his head. The woman opposite him was tiny and hunched, and the knife and fork in her trembling, mottled claws rattled when they touched her plate. 'Do you know him?'

'No,' Rose said. 'But I know an attentive and hopeful nephew when I see one. The point is, when we walked in here he turned to look at us. Or at you, rather. His eye glided over me without the slightest flicker.' She made a wry mouth. 'It was not ever thus, my dear.'

Rose ordered sole for them both, and a bottle of Chablis. The sun through the window made the linen tablecloth shine like bullion and laid a burning speck on the rim of each of their wine glasses.

'Where's that father of yours?' Rose demanded. 'I expected him to dance attendance on me, but I haven't seen him since the day I arrived. What does he think I do with myself all day long? I know no one in this city.'

'Why do you stay?'

Rose opened wide her eyes in exaggerated surprise. 'Why, my dear! Do you want to get rid of me?'

'Of course not. Only . . .'

'Oh, you're right—why *do* I stay? I don't know. Somehow your grim little country is growing on me. I never knew I was a masochist.'

Phoebe smiled one of her ghostly, melancholy smiles. 'Is it because of Quirke that you stay?'

Rose did not look at her. 'I shall ignore that, young lady,' she said.

The waiter came and, with a flourish, presented the wine bottle for Rose's inspection, like a conjuror showing a dove preparatory to making it disappear. When he had poured and gone she held up her glass to the light and asked, in her indolent drawl, 'And what are you up to, young lady?'

Phoebe had to bite her lip to keep herself from grinning like an idiot. This was what it must feel like to be pregnant, she thought, the same hot, thrilling, secretive sense of being all the time about to brim over. She stared innocently. 'Up to?'

'Yes. Don't try to fool me. You're up to something, I can tell.'

'How? How can you tell?' She could not keep the eagerness out of her voice. If only Rose would guess her secret, then it would not be her fault, she would not be the betrayer, and then they could talk.

'Oh, I don't know,' Rose said. 'You have a glow—no, a glitter. There's quite a wicked light in your eye. I think you *are* having an adventure, aren't you?'

Phoebe looked down at the table. She did not often blush but felt she might be blushing now. She was glad when their sole arrived, swimming in brown butter on oval pewter platters. She did not care for fish, but Rose, in her blandly commanding way, had not consulted her before ordering. It did not matter: Phoebe rarely ate lunch, and would probably not eat this one. She took a draught of the Chablis and felt it go straight to her head, like a flash of lemon-yellow light.

'There was a coincidence,' she said, measuring her words.

'A coincidence? What do you mean?'

'Somebody that Quirke knew came to him and asked him not to perform a post-mortem.'

'*Not* to?'

'Yes.'

'On whom?'

'On his wife. This man's wife. She died.'

'Well, yes, I gathered that, if there was or wasn't going to be a post-mortem. Who were, are, these people?'

'It doesn't matter. Just . . . people. I knew the wife—I mean, I didn't know her, but . . . She ran a beauty parlour, I bought things from her.'

'What sort of things?'

'Just face cream, hand lotion, you know. And then . . .' She stopped. She had a sensation of helpless, slow, not wholly unpleasurable falling, as in a dream. Her hand, she noticed, was shaking, and she was afraid that, if she let it, her knife, too, like the old lady's, would rattle against the ridiculous pewter plate. 'She killed herself,' she said. How stark it sounded, how matter-of-fact. She used to think of death as a mysterious, a mystical thing; not any more.

Rose had stopped eating and was watching her with a bright, birdlike stare; Rose recognised the moment when mere talk turned into something else.

'Phoebe,' she said, 'has Quirke got himself involved in more trouble?'

She wondered, Phoebe, when last, if ever, she had heard Rose call her by her name. But then, she reflected, Rose was not really on first-name terms with the world in general. And she had missed the point, here; Quirke was not the one who was in trouble. She lifted her glass and looked at it, but did not drink. Rose was still watching her with a raptor's eye.

'Trouble?' she said. 'No, I don't think Quirke is in trouble.'

The unctuous waiter glided up and refilled their glasses, and when he had done so Rose, without looking at him, motioned him away with an impatient flick of an index finger. She took a sip of her wine. The glint of concern in her look was waning, and suddenly Phoebe knew, suddenly and certainly, that Rose was indeed in love with Quirke. She was surprised not to be surprised.

'You mentioned a coincidence,' Rose said.

'This woman, the one who died, Laura Swan—I knew her partner, too.'

'What sort of a partner?'

'He was in the business with her, the beauty-parlour business. Leslie White is his name.' Had there been a tremor in her voice when she said it? She hastened on. 'Quirke seems to think there was something odd, I mean something odd about her death, Laura Swan's, or about her husband coming to him . . .'

She faltered into silence. Her voice must have quivered when she said Leslie's name, for Rose's attention had snagged on it.

'Leslie White,' she said slowly, looking at her, and made a low, humming sound behind pursed lips. 'Is that what he's called, your adventure?'

'Oh, no, no. No, I mean, he, that is, Quirke, he—he can't seem to leave anything alone.'

Rose nodded. 'That's certainly true.' She turned her attention to her plate and speared a fragment of fish. Phoebe watched in peculiar fascination the morsel of white flesh with its broken threads of bright-pink vein passing into Rose's painted, blood-red mouth. There were tiny striations on her upper lip, as if the skin there had been stitched all along with a marvellously fine, transparent filament.

'How is it, between you and your father?' she asked.

Phoebe always experienced a pause, a mental stumble, when she heard Quirke referred to as her father.

'All right,' she said neutrally. 'He buys me dinner once a week.'

'And has his glass of wine.' Rose's smile was as dry as the Chablis.

'Our lives don't really . . . cross,' Phoebe said, looking at her plate again.

'Hmm. Except when there's a coincidence, like this one with—What's his name again? Leslie who?' Phoebe, looking resolutely down, did not answer. Rose crossed her knife and fork on her plate and leaned her elbows on the table and folded one hand into the other and laid her lips a moment against the knuckle of a forefinger. 'Did you know,' she asked slowly, 'about all the things that happened that time, in Scituate, and before that, here, in Dublin? About Judge Griffin and your father—Quirke, I mean—and the girl who died. I've forgotten what she was called, too.'

'Christine Falls,' Phoebe said, surprised at herself—how had she remembered that name, so surely and so quickly?

'Well, then, obviously you did know,' Rose said. 'Who told you?'

'Sarah.'

'Ah.'

'But I had guessed a lot of it.'

'You know Quirke tried to destroy the Judge's career?—your grandfather, who has just died.'

'Yes. I know. But it was all hushed up.'

Rose sniffed. 'And quite rightly, too. It was a nasty business. That's why I asked you if Quirke was getting himself into more trouble. I think he's still a little bruised from all that—I wouldn't like to think of him becoming embroiled again, in some new scandal. He's not exactly the knight in shining armour that he thinks he is.' A soft breeze swooped down on them from the tall, open window beside their table, bringing a scent of trees and grass from the park across the road, and the dry hay-stink of the cab-stand where the jarveys in their battered top hats waited on the lookout for moneyed tourists. 'You should forgive him, you know,' Rose said. Phoebe gazed at her steadily. 'Oh, I know it's no business of mine. But, my dear, you owe it to yourself, if not to him.' She looked up brightly, smiling. 'Don't you think?' Still Phoebe said nothing, and Rose gave the faintest of shrugs. 'Well now,' she said, 'why don't we have some of this delicious-sounding strawberry shortcake, and then take a stroll in the park over there?'

'I have to go back to work,' Phoebe said.

'Can't you take a little time off, to promenade with your lonely old step-grandmother?' At times, for no apparent reason, Rose exaggerated her Confederate accent—*Cain't yu taike . . . ?*—while laughing a little at herself, an unlikely Southern belle. Phoebe shook her head. Rose sighed, lifting her narrow, pencilled eyebrows. 'Well, then, have some coffee at least, and we'll call it quits.' She considered the young woman before her for a moment, her head tilted at a quizzical angle. 'You know, my dear,' she said, in the friendliest fashion, 'I don't think you like me much, do you.'

Phoebe considered. 'I admire you,' she said.

At that Rose threw back her head and laughed, a sharp, brittle, silvery sound.

'Oh, my,' she said. 'You certainly are your father's daughter.'

She did not go straight back to the shop, but walked across the Green and up Harcourt Street, and let herself into the unaccustomed early-afternoon silence of the house. Today she did not hurry on the stairs, but plodded slowly, gripping the banister rail as she went. Somehow she knew, even before she opened the door of the flat, that Leslie was gone. The blanket and the cushion were still on the sofa, and there were empty sweet papers on the carpet, and his gin glass and a crumpled copy of last evening's *Mail* were on the coffee-table. She stood for a long time, her mind slowly emptying, like a drain. She saw again the baby hares panting in their nest of grass. No fox or weasel would have got Leslie, there was that, at least, though who knew what other dangers might be lying in wait for him? She heard herself sob, almost perfunctorily, heard it as from a distance, as if it were not she who had made the sound but someone in an adjacent room. She put her handbag on the table beside the glass—there was still a bluish drop of gin in the bottom of it—then went and lay down on the sofa, fitting her head into the head-shape he had left in the cushion, and pulled the blanket up to her cheek, and closed her eyes, and gave herself up, almost luxuriously, to her tears.

4

THEY HAD KNOWN, without the slightest doubt, that they would meet again. Quirke waited two days after that first visit to her house before telephoning her. When he took up the receiver he was aware of a tremulous sensation in the region of his diaphragm, which gave him pause. What was it he was embarking on here, and where would the voyage end? He was by nature cautious in matters of the heart. It was not that, after Delia, this organ had ever again suffered a serious breakage, but he preferred to avoid the risk, now that he had come through safe into the middle passage of his life. The very fact of his hesitancy made him more hesitant still. It was apparent, as that warning inner wobble told him, that Kate White offered more than the prospect of what he was in the habit of asking of a woman. Slowly he put down the receiver, and took a breath. It was well into July already, a Sunday afternoon, and the wedge of sky he could see between the rooftops if he leaned forward and squinted up through the window of his living room was a clear, warm, cobalt blue that seemed the very shade of all of summer's possibilities. He conjured up Kate's rueful, damp-eyed smile. What could he lose that would outweigh all he might gain?

He picked up the receiver, and dialled.

Oh, he could lose much, much.

They took a trip to Howth together. Quirke had suggested it; there was a pub in the village where he used to drink that he said he thought she would like. Neither had raised the larger question of what might be done with the remainder of the evening. He arrived by taxi at Castle Avenue and marvelled again at the stolid, four-square ugliness of the house, with its big, glaring windows and slatted blinds and its bricks the colour of dried blood. He found it hard to picture Leslie White here, returning home from a hard day managing the affairs of the Silver Swan and settling down after dinner with his slippers and the evening paper. Yet it was Leslie, according to his wife, who had fixed on the house in the first place, when somebody he knew in the hairdressing business had put him on to it. 'I think he thought it would be the kind of thing I'd like,' Kate had said, pulling a clown's grimace. 'He has terrible taste and imagines I share it. Poor old Les.'

She had come to the door smelling of lemon soap. She had been in the bath. When she saw it was him she put her head on one side and contemplated him for a moment in silence, smiling. 'It's kismet,' she said. 'Obviously.' Her hair today was tied back behind her ears with a black band, and she wore no makeup except lipstick. Her dress was pale yellow with a design of large blue splashes in the shape of giant cornflowers.

'How is the cut?' he asked.

'What? Oh.' She held up her thumb to show him the

neat circlet of sticking-plaster. 'Healing nicely. You should go into medicine.'

She invited him to step inside for a moment while she went to fetch her handbag. He waited in the hall, and a feeling of unease broke out on his skin like sweat; other people's houses, their other arrangements for living, always unsettled him. When Kate came back he saw that she, too, was ill at ease—was she having second thoughts about Howth, and him?—and she avoided looking at him directly. The taxi man, hunched toadlike behind the wheel of his car, eyed her with disdainful lasciviousness as she came out on the pavement, her light dress swishing about her tanned, long legs.

'Oh, not a taxi,' she said. 'Let's take the bus. I'm in a democratic mood, today.'

Quirke did not protest. He paid the driver, who shot away from the kerb in a resentful snarl of exhaust smoke. They set off walking together down the hill road to the seafront. For Quirke there was something at once dreamy and quintessential about summer afternoons, they seemed the very definition of weather, and light, and time. The sunlit road before them was empty. Heavy frondages of lilac leaned down from garden walls, the polished leaves mingling their faint, sharp scent with the salt smell of the sea. They did not speak, and the longer the silence between them lasted the more difficult it was to break. Quirke felt slightly and pleasantly ridiculous. This could only be called a date, and he could not remember when he had last been on one. He was too old, or at least too unyoung, for such an outing. He found this fact inexplicably cheering.

The lower deck of the bus was full of raucous families,

bristling with fishing rods and sand shovels, off to spend the long summer evening by the sea. They climbed the narrow, winding stairway to the upper deck, Kate going first and Quirke the gentleman trying not to look at her behind. He found a seat for them at the front. The sky was clear, a flat blue plane clamped squarely along its lower edge to the horizon; there was a strong breeze and the salt-laden light out over the bay had a bruised cast to it. Before them, Howth Head was a low, olive-green hump dotted with bursts of yellow gorse.

Kate was the first to speak. 'You look very smart,' she said.

Startled, he glanced down at himself dubiously, taking in his pale-blue shirt, his pale-grey suit, his suede shoes—he was never sure about suede shoes. He recalled Leslie White sloping round the corner of Duke Lane, with that silver helmet of hair, those boneless wrists; Leslie would be a born suede-shoe-wearer. Kate laughed briefly. 'I'm sorry,' she said, 'I see I've embarrassed you. I'm always doing that, making people feel self-conscious and awkward and hating me for it.'

In Howth the bus stopped at the railway station and they walked along the front and turned up Church Street. The Cock Tavern was dim inside and slightly dank. A single shimmering blade of sunlight slanting down from the unpainted strip at the top of the window was embedded at an angle in the centre of the floor. Three dusty cricket caps were pinned to a board on the wall, and there was a chart of the coast hereabouts with all the lighthouses marked. They sat at a low table near the open doorway, from where they could see the sunlight in the street. Quirke drank a glass of tomato juice and Kate a Campari and soda. Through the stuff of her dress he could make out the broad bands of her stocking-tops and the imprint of a suspender clasp. He approved of the way she dressed, the freedoms she allowed herself; the women he was used to wore too many clothes, belts and straps, corsets, rubber roll-ons, and came heaving into his arms with all the voluminous rufflings and strainings of an old-style sailing ship in full rig.

'They lived not far from us, you know,' Kate said suddenly, the conclusion, it seemed, to a lengthy and sombre train of thought. He looked at her. She was running a fingertip pensively round the rim of her glass. 'The bitch and her husband—Laura Swan, I mean. I suppose he must live there still. One of those streets of little red-brick terraces over by St Anne's. The height of respectability, as she would have said herself, I'm sure. I can just see it, plaster ducks flying up the wall and a fluffy cover on the lavatory lid. To think of my Leslie there, snuggling down with her of an afternoon under her pink satin eiderdown—oh, yes, she let him come to her, apparently, while hubby was away. God, it's so humiliating.' Now she looked at him. 'How could he?'

When they had finished their drinks they crossed the road and went down the narrow concrete steps between the houses to Abbey Street and the harbour. On the west pier sailors in clogs and smeared aprons were packing salted herring into iron-hooped wooden kegs. Farther on, a squad of trawlermen was mending an immense fishing net strung between poles, vaguely suggestive of harpists in their deft, long-armed reachings and gatherings. There were other couples like themselves, out strolling in the clear, iodine-scented air of evening. A grinning dog raced along the edge of the pier, barking wildly at the gulls bobbing among the boats on the harbour's oilily swaying, iridescent waters. Quirke lit a cigarette, stopping to turn aside and cupping his hands round the lighter and its flame. They walked on. Kate took his arm and pressed herself against him, and he felt the firm warmth of her hip and the slope of a breast in its crisp silken cup.

'Tell me something,' she said.

'What?'

'Anything.'

He thought for a moment.

'I saw your husband,' he said.

She stiffened, still leaning against him, and suddenly she seemed all bone and angles. 'Where?'

He shrugged. 'In the street.'

'Do you know him? I mean, had you met him?'

'No.'

'Then how did you know it was him?'

He hesitated, and then said: 'He was with my daughter. Or he had been.'

He did not know why he had told her. He was not sure that he had even meant to. He thought it might be because, for a brief moment, there on the quayside, with the couples strolling, the dog barking and this bright, full, warm woman leaning on his arm, there had seemed the possibility of happiness. For there was another version of him, a personality within a personality, malcontent, vindictive, ever ready to provoke, to which he gave the name 'Carricklea'. Often he found himself standing back, seemingly helpless to intervene, as this other he inside him set about fomenting some new enormity. Carricklea could not be doing with mere happiness or the hint of it. Carricklea had to poke a stick into the eye of this fine, innocent, blue-and-gold summer evening that Quirke was spending by the sea in the company of a handsome and probably available woman. Carricklea did not go on *dates*, or not willingly, and now, when it had been forced to, it was making sure to have its revenge.

The journey back from Howth was fraught and wordless. That was how it always was when Carricklea had done its worst, a pall of rancorous silence over everything, and all concerned hot and tight-lipped and grim. Quirke had hailed a taxi outside the station and this time Kate had not protested. In the back seat they sat side by side but apart, Leslie White and all that he entailed squatting between them, invisible yet all too palpable. Kate was deep in thought, he could almost hear the ratchets of her mind meeting and meshing. Had he spoken to her of Phoebe before now? Had he even mentioned her? He thought not. Why then was she not plying him with questions? Through the window beside him he watched the dusty, sun-resistant façades of Raheny and Killester sliding past, and sighed. The questions, he was sure, would come. The questions were what her mind was working on, even now.

At the door of the house on Castle Avenue they both hesitated, and then Kate, not looking at him, asked if he would like to come in, and presently he found himself sitting at his unease among the cuboid furnishings of—what had she called it?—'the den', smoking a cigarette and sipping at a cup of coffee that had, for him, no taste. He watched Kate doing the things that women seemed all to do at moments such as this, vigorously plumping up a cushion, picking up a hairpin from the carpet, standing before the window and frowning at the garden as if something were seriously amiss out there that only she could see. At last, chafing under the weight of the room's silence, he put down his coffee cup on the tiny glass table beside him and said: 'Look, I'm sorry.'

He had agreed with himself that if she pretended not to know what he was apologising for he would get up at once and leave. But all she said was 'Yes,' vaguely, letting her voice trail off. Then, suddenly brisk, she sat down opposite him on the white sofa, her shoulders hunched and her hands clasped together on her knees, and gazed at him for a long moment, holding her head to one side in that way she had, as if he were an example, a specimen of some special, rare or hitherto unknown kind, that she had been directed to evaluate.

'Why did you come here, that day?' she asked calmly, in a spirit of pure enquiry, it might be, with not a hint of challenge or resentment detectable in her tone. 'What were you after, really?'

He did not hesitate. 'I don't know,' he said. It was the truth. 'I told you, I'm curious.'

'Yes, so you said. "I suffer from an incurable curiosity," those were your very words.'

'And you didn't believe me.'

'Why would I not believe you? Besides, I was three-quarters drunk. Otherwise I'm sure I wouldn't have let you in the house.'

He looked away from her unsettlingly scrutinising gaze.

It was growing late and the air in the garden had turned a luminous grey. Everything out there seemed touched with an inexplicable, sweetish melancholy, as in a dream. He thought of Deirdre Hunt dead on the slab, her chest cut open and folded back on both sides like the flaps of a ragged and grotesquely bulky, bloodstained jacket.

'It's not just curiosity.' He paused. 'A couple of years ago,' he said slowly, 'I became involved in something that never got finished.'

'What sort of something?'

'Oh, a scandal. A young woman died, and then another one was killed. People close to me were involved. It was hushed up afterwards.'

She waited. He felt in his pockets for his propelling pencil, but then remembered that he seemed to have lost it, somewhere, somehow.

'I see,' she said. He studied her. Did she? Did she see? She said: 'You've sniffed another scandal, and this time you want to make sure it's not hushed up but brought out into the open. Yes?'

'No. The opposite.'

'The opposite?'

'I want it to stay hidden.'

'"It"?'

'Whatever it is. Whoever is involved.'

'Why—why do you want to keep it hidden?'

'Because I'm tired of'—he shrugged—'I'm tired of dealing with people's filth. I've spent my life plunged to the elbows in the secrets of others, their dirty little sins.' He looked to the window again and the greying light. 'One of the first PMs I ever did was on a child, a baby, six months old, a year, I can't remember. It had been beaten black and blue and then strangled. Its father's thumbprints were on its throat. Not just the mark of his thumbs, but the actual prints, engraved into the skin.' He stopped. 'What does it matter what people do? I mean, when it's done it's done. I nailed that bastard for strangling his child, but that didn't bring the child back.' He stopped again, and touched a hand to his brow. 'I don't know what I mean. Look'—he stood up suddenly—'I should go.'

She did not move, but lifted her eyes to his. 'I wish you'd stay.'

'I can't.'

'It's not an offer I make to every strange man who comes to the house asking mysterious questions.' He said nothing. He was on his way to the door. Still she stayed as she had been, sitting there on the edge of the sofa with her hands clasped together and resting on her knees. He walked out to the hall. His hat was on the peg behind the door. He took it down and ran a finger round the brim. His throat felt constricted, as if something were welling up in him, a bubble of bile. *Why had Phoebe been with Leslie White?* That was the question he wanted to ask. But of whom could he ask it, who would have the answer? When he turned, Kate was standing in the doorway behind him, just as she had stood the first time he saw her, one arm lifted against the jamb and her head tilted to one side.

'If you leave,' she said, 'I won't ask you back.' He was still fingering his hat. She turned her face violently aside, as if she might spit. 'Oh, go then.'

*

He walked down to the front and crossed the road and stood by the sea wall. The day was at an end and the sea was lacquered with streaks of sapphire and leek-green and lavender-grey under a violet dome of sky. On the other side of the bay—was that Dun Laoghaire?—the lights were flickering on, and farther off the mountains had lost a dimension and seemed painted flat, as on a backdrop. Vague brownish bundles of cloud hugged the horizon, where night was gathering. His thoughts were a blank, were not thoughts at all. He had a sense of being bereft, bereft not of some definite thing, but in general. But what had he lost? What had there been for him to lose? A light winked far out to sea: a boat? A lighthouse? He turned, and walked back over the grass margin to the road.

When she opened the door she was wearing a blue calico nightgown, and was barefoot. She showed no surprise to find him there. She said: 'Kismet revisited.' She did not smile. 'I was going to have a bath.'

'I thought you had one earlier,' he said.

'I did. I was going to have another. But now I won't.'

He sat at the kitchen table, smoking, while she cooked. The window above the sink grew glossy with darkness. She fed him a lamb chop and tomatoes and asparagus with mayonnaise. He asked why she was not eating and she said she had eaten already, and though he did not believe her he said no more. He let his thoughts wander. He was prey to a strange lethargy; he felt as if he had travelled a long way to come to this place, this room, this table. He ate with scant relish. Food that someone else had prepared, had prepared like this, in a kitchen and not a restaurant, always tasted strange to him, not really like food at all, although he knew it must be tastier than anything he ate elsewhere, tastier certainly than the stuff he prepared for himself. Moly—was that the word? Food of the gods. No, ambrosia. Kate sat opposite him and watched him with a matronly intentness as he ate, doggedly consuming the meat, the red pulp of the tomatoes, the limp green spears. When he had finished she took his plate and put it in the sink, and with her back turned to him said: 'Come to bed.'

'Oh,' she cried, and rolled her head on the pillow to one side and then to the other, biting her nether lip. Quirke loomed above her in starlight, hugely moving. 'Oh, God.'

In the early hours they came down and sat again at the kitchen table. Kate had offered to make more coffee but Quirke had declined. He was barefoot now, as she was, and had on only his shirt and trousers; in the bedroom she had brought out Leslie White's dressing-gown but he had given her a look and she had said 'Sorry' and put it back on its hook. Now in the kitchen the blue-black night was pressed against the window-panes, an avid darkness. There was not a sound to be heard anywhere, they might have been alone in the world. She watched him smoke a cigarette. He was just like every other man she had ever been to bed with, she saw, uneasy now that the main event was done with, trying not to twitch, his eyes flicking here and there as if in search of a means of escape. She knew what was the matter with him. It was not that sadness men were supposed to feel afterwards—that was just an excuse, thought up by a man—

but resentment at having been so needy and, worse, of having shown that neediness. But why was she not resentful of his resentment? She could not be angry with him. An upside-down comma of blond hair stood upright on the crown of his great solid head, and she saw for a second how he would have been as a child, big already and baffled by the world and terrified of showing it. When he came to the end of his cigarette he lit another one from the stub.

'You could enter the Olympics,' she said. He looked at her. 'As a smoker. I'm sure you'd win a gold medal.' He smiled warily. Jokes, she had often noticed, did not go down well at moments such as this. He fixed his eyes on the table again, breathing hard. 'It's all right,' she said, and tapped him lightly on the back of the hand with a fingertip, 'you don't have to say you love me.'

He nodded in hangdog fashion, not looking at her. Presently he cleared his throat and asked: 'Why did your husband go into business with Deirdre Hunt?'

She laughed. 'Is that all you can think to talk about?'

'I'm sorry.'

Again a quick, hare-eyed glance. Was he really so frightened of her?

'You are an old bulldog, aren't you?' she said. 'You've got hold of this bone and just won't let go.'

He shrugged, dipping his enormous shoulders to the side and sticking out his lower lip. She had a strong urge to reach out and press down that rebellious blond curl. Instead she rose and went to the sink and filled a glass of water.

'I don't know why he got involved with her,' she said, sipping the water—it tasted, as it always did, faintly, mysteriously, of gas—and looking through the window at the garden with its sharp-edged patches of stone-coloured moonlight and purple-grey shadows. On the night after she had thrown Leslie out she had stood here like this, willing herself not to weep, and had seen a fox crossing the lawn, its tail sweeping over the grass, and she had laughed and said aloud, 'Oh, no, Leslie White, you're not going to trick me so easily and slink back in here.' Now she turned from the sink and contemplated Quirke again, hunched at the table with the cigarette clamped in his huge fist. 'Leslie was always up to something,' she said, 'doing deals and offering to cut people in on them. A dreadful spiv, really. I can't think why I didn't see through him at the very beginning. But then'—a wry grin—'love is blind, as they say it is.'

She came back to the table and sat down opposite him again and took the cigarette from his fingers and drew on it once and gave it back. He hastened to offer her the packet but she shook her head. 'I've given them up.'

They were silent for a time. A clock somewhere in the house chimed three.

'I'd better go,' he said.

She pretended not to hear. She was looking again to the window.

'Maybe they were having an affair already,' she said. 'Maybe that's why they went into business together—' She broke off with a bitter laugh. 'Business! I don't know why I use the word when talking of Leslie. He really was hopeless. Is.' Quirke rolled the tip of his cigarette along the edge of the ashtray, making a point of the ash, and she experienced a faint twinge in her breast, not a pain, but the memory of a pain. Leslie, too, used to do that with his cigarette, perhaps was doing it now, at this very moment, somewhere else. 'I wouldn't be surprised if he got money out of her,' she said. 'The hairdressing salon had failed—it was called the Clip Joint, appropriately enough—and he'd already got a couple of hundred quid out of me, which of course he threw into the money pit to be swallowed up. I told him there would be no more where that came from. Which didn't improve domestic harmony. I'd sue him, if I thought I had any chance of getting the money back.'

'Would *she* have had money, Deirdre Hunt?'

'*You mean Laura Swan*—I don't know why it irritates me so when you call her by that other name.' She put a hand briefly over her eyes. 'Money?' she said. 'I don't know—you tell me. But Leslie tended not to get interested in anyone who hadn't money, even a little sexpot like her.' She smiled a thin and bitter version of her anguished smile.

He asked: 'How did they meet?'

'Oh, God knows—or wait, no. It was through some sort of doctor they both knew. An Indian, I think. Very odd name, though, what was it. Krantz? Kreutz? That was it. Kreutz.'

'What kind of doctor?'

'I don't know. A quack, I imagine. I don't think Leslie knew anyone that wasn't a fraud of some sort.'

When one or the other of them was not speaking the silence of the night came down upon the room like a dark, soft cloak. Quirke drummed his fingers on the table.

'Kreutz,' he said.

'Yes. With a *k*.'

He sat thinking, then said: 'You mentioned photographs, letters.'

'Did I?'

'Yes, you did.'

She made a disgusted grimace. 'They were in an attaché case under our bed. Just lying there, just like that. I think he must have wanted me to find them.'

'Why? I mean, why would he want you to find them?'

'For amusement. Or to give himself a thrill. There's a side to Leslie that's a little boy with a dirty mind, showing his thing to the girls to make them squeal.' She looked to the side, seeming baffled. 'Why did I ever marry him?'

He waited a moment, cautiously.

'Who were the photographs of?' he asked.

'Oh, women, of course.'

'Women you knew?'

She laughed. 'God, no.'

'Prostitutes?'

'No, I don't think so. Just ... women. Middle-aged, most of them, showing themselves off while they still had something to show, just about.' She gave him a brittle glance. 'I didn't look at them very closely.'

'Were there any of Deirdre—Laura Swan?'

'No.' She seemed almost amused by the possibility. 'I would have noticed.'

'And who took them—Leslie?'

'I don't know. Him, or the Indian, Kreutz—all his patients, so-called, were women, so Leslie said.'

'And the letters?'

'They were hers, the Swan woman's. Not letters, really, just jumbles of filthy things, images, fantasies. I'm sure Leslie got her to write them for him. He liked hearing that kind of thing—' She stopped, and looked down, biting her lip at the side. 'That's another thing when a marriage breaks up,' she said softly, 'the sense of shame it leaves you with.' She stood up, seeming suddenly exhausted, and walked to the sink and filled another glass of water. She drank thirstily, facing away from him. He was afraid she might be weeping, and was relieved when she turned to him with a strained smile. 'The beauty parlour was in trouble too, at the end. God knows what kind of legal chicanery Leslie had been up to. He probably had his hand in the till, too, if I know him. He really didn't have an honest bone in his body.' She checked herself. 'Why do I keep talking about him in the past tense?'

He smoked in silence for a moment and then asked: 'Did you ever meet her, Deirdre Hunt?'

She pulled a face of agonised annoyance. 'I *told* you, her name was Laura Swan. And no, I never met her. Leslie would not have been that stupid.' She paused. 'A wife always knows, isn't that what they say? Or is it that a wife *never* knows? Either way, Leslie was careful to keep his doxy out of my line of fire.'

'And the photos, the letters, where are they now?'

'Gone. I burned them. It took forever. There I was, kneeling in front of the fireplace out in the den, feeding all that filth into the flames and crying like an idiot.'

He said nothing, and after a moment he crushed out the last of his cigarette and stood up. She watched him, and said: 'You could stay, you know.'

He shook his head. 'No, I . . .' She saw him trying to think of a reason, an excuse, to be gone.

'It's all right,' she said.

'The thing is, I—'

She held up a hand. 'Please. Let's not start lying to each other already.'

He hovered barefoot on the rubber tiles, looking at her helplessly. Yes, she thought, they're all the same, all just overgrown infants. Once they've had the breast they lose interest.

He went upstairs to fetch the rest of his clothes, and when he was dressed she saw him to the door. On the step they lingered. The dark air was moist and chill, and fragrant with the scent of some night-flowering plant. She asked if he would come back to see her and he said of course he would. He plainly could not wait to be away, and at last she took pity on him and kissed him quickly on the cheek and put a hand to his shoulder and gave him a soft push. When she had shut the door on him she leaned her forehead against the wood and closed her eyes. She had not even asked him for his phone number. But, then, he had not offered it, either.

5

IT WAS AMAZING how quickly they got the salon up and going. Deirdre never doubted it would be a success, but she had not dreamed it would all be so smooth and so easy. She discovered what a flair she had for business, not only the treatments and the selling of things but the finance side as well. Yes, she had a real head for money. When she had first heard that Leslie White ran a hairdressing salon it had been, though she tried to deny it to herself, a definite let-down. At first she thought it meant that *he* was a hairdresser, and that was a real shock, for she knew what *they* were like, most of them. But he had laughed, and asked how she could have had such a notion—what did she take him for, a pansy? She said of course not, that the thought had never entered her mind, though it had, if only for a second. After all, sometimes it was hard to tell whether a man was that way inclined; not all of them were limp-wristed or spoke with a lisp. And in fact, when she thought about it, it struck her that Leslie's own wrists were not the stiffest, and on certain words he did lisp a bit. Still, she was sure he was normal, and yet she could not get rid of the touch of disappointment that he was in that line of business. She was not sure what she had expected him to be.

Something more romantic, certainly, than the proprietor of the Clip Joint, as it was named—which she had to admit was funny—or as it had been named, for the place had just been shut down.

Leslie talked about the failure of the Clip Joint light-heartedly, with a show of cheerful indifference. To listen to him you would not think it had failed at all, but that he had let it run itself gently into decline because he was bored and wanted to move on to something more exciting and worthier of his talents. He had plans, he told her, oh, yes, indeed, big plans. He had brought her to see the premises in Anne Street, a big, white-painted room on the first floor with its own entrance up a flight of stairs beside an optician's. Everything movable had been cleared out, but the wash-basins were still there, standing in a row along one wall, making her think, with shamefaced amusement, of a gents' toilet. Leslie stood in the middle of the floor in his camel-hair coat and looked about, and could not keep, she saw, the look of misgiving out of his eyes. But he tried to be all bounce, talking airily of the contacts that he had, the money-men and the entrepreneurs he was intimately acquainted with, who as soon as they heard his plans would be falling over each other to invest, there was no doubt of that.

'A beauty parlour,' he had said, his face alight, 'that's the thing. Hairdressing is fine for your average hairdresser, who doesn't know how to do anything else. But the full package, the all-over treatment for the whole woman, that's where the profits are.'

She had the clear impression that none of this was original. It was the kind of thing he would have heard from one of his contacts, one of the money-men, the 'chaps with vision', as he called them. He caught the sceptical glint in her look, though she had tried to hide it, but all he did was smirk and bite his lip, like a little boy caught out in a fib. That was one of the things she liked about him, perhaps the thing she liked best, the merrily offhand way in which he dismissed all reversals of fortune, treating them as mere stumbles along the path to unimaginable success, and riches, and happiness.

There was, though, another side to him, and it had not taken her long to see it. When he spoke of his wife, for instance—'that stuck-up bitch', as she thought of her, though she had never even seen her—his pale long face would flush, and his eyes would take on what she could only describe as a dirtied, a muddied look, and he would make a sucking motion at the side of his mouth, peeling his lip upwards to reveal a slightly tarnished eye-tooth. But this show of rage and vengefulness would last only a second or two, and then he would be his old playful self again, and he would do that sort of dance step that he did, prancing nimbly sideways towards her and lifting one hand with palm upturned and touching her teasingly under the chin with the tip of an index finger, humming some tune buzzingly with lips tight shut.

He had lost no time in attempting to get her to go with him, of course. She admitted candidly to herself that he probably would have succeeded straight away if there had been any surface in the Clip Joint more accommodating than the floor for them to lie down on. Yet he did not try it on with her the way she was used to from other fellows. He did not make a grab at her, or attempt to put his hand up her skirt or down her front. He was more like a wonderful and exotic bird, a peacock, maybe, dancing round her and showing off his plumage, smiling and cracking jokes and making her laugh, often despite herself. Oh, yes, he knew how to make a woman feel good, did Leslie White, knew how, in fact, to make her feel like a woman, not the way most of the men she knew did, treating her as if she was a piece of moving furniture, a sofa, say, or a lumpy old mattress, on which to fling themselves down, snuffling and snorting like a pig.

Billy was like that, sometimes.

It had not taken her long to find out that Leslie was married. She had assumed from the start that he was. He did not tell her much about his wife. She had money, it seemed—she was in business herself, something to do with the rag trade—but kept it safely locked away from him. He did let it slip that she had on at least one tricky occasion in the past stepped in and saved the Clip Joint from closure. Maybe, Deirdre thought, it was that experience that had soured Mrs High-and-Mighty White on her feckless husband. He was living with her still, although as far as he was concerned the marriage was over, and as soon as he got the new venture under way he would be moving out, so he assured her. All this she took with a certain reservation. She was not a fool; she knew men, and how they talked; she knew what their promises and declarations were worth. Yet there was something about Leslie White that she could not resist, she knew it, and he knew it, too, and meanwhile everything had come to a point from which there would be no turning back. She was the girl in the canoe and the brink of the waterfall was getting steadily nearer and nearer.

In the end it was the photographs that had done it. She often wished, afterwards, that he had not shown them to her. She knew, of course, why he had. It was partly out of simple mischievousness, that schoolboy urge he had to show off the secret he had discovered, but also he had gauged, correctly, as it would turn out, that there was a part of her, buried deep down, so deep that she had been hardly aware of it before now, a part that was, she had to admit it, just as gleefully dirty in its desires as Leslie White was—as any man was. All the same, they were a shock, the photographs, at least at first. When he showed her the one of the woman in the fox-fur stole—they were in the empty room above the optician's shop—she felt hot and excited and almost frightened, in a way that she had not felt since she was a little girl. It was a big photograph, twelve inches by nine or so, but very sharp and clear, all silver-greys and soot-blacks, and finely detailed. 'Exposure' was the word, all right. The woman, very slim, pale, small-breasted, was lying diagonally across a sofa—Deirdre recognised it at once—with one leg thrown wide, the slender foot resting on a cushion on the floor. She was naked except for the fur that was wound around her neck, with the fox's sharp little muzzle seeming to bite into the flesh at the soft incline of her left breast. Her right hand was stretched out to the side, dangling languidly by the splayed right leg; the left hand was in her lap, the thumb and second finger holding wide apart the dark lips there and the index finger stuck inside herself right up to the knuckle. The woman was smiling into the lens, at once brazen and guilty, and her head was turned a fraction to one side, as if she was inviting the person behind the camera, and anyone else who might chance to look at the cameraman's handiwork, to come and join her, where she lay.

Deirdre took all this in, the foot on the cushion, the fox's clenched muzzle, that dangling hand, those lips agape, and immediately shut her eyes tight and turned the photo face down with a snap. She could hear herself breathing. The feeling she had was that feeling, hot all over and at the same time somehow cold, that she would have when she woke as a child in the cot-bed in her parents' bedroom and realised that she was wetting herself, wetting herself and horrified to be doing it and yet unable to stop for the shameful pleasure it gave her. And she was not able to stop now, either, not able not to open her eyes and turn the picture over and look at it again. She was disgusted with herself, yet excited, too, in a horrible way that made her think she should be ashamed, though she was not, not really.

There were other pictures, twenty or thirty of them, which Leslie kept in an old music case that fastened with a metal thing like a horse's bit that came down over the flap. Some were of the same woman, the woman with the fox fur, and some were of others, all of them naked, all shamelessly on display, some of them doing even worse things than the woman was doing with her hand down there, and all smiling that same dirty smile into the camera. At first she had not been able to meet Leslie's eye, and now, when she did look at him at last, she knew her face was burning. He was watching her, and smiling, with one eyebrow wickedly lifted, enjoying her discomfort. It came to her that she would remember this moment for the rest of her life, the chill in the bare room, the winter light on the white walls, the dull and somehow sullen gleam of the washbasins, and Leslie there with his overcoat open, leering at her.

'Where did you get these?' she asked, in a voice that dismayed her, it was so steady. Had she no shame, really?

'Simple,' Leslie said, and tapped a fingernail on the one of the woman in the fur stole. 'She gave them to me.' Then he told her, pacing the floor with his hands in his coat pockets, how he had met her, the woman, one afternoon in a basement pub in Dawson Street where he used to drink— he would not tell her the woman's name, said she might recognise it, since her husband was well known, and would only call her Mrs T.—and how he had made friends with her in the hope that she might put some cash into the Clip Joint, which was just starting to run into trouble at the time. He had seen straight off, despite the fact that she frequented Wally's place, which had about as bad a reputation as a pub or drinking club or whatever it was could have, that she was well connected. That end of the thing had not worked out, however—Mrs T. was cautious when it came to money— but she was good company, and a real sport. It was through her that he had come in contact with Dr Kreutz, and now he and Kreutzer, as he called him, were—he laughed—'Oh, the best of pals.'

She thrust the bundle of photographs back into his hands. 'They're disgusting.'

'Yes, they are, aren't they?' he said happily.

'Why did she give them to you—how could she?'

'Well, I suppose she's a bit of an exhibitionist. She thought I'd like them. And, of course, she didn't know I'd show them to you.'

'Which you shouldn't have.'

'No, I suppose not.' He lowered his head and looked up at her from under his eyebrows in the way that made him seem a bit like a smiling, silver-haired devil. 'But you're glad I did,' he said softly, 'aren't you?'

'I certainly am not.'

But was she not, really? She did not know. She was confused. Certainly she was shocked to think that Dr Kreutz would take such pictures—for she was certain, without having to ask, that it was he who had taken them. So these were his *clients*, so this was *spiritual healing*. Leslie, of course, could see what she was thinking.

'I warned you about him, didn't I, old Kreutzer?'

She shook her head. 'But why?' she said. 'How?'

He looked surprised. 'Why did he take them? Because they wanted him to. Some people like to see themselves doing naughty things. Good, aren't they—as photographs, I mean? Look at the technique. He has quite a knack.' He chuckled. 'Comes from long practice, I imagine.'

She knew she should break with Leslie White there and then. Nothing would be the same between them after she had seen those pictures. And yet she could not do it. When the thought of those women, so lewd, so shameless, came into her mind she experienced a thickening in her throat, as if something soft and warm had lodged there, and she felt a panicky sensation that had as much of pleasure in it as anything else. Yes, pleasure, dark and hot and frightening. Billy her husband noticed this new excitement in her, although of course he did not know what was causing it, and when he was home he followed her round the house like—she hated to think it but it was true—like a dog sniffing after a bitch that was in heat, and as for the things he tried to get her to do now when they were in bed . . .

Billy. She knew she must make herself sit down and consider what was to be done about Billy. Sooner or later she would have to tell him about Leslie White, tell him, that is, that she had met this man who wanted her to go into business with him. That was as much as she would need to say, for now; it was also as much as she would dare to say. For the fact was she had accepted Leslie White's proposal—oh, my God, what a word to use!—his *business* proposal, she meant, to open a beauty parlour with him. It was all arranged. The premises was there already, over the optician's—he talked to her about ninety-nine-year leases and ground rents and tenants' options until her head was spinning—and the shopfitters would be coming in any day now.

Yes, it was all arranged, all agreed. One rainy January morning Leslie had taken her to a lock-up in Stoney Batter in order to get her opinion, so he said, on a doctor's trolley thing, a sort of high, narrow, flat couch on wheels, which some friend of his was selling and which would be ideal for doing massages on. The friend, a shifty-looking fellow in broad pinstripes who had the worst smoker's cough she had ever heard, went off and left them alone—had Leslie arranged that, too?—and something in the moment affected her, perhaps it was the sense of sudden intimacy that she felt, despite the damp and the gloom of the place, and before she knew it she was on the trolley in Leslie's arms, biting the back of her thumb to stop herself crying out, and the trolley was moving on its wheels with every rapturous move they made. Afterwards she had pulled his coat over herself—that famous camel-hair coat!—because she was cold and because the champion cougher might come back at any minute. Leslie had got up, since there was not enough room on the narrow rubber mattress for them to lie side by side, and when he had fixed his clothes he lifted the coat by a corner so he could get a look at her. 'My my,' he said, grinning. 'Wouldn't the Doc be delighted with you.' It took her a moment to realise what he meant, and she turned her face aside so as not to let him see her blushing, and smiling, and twitched the coat away from him and wrapped herself up in it. 'Snap snap,' he said gaily, holding an invisible camera to his eye.

She had to let some weeks go by before she could face Dr Kreutz again. Yes, everything was changed. It was not just that she had seen the photographs—that, in a way, was the least of it by now—but there was the fact of her and Leslie, too. He saw it in her eyes, she could see him seeing it. What woman could hide the simple truth that she was in love? Thinking this, she paused. Was that what it was—love? The word had not entered her head before this moment. She softened. Why be surprised that she should think of love in Dr Kreutz's presence? Had he not taught her about such things, the things of the spirit? What did it matter if he liked to take pictures of naked women? Perhaps it was part of the treatment, perhaps it was a way of helping those women by letting them see themselves as they were, in all their womanliness. Perhaps it did heal their spirits— who was she to say otherwise, she who had lain a-sprawl on that rubber mattress on the trolley in that dirty shed, and on other beds, on other days, with every fibre of her on fire under Leslie White's admiring gaze?

Besides, it was Dr Kreutz who was financing the setting

up of the beauty parlour. Leslie had gone to him and asked for the money and he had agreed, as simple as that. Or so Leslie said.

Now Dr Kreutz made a pot of herbal tea and invited her to kneel with him on the cushions on the floor before the low table with the copper bowl. By now it was almost spring, and through the window she could see black branches that were already budding and, behind them, a sky of nude white with scraps of cloud flying diagonally across it. She had a feeling of pent-up happiness that might burst out at any moment. She knew, of course, that there were things that could go wrong. It would take work and a lot of luck to keep the Silver Swan going at the rate that it had been going at so far—she could hardly keep up with the numbers of new customers coming in every week, and was already thinking of when would be the time to hire an assistant—but she could not believe that between them, she and Leslie and Dr Kreutz, they would not continue the success they had achieved so far. It was true that the Clip Joint had failed, but Leslie had explained how that had happened, and if she did not understand all the technicalities that did not mean his explanation was not the true one. What they had between them, Leslie and she—their *love*—would overcome any number of difficulties that might arise.

Love. She sipped her tea and in her mind tried out the new word for size, for weight. She would have to use it sparingly. Leslie, she had already learned, did not take kindly to being *mauled*—that was his word for the kisses and caresses by which, since the day in the lock-up, she had tried to show how she felt for him. That was because of his being English, she reasoned, since the English were all supposed to be reserved and not willing to let on how they were really feeling. He had a way at times of drawing back from her, his head lifted on its long, pale neck, and looking down at her with an expression that was less a smile than a wince, and giving a little puff of laughter through his nostrils, as if she had done something too foolish for words. He was rough with her, too, sometimes. By now they had a place where they could be together, a bedsitter in Percy Place, rented, or borrowed, more likely, from another of Leslie's friends. They would go there in the afternoons, and pull the curtains, and he would undress her slowly and almost as if absent-mindedly, and then take her in his arms and press himself against her, trembling in that peculiar way that he did—girlishly, almost—which excited her and at the same time made her want not so much to make love to him as to cradle him in her arms and rock him to sleep. But he was no baby. He would bite her lips until they bled, or twist her arm behind her back and make her gasp, and once, when he could not manage to do anything and she laughed it off and said it did not matter, instead of being grateful for her understanding he smacked her across the face, hard, so that her head flew back and banged off the headboard and she saw stars. And then there was the night when she and Billy were getting ready for bed—what a trial it was for her now, being in bed with poor Billy—and he saw the red weals on the backs of her legs where Leslie had whipped her with his leather belt—God, how she had moaned—and she had to make up an excuse, which she could not believe he believed, about having been sitting on a chair that had slats in the seat. And yet she—

'More tea?' Dr Kreutz asked.

She blinked, waking out of her reverie. She noticed again now, as she had already noticed, that he had hardly looked at her directly since she had arrived. She wondered if he might be jealous, for surely he must have guessed that what she and Leslie had going was more than a business partnership. The thought made her flare up in annoyance. She had enough to do keeping Billy's suspicions at bay. Billy had talked to Leslie only once, when the three of them met by arrangement for a drink in the bar of Wynn's Hotel. It was a Sunday evening and behind them three red-faced priests were drinking whiskey and talking loudly about a hurling match they had been to in the afternoon. Billy had been shy of the Englishman with his hoity-toity accent, as he described it afterwards, and his silver cravat, and had looked at his boots and talked in a mumble—not that he had much to say, anyway—his nearly colourless eyebrows meeting in a frown and the tips of his ears bright pink. When she looked at him she had felt not so much guilty as . . . *sorrowful*; yes, that was the only word for it, she felt sorrow for him, the soft-hearted poor lummox. And, more strangely, it seemed to her that she had never loved him as much, with such tenderness and compassion and simple concern, as she did in that half-hour in that smoky bar with the voices of those priests breaking in on them and Leslie and she trying not to look at each other in case they might burst out laughing.

Leslie had been very good with Billy, had really acted the part of the businessman, going on about overheads and annual turnover and broad profit margins and all the rest of it. She had to admire him—what a bamboozler he was. He pretended to listen to Billy's mumbles, nodding solemnly with his lips pursed, and made sure to remember to call her

Mrs Hunt and not by her first name. To hear him you would think it was a hospital or something the two of them were setting up. When he said that 'Mrs Hunt would make a great contribution to the salon'—he had learned to follow her example and call it a beauty *salon* instead of a beauty *parlour*, which she thought sounded common—'because of her long experience as a pharmacist', Billy blinked. She wondered how much of Leslie's palaver he was swallowing. He knew a bit about business himself, and he was no fool when it came to dealing with people. She told herself not to say too much but to keep quiet and let Leslie do the talking. She limited herself to a glass of Babycham and nursed it for the whole time they were there, for drink went straight to her head on occasions like this—although when in her life, she asked herself, had there been another such occasion?— and above all she must not show how excited she was. For the fact was, it was only now, as she stood there in her sensible shoes and the charcoal-grey two-piece costume she had bought to be her business suit, listening to Leslie fast-talking her husband, that the full realisation came to her of just what an adventure it was that she had embarked on. The future suddenly was—

'You must, you know,' Dr Kreutz said, 'you must be careful—very very careful.'

She looked at him blankly. What was he talking about?

'Careful of what?' she asked.

He shrugged uncomfortably. Today he was wearing a blue silk kaftan—it was another of the exotic words and names for things that he had taught her—and under it his shoulders looked more than ever like a coat-hanger.

'Why, all this,' he said, 'this business you have started.'

There was a new, plaintive note in his voice, she noticed, and between phrases he kept making a sort of humming sound under his breath. 'Mr White's previous enterprise failed, you know—hmm hmm—and Mr White himself maybe is not—hmm—everything that he seems.'

Well! she thought. Talk about the kettle calling the pot black. She felt like enquiring where his *camera* was today, and how many *clients* he had taken pictures of recently. But she could not be indignant with him for long. In her new-found state of bliss she could not be indignant with anyone, even Billy, or not for long, anyway. Of course Leslie was not all that he seemed, but she knew that, if he was anything, he was more of it rather than less. Only that *more*, of course, was something Dr Kreutz would not understand. Now she pushed her cup away—it had a peculiar aftertaste, cloying and sickly sweet—and said that she must be going. When she stood up, however, she felt suddenly light in the head, and it seemed for a moment that she might fall over. The doctor was on his feet in a flash and holding her hand, and with his other hand under her elbow he led her to the sofa—*that* sofa—and lowered her gently on to the cushions and stood back, watching her, his head on one side and his lips set in the downturned way that he had, which was the nearest he ever came to a smile.

'Rest,' he said softly. 'Rest now, my dear lady, my dear dear lady.'

She thought of all the women who had lain down there, naked and showing themselves off. She wondered what it would feel like, to be exposed like that, not in front of a man, exactly, but a camera. And wondering that, she fell into a deep and dreamless sleep.

6

MAISIE HADDON—or Nurse Haddon, which was how she liked to be known, in private as well as in public—had a soft spot for Quirke, and frequently assured him so, especially after a second or a third rum and blackcurrant juice, which was her tipple. They had arranged to meet, as they usually did, in a murky little pub on a side-street behind the Gaiety Theatre. They arrived simultaneously, he on foot and she in her open-topped miniature red sports car that always reminded him of a scuffed and slightly battered ladybird. She wore dark glasses with white frames, and was smoking a cigarette in an ebony holder. Despite the warmth of the day she sported a mink jacket and a long yellow chiffon scarf, one end of which was flung back dramatically over her right shoulder. She pulled in to the kerb with a shriek of tyres and the little car mounted the pavement and stopped and the engine gave a final, rivet-loosening roar before she switched it off.

'Howya, handsome,' she said, leaning over the low door and offering him a lace-gloved hand.

He bowed and brushed his lips against a bony knuckle, catching a sharp waft of her perfume. 'I tell you, Maisie,' he said, 'one day you'll end up like Isadora Duncan.'

She took up her handbag from the passenger seat and clambered out of the car. 'Who's she when she's at home?'

'Dancer. Her scarf got caught in the back axle of a sports car and broke her neck.'

'Jesus,' she said, 'what a way to go.'

They entered the pub. It was a Saturday afternoon and the usual rackety crowd was in. When Maisie paused on the threshold to scan the room through her white-framed specs a dozen heads lifted; there were few here who did not know who Nurse Haddon was. She walked to the bar with Quirke in her wake and perched herself on a high stool, smoothing her tight skirt over her knees with a demure little gesture that made Quirke smile. In his way he, too, had a soft spot for her, this preposterous creature. He wondered what age she was, exactly—it was impossible to tell from her looks or figure. Her big, square, countrywoman's face showed hardly a wrinkle, and her hair, if it was dyed, was blonde to the roots, so far as he could see—he did not dare look too closely for Maisie was quick to anger and was said to have once knocked out cold a Garda detective who was trying to arrest her. It amused Quirke to think, not for the first time, that he was probably putting his professional reputation at grave risk by being seen with her, and in a public house, at that. For Maisie Haddon was the city's most notorious, most successful and busiest back-street abortionist.

He ordered drinks, her rum and black, and a tomato juice for himself.

'Are you off the gargle?' she said, incredulous.

'Six months now.'

'Holy God.' She still had the accent, raw and flat, of wherever it was she hailed from, over in the west. 'Did you have a conversion, or what?' Their drinks arrived and she clinked the rim of her glass against his. 'Well, I hope you get a high place in Heaven.'

He offered her his cigarette case and flipped the lid of his lighter. She screwed up her mouth and blew smoke sideways, and touched the tip of a little finger delicately to one corner of her mouth and then to the other.

'So,' she said. 'What is it you're after?'

He pretended puzzlement. 'What do you mean?'

'I know you—you're always after something.'

'Only your company, Maisie.'

She flexed a sceptical eyebrow. 'Oh, sure.'

Maisie had spent two stretches in jail. The first time was twenty years before, when she had been charged with running a nursing-home, so-called, where women with inconvenient pregnancies came in secret to have their babies, many of which were left for Maisie to dispose of, often in a bundle of swaddling on the side of a country road at dead of night. When her sentence was served she had promptly rented a room in Hatch Street and started in the abortion trade. Shortly afterwards her clinic, as she called it, had been raided by the Vice Squad and she had done another two-year stretch in Mountjoy. Released again, and undeterred, she had gone straight back to work. Maisie was the keeper of many secrets. She knew Malachy Griffin and claimed to have worked with him at the Holy Family hospital in the days when she was still a real nurse, a claim, Quirke reflected, that no doubt Malachy would not wish to hear too often or too loudly put about.

'How is business?' Quirke asked now.

'Never better.' She took a slug of her rum and fitted

another of his cigarettes into her ebony holder. 'I tell you, Quirke, the women of this town must never have heard of a french letter.'

'Hard to come by.'

She cackled, and poked him in the chest with a fore-finger. '*Hard to come by*—that's a good one.' Her glass was empty already, and he signalled to the barman for a refill. 'Anyway, they're not,' she said. 'I have a fellow brings them in by the suitcaseful through Holyhead. I offer them to my clients. "Here," I say, "take a couple of dozen packets of them with you, for I don't want to see you here again for a good long while, and preferably never." But will they take them?' She put on a whining tone. '"The priest will give out to me, Nurse. My fella won't hear of it, Nurse." Bloody little fools.'

Quirke toyed with his glass. 'Ever come across a woman called Hunt?' he asked. 'Deirdre Hunt?'

She gave him an arch look. 'Oho,' she said. 'Here it comes.'

'She also called herself Laura Swan.'

She was still looking at him hard along one side of her nose.

'Do you know what it is, Quirke,' she said, 'but you're a terrible man.' Putting on a show of unwilling surrender she rummaged in her handbag and brought out a dog-eared address book bound in leather. This was her famous little black book, which, as she declared frequently in her cups, she intended one day to sell to the *People* or the *News of the World*, to keep herself in comfort in her declining years. She flipped through the pages, reading off names under her breath. It was all show, Quirke knew: there was not a woman Maisie had treated, in the three decades and more in which she had been in business, whose name, address and telephone number she could not recite from memory at a moment's notice. 'No,' she said, 'no Hunt. What was the other name—Swan? No Swan, either. Who is she?'

Quirke raised one shoulder an inch and let it fall again. 'Was,' he said.

'Ah. So that's the way it is.' She shut the address book with a slap and thrust it back into the depths of her bag. 'In that case, I certainly do not know and have never known any person or persons of that name or names. Right?' She finished her second drink and fairly banged the glass down on the bar.

Quirke lifted a finger to the barman. 'In fact,' he said, deliberately pausing, as if in judicious scruple, 'in fact it wasn't her, Deirdre Hunt, that I was particularly interested in. She wouldn't have been one of your customers.' She looked at him. 'I did a post-mortem on her,' he said. 'She had never been in the family way.'

A small man wearing a puce-coloured tie, on his way to the gents', staggered as he was going past and jogged Maisie's elbow, and a drop of rum from her glass splashed on her chiffon scarf.

'*Bloody queers*,' Maisie muttered, glaring after the little man and plumping herself up like a ruffled hen. She turned her attention back to Quirke. 'So what,' she asked, 'was the matter with her, then?'

The fumes of the rum she was breathing over him were making Quirke's head swim. His mouth was dry and his fingers had the arthritic ache in the joints that came on when he was most in need of a drink. Would it never abate, he wondered, this raw craving? Perhaps he was an alcoholic, after all, and not just the heavy drinker he had always told himself he was. Suddenly he wanted to be away from here, from this reeking place, these jabbering, reeling people, this woman with the blood of countless embryos on her hands, and of more than one misfortunate mother, too, if the stories whispered of her were true.

'Do you know—' he began, and had to stop. His thirst was a rage now, his mouth drier than ever and his forehead moist with a chill sweat. He ran a hand over his eyes, his nose, his mouth. 'Do you know a man called Kreutz?' he asked, clenching his fists under the rim of the bar and digging his fingernails into his palms.

She focused on him, frowning. 'How do you spell that?' He spelled it. 'Oh, I know him, all right,' she said, and gave a low laugh. '"Doctor" Kreutz, so-called. The darkie. Has a place in—where is it? Adelaide Road, that's right.' She chuckled again. 'I've had a few of that gentleman's patients referred to me.'

'What does he do?'

'I don't know, some kind of mumbo-jumbo. Healing for the spirit. Incense and fruit diets, that kind of thing. Women go to him.'

'And he sent some of them to you?'

She grew wary, and looked into her drink and shrugged. 'A couple. Why?'

'Was it the usual trouble?'

'What do you mean?'

'The reason he sent these women to you, was it the usual?'

'No,' she said with harsh sarcasm, 'they were in need of

further spiritual guidance and advice on their complexions.' She leaned her face into his. She was not drunk, but she was not any longer sober, either. 'Why the fuck do you think he sent them to me?' She guzzled another go of her drink. A thought struck her. 'What has he to do with the other one, what's her name—Hunt?'

'I don't know,' Quirke said. He slid himself cautiously off the stool. This was how their meetings most often ended, with Maisie tipsy and morose and him sidling for the door and escape. Behind Maisie's back, and with a finger to his lips, he paid the barman for another rum and black and stepped away from the bar nimbly. Maisie looked over her shoulder and watched him go. For such a big fellow, she blearily mused, he could move awful fast.

The sunlight in the street blinded him. An enormous Guard was examining Maisie's car where she had left it skewed at an angle with two of its wheels on the pavement. Quirke veered aside and made off.

Everywhere he turned in the business of Deirdre Hunt things that had seemed substantial evaporated into smoke and air, and what had appeared open and inviting entryways were suddenly slammed shut in his face.

When he had rounded the corner from Merrion Square and was walking up Mount Street he spotted a figure sitting in the sun on the steps outside number thirty-nine and knew at once who it was. Even at that distance there was no mistaking the big head with its cap of carroty hair and monk's tonsure. He thought of turning back before he was spotted himself, but instead went on, for lack of will. His rage for a drink had abated but he had a dry hangover now, and there was a pounding in his head and his eyes scalded in their sockets.

Billy Hunt was sitting on the steps with his back sloped and a hand under his chin, like Rodin's *Thinker*. Quirke wondered what had possessed him to get involved with the likes of Deirdre—what was her maiden name?—Deirdre Ward. But then, what possessed any man to fix on any woman, or any woman to fix on any man? In the case of his own marriage the answer had been simple, and Sarah, dead Sarah, his dead wife's sister, had enunciated it clearly for him: Delia had been willing to sleep with him without a wedding ring, and Sarah had not, and on that basis he had made his choice. But Delia, the lovely, dissatisfied, danger-ous Delia, why had *she* accepted *him*, knowing, as she must have known—for Delia was clever, and missed nothing—that it was her sister he had really wanted? Had she, he wondered now—it had never occurred to him before—had she done it to spite her sister? God knows, Delia would have been capable of it; Delia, he thought, would have been capable of anything.

He stopped at number thirty-nine and stood with one foot on the lowest step, his hat tipped back and his jacket over his shoulder with a thumb hooked in the tag.

'Hot day,' he said.

Billy lifted a hand to shade his eyes and squinted up at him. 'Ah, Quirke, there you are. I said I'd buy you a drink.'

Quirke shook his head. 'I told you, Billy, I don't drink.'

'Did you? I forget things all the time, these days. There's

a permanent fog in my head. Anyway, you must drink something—tea? Coffee? A bottle of minerals?'

Quirke smiled. *A-boddle-a-minerls.* Billy would always be the boy from Waterford.

They went round by the Peppercanister church and crossed the road to the canal. They did not speak. The trees, hotly throbbing, hung their heads out over the unmoving water. A Swastika Laundry van, comically high and narrow, appeared on Huband Bridge, its electric engine purring. Billy Hunt was tall, Quirke had no more than an inch or two on him, and he walked with a sportsman's muscle-bound shamble. Percy Place was cloven down the middle, with glaring sunlight along one side and a wedge of shadow along the other. At the door of the *47* Quirke caught the familiar pub reek of alcohol and male sweat and ancient cigarette smoke that he used to savour so and that now made him feel nauseous. When they were at the bar Billy Hunt asked him what he would have and he asked for a soda water—by now he thought he might never again manage to drink another tomato juice—and Billy ordered it without comment, and a pint of stout for himself. Quirke watched him drink off the pint in two goes. He seemed to have no swallow mechanism, merely opened his mouth impossibly wide and tilted the heavy black liquid straight down his throat.

'So,' Quirke said, hearing how wary his own voice sounded, 'how is it going?'

Billy tucked his chin into his chest and belched.

'I appreciate you doing that thing for me,' he said. Quirke said nothing. Billy Hunt belched again, less loudly.

'That detective called me in,' he said. He was looking at his reflection in the mirror behind the bar above a shelf full of bottles. He rubbed a hand back and forth on his chin, making a rasping sound. 'What's his name? Hackett.'

'Oh, yes?' Quirke said. Johnnie Walker, Dimple Haig, Jameson Twelve-year-old. A tin sign assured him that *Players Please*. 'And?'

'You may well ask.' He put his empty glass on the bar and looked at the barman, who took the glass and produced a clean one and set it under the Guinness tap and pulled the club-shaped wooden handle. All three men watched the sallow gush of stout turning black in the bottom of the glass. 'He talked about the weather,' Billy said. 'Wanted to know if Deirdre was able to swim. Asked me where I was the night she died.' He turned suddenly and looked at Quirke with his ox's injured eyes. 'He wasn't fooled.'

'Wasn't fooled about what?'

Suddenly he saw, for the first time, really, just how angry Billy was. Anger, he realised, was his permanent condition now. And that would never change. Not only his wife, but the whole world had wronged him.

'He knows it wasn't an accident,' Billy said.

'Knows? Knows for a fact, or is guessing?'

Billy's new pint arrived. He considered it, turning the glass round and round on its base.

'The coroner didn't believe it, either, did he?' he said. 'I could see it in his eye. And yet he let it go.' Quirke said nothing, but Billy nodded, as if he had. 'What did you say to him?'

'You heard the evidence I gave.'

'And that was all?'

'That was all.'

'You didn't have a word with him beforehand?' Once more Quirke chose not to answer, and Billy nodded again. 'There wasn't anything in the papers,' he said.

'No.'

'Did you fix that, too?'

'I haven't got that kind of influence, Billy.'

Billy chuckled. 'I bet you have,' he said. 'I bet you have a cosy little arrangement going with the reporters. You're all the same, you crowd. A cosy gang.'

This time Billy sipped his pint instead of devouring it, pursing his mouth into a beak and dipping it delicately into the froth like a water bird breaking the scummed surface of a rock pool. Then he wiped the back of a hand across his lips and frowned into the mirror before him, the surface of which had a faint, inexplicably pink-tinged sheen.

'That's the thing I can't understand,' he said. 'She would never have wanted to make a show of herself like that. Being found on the rocks, with no clothes on her.' He paused, thinking, remembering. 'I never saw her naked, you know, when she was alive. She wouldn't let me.'

Quirke coughed. 'Billy—'

'No no, it's all right,' Billy said, waving one of his great, square hands. He bent his face wader-like again over his pint, and drank, and again swabbed his lips with the back of his knuckles. 'That's the way she was, that's all. So I can't understand it, her doing what she did.' He looked at Quirke. 'Can you?'

Quirke was lighting a cigarette. 'I didn't know your wife, Billy,' he said. 'I'm sure she was . . .'

Billy was still looking at him. 'What?'

Quirke took a long breath. He had the strange and surely mistaken feeling that Billy was laughing at him. He drank his soda water. 'It doesn't do, Billy,' he said, 'to keep going over things. The past is the past. Death is death. It doesn't give up its secrets.'

For a moment Billy did not respond, then he made a muffled, snuffling sound, which after a moment Quirke realised was indeed laughter. 'That's good,' Billy said. '"Death is death and doesn't give up its secrets." Did you rehearse that, now, or make it up on the spot?'

Quirke felt himself flush. 'I meant—' he began, but Billy interrupted him by lifting that meaty hand again and laying it with complacent heaviness on his shoulder. Quirke flinched. He did not like to be touched.

'I know what you meant, Quirke,' Billy said. Again he twirled his glass slowly on its base. The cork mat it stood on had a cartoon of a pelican with a yellow beak. *Guinness Is Good For You*, yes, and *Players Please*. What an agreeable place the world might be, with merely a little adjusting. 'One of the things about being in my position,' Billy said, in a now seemingly relaxed, conversational tone, 'is the way people talk to you. Or I should say, the way they *don't* talk to you. You can see them watching every word they're saying, afraid they'll make some blunder and remind you of "your loss", as they call it, or "your trouble", then the next minute they'll suddenly blurt out some saying, or some proverb, you know—"she's in a better place", or "time is a great healer", that sort of thing—which you're supposed to be grateful for.' He nodded again, amused and sardonic. 'And the other thing is that you have to listen to all of them, and pretend to *be* grateful, and not say anything back that might upset *them*. Because, of course, when someone has died on you, suddenly you must be the nicest, most forgiving, most understanding, most *harmless* person in the world.' He gripped his glass where it stood on the bar, and Quirke could see his knuckles whiten. 'But I'm not harmless, Quirke,' he said, with almost a sort of grim gaiety. 'I'm not harmless at all.'

They left shortly afterwards. Billy Hunt's mood had shifted again. A light had gone out in him and he had a hazed-over aspect. He looked, Quirke thought, sated, sated and—smug, was it?—as if he knew a thing that Quirke and everyone else did not. At the door of the pub they parted, and Billy shambled away in the direction of Baggot Street. Quirke crossed over the little stone bridge. The trees along the canal seemed to lean lower now, exhausted in the heat of the day, yet to Quirke the sunlight was dimmed, as if a fine dust had sifted into the air, thickening and sullying it.

7

DEIRDRE REALLY DID wish sometimes that Leslie had never shown her those pictures. It was not that she was shocked by them—on the contrary, they fascinated her. And that was the trouble. It was the fascination that led her on to other things, things that she would not have thought herself capable of. For a start there were the letters that Leslie got her to write to him. Not that they were letters, really, more like those accounts of her dreams that she used to scribble down when she was a girl, because she had heard someone say that you could tell the future from your dreams. Only no girl would write the kind of things that she wrote for Leslie. He said she was to put down any thought that came into her head, any thought at all, so long as it was dirty. At first she had laughed and said she would do no such thing, but he kept on at her and would not take no for an answer. What she should do, he said, was imagine that he was a prisoner and she was the prisoner's girlfriend and that she was writing to him to keep his spirits up—'And not only his spirits,' he murmured, nuzzling her ear and softly laughing. In the end she said all right, that she would try, but that she was sure she would not be able to do it. It turned out that she *was* able, though, and more than able.

And the things she wrote! She carried a pad of pale-blue Basildon Bond writing paper everywhere with her in her handbag—and envelopes, too, for Leslie insisted they should be like real letters—and whenever she got the chance would take it out and start scribbling with an indelible pencil, not thinking of what she was writing only letting it pour out of her, blushing half the time and biting her lip, hardly able to keep the lines straight, hunched over the page like she used to do in school when the girl she shared a desk with was trying to copy off her. She took terrible risks, she seemed to have no fear. She wrote at her dressing-table in the bedroom while Billy was in the bathroom shaving, or at the desk in the cubbyhole behind the treatment room in the Silver Swan when she was between clients. She wrote on park benches, in cafés, on the bus if there was nobody beside her. Once even she slipped into Clarendon Street church and sat hunched over in a pew at the back with the pad on her knee, panting almost in the midst of that holy hush, the waxy smell of burning penny candles reminding her of other and very different smells, night smells, Leslie smells. As she wrote she grew more and more excited, and almost frightened. It made her think of that time when she was working at the pharmacy and she went to confession and told the priest a screed of made-up sins, about sucking Mr Plunkett's thing and doing it with an alsatian dog, just to shock the old boy behind the grille and hear what he would say.

Were the things that she wrote down that day in the church filthier than usual, or did they only seem worse, because of the surroundings? She got herself in such a state, her pencil flying over the page, that she had to stop writing and undo the button at the side of her skirt and put a hand

BENJAMIN BLACK

inside her pants, into the hot moistness there, and use her finger to make herself come. The pleasure was so intense she had to clench her teeth and shut her eyes tight to keep from crying out. Luckily it was morning and there was no one else in the place, except a bald and bent old sacristan in a rusty surplice who kept crossing back and forth in front of the altar, stopping always in the middle to genuflect before the Blessed Sacrament, and who did not even glance in her direction. When she was leaving, her pants all wet between her thighs, she could feel the red beam of the sanctuary lamp boring into her back like an accusing eye. To think she had done those things in a church! She knew she should be ashamed, but she was not; she was exultant.

All this delighted Leslie, of course. 'Well well,' he said to her, chuckling, 'I'd no idea what a filthy mind you had.' Although he pretended it was all just a bit of fun that he had thought up for his amusement, it was plain that he really was impressed by how much she wrote and how detailed it was. She could see he could hardly believe his luck in having found someone who was willing—who was, if she was to tell the truth, only too eager—to let him know all the darkest and most disgusting things that went on in her mind. They would lie twined together naked in the narrow bed in the room in Percy Place—that name always made Leslie laugh—and he would read aloud what she had written for him since she had seen him last. While he was reading she would bury her face in the hollow of his shoulder, flushing to the soles of her feet, but making sure not to miss a word, hardly able to believe it was she who had written such things. She loved Leslie's voice, his accent like you would hear in the pictures, so that what he read out sounded different from how it had sounded in her head when she was writing it. In Leslie's mouth it seemed serious, somehow, and—and authoritative, that was the word; just like, in fact, it suddenly struck her, just like how the actor doing the voiceover in a film would sound, only not—she laughed to herself—not the kind of film that was ever likely to be shown in a picture-house in this country.

Leslie got as excited as she was by what he was reading out, and would stop in the middle of some really spicy bit and lie back against the pillow and twist a handful of her hair round his fist the way her brothers used to do and push her head into his lap. How silky he was there, how hard and hot and silky, when she pulled the skin back from the helmet-shaped head with the funny little slit in the top like an eye winking at her and put her lips delicately round it. She liked doing it that way, liked to make him writhe and groan, knowing that she was the one who was in charge, that she was the one with power.

She would never have dreamt of doing it like that with Billy.

Whenever the thought of Billy came into her mind now she would immediately hurry on and think of Leslie instead. Did that mean she really was in love with Leslie? A girl in school years ago had told her, and she had believed it, that when you thought of one fellow and then immediately of another it was the second one you really loved. But the fact was she did not know what she felt for Leslie. She was not even sure that she liked him, which was strange—how could you be with someone as she was with Leslie if you did not like him? He was good-looking, of course, in a thinned-out sort of way. In bed, when he had not taken anything, he could keep going for ages. It was easy to tell he had been with a lot of women, and knew what he was doing. And he was funny. He would do imitations of Dr Kreutz and even, though she tried to stop him, of Billy—he had nicknames for him, such as Billy in the Bowl, or Billy the Kid, or the Old Boy—which made her scream with laughing. He would get her down on the floor and sit on her and tickle her, as if they were a pair of kids. Sometimes when he was about to go into her he would stop for a second and raise himself above her on his arms and enquire, putting on the fruity voice of that woman who had stopped them in the street one day to ask directions, 'Is this Percy's Place?' Yet for all that it sometimes seemed to her—and this was *really* strange—that she would prefer him to be not real but a part of her fantasies. That way it would be so much easier. Billy, and their little house on St Martin's Drive, and her work in the salon, and her mother who was sick now and her father she was still afraid of and her brothers that she never saw— that was life, real life, and though none of it could compare in intensity with what she had here in this shabby little room below street-level, with the net-curtained half-window looking directly on to the pavement, and the worn lino and the lavatory down the hall and the cracked handbasin and the bed that sagged in the middle, still she valued that other life, the normal one, and wanted to keep it separate from all this with Leslie, separate, and uncontaminated.

Nothing was simple, though Leslie tried to make her think otherwise. She did not believe they were just having a bit of fun together, *a bit of a lark*, as he said. Sometimes she was shocked by the mixed-up feelings she had for him. For instance, there was the time when he told her there was no danger of her getting into trouble because he and his missus had both been tested and it had been found that he could not make a child. He thought she should be relieved, and happy, even, and she supposed she should be, but she was not. She knew how unlikely it was that a time would come when they could have a baby together, yet the fact that it could never happen, not ever, gave her a sort of empty, hollow feeling in her stomach, as if a part of her had been removed.

No, nothing was simple. And to make it all even more complicated, as well as their very private life together she and Leslie had a sort of a public one, too, in which she had to pretend to be nothing more than his business partner. The Silver Swan was doing well, better than she, or Leslie, either, she suspected for all his confident talk, would have dared to hope. There were more rich, bored women in this city than she could have imagined. Nor could she have imagined how many of them would be funnily inclined: hardly a week passed that she did not have to fend off the advances of some stark-faced viper with razor-sharp finger-nails and eyes like bits of ice. In time she came to think of these women—they claimed to be women though they were more like men than some men were—as hazards of the trade, and added a hefty premium to their bills.

And how the money rolled in. It had been a surprise to discover what a shrewd head for business she turned out to have, but it was just as well she had, for Leslie, as she very soon discovered, was hopeless—charming, but hopeless. In fact, his sole asset was his charm, and there were many among her clients, she knew, though obviously not the icy-eyed ones, who came to her chiefly in the hope of cornering him for a cosy chat, at least, and no one did cosy chats better than Leslie. She made a point of not criticising him for his incompetence or his laziness. Why should she complain? For the first time in her life she felt fulfilled. She had confidence, security, money in her purse and a brand-new Baby Austin to drive, and next winter, if things continued as they were going, she would be able to buy herself a mink coat. In other words, she was no longer Deirdre Hunt—she had become Laura Swan. And she had Leslie, too, into the bargain.

He showed her how to do things that, before she knew him, she would not have thought of even in her most secret fantasies. They were things that made her ashamed at first, which of course was a big part of the pleasure of them, but soon they became a source almost of pride to her. It was like learning a new skill, training herself to new levels of daring and endurance. She had always been shy of her body, she supposed it was because of being brought up in the Flats and having to sleep in her parents' room even when she was well past being a child, with no privacy anywhere, even in the lav, since her father would not fix the lock that had been broken for longer than anyone could remember. Now all that awkwardness had disappeared, Leslie had seen to that.

There was only one worry that she had, which was that Billy might notice the change in her. One night in bed she forgot herself and guided him into a place he had probably thought she would never allow him even to touch—she had been fantasising that he was Leslie—and afterwards he had heaved himself off her and flopped down on his belly, panting, and asked in a muffled voice where she had learned that sort of thing. In a panic she said she had read about it in a magazine that someone had lent her, and he had snorted and said that was a nice kind of magazine for her to be reading. The next morning when she looked at herself in the mirror she saw for the first time something in her face, a new hardness, a sort of tinny sheen, and, worse than that, a look she had never noticed before: it was, though it shocked her to have to admit it, a look of her father.

Yes, this place Leslie had brought her to was a different place, a place she had not known existed, and yet somehow it felt not at all strange to her. It was like a place she had been to in childhood and had forgotten about and then had come back to suddenly, unexpectedly. What she felt when she thought of Leslie was the same feeling that she would have when they played games of blind man's buff at home at Christmas time. It was a mixture of giddy anticipation and gleeful terror, and it made her skin tingle and her throat go thick. Or maybe it was a feeling she had known even further back, when she was baby, yes, that was it: with Leslie she was a baby again, a babe in arms. She had tried to explain this to him one day but of course he had only laughed at her, and said sure, she was a babe, all right, his babe, and he had pinched her breast so hard with the long, pearly nails of a finger and thumb that it had made her gasp.

It was strange, too, that she was not jealous of the woman in the fox fur, the woman she had seen Leslie meeting in the bookshop on the bridge, the one showing herself off so brazenly in the photo. When she asked Leslie about her he had given that smiling shrug of his and said that of course he had fucked her—the word made the blood rush to her cheeks—and then picked up the other photographs and splayed them under her nose like a hand of cards and grinned in that cold-eyed way that he did sometimes when he wanted to hurt her and said, 'Fucked them all, didn't I?' She did not know whether to believe him or not, but it did not matter: she did not care if he was telling the truth or lying just to tease her. No, she did not care; she was not jealous. Where she was now, the old rules did not apply. It was all right if Leslie had slept with Foxy—that was the nickname she had invented for Mrs T., since Leslie still refused to tell her the woman's real name—and even if he had slept with every one of those women in the photos, that was all right, too. Somehow, they did not matter, they were like the people in the fantasies she wrote out for him, not real at all. Leslie, for his part, said he did not mind if she went with other men. In fact, he wanted her to find people to sleep with, men, women, anyone, so long as she would tell him about it afterwards. On that one thing she was adamant, though: she would never go with anyone but him.

'Oh, yes,' he said, 'and what about old Billy Boy?'

That, she had discovered, was Leslie's one big weakness: she might not be jealous of his women, but he was certainly jealous of Billy. The thought of her husband so much as touching her made him furious. She had to pretend to him, had to swear to him, that she would not let Billy near her, ever again. It was hard to convince him. When he had first demanded that she promise it she had asked, off-handedly, almost laughing, just how she was supposed to fend Billy off, for he was a strapping fellow and insisted on his conjugal rights. Leslie had given her a frightening look then, his head at an angle and his eyes seeming to draw even closer together, and had said nothing. Only when, a little later, they were in bed together, he had twisted her arm up behind her back until she thought it might break, and had breathed into her ear the one word, '*Remember.*'

Yet he could be gentle, too, and even kind, sometimes. She hated her hands, they had never been anything but square and blunt, but now they were all sinewy, the veins in the backs of them almost like ropes, a masseuse's hands, yet Leslie always said they were lovely, and twined his slender, pale fingers in her sausagey ones and lifted them to his lips and kissed the tips of them, one by one, smiling at her with his eyes.

He brought things for her to take when they were in bed together, pills, and drops of odd-tasting oily stuff out of little glass bottles. There was a powder that he mixed into sugar and coaxed her to eat, which just gave her an itch and made her feel bilious, and which only afterwards he told her was spanish fly. Then one afternoon he produced a velvet-lined box with a hypodermic syringe in it, and a handful of ampoules of liquid clear as water, and offered her a 'toot', as he called it. She drew the line at that. 'It's good for you,' he said, in that crooning way that he had when he was trying to get round her. 'It's made from poppies. It's like a health food.' Oh, no, she said, oh, no you don't. She had not worked in a chemist's shop all those years without being able to recognise dope when she saw it. He said she did not know what she was missing. All the same, when he had rolled up his sleeve to give himself the injection she noticed that he turned away from her and held his arm pressed in close against his side—how naked it was, suddenly, that arm, how naked and white—and she was reminded of a cat doing its business and trying not to be seen. Yet how beautiful he looked there, too, sitting half turned away from her on the bed with his leg bent in front of him and one foot on the floor, the overcast day's pale dry light from the window falling across the side of his face with its long sharp jaw and sharply pointed chin. When the stuff had taken its effect he lay down on his side on the bed, and she lay down too and put her arms round him, and so they remained for a long time, so peaceful, he with a hand under his cheek, gazing up at the window, and she looking into his face, which seemed, with the window-light still on it, to be made of silver, a different silver from his hair, and so like the face of a saint, a martyred saint, in an old painting. He slept for a while, breathing like a baby, and when he woke up they made love, and he was so dreamily tender that she almost cried in his arms. 'Next time,' he murmured into her hair, in a slowed-down, underwater voice, shivering a little, 'next time you'll have to try a toot of joy-juice.'

She supposed she should not have let him come to the house. She supposed that was the worst thing she could have done to Billy, or would have been if he knew about it, which God forbid. Billy was away in Switzerland, hob-nobbing with the swanks, and maybe it was out of resent-ment—before they were married he had been full of promises about taking her with him to Geneva, but he never had—that she said yes when Leslie asked if he could 'pop out' to Clontarf and see her. He was just itching to get into the house and have a look, of course, that was all, she knew that. She let him in from the laneway at the back, afraid some busybody on the street would spot him. She was determined to get him out again double quick, for already she was having cold feet, but no sooner was he in the back door than he swept her into his arms and kissed her on the mouth so hard and deep that she forgot about the danger and the hurt she could be causing Billy.

Leslie walked all round the house, with his hands in his pockets and bouncing on his tiptoes—he had a way of walking that reminded her of a tennis player—smiling delightedly and saying how fascinating everything was, the wedding photos on the sideboard, the silver-plated tea service her Ma and Da had given her, Billy's salesmanship diploma in a gilt frame, and the Sacred Heart lamp and the reproduction of the *Monarch of the Glen* over the fireplace. She trailed behind him in silence. Instead of being pleased that he liked the place—*her* place, since Billy had no interest in it except as somewhere to eat and sleep and slump in an armchair on a Sunday afternoon listening to the football matches on the wireless—she felt a growing sense of doubt, of misgiving. The things after Leslie had looked at them seemed changed, dimmed, somehow, as if he had breathed on them and left them covered with a fine, grey mist that, unlike real mist, did not fade. But then he made her take him upstairs, into the bedroom, hers and Billy's, and took off her clothes in that slow, dreamy way that nearly drove her mad with desire for him, and they lay down on the bed, and she lost consciousness of everything except his lips, and his hands on her, and his pale, cool, glimmering skin pressing against hers.

Afterwards, of course, he had to have a *toot*, and she warned him not to forget to take all that stuff away with him, the needle and the empty phial and the cotton wool and the little bottle of alcohol he was so careful to swab his arm with before injecting himself. Those would be nice things for Billy to happen on when he came home.

That was the evening that she told him about the time in Dr Kreutz's office when she had drunk the herbal tea and passed out. She had said to Leslie, while she was getting dressed, that she supposed he had got that stuff, the spanish fly and the dope and so on, from the Doctor—nothing any more would surprise her about the man she used to think so highly of—and then she heard herself blurting out about how she had woken up on the sofa that day feeling as if she had been hit over the head. No sooner had she spoken than she regretted it. Suddenly, for the first time, it was clear to her what had happened, what she had known without knowing had happened, and her heart froze. So that was the reason her clothes had felt as if they were on back to front. Why, the dirty old . . . Even though he was half doped Leslie had been listening, and had heard even more than she had said, for Leslie had an ear for such things. He was still in the bed, lying on his back with the sheet pulled up to his chin, like a patient after an operation; it gave her a shiver to see his head where she was so accustomed to seeing Billy's. He swivelled his eyes until the big pupils of them were focused on her, and waited, and of course she had to go on then, though she tried to make light of it. 'There must have been something in the tea,' she said, with a little laugh that sounded even to her a bit hysterical. She sat down on the bed to fasten her suspenders, her fingers nervously fumbling with the clips. 'I suppose it was something relaxing that he gives his clients. I must say, I did have a good sleep.' Leslie made no comment, only went on watching her, and then, slowly, he smiled. She knew that smile. It frightened her, though she tried not to show it. 'Right, Mister,' she said, smacking her hands on her thighs and rising smartly to her feet, 'you better be off.' He made no move to get up, though, only turned his face away and sighed. His long thin white feet were sticking out from under the sheet.

Again she had the icy sensation in her chest. If Kreutz had knocked her out to take pictures of her, what was he going to do with them?

She found out soon enough. When the morning post was delivered at the salon a couple of days later and she saw the big brown envelope, with the square handwriting on it that looked so innocent, somehow she knew straight away what would be in it. She had a client on the table—she was getting to be good, really professional, at massage, even though she had no training and had only read it up in a book—but she had to stop immediately and wipe the oil off her hands and open the envelope, though it was addressed to Leslie. When she saw the photograph the blood seemed to drain straight down out of her brain and she almost fainted. She must have caught her breath out loud, for the client, a crotchety, fat old bitch with asthma, lifted herself up on her elbows with her eyes out on stalks to try to see what the picture was of. She turned away and hurried into the cubbyhole behind the curtain and sat down at the desk there and made herself take three or four deep breaths. She had thrust the photo back into the envelope—was it really her?—and though she tried to she could not bring herself to look at it again. She had gone white first but now she could feel herself turn bright red with shame. How could he, the dirty brute? It was as if a bucket of slops had been flung into her face. Even the things her Da used to do to her when she was little seemed not as bad to her now as the way Kreutz had betrayed her. *How could he?*

Leslie only laughed, of course, and held the photo at arm's length and pretended to study it as if it was an old-master painting or something, shutting one eye and tilting his head first to one side and then the other. 'He definitely has a flair, old Kreutzer,' he said. 'He should take it up professionally'—he grinned—'photography, I mean.' They were in the room in Percy Place, and he was lying on his back on the bed with his jacket still on and one leg flexed and a skinny ankle propped on a knee. There was a summer storm, and the wind was blowing rain in sheets diagonally across the light from the street-lamps. She had bought cheese and a Vienna roll and a bottle of Liebfraumilch for their supper. Leslie was still chuckling. She said it was not funny, and asked if there was nothing he would not laugh at. Could he not understand how ashamed it made her, to see herself like that, with her dress up around her and her legs all over the place and every bit of her on show? 'He's made you look quite the doll, I think,' Leslie said. 'Quite the pin-up.'

She said she did not look anything of the kind, and that it was only what it was, a dirty picture.

'Oh, I don't know,' he said slyly. 'I'm sure I could find some connoisseur who'd pay a pretty penny for a framed copy of this.'

'Don't you even think about it, Leslie White,' she cried.

She knew he was joking about selling it, but even so the

very idea made her go hot all over. When she was handing him his glass of wine she could not help glimpsing the photo again, where he was holding it up to the light to study it, and she shivered. Strangely, the worst part of it for her, though she did not say so, was the fact that in the photo her eyes were shut. It made her look like a corpse.

'What was it he gave you, I wonder,' Leslie said. 'Must have been something pretty good, for you to stay knocked out while he was setting up this little scene.' He threw her an impish look, the sharp little tip of his tongue showing. 'You're sure you weren't just pretending?'

She did not deign to answer him. The whole thing was disgusting, and yet somewhere inside her, deep, deep down inside her, a small flame flared at the thought of herself sprawled unconscious there on that sofa, on the red blanket, and Kreutz, with the camera around his neck, leaning over her and pulling up her dress and taking off her pants and parting her knees . . . Leslie was watching her. He always knew what was going on in her mind. He laid the photograph flat on his chest and reached out a hand to her. 'Come here,' he said softly. She wanted to say no, that she was too upset, that she felt dirty and ashamed. But in the end, of course, she could not resist him. As he undid the buttons of her dress he hummed under his breath, as he always did, as if she was a job of work he was about to get busy on.

'I want that photo,' she said.

'Mmm?'

'I'm going to tear it up. I'm going to burn it.'

'He'll have copies. He'll have a negative.'

'You could get them from him. Will you do that, for me? Get them and burn them, burn them all?'

'Mmm.'

He thought it was funny that Kreutz would dare to try to blackmail him—why else had he sent the nudie photo of D.?—and would have dismissed the whole thing if D. had not kept on at him so. In the end, to shut her up, he had said that he would go round in the morning and call on Kreutz and give him a talking-to. He had not expected to keep his promise, yet next day early—it was early for him, anyway—he found himself bowling up Adelaide Road in the Riley. The storm of the night before had blown itself out, and the sun was shining, and the smell of rain drying on the pavements and the look of the rinsed trees all in full leaf cheered him up. He had stopped at a postbox on Fitzwilliam Square and dropped in the resealed envelope with a forwarding address on it, and a girl in a white blouse going past had given him a hot look. He drove on, whistling through his teeth and smiling to himself, with the wind ruffling his long hair.

At Kreutz's place he parked at the kerb and went through the iron gate and hammered on the door and waited. When paying a call such as this one was likely to be, a fist on the wood and plenty of noise, he considered, was a better way of announcing his arrival than merely pressing the bell; it put the wind up those indoors and at the same time got his own adrenalin going. He thumped on the panels again but still no one came. He retraced his steps to the gate and glanced up and down the street—it was empty, at this hour in the middle of a sunny summer morning—then went back to the door and took from a zipped pocket of his wallet a gadget made of toughened, tensile wire, intricately bent. It looked as harmless as a hairpin. He inserted the business end of it in the keyhole and turned it delicately this way and that, thinking with idle satisfaction how wise he had been to bone up on so many useful skills when he was young, and presently he felt, with almost a sensual satisfaction, the oiled yet resistant shift and slide of the engaged tumblers as they gave way and turned. He pushed the door open hardly more than a hand's width and stepped sideways smartly into the hall and stood listening, holding his breath. He liked breaking and entering; it gave him a real thrill. Then his heart did a bounce and he almost shouted out in fright. Kreutz was standing motionless in the shadows at the end of the hall, looking at him.

He had never really understood Kreutz. Not that he expected to—wogs were different, in all sorts of ways—or cared to, for that matter. There was something in the way the fellow had of moving, though, or of not moving, more like, that he found uncanny. And quiet, too, he was always very quiet. It was not just that he said little and moved lithely, no, his kind of quiet was more a way of not being there—of being there, that is, and, at the same time, not. Inscrutable, that was it—or was that Japs? Anyway, Kreutz was a man it was hard to scrute, if there was such a word. He was barefoot today, and wore a collarless tunic of dark-red silk buttoned to the neck and some sort of baggy Ali Baba trousers or pyjama bottoms that seemed to be made of silk, too. To cover his initial shock Leslie laughed and said: 'Jesus, Doc, the way you're standing there I thought someone'd had you done in and stuffed. And why didn't you answer my knock?'

Kreutz seemed to ponder the question seriously, then asked: 'What do you want?'

Leslie sighed, shaking his head in a show of regretful sorrow. 'I ask you, Doc, is that any way to greet an old pal? Where's your warmth? Where's your hospitality? Why don't you invite me in to share a pot of your special tea? Why don't you do that, eh?'

The Doctor seemed to be pondering again. Leslie wondered if he was thinking of putting up a fight. That would be a laugh, if he tried it. But he would not, of course, being a Buddhist or whatever he was. Leslie was aware of a faint regret. He had that tickle in the palms of his hands that he knew of old, the tickle of wanting to hit something or someone, provided the someone or something, a woman, preferably, could be counted on not to hit back, or not seriously, anyway. And Kreutz was as good as a woman, in that regard. Without a word now he turned on his bare, horny-rimmed heel and walked into the living room. Leslie followed, and stopped in the doorway and leaned against the jamb in a negligent pose with his hands in his pockets and his ankles crossed. He looked down at his shoes, admiring them absently: brown loafers with tassels, old but good. Kate always made fun of the way he dressed, saying he looked like a successful spiv. 'Instead of,' he would say, with one of his laughs, 'an unsuccessful one, which is what you think I really am.' And then the fight would start. She was a good fighter, was Kate. In the early days their rows always ended in bed; not any more. He waggled the toes of his right foot inside the shoe. Good old Kate.

'What do you want?' Kreutz asked again, bringing him out of his reverie.

'I told you—nice cup of tea.' The room was brightly, almost garishly, lit by a great panel of sunlight slanting down through the window from above the roof of the hospital opposite. Leslie could see how worried Kreutz was by the way he was standing, his arms rigid at his sides and his fingers jiggling and the whites of his eyes flashing. Well, good; he should be worried. 'Go and put the kettle on,' Leslie said, 'there's a good lad.'

Kreutz did not stir, just stood there beside the low table with his arms held in that stiff way, like, Leslie thought, a squaddie standing to attention; he would be saluting, in a minute. Not that Leslie knew much about army life, having been clever enough to avoid the war and, afterwards, National Service, too. Kreutz took a deep breath, almost a gulp, and said: 'I expected you would come.'

'Oh? Why was that?'

Kreutz blinked a number of times rapidly. 'I sent you something.'

Leslie put on an act of remembering, smacking a palm softly to his forehead. 'Why, so you did,' he said. 'How could I have forgotten?'

'I make the tea,' Kreutz said shortly, and turned and loped off to the kitchen on his skinny, stork's legs. Even on level ground, Leslie thought, Kreutz always looked as if he was scaling an awkward incline. There were kettle noises and tap noises, clatter of tea caddy and spoon and crockery—the Doc was nervous, all right. Leslie went and stood in the kitchen doorway, again with his hands in the pockets of his slacks and one ankle crossed on the other. Kreutz was spooning dried leaves of something or other into a pot that had a long, curved spout.

'Yes, that photo,' Leslie said. 'Very nice. You made old Deirdre look as pretty as a picture. You have a flair. I said it to Deirdre, I said to her, "The Doc has a real flair for taking snaps."' He brought out cigarettes and a lighter. 'I posted it on, by the way,' he said, blowing smoke upwards.

A sort of ripple passed over the Doctor's smooth brown polished face; it took Leslie a second to recognise it as a frown.

'What?' he asked.

'The photo. I sent it on. Forwarded it. It'll probably come back to you—I put your name on it, and the address here. Thought we might get a round-robin kind of thing going. You to me, me to someone else, someone else to you. You know.'

Kreutz did not look at him. 'Who did you send it to—why?'

'That's no matter.' He picked a fragment of tobacco from his lower lip. 'Tell me why you sent it to me in the first place. Did you think I'd be worried because you had a snap of Deirdre with her twat on show, like the ones you took of all those tarts you pretend to treat?' He chuckled. 'Thought I'd be concerned for my girl's honour, did you?'

Kreutz did not look at him. 'I can't pay you any more,' he said sulkily. 'It's too much for me, I cannot support that place you and she are running. When will it start making money? You are supposed to repay me what I have already given you.'

The kettle boiled, and set up a whistle through its spout, first quavering and then increasingly strong and shrill. 'Here, let me,' Leslie said, and stepped forward and turned off the gas flame. He lifted the kettle and pulled the whistle thing gingerly off the wide neck of the spout. Then, so fast that it was done it before he knew he was going to do it, he seized Kreutz by his left wrist high up and jerked him to the sink and poured a gout of the boiling water straight on to the back of his hand. Kreutz hardly had time to realise what was happening before the water was rolling and seething over his skin. He gave a peculiar, stifled shriek and leaped back, brandishing his scalded hand aloft and waggling it, like a voodoo dancer, or some sort of dervish, Leslie thought. He dropped the kettle into the sink. Some of the water had splashed on his own hand, and he turned on the tap now and held it under the cold stream. 'Now look what you've done,' he said crossly. 'You've gone and made me scald myself.'

Kreutz came crowding forward and tried to thrust his hand above Leslie's under the gushing water, making a high-pitched, nasal, whining noise.

'Oh, stop the racket, will you?' Leslie snapped. 'You'll have the rozzers in on us. Aren't you supposed to be some sort of Buddhist who can put up with pain?'

'You have destroyed my hand!' the Doctor cried. 'My hands are my living!'

'Serves you right. Teach you to keep them to yourself.' Leslie was examining his own hand; it was mottled with angry red patches, but not blistering. By now he really was very cross indeed. He grabbed Kreutz by the shoulder and spun him around to face him and got him by the throat with his good hand and pressed him backwards until his back was arched against the draining-board. He was all skin and bone, like a long, brown bird. 'Listen, you nigger or kraut or whatever it is you're supposed to be—did you think you could blackmail me? Did you?'

Kreutz, in his pain and fright, was making gargling sounds, his eyeballs popping whitely in a swollen face growing ever darker with congested blood. Leslie released him and stepped back, wiping the palm of his hand on the side of his jacket and grimacing in disgust.

'I want the negative of that picture,' he said, 'and any prints you've made. If I see it anywhere, in anybody's hands but mine, I'll come back here and break your fucking neck for you, you black bastard. Understand?' The Doctor had his hand under the tap again. Leslie moved forward quickly and stamped hard with the heel of one of his tasselled shoes on the instep of the fellow's bare left foot. '*Do you understand?*' Kreutz did his stifled scream again, and despite his annoyance Leslie had to laugh, so comical did the old boy look, hopping on one leg and flapping his blistered hand in the air, more than ever like a stringy old bird with a damaged wing.

'Come on,' Leslie said, 'get those pictures.'

There were half a dozen prints, and the negative. He handed the lot to Deirdre when she came to Percy Place that evening, and she burned them in the mean little fireplace, filling the room with a scorched, chemical stink. He did not tell her what he had done with the first print, the one Kreutz had sent him, or that he had kept another one for himself, *for old times' sake*, he thought, and then caught himself up, startled—old times? But when he considered the matter he realised it was true: their time together was up, his and Deirdre's. It had been fun, and she was a good girl in many ways, but it was over. He lolled on the bed with a cigarette and contemplated her where she squatted in front of the grate, poking with the blade of a table knife at the still smouldering remains of the photographs. He admired absently the taut, full curve of her behind, the pert, freckled nose, the plump bosom. She was saying something to him but he was not hearing her; it was as if she was too far away, as if she was out of earshot. Suddenly he hardly knew her—she might have been a stranger, a servant tending the room, or a waif who had wandered in from the street; she might have been anyone. Strange, the way things had of resolving themselves while a body was blissfully unaware of what was going on. He had used her up without knowing it, and now it was done. There would be the usual fuss, tears and pleas, screams, recriminations, but all that would not last long. He was an old hand at ending things.

8

MAISIE HADDON telephoned Quirke and said she wanted
to see him. She suggested they should go to the Gresham
Hotel, for a change. He tried to get her to say what it
was she had to tell him but she would not. 'Just meet me
there,' she said, in her truculent way. 'In the bar.' It was
mid-afternoon when he got to the hotel and when he came
in out of the sunlight he was half blinded at first, but there
was no missing Maisie Haddon. Today she wore a white suit
with padded shoulders and broad lapels, large white high-
heeled shoes, a crimson blouse and a scarf of gauzy, lime-
green silk. She had a hat, too, a boat-shaped concoction
of green felt sailing at a jaunty angle above the waves of
her bright-yellow perm. She was sitting on a stool at the bar
with her legs crossed. Today, in deference to the venue, she
was drinking a brandy and port. 'For the innards,' she said.
'They're very delicate, the innards.' He complimented her
on her hat and she gave an angry laugh. 'It should be nice,'
she said. 'It cost a bloody fortune. How she gets away with
it, that old hake Cuffe-Wilkes, as she calls herself, I don't
know. Maison des Chapeaux how are you. Maison de Clappo,
more like.' Despite the accustomed raucous tone she seemed
subdued; Quirke suspected she was intimidated by the hotel's

grand appurtenances, the chandeliers and high, gleaming mirrors, the polished marble floors, the soft-footed waiters in morning-coats and the waitresses in white bibs and black stockings and little silk mob-caps.

'Mickey Rooney stayed here, you know,' Maisie said, looking about her appraisingly. 'And Grace Kelly.'

Quirke lifted an eyebrow. 'Together?'

She gave him a shove with her elbow.

'No, you clown,' she said, laughing. 'But I saw the Aga Khan and Rita Hayworth here one time, when they were married.'

'Aly,' Quirke said. She glowered at him. 'It was Aly Khan that was married to Rita Hayworth,' he said, 'not Aga.'

She bridled. 'Aly, Aga, what does it matter? If you know so much, Mr Smarty-Pants, tell me this—what other film star was Rita Hayworth a cousin of?'

'I've no idea.'

She grinned triumphantly, showing most of her large, slightly yellowed teeth. 'Ginger Rogers!'

'Maisie, you're a walking encyclopedia.'

At that she scowled. Maisie was touchy, and never more so than when she thought she was being mocked. He ordered another drink for her, and for himself a glass of plain water.

'Are you still off the gargle?' she demanded. 'Would you not have something, to keep a girl company?'

He shook his head. 'If I have one I'll have another, and then another, and another after that, and then where will I be?'

'Christ, Quirke, you're no fun any more, do you know that?'

When, Quirke wondered idly, had he and Maisie had fun together?

'That one you were asking me about,' Maisie said. 'The one that topped herself.'

'Yes?'

He had paused before responding. Maisie liked everyone to keep a leisurely pace. She was gazing into the ruby depths of her second and already half-drunk drink.

'I enquired around,' she said. 'No one knew anything, or not anything that would be likely to interest you, anyway. Then I spoke by chance to a former client of mine that lives out in Clontarf. A former nun, she is, living with a former priest—would you believe it? Came over from England, the two of them, on the run from the bishops, I suppose, or the peelers, I don't know which. She bought a ring, or got one out of a Hallowe'en brack, and they set up house together, as respectable as you like.'

'How did you come to know her?'

She gave him a look. 'How do you think? A ring is one thing, but a bouncing babby is another. Anyway, here's the thing, here's the coincidence. When I asked her about this one Deirdre Hunt, had she known her, or heard of her, she gave a laugh and said, "Deirdre Hunt, is it? Sure, doesn't she live across the road from me."'

'In Clontarf,' Quirke said.

'St Martin's something—Avenue, Gardens, Drive, I can't remember. Isn't that a queer thing, though, me ringing her up asking her about someone who turns out to be her neighbour opposite?'

Quirke waited again, and took a lingering sip of water. 'Did she know her?' he asked. 'I mean, to talk to.'

'They kept themselves to themselves.'

'Which? The nun and her priest, or the Hunts?'

She turned and studied him for a long moment, shaking her head slowly from side to side. 'I sometimes wonder, Quirke, if you're as slow as you seem, or are you only pretending?'

'Oh, I'm very slow, Maisie, very slow.'

'Sure you are,' she said with a scathing chuckle. 'Sure you are.'

Her glass was empty, and now she waggled it meaningly. He said: 'But your nun—what's her name, by the way?'

'Philomena.'

'—she must have had some contact with the Hunts?'

'Only to say good morning and hello to, that kind of thing. "A nice quiet couple," Philomena said they seemed. She couldn't believe it when she heard that the wife had drowned herself. "Must have been an accident," she said, "must have."' Maisie turned again and this time gave Quirke a searching look. 'Was it?'

He returned a blank gaze of his own. 'Was it what?'

Maisie nodded knowingly. 'You wouldn't be interested in it if it was an accident,' she said. 'I know you, Quirke. And by the way'—she tapped a finger on his wrist—'you may have given up the sauce, but some of us around here are dying of the thirst.'

So he ordered her another brandy and port and waited while the barman poured it, both of them watching him as he worked. He was young, with a short-back-and-sides haircut and a pustular neck. He wore a white shirt and a black waistcoat. Quirke noted a frayed cuff, a greasy shine at the pockets of the trousers. This country. Someone recently had offered Quirke a job in Los Angeles. Los Angeles! But would he go? A man could lose himself in Los Angeles as easily as a cufflink.

Maisie took up her drink, and resettled herself contentedly, henlike, on the stool's high perch.

'The night Deirdre Hunt died,' Quirke said, 'did Philomena notice anything out of the ordinary?'

Maisie Haddon fairly tittered. 'You talk like a detective in the pictures. Humphrey Bogart. Alan Ladd. "Notice anything suspicious, lady?"' Laughing, she took up her drink, little finger cocked, and delicately sipped. 'Do you know where Philomena insisted on meeting me?' she asked. 'In the church in Westland Row. What do you think of that? You'd imagine she'd be too ashamed to show her face in God's house. "Why not Bewley's?" I said. "Or the Kylemore?" but no, St Andrew's it had to be. There was a Mass ending, we had to sit in the far back, whispering. Philomena kept blessing herself and looking pious. The rip! She goes in for stylish outfits, you know—the sky-pilot she's living with must have money—nylons, makeup, perfume, the lot. But do you know what it is?' She paused for effect. 'She still smells like a nun. That musty whiff, there's no getting rid of that.'

Quirke was bored, and his damaged knee ached, and, as always in Maisie's company, he was beginning to want a drink badly. Maisie had nothing to tell him. Why had she asked him to come here? Perhaps she had been bored, too. He thought of slipping away, as he usually did, and had even begun to ease himself off the stool in preparation for flight, when Maisie, looking into her glass, a little bleary now, told him, with blithe offhandedness, what it was she had summoned him to hear.

9

THEN ONE DAY without warning her world just fell asunder. That was the way she thought of it, that was the phrase she kept saying over and over in her mind: *The world has fallen asunder.* At the start it seemed a day like any other. True, Billy had hardly spoken a word to her, and ate his breakfast on his own in the kitchen and then departed without even a goodbye, lugging his bag of samples. Either he had used too much aftershave lotion or his face was flushed, as it tended to be when he was angry. But he did not seem angry, only in a mood of some sort. The kitchen when he was gone from it was left smouldering, the lingering smoke of his cigarette rolling in slow, grey-blue billows in the big shaft of sunlight through the window beside the back door. She had poured herself a cup of lukewarm tea from the brown china pot and sat with it at the littered table half listening to the wireless. Billy had left a smear of marmalade on the white tablecloth, it glittered like a shard of glass. In the garden a bird was whistling its heart out. She reminded herself that before she set off for work she must start the laundry, in the brand-new washing-machine that was another little luxury the bountiful Silver Swan had brought to her.

Yes, a day like any other, so it seemed.

When the telephone rang it made her jump. Who would be calling, at this early hour? She hurried into the hall. At first she could not make out who it was on the line. Hardiman, he said his name was. Did she know anyone called Hardiman? Then he said he was with the bank. Her mouth went dry, and she felt her heartbeat suddenly slow to a dull, effortful thumping, as if something was climbing up laboriously inside her. Dealing with the bank had been the part of the business that she secretly hated. Banks terrified her, she had never been in one before she was in her twenties. They were so big, with such high ceilings, and so many counters with so many people behind them, all wearing ties, or twin-sets, while the men in the back, the managers or whatever they were, all wore pin-striped suits. She was frightened even by the smell, dry and papery, like the smell in the head nun's room at school. Hardiman was saying something about 'some matters', and 'these figures', and 'these cheques signed by Mr White'. He asked her to come in and see him. Somehow she managed to get her voice to work, and said she was very busy today, and would Monday do? There was a silence on the line then, a silence that was more alarming even than the man's voice, and then she heard him give a little cough—though she had never even met him she could see him, grey and precise, with dandruff on his collar, sitting at his desk with the phone in one hand and the knuckle of an index finger pressed to his pursed lips—and he said that no, no, it would not keep till Monday, that it would be better if she came in right away. She tried to protest but he cut her off, and with a new sharpness. 'Really, Mrs Hunt, I think it will be in all our interests for you to come in, now, and see if we can sort this out.'

When she put the phone down she had to run upstairs, into the bathroom, and sat on the lavatory with the pee gushing out of her, just gushing and gushing, she could not think how there could be so much of it inside her. When she touched her face it felt as dry as dead leaves, no, not leaves, but ashes, yes, and her throat was so constricted she could hardly swallow, and her eyelids were burning and even her hair pained her, if that was possible. Despite all this, the fright and the panic and the helpless peeing, she was not surprised. This, she suddenly saw, this was what she had been waiting for all along, since that very first day in the pub on Baggot Street when she had sat at the bar listening to Leslie White telling the barman exactly how he wanted their hot whiskeys prepared—'Hot water, mind, not boiling, and no more than three cloves in each glass'—and she was so excited to be in a pub in the middle of the afternoon drinking with this beautiful, silver-haired creature that she had been afraid she might fall off the stool in a swoon straight into his arms. What had made it all so thrilling, in its horrible way, she realised now, was not the success of the salon, or the money, not Leslie's playful talk or the intoxicating feel of his fingers on her skin, no, not even love, but the unacknowledged prospect of this, the telephone call at nine in the morning of an ordinary day, the call to announce that the catastrophe had come. That was strange.

The interview with Hardiman passed for her in a hot blur. She had been wrong about him, he was not the weedy, dry stick she had pictured, but a big, white-haired, red-faced, worried man in a blue suit who leaned forward intently with his elbows on the desk and his huge, meaty hands clasped before him, telling her in a voice resonant with sadness how Leslie White had ruined the business. She did not understand, she could not take it in. It seemed that for every pound she earned Leslie had spent two. He had used the salon as security to raise a mortgage with another bank, but that was spent, too. There were cheques that had not been 'made good', Hardiman said. She stared at him, slack-jawed, and he looked down at his hands and then back at her and sighed and said, 'Bounced, Mrs Hunt. The cheques bounced.' But where had the money gone? she asked, pleading for enlightenment. What had Leslie spent it on? Mr Hardiman lifted his big, blue-clad shoulders and let them fall again, as if the weight of the world was on them. 'That's something the bank is not privy to, Mrs Hunt,' he said, and when she went on gazing at him helplessly he blinked and frowned and said harshly, 'I mean, we don't know what he spent it on. Perhaps that's a question'—he checked himself, and softened his tone—'perhaps it's a question you should ask him, Mrs Hunt.'

She walked out into the summer morning, feeling as if she was the sole survivor of a huge and yet entirely soundless disaster. The sunlight had a sharp, yellowish cast, and hurt her eyes. A coal merchant's cart went past, the black-faced coalman standing up on the board with the reins in one hand and his whip in the other and the big horse's nostrils flaring and its lips turned inside-out and foam flying back from them. A bus blared, a newsboy shouted. The world seemed a new place, which she had never seen before, only cunningly got up to look like the old, familiar one. She stepped into a phone box and fumbled in her bag for coppers. She had none. She went to a newsagent's and bought a newspaper, but the change was in silver and she had to ask for pennies, and the newsagent scowled at her and said something under his breath, but gave her the coins anyway. She telephoned the salon, but there was no reply. She had not expected Leslie to be there, of course, but there was a tiny comfort in dialling the familiar numbers, and hearing the phone ring in the empty room. Then, before she knew what she was doing, she called his home. Home. The word stuck in her heart like a splinter of steel. His home. His wife. His other life; his real life.

Kate White answered. The English accent was a surprise, though it should not have been. It seemed so strange to her now that they had never met, she and Leslie's wife. At first she could not speak. She stared through the grimy panes of the phone box at the street, the passing cars and buses sliding sinuously through the flaws in the glass.

'Hello,' Kate said. 'Who is this?' Bossy; in charge; used to being obeyed, to her word being hopped to.

'Is Leslie there?' she asked, and sounded to herself like a little girl, a schoolgirl afraid of the nuns, afraid of the priest in the confession box, afraid of Margy Rock the school bully, afraid of her father. There was a silence. She knew Kate knew who she was.

'No,' Kate said at last, coldly, 'my husband is not here.' She asked again: 'Who is this?'

She could not bring herself to say her name. 'I'm his partner,' she said. 'I mean, I work with him, at the Silver Swan.'

At that Kate snickered. 'Do you, now?' she said.

Another silence followed.

'I need to talk to him,' she said, 'urgently. It's about the business. I've been to the bank. The manager spoke to me. It's all . . .' What could she say? How could she describe it? The thing was so vast, so terrible, so hopeless and so shaming.

'In trouble again, is he?' Kate said, with a sort of trill in her voice, a mixture of bitterness and angry amusement. 'That doesn't surprise me. Does it surprise you? Yes, I should think it would. You haven't as much experience of him as I have, whatever you might think. Well, I hope he doesn't imagine I'm going to bail him out again.' She paused. 'You're in this together, you know, you and him. As far as I'm concerned, you can sink or swim. *Can* you swim, *Deardree*?' And she hung up.

When she got home she decided, although she was not hungry—she thought she might never be hungry again—that she must eat something, to keep her strength up. She made a ham sandwich, but had got only half of it down when she had to scamper to the bathroom and throw it back up. She sat on the side of the bath, shivering, and a cold sweat sprang out on her forehead. The nausea passed and she went downstairs again and got out the vacuum-cleaner and vacuumed the carpet in the parlour, pushing the brush back and forth violently, like a sailor on punishment duty swabbing a deck. It had never struck her before that it was not possible to get anything completely clean. No matter how long or how hard she worked at this carpet there would be things that would cling stubbornly in the nap, hairs and bits of lint and tiny crumbs of food, and mites, millions and millions of mites—she pictured them, a moving mass of living creatures so small they would be invisible even if she were to kneel and put her face down until her nose was right in among the fibres.

She remembered the bottle of whiskey that someone had given them for Christmas. It had never been opened. She had put it on the top shelf in the airing cupboard, along with the mousetraps and the caustic soda and the old black rubber gas mask left over from when the war was on and everybody expected the Germans to invade. She turned off the vacuum-cleaner and left it there in the middle of the floor, for the mites to crawl over, if they wanted.

The whiskey seemed to her to have a brownish tinge. Did whiskey go off? She did not think so—they were always talking about it being better the older it was. This one had been twelve years old when it was bottled, the same age as the gas mask, the same age as she was when she turned on her Da at last and threatened to tell Father Forestal in St Bartholomew's about the things he had been doing to her since the time she had learned to walk. Never the same in the flat again after that. The strangest thing was how furious her Ma was at her—her Ma, who should have been protecting her all those years! How she wished, then, that she knew where Eddie was, Eddie her brother who had run away from school and gone to sea when he was still only a boy. At night in bed, listening with a sick feeling for her father's step on the landing, she would make up stories about Eddie, about him coming home, grown-up, in a sailor's vest and bell-bottom trousers and a hat like Popeye's on the back of his head, Eddie smiling and showing off his muscles and his tattoos and asking her how she was, and her telling him about Da, and him going up to his father and showing him his fist and threatening to knock his block off if he ever again so much as laid a finger on his little sister. Stories, stories. She drank off a gulp of whiskey straight from the bottle. It burned her throat and made her gag. She drank again, a longer swallow. This time it burned less.

It was late in the afternoon when Kate White came. When she heard the bell she thought it must be Leslie, and she ran to the door, her heart going wildly, from the whiskey she had drunk as much as from excitement and sudden hope. He had come to apologise, to explain, to tell her it was all a misunderstanding, that he would fix it up with the bank, that everything would be all right. When she opened the door Kate looked at her almost with pity. 'My God,' she said, 'I can see what he's done to you.' She led the way into the parlour. Kate looked at the vacuum-cleaner, and Deirdre picked it up and put it behind the sofa. She could not speak. What was there to say?

Kate paced the floor, with her arms folded across her chest, smoking a cigarette in fast, angry little puffs. She had found the photographs, and the letters. Leslie had left them in the bag under his bed—their bed. She gave a furious laugh. 'Under the fucking bed, for God's sake!' She supposed he had wanted her to find them, she said. He had wanted an excuse to leave, and this way it would be she who would have to throw him out. She laughed again. 'He always liked to leave decisions to someone else.' She did not know where he had gone. She said she supposed the two of them had a love nest, he would probably move in there. She stopped pacing suddenly. '*Have* you somewhere?' She told her yes, they had a room, but she would not say where it was. Kate snorted. 'Do you think I care where you did your screwing? By the way'—she looked up at the ceiling—'did you ever do it here? I'm interested to know.'

Deirdre lowered her eyes and gave the barest of nods. Yes, she said, Leslie had stayed one night when her husband was away, in Switzerland. Kate stared, and she had to explain that Billy sometimes had to go to Geneva, for conferences at the head office of the firm he worked for.

'Conferences?' Kate said, with another snort. 'Your husband went to conferences?' The idea seemed to amuse her. 'The poor fool.'

But Kate, she could see, was not as angry now as she had been when she had arrived. She supposed Kate felt sorry for her, or maybe it was just some feeling of solidarity between the two of them. After all, Leslie had done wrong to them both, to her as much as to Kate. Now Kate, as if thinking the same thought, stopped pacing again and looked at her closely, for the first time. 'Are you drunk?' she asked. She said no, she was not drunk, but she had been drinking whiskey, and she was not used to it. 'I'll give you a piece of advice,' Kate said. 'Don't take to drink.' Abruptly she sat down on the sofa with her knees together and her fists pressed on her knees. 'Christ almighty,' she said, 'look at us, taken in by that ... that *rat*.' And amazing as it was, Deirdre at that felt a protest rising in her throat, a cry of denial and defence. In that moment, for the first time in this long day, she was pierced by the inescapable realisation of all that she was losing. Not money, not the business, not her new car and her frocks and next year's mink coat—none of that mattered—but Leslie, Leslie who she loved, as she had never loved anyone before and never would love again. She felt something shrivel in her, shrivel and crumble, as the photographs had crumbled into ash when she had burned them in the grate that day in Percy Place.

Kate stood up. 'I'm sorry,' she said. 'I don't know why I should be, but I am. I came here to scream at you for stealing my husband. I had fantasies of hitting you, of scratching out your eyes, all those things you imagine you'll do at a time like this. But all I feel is sadness.' She stepped forward, and lifted a hand as if indeed to strike, but instead merely touched her lightly, fleetingly, on the cheek with her fingertips. 'You poor, stupid bitch,' she said. And then she left.

The day wore on, grindingly. The air in the house was suffocating yet she did not dare go outside, even into the back garden, she did not know why, except that the outdoors now seemed a hostile place, smoky and sulphurous. She went into the kitchen, still hugging the whiskey bottle, and got a glass and sat at the table and filled the glass to the brim, so full that she had to lean down to take the first sip from the rim. Her eyes felt like live coals and her tongue and the insides of her lips were raw and pulpy. She drank on. Then she slept for a while, still sitting at the table, with her head on her arms. When she woke it was twilight. Where had the day gone? It seemed such a short time ago that she had been at the bank, with Mr Hardiman. The house was unnaturally silent. She sat motionless for a long time, listening, but heard no sound except a steady, dull hum that she knew was only in her head. Her skin itched under her clothes. She felt unclean—not dirty, but just that, unclean. She took the bottle and went upstairs, pressing it to her chest and supporting herself with an elbow along the banister rail. At the top of the stairs she saw herself like that in the full-length mirror on the wall outside the bathroom, with her elbow out and her fist with the bottle in it turned in against her breast, as if she had the palsy or was crippled or something.

In the bathroom she set the bottle carefully on the shelf at the head of the bath and got down the toothglass. When she leaned forward to put in the bath plug she almost toppled over headlong. She took off her clothes, shedding them about her like so many swatches of sloughed skin. The sharp non-smell of steam stung her nostrils. She climbed into the water—it was so hot it was hardly bearable—and lay down with a sigh. She looked at her pale body under the water, its shifting lines, its wavering planes. Then she kneeled up and poured the last of the whiskey into the glass—had she really drunk the whole bottle?—and lay down again up to her neck in the water, holding the glass between her sluggishly buoyant breasts. Her mind wandered in vague distress over scenes of her past life, the Christmas when her Da brought her the present of the bicycle, the day she knocked out Tommy Goggin's tooth, the glorious morning when she marched into the pharmacy and told that dirty old brute Plunkett that she was resigning and off to start up a business of her own.

She dozed for a while, until the bathwater went cold and she woke up shaking. She wrapped herself in a towel and went into the bedroom, staggering in the doorway and hurting her shoulder against the door jamb. It was dark by now but she did not bother to put on the light. The shaking had lessened but her teeth were chattering. She drew back the bed covers and, still wrapped in the damp towel, lay down and pulled the sheet to her chin. There was a full moon shining in the window, watching her like a fat and gloating eye. She cried for a while, the shivering making hiccups of her sobs. What was she crying for—what good would crying do? Everything had fallen asunder.

She watched the moon, and suddenly saw herself, so clear, in radiant light, standing those summer evenings at the window in the flat when she was a girl, smelling the lovely smell from the biscuit factory and listening to the bird singing on the black wire. She had stopped crying. Maybe something was still possible, maybe something could be salvaged from the wreck that Leslie had made of things. 'Yes,' she said aloud, 'maybe we can save something, after all.' Then she remembered Kate White touching her face with her fingers, so gently. She had liked her, despite everything. They might have been friends, if things had been different. They might even have gone into business together, might have started up another salon, without Leslie. Thinking these consoling thoughts she sighed, and smiled into the moonlit darkness, and closed her eyes. And closed her eyes.

III

1

LESLIE WHITE COULD not think why he had abandoned a perfectly good billet at the girl's flat after less than a week and holed up instead by himself in the room in Percy Place. What had he been thinking of? First of all there were so many things in the Percy Place room to remind him of Deirdre—starting with the bed—poor bloody dead Deirdre, and he could certainly have done without that. He missed her, he definitely missed her. She had been a good girl, and a hot little number, God knows. In the end of course she had to go, and go she did. He could not pretend to be heartbroken. After all, if you wanted to talk about billets, she was the cause of his being kicked out of the best one he had ever had, when Kate found the photos and, worse, the dirty letters. Funny, though, how after those bastards had beaten him up he had gone instinctively to the girl's place, never doubting she would give him shelter and look after him. And as it happened he could not have done better, for although she looked and acted like the ice maiden, she had melted pretty quick. In fact, she had turned out to be a hot little number herself, though obviously not much experienced, a condition that by the end of the four days they spent together he had gone a good way to curing, despite his bruises and his aching ribs. So why had he left?

But he knew he could not have stayed with her for long. She was that type, sex-starved and nervy and too bright for her own or anybody else's good, who given encouragement would cling, and before he knew it would be moaning about love and all the rest of it. He had been with a few such in his time—they were the devil to get rid of if you hung about for more than a few days. So he had made a run for it, and now here he was in Percy Place—what a name, it still made him laugh—hiding behind the dusty net curtains and nursing himself back to health and vigour as best he could. It was not easy.

The first thing he had to do was to get his hands on a supply of medicine, and he lost no time in setting off on his rounds, keeping an eye out in case those fellows with their bats—some sort of wooden axes, they had seemed—might be lying in wait to give him another going over. It did not take him long to locate what he was after. Maisie Haddon was always good for a fix, and sure enough when he went that night to her snip-shop in Hatch Street she did not let him down. However, when she saw what a bad way he was in and how needy for the stuff he was she tried to charge him for it, and he had to threaten to give her a tap if she did not hand it over sharpish. Not that Maisie had not taken a good many hard taps in her time, but she knew the things Leslie had on her, and what he would do with them if she held out, and that was more persuasive even than the prospect of a black eye and a few broken teeth.

Mrs T. was more accommodating. Her husband was a doctor who had kicked her out and now refused to see or speak to her, but kept her well supplied so she would not come and stand screaming for the stuff outside his fancy consulting rooms in Fitzwilliam Square. Leslie arranged to meet her at the bookshop as usual. Though she was obviously shocked by the state of his face, the bruising and the black eyes, he was afraid for the first minute or so that she would throw herself on him right there and then, in the middle of the shop, she had missed him that much, so she said. She wanted him to take her somewhere immediately, and he had to think fast and say that there was nowhere they could go, since the salon was closed and he had made it up with Kate and was living with her again, which was a lie, of course—Kate, he was fairly certain, would never have him back. He could see Mrs T. did not believe him—he had made the mistake of taking her to Percy Place a couple of times when Deirdre's back was turned, so she knew about the room, which he also had to swear now that he had given up—but he had more important things to worry about than Mrs T.'s disappointment at not being able to get him between the sheets. He escaped from her finally, after she had handed over the stuff, by promising to meet her that night in the Shelbourne—'I'll take a room,' she purred, gazing up at him slit-eyed like a cat and clawing softly at the lapels of his linen jacket, 'we can give a false name'—a promise he had no intention of keeping.

As he drove off along Baggot Street she stood on the bridge in the sunlight looking after him, in her white-rimmed sunglasses and her flowered frock that was too young for her, and when he glanced back over his shoulder she lifted a white-gloved hand and waved weakly, sadly, and he knew he would not see her again—unless, of course,

Maisie Haddon and his other contacts should suddenly dry up. Mrs T. was another one he would miss, he really would. She was forty-five if she was a day, and as thin as a whippet, but there was something about her, something about those bony wrists and spindly ankles of hers, so frail, so breakable, that had got a little way under even his tough hide. He remembered how easy it had been to make her cry. Yes, he would miss her. But, Christ, all these bloody women, hanging out of him and telling him they loved him, and then turning awkward—what was a fellow to do?

It was funny, but when he walked out of the front door in Percy Place into the hot, muggy grey morning, he was stopped in his tracks by a feeling that at first he could not identify, a sort of heaviness in the chest, as if a weight had dropped on his heart. He climbed gingerly into the Riley, careful of his strapped-up ribs. He did not start the engine at once, but sat behind the wheel trying to discover what was the matter with him. He had been thinking of Kreutz, and Deirdre, and the dirty photo Kreutz had taken of her, the photo that he had posted on, for a lark. Now he closed his eyes for a moment. Christ. What had he done? And then he realised that what he was feeling was guilt. Yes, guilt. That was what had stopped him in mid-stride, that was the weight pressing on his heart. He opened his eyes again and looked about the empty street in a kind of amazement. Leslie White, feeling guilty—now there was a thing. Then he started the engine and gave the accelerator a few hard punches. What was done was done. Things had turned serious, but was that his fault? The trouble was, he thought, as he drove out into Haddington Road, people did not understand him, women especially. They wanted things from him that it simply was not in him to give. Yes, that was the trouble, people expecting things that he did not have.

He ran a yellow light at Baggot Street and shot on to Mespil Road in a whoosh of exhaust smoke. The trees by the canal gleamed grey-green in the overcast air. The water had the look of polished tin. He pushed a hand through his hair, feeling with pleasure its silky texture. The breeze was pleasantly cool against his bruised face. What had it been but a jape, after all, posting the picture on? He had not meant to make so much mischief. That was another thing people did not understand about him: his essential innocence, his blamelessness. Nothing he did was ever meant, not really.

He was beginning to feel jumpy, and thought of stopping the car and nipping into a pub and locking himself in a cubicle in the gents' and giving himself a shot of joy-juice, but decided instead to wait. He had things to do, and he needed to stay sharp until they were done. There was old Kreutzer, for a start. He was certain it was Kreutz who had sent those johnnies to beat him up, so that would have to be sorted out, and retribution administered. Old Kreutz had not been nice to the girl when he had sent her to him that night of the beating to fetch his medicine. She was his angel of mercy and Kreutz had spurned her, had turned her from his door. Mind you, that was better than giving her a cup of his special brew and taking an artistic study of her, too, as he had done with poor Deirdre. How had the bloody wog found the nerve, first to try blackmailing him and then hiring a squad of thugs to give him a going-over? Yes, the Doctor was in need of a serious seeing-to.

Adelaide Road was deserted as usual this afternoon. Strange, how little movement there was about here always, only the occasional car, and hardly ever a pedestrian. Why was that? he wondered. Surely there should be hospital traffic, and there were plenty of houses and flats, so where were the occupants? He would not mind having a place here, a bolthole, amidst all this peace and leafy quiet. The question of where to live was much on his mind these days, since the bust-up with Kate and then Deirdre's going. The room in Percy Place had been all right for the purpose he had borrowed it for, but it would not do for a roost in the long-term. There was the problem of funds, of course, which were in decidedly short supply since the salon had sung its swan-song and gone under. Kreutz would have to be made to resume payments, or certain respectable husbands would shortly be receiving in the post some very interesting snaps of their lady wives. The difficulty there, of course, was that Kate, damn her, had burned the bloody photos. Nothing for it but to obtain a replacement set from Kreutz, which he imagined would entail a certain amount of arm-twisting.

He was smiling to himself as he drew up to the kerb and parked. What a wheeze it would be to make Kreutz hand over the very material that Leslie would then use to squeeze money out of him. *Blackmail* was a word, by the way, at least when he was the one who was doing it, that he certainly did not think was ugly, despite what everyone was always saying in detective stories; on the contrary, it smacked to him of dark deeds of elegant risk and feats of derring-do. He pushed open the iron gate—*eek, eek*—and walked up the short path to the door, a hand in the pocket of his jacket rolling the ampoules Mrs T. had given him through his fingers like glass dice, liking the clunky, cool, happiness-promising feel of them.

Once again Kreutz was not answering the door, and he got out his clever bit of wire and, having checked the street, went to work on the lock. In the dim hallway there was a faint but definite and distinctly unpleasant smell. He walked forward softly. He wondered where Kreutz would be hiding. Well, it did not matter, he would find him.

When the telephone rang Quirke somehow knew, in the second before he picked up the receiver, who it was that was calling. He was at his desk in his underground office beside the body room, where Sinclair was at work, preparing a corpse for cutting. It was close to six o'clock on a busy working day and the phone seemed to have been going all afternoon, shrill and demanding as a baby wanting its bottle, so what was it about this particular call, he wondered, that he should be able to tell who was on the line? Yet when the policeman announced himself—'Inspector Hackett here'—he felt the usual twinge of foreboding. Hackett took his time in coming to the point. He talked about the weather— the topic was for Hackett what mother-in-law jokes were for comedians, always dependable—saying the heat was getting him down, though the wireless was forecasting rain, which would be a welcome relief, a thing he knew he should not be saying, there were so many people out enjoying the sun, he had seen them in the Green when he was walking up here, lying on the grass, getting burned, the half of them, he had no doubt, which they would know all about come nightfall . . . Where was it, Quirke was wondering, that the Inspector had 'walked up' to? When he said where he was, at an address in Adelaide Road, Quirke had another moment of telepathic recognition, and knew the name that was coming.

'Seems to have met with a bit of an accident,' the inspector said. 'More than a bit, in fact, and more than an accident, too, if I'm not mistaken. Do you think you could spare a minute to come up here and have a look?'

'Officially?'

A soft chuckle came down the line. 'Ah, now, Mr Quirke . . .'

Over every scene of violent death that Quirke had attended in the course of his career there hung a particular kind of silence, the kind that falls after the last echoes of a great outcry have faded. There was shock in it, of course, and awe and outrage, the sense of many hands lifted quickly to many mouths, but something else as well, a kind of gleefulness, a kind of startled, happy, unable-to-believe-its-luckness. Things, Quirke reflected, even inanimate things, it seemed, love a killing.

'A right mess, all right,' Inspector Hackett said, nudging gingerly with the toe of his shoe a copper bowl overturned on the blood-spattered floor.

The dark-skinned man lay in a curious posture in front of the sofa, face down with his arms upflung above his head and his bare feet pointing downwards. It was as if he had rolled, or had been rolled, across the room until he had come to a stop here. Death is a rough customer. One of the man's hands was wound thickly in a not very clean bandage.

'What happened?' Quirke asked.

The inspector shrugged. 'Took a hiding,' he said. 'Fists, kicks. The bandaged hand seems to be a burn, or a scald.' He was wearing his blue suit, the jacket tightly buttoned in the middle, but his shirt collar was undone and the noose of his tie loosened, for it was hot and airless in the room. He was holding his hat in one hand, and there was a faint pink weal across his forehead where the hat band had bitten into the sweat-softened skin. 'There must have been some racket. Surprising no one in the houses round about heard anything—or if they did, no one reported it.' He walked forward and stood over the body, pulling at his lower lip with a thumb and forefinger. He glanced at Quirke. 'Do you mind my asking how you knew of him?'

'How did you know I knew?'

The detective grinned and bit at the inside of his jaw. 'Ah, there's no catching you out, Mr Quirke.' He twirled his hat in his hand. 'Billy Hunt mentioned him.'

'Then I suppose he must have mentioned him to me, too.'

Hackett nodded. 'Right,' he said. 'Right. His wife knew him, it seems—Billy's wife. There's a coincidence, what? First she dies, and now this poor fellow is killed. And'—he wagged a finger to and fro, as if counting sides—'here's you, and me, and the grieving widower, and God knows who else, and all of us somehow connected. Isn't that strange?'

Quirke did not respond. Instead he asked again: 'What happened?'

'Must have been someone he knew. No locks were forced, no windows broken, as far as I can see.'

Something struck Quirke. 'You haven't called in Forensics?'

The inspector gave him a sly smile. 'I thought I'd have a word with you first,' he said, 'seeing as you were the one who came to me about Deirdre Hunt, and now Deirdre Hunt's pal here is after being knocked into the next world.'

'I don't know anything about this,' Quirke said flatly. 'I never saw this fellow before—what's his name again?'

'Kreutz. Hakeem Kreutz. It's written on the board out on the railings.'

'Do you know anything about him?'

'Aye, I did a bit of investigating. He claimed to be Austrian, or that his father was Austrian, anyway, and that his mother was some class of an Indian princess. In fact, he was from Wolverhampton. Family kept a corner grocery shop.'

'How did he come to be Kreutz?'

'It's just what he called himself. I suppose he liked the sound of it, "Dr Kreutz". Real name Patel.'

Quirke hunkered down beside the body and touched the cheek; it was cold and stiff. He got to his feet, brushing his hands together, and said: 'I don't see what the connection could be between this and Deirdre Hunt's suicide.'

Hackett took it up sharply. 'Her suicide?' He waited, but Quirke said nothing. 'Are you sure, Mr Quirke, there isn't something you're not telling me? You're a fierce secretive man, I know that of old.'

Quirke would not look at him. 'As I've already said, I don't know anything about this.' He was studying a dried puddle of blood, gleaming darkly like Chinese lacquer against the red-painted floorboards. 'If I did, I'd tell you.'

There was a lengthy silence. Both men stood motionless, each turned somewhat away from the other.

'All right,' the inspector, sighing, said at last, with the air of a chess player conceding a game, 'I'll believe you.'

Leslie White had the jitters so badly that even a hefty toot of Mrs T.'s poppy-juice, administered in the basement lavatory of the Shelbourne, had not steadied him. He nosed the little car in and out of the evening traffic, clutching the wheel and blinking rapidly and shaking his head as if trying to dislodge an obstruction from his ear. He had been driving round and round the Green for what seemed hours. He did not know what to do, and could not think straight. The dope had strung scarves of greenish gauze in front of his eyes, like a forest of hanging moss, behind which he could still see blood, and the copper bowl on the floor, and Kreutz dead. He desperately wanted to be inside, away from the streets and the cars and the hurrying crowds. Was the daylight as dim as it seemed? Was it later than he thought? He longed for nightfall and the concealing dark. It was not so much that he was afraid, but this inability to decide what to do next was awful. He veered into the path of a bus and it trumpeted at him like an elephant, so that he wrenched the wheel and almost ran into a big Humber Hawk that had been waddling along beside him. He knew he should stop and park the car, go into a pub, have a drink, try to calm down, try to think. And then, suddenly, he knew what he should do, where he should go. Of course! Why had he not thought of it before? He sped along to the corner of

Grafton Street and turned with a squeal of tyres and headed west.

Phoebe had got into the habit of stopping in the front doorway and looking carefully in all directions before venturing into the street. The feeling of being watched, of someone spying on her and following her, was stronger than ever. She would have believed it was all in her imagination—an imagination, after all, that had been for so long a house of horrors—had it not been for the telephone calls. The phone would ring, at any hour of the day or night, but when she picked it up there would be nothing but a crackling silence on the line. She tried to catch the sound of breathing—she had heard of other women's experiences of heavy-breathers—but in vain. Sometimes there was a muffled sensation, when she thought that he—and she was certain it was a he—must have his hand over the mouthpiece. Once, and only once, she had caught something, a very distant faint tiny clinking sound, as of the lid of a small metal box being opened and shut again. It was maddeningly familiar, that clink, but she could not identify it, try as she would. She had become used to these calls, and although she knew it was perverse of her, she sometimes welcomed them, despite herself. They were by now a constant in her life, fixed pinpricks in the bland fabric of her days. Sitting there on the bench seat at the wide-open window with the phone in her lap and the receiver pressed to her ear, she would forget to feel menaced, and would sink down almost languorously into this brief interval of restful, shared silence. She had given up shouting at whoever it was; she no longer even asked who was calling, or demanded that he identify himself, as she used to do in the early days. She wondered what he thought, what he felt, this phantom, listening in his turn now to *her* silences. Perhaps that was all he too wanted, a moment of quiet, of emptiness, of respite from the ceaseless din inside his head. For she was sure he must be mad.

In the street this evening there was the old man walking his dog whom she had seen many times before—man and dog were remarkably alike, short and squat in identical grey coats—and a couple going along arm and arm in the direction of the Green, the girl smiling at the man, showing her upper teeth all the way to the gums. A boy bent low on a racing bike went past, his tyres sizzling on the tarred roadway that was still soft from the day's heat. A bus stopped, but no one got off. She stepped out into the gloaming. A waft of fragrance came up from the flowerbeds in the park. Why did flowers put out so much scent at evening? she wondered. Was that the time when the insects came out? So many things she did not know, so many things.

She got on to a bus at Cuffe Street, and just missed seeing the low-slung apple-green roadster cross the junction and speed on up in the direction from which she had just come.

2

FOR A LONG time Maggie the maid had been hiding the fact that she was going blind. She was convinced that Mr Griffin would get rid of her if he knew—what good would a blind maid be to him? That was one reason why she pretended not to hear the doorbell, for she was afraid that if she opened the door she would not be able to make out who it was that was there, and if it was someone she was supposed to know by sight she would be shown up. So that evening she hid in the basement pantry and let Mr Griffin answer the door himself, and did not come out until she had counted in his three guests. These were Mr Quirke and Phoebe, and that one from America, the old hake trying to be young, Rose whatever-she-was-called. It would be a dismal sort of occasion. Not like the parties there used to be when Missus was still here. Not that Missus was much of a live-wire, but at least she got in decent food and drink and dressed herself up nicely when there were people coming.

She was looking forward to seeing Mr Quirke. She was fond of him, and always had been, even when he had drink taken. He was off the booze now, so he said. It was a pity, for when he was half-cut he used to tease her and make her laugh. No laughing in this house, these days.

She nearly fell over the dog when she was carrying up the tray of sandwiches. She got a kick in at the beast, and it scuttled off, whimpering. She had a plan to get hold of a tin of rat poison from the chemist's on Rathgar Road one of these days and put that animal out of its misery. Nobody wanted it here, not even Mr Griffin, who was supposed to be its master. Young Phoebe it was that had got it for him, to keep him company when he came home from America after Missus had died. Company! The thing was more of an annoyance than anything else. This family had a fondness for taking in strays. First, years ago, there was that one Dolly Moran that later on got killed, and then the other one, Christine somebody, the brazen hussy, that had died too. And Mr Quirke himself had been an orphan that old Judge Griffin had rescued from the poorhouse somewhere and brought to live here as if he was one of his own. Maggie, shuffling along the dim hallway with the tray in front of her, chuckled. Aye, she thought—as if he was one of his own.

In the drawing room Quirke took the tray from Maggie and thanked her and asked her how she was. The french windows were open on to the garden, where a brooding lilac light lay on the grass under the drooping trees. Rose Crawford, wine glass in hand, stood in the window with her back turned to the room, looking out. Mal, in a funereal dark-grey suit and dark-blue bow-tie, stood with her; they were not speaking; they had never had much to say to each other. Phoebe was sitting in an armchair by the empty fireplace, idly turning over the pages of a leather-bound photograph album. Quirke set the tray down on the big mahogany table, where there were bottles and glasses, and bowls of nuts, and plates of sliced cucumber and celery sticks and quartered carrots. It was the second anniversary of Sarah's death.

He carried his glass of soda water across the room and sat down on the arm of Phoebe's chair and watched as she turned the pages of the album. 'So sad,' she murmured, not raising her eyes. 'How quickly it all goes.' He said nothing. She had stopped at a page of photographs of Sarah on her wedding day, stiff, formal pictures taken by a professional. In one she stood in her long white dress and bridal veil beside a miniature Doric pillar, holding a clustered posy of roses in her hands and peering into the camera lens with a faintly pained smile. Despite the obvious fakery of the setting the photographer had achieved a real suggestion of antiquity. Phoebe was right, Quirke thought, it had all gone so quickly. He remembered the day that photograph was taken—which was a wonder, considering how deeply he had drowned his sorrow that day at having thrown away his chance with her.

Rose Crawford turned from the window and walked to the table and refilled her glass. She wore a tight-fitting frock of night-blue silk that shimmered in angled shapes like metal when she moved. Her shining black hair—she must be dyeing it by now, Quirke thought—was cut short and swept back from her face in two smooth wings, which emphasised the classic sharpness of her profile and gave her a fierce, hawklike look. He left his place on the chair-arm and went to her. She had bitten the corner from a crustless triangular sandwich, and as he approached she stopped chewing and put down her wine glass and with her fingers extracted from her mouth a long, grey hair.

'Oh, my,' she wailed faintly, 'it's the maid's, I recognise it.'

'Maggie?' Quirke said. 'She's half blind.'

Rose sighed, and put down the bitten sandwich and took up her glass. 'I don't understand you,' she said. 'The things you accept, as if there was nothing to be done about anything.'

'Do you mean just me, or all of us in general?'

'You people, in this country. I've been amazed since I've been here.'

'What in particular amazes you?'

She shook her head slowly from side to side. 'The quietness of everything,' she said. 'The way you go about in a cowed silence, not protesting, not complaining, not demanding that things should change or be fixed or made new.' She looked at him. 'Josh wasn't like that.'

'Your husband,' he said, 'was a remarkable man.'

She laughed, it was no more than a sniff. 'You didn't admire him.'

'I didn't say he was admirable.'

At that, for no obvious reason, they both turned and looked across at Mal, as if it were he and not Josh Crawford they had been speaking of. He stood somewhat stooped, seeming in faint pain, with a vague, helpless look, the light from the garden giving him a greyish pallor. Rose turned her attention to Phoebe where she sat in the armchair by the fireplace, with the photograph album. 'How is she?' she asked quietly.

Quirke frowned. 'Phoebe? She's all right, I think. Why do you ask?'

'She's not all right.'

'What do you mean?'

'She has a secret. And it's not a nice secret.'

'What secret? How do you know? Has she spoken to you?'

'Not really.'

'Then—'

'I just know.'

Quirke wanted Rose to tell him how she could 'just know' things, about Phoebe or anybody else. He never knew anything until he had dismantled it and examined the parts.

'You're her father,' Rose said. 'You should speak to her. She needs someone's help. I can't do it. Maybe no one can. But you should try.'

He looked down. What could he say to Phoebe? Phoebe would not listen to him. 'Sarah could have done it,' he said.

'Oh, Sarah!' Rose snapped. 'Why you all go on so about Sarah I don't know. She was a nice woman, harmless, did her best to be pleasant. What else was there to her? And don't look at me like that, Quirke, as if I'd kicked your cat. You know me, I say what I mean. I so hate your Irish mealy-mouthedness, the way you treat your women. You either makes saints of them and put them on a pedestal or they're witches out to torment and destroy you. And you of all people shouldn't do it. I'm sure your wife—what was her name, Delia?—wasn't the Jezebel you pretend she was, either.'

'Why me,' he asked, '"of all people"?'

She considered him in silence for a moment. 'I told you

before, a long time ago,' she said. 'You and I are the same—cold hearts, hot souls. There aren't many like us.'

'Maybe that's just as well,' Quirke said. Rose only put back her head and smiled at him with narrowed eyes.

Mal joined them. He tapped a fingertip to the bridge of his spectacles. 'Did you get something to eat?' he asked of them both. He looked doubtfully at the tray of wilting sandwiches. 'I'm not sure what Maggie has prepared. She gets more eccentric every day.' He gave a faint, hapless smile. 'But then, what can I expect?'

Rose shot Quirke a look, as if to say, *You see what I mean?* 'You should sell this house,' she said briskly.

Mal looked at her in slow astonishment. 'Where would I live?'

'Build something else. Buy an apartment. You don't owe anyone your life, you know.'

It seemed he might protest, but instead only turned aside, in an almost furtive way, the lenses of his glasses shining, which somehow made him seem to be weeping.

The evening crawled on. Maggie came back and cleared the table, muttering to herself. She appeared not to notice that no one had eaten the sandwiches. They drifted into the garden two by two, Mal with Rose, Quirke with Phoebe, like couples progressing towards a dance.

'Rose says you have a secret,' Quirke said quietly to his daughter.

Phoebe was looking at her shoes. 'Does she? What kind of secret?'

'She doesn't know, only she knows you have one. So she says. When I hear women talking about a secret, I always assume the secret is a man.'

'Well,' Phoebe said, with a cold little smile, 'you would, of course.'

The soft grey air of twilight was dense and grainy. It would rain later, Quirke thought. Rose had stepped away from Mal and now turned about to face the others, and looked askance at the ground, turning the stem of the wine glass slowly on the flattened palm of her hand. 'I suppose,' she said, raising her voice, 'this is as good a moment as any to make my announcement.' She glanced up, smiling oddly. They waited. She touched a hand to her forehead. 'I feel shy, suddenly,' she said. 'Isn't that the darnedest thing? Quirke, don't look so alarmed. It's simply that I've decided to move here.'

There was a startled pause, then Quirke said, 'To Dublin?'

Rose nodded. 'Yes. To Dublin.' She laughed briefly. 'Maybe it's the biggest mistake I've ever made, and the good Lord knows I've made many. But there it is, I've decided. I have'—she looked at Quirke—'no illusions as to what to expect of life in Ireland. But I suppose I feel some kind of—I don't know, some kind of responsibility to Josh. Perhaps it's my duty to bring his millions back to the land of his birth.' This time she turned to Mal, almost pleadingly. 'Does that seem crazy?'

'No,' Mal said, 'no, it doesn't.'

Rose laughed again. 'I can tell you, no one is more surprised than I am.' She seemed to falter, and cast her eyes down again. 'I guess the dead keep a hold on us even after they've passed on.'

And at that, as if at her summoning, Sarah's voice spoke in Quirke's head, saying his name. He turned without a word and walked into the house. In the past long months of sobriety he had never wanted a drink so badly as he did at that moment.

He walked with Phoebe along the towpath by the canal. Night had fallen and the smell of coming rain was unmistakable now, he even fancied he could feel a breath of dampness against his face. Beside them the water shone blackly, like oil. They passed by courting couples huddled in pools of darkness under the trees. A bearded tramp was asleep on a bench, lying on his side in a nest of newspapers with a hand under his cheek. Neither Quirke nor Phoebe had spoken since they had left the house in Rathgar. The shock at Rose's announcement had lingered, and the party, such as it was, had come to an abrupt end. Rose had taken a taxi back to the Shelbourne, and had offered Quirke and Phoebe a lift, but they had preferred to walk. Quirke was still feeling the effect of Sarah's sudden presence, after Rose's words had somehow conjured her for him in that moment in the twilit garden, under the willow tree that she had planted. He said now: 'A man was killed today. Murdered.'

For the space of half a dozen paces Phoebe gave no response, then only asked, 'Who?'

'A man called Kreutz. Dr Kreutz, he called himself.'

'What happened to him?'

In the light of a street-lamp a bat flickered crazily in a ragged circle about the crown of a tree and was gone.

'He had a place not far from here, in Adelaide Road. He was a healer of some sort—a quack, I'm sure. And someone beat him to death.' He glanced sidelong at her but she had her head bent and he could not make out her expression in the darkness. 'He knew Deirdre Hunt—Laura Swan—and her business partner, Leslie White.' He paused. The sound of their footsteps startled a moorhen and it scrambled away from them, making the dry reeds rattle. 'And you've been seeing him, haven't you, Leslie White?'

She showed no surprise. 'Why do you say that?'

'I saw you together one day, in Duke Street, near where Laura Swan had her beauty salon. It was by chance, I just happened to be there. I guessed you'd been with him, in a pub.'

She made an impatient gesture, flicking a hand sideways in a chopping motion. 'Yes, I know, I remember.'

They came to the bridge at Ranelagh and crossed over. Below, the reflection of a street-light in the water crossed with them.

'Is he your secret,' Quirke asked, 'Leslie White?'

It was again a long time before she answered. 'I don't think,' she said at last, 'that's any of your business.' He made to speak but she prevented him. 'You have no rights over me, Quirke,' she said evenly, in a low, hard, calm voice, looking straight before her along the deserted roadway. 'Whatever right you might have had, whatever authority, you forfeited years ago.'

'You're my daughter,' he said.

'Am I? You hid that fact from me for so long, and now you expect me to accept it?' She still spoke in that level, almost detached tone, without rancour, it might be, despite the force of the words. 'You're not my father, Quirke. I have no father.'

They turned the corner and walked down Harcourt Street. The darkness seemed more dense here in this canyon between the high terraces of houses on either side.

'I worry about you,' Quirke said.

Phoebe stopped, and turned to him. 'There's no need for that,' she said, suddenly fierce. 'I forbid you. It's not fair.'

A low-slung sports car, painted green but seeming black in the dim light, was parked on the opposite side of the road. Neither of them noticed it.

'I'm sorry,' Quirke said. 'But I think Leslie White is a dangerous man. I think he killed Deirdre Hunt. I think he killed this fellow Kreutz, too.'

Phoebe's eyes glittered in the shadows. She was smiling, almost savagely, and he could see the tips of her teeth. 'Good,' she said. 'Maybe he'll kill me, too.'

She turned then and walked swiftly away. He stood on the pavement, watching as she went. She stopped at the house and found her key and climbed the steps and let herself in at the front door and shut it behind her without a backward glance.

He lingered a while, and then went on, in the direction of the Green. At the junction he paused at the traffic-lights, and heard behind him the flurried cry and the brief, winglike rushing in the air and then the clang and crunch and he turned and in the street-lights' sulphurous glow saw the man in the white suit impaled through the chest on the spears of the black railings, his arms and legs still weakly moving and his long, silver hair hanging down.

*

She had felt there was something wrong from the moment she shut the front door behind her, and as she climbed the stairs the feeling grew stronger with every step. She supposed she should have been frightened but instead she was strangely calm, and curious, as well, curious to know what it was that awaited her.

On the second landing she stopped and stood a moment, listening. It was a quiet house at all times. The other tenants were an elderly spinster on the ground floor, who kept cats the smell of which permeated the hall, and on the first floor an elusive couple she suspected of living in sin; an artist had her studio in the second-floor flat but was rarely there, and never at night, and the third-floor flat had been empty for months. Now she could hear nothing, not a sound of any life, strain as she would. A faulty cistern above her gurgled, and from away off somewhere in the streets there came the wail of an ambulance siren. She looked up through the well of the stairs, into the upper dark. There was someone up there, she was sure of it. She went on, avoiding those places where she knew the stairs would creak.

On the third floor she pressed the switch that lit the yellow-shaded light on the landing above, outside her door. She paused again, and again looked up, but saw no one. Outside her flat, to the right, there was a dark alcove where a small door gave on to the attic stairs. She did not look into the alcove. She could feel the small hairs prickling at the nape of her neck. She was trying to remember the name of a girl she had known at school who had walked out of her parents' house one morning in her school uniform and was never seen or heard of again. There had been stories that she had eloped. Her schoolbag had been found discarded in a front garden in the next street.

She opened the door to the flat.

The first thing to strike her was how odd it was that Quirke should somehow have managed to get into the house in front of her and hurry up the stairs to hide in the alcove. It seemed impossible, but there he was, rushing past her in the doorway, just as Leslie White came out to meet her from the living room, with a cigarette dangling between his middle and third fingers, saying something. When he saw Quirke he put up both hands, still holding the cigarette, and retreated the way he had come. Quirke rushed at him, head down, like a rugby-player charging into a scrum. Leslie gave a squeak of alarm and the two of them disappeared into the room, Leslie going backwards with Quirke's arms thrown round him and Quirke bent double. She had trouble getting her key out of the lock—she was trying to pull it out at a bias—and she abandoned the struggle and hurried after the two men. She heard Leslie cry out again, much more piercingly this time. When she came into the room there was only one man there, leaning out of the wide-open window with his hands braced on the window-seat.

'Quirke?' she said, feeling more puzzlement than anything else.

When the man straightened up and turned to her she saw that it was not Quirke, but someone she had never seen before. He was almost as big as Quirke, and had a large, square-shaped head and thinning, rust-red hair. His mouth hung open like the mouth of a tragic mask, though the effect was not tragic but comic, rather, in an odd, grotesque way. She noticed the beads of sweat glistening in his hair like tiny specks of glass. And at that moment, simultaneously, and with fascinating inconsequence, she remembered the surname of the girl in school who had disappeared—it was Little, Olive Little—and realised that the clinking sound she had heard that time behind the phantom telephone caller's silence was the sound of the lid of a cigarette lighter being flipped open and shut.

The doorbell began to buzz, and went on buzzing for fully ten seconds, and then in shorter but no less insistent bursts. She had an image of someone down on the front step, with a finger on the bell button, dancing in impatience and fury, and that, too, was comical, and she almost laughed. The red-haired man advanced on her, holding out his hands before him as if to show her something in them, though his palms were empty. He stopped and stood still in a curiously supplicatory pose. She felt no fear, only continuing surprise and lively puzzlement, and still that tickle of incipient laughter.

She did not realise what she had been searching for in her handbag until she found it. She ran forward lightly, almost trippingly—'fleet' was the word that came to her mind—with an elbow raised against him for protection and lifted high her arm and plunged the silver spike into the hollow place where his chest met his left shoulder. The tissue was more resistant than she had expected and she felt the metal go in grindingly and meet something, bone perhaps, or gristle, and stop. The man drew back with a grunt, more surprised it seemed than anything else, goggling. She pulled the weapon free of where she had stabbed him and dropped it on the table. It landed with a metallic, joggling sound, rolled quickly to the edge and fell to the floor, leaving a bloodstain on the table in a fan shape. The man sat down suddenly, heavily, on a bentwood chair—it gave a loud and seemingly indignant crack—and looked from his wounded shoulder to the girl and back again. She dodged past him, and went and leaned out of the window. The lower sash was lifted all the way up, she had left it that way when she went out. The doorbell was still shrilling. The night air was damply cool against her face. She still felt no fear, though for all she knew the wounded man might be creeping up behind her, bleeding and in a murderous rage and ready to kill her. She did not care. She peered down into the street. Quirke was there, standing on the step, looking up at her. It was he who was ringing the bell. His arm was extended sideways and he was pressing it even now, and this, too, seemed wonderfully comic, him being there pressing on the bell that was ringing behind her. He called up to her, but she could not make out what he was saying. Then she saw the thing on the railings.

She turned back to the red-haired man. He was still sitting as before, with a hand pressed to his shoulder, and there was blood on his fingers. He had a bewildered look. She said:

'What have you done?'

3

QUIRKE HAD NEVER had so many calls upon his attention, so many things that needed to be done. In the small hours of the morning, after the ambulance men had gone and the Guards had taken Billy Hunt away, he had brought Phoebe down from her flat, wrapped in a blanket, and had taken her in a taxi to Mal's house. Mal came down in his pyjamas, scratching his head and blinking. Few words were exchanged. Phoebe would stay with Mal, for now, at least. The two of them would take care of each other. After all, this had been her home, she had grown up here. Quirke, leaving, paused at the gate and stood a moment in the damp darkness that was laden with the cloying scent of night-stock, and looked back and saw in the lighted window of the drawing room the two of them there, Phoebe hunched in an armchair and Mal in his absurd striped pyjamas standing over her, speaking. Then he turned and walked away into the night.

He thought he would not sleep, but when he got to the flat and stretched himself on his bed he plunged at once into a troubled sea of dreaming. He heard cries and calls, and saw bodies plummeting from the sky, whistling in their flight. At seven he woke with what felt like a hangover. He wanted to pull the blanket over his head and not get up at all, but there were, he knew, two visits that must be paid. He did not relish the thought of either of them. He decided to go first to Clontarf.

It was a grey, damp morning—the balmy weather of midsummer was past—and a fine mist was dirtying the light over the bay. The tide was far out and even with the windows of the taxi shut he caught the bilious stink of sea-wrack. He left the taxi at the front and walked up Castle Avenue. The bricks of the houses he passed by seemed today a deeper shade of oxblood, and in the gardens lush, damp dahlias hung their scarlet heads as if exhausted after the effort of coming into such prodigious bloom. He turned in at the gate and rang the doorbell and waited, eyeing the violent flowers. He took off his hat and held it in his hands; the dark felt was finely jewelled with mist.

What was he to say to her?

She did not seem surprised to see him. 'Oh,' she said flatly, 'it's you.' She was wearing the same outfit, black slacks and a black, high-necked pullover, that she had changed into the first day that he had been here. 'You may as well come in.'

She led the way out to the kitchen. There was a coffee cup on the table, and a copy of the *Irish Times* open at the death notices. 'I was studying them,' she said. 'When I rang up they asked how I'd like the wording. I had no idea. What on earth is there to say about someone like Leslie? "Beloved husband of" doesn't seem quite right. What do you think?'

He stood in the middle of the floor fingering the brim of his hat. 'I'm sorry,' he said. 'About everything.'

She asked if he would like a cup of coffee. He said no. The atmosphere in the room tightened another turn. She carried the cup to the sink and emptied out the remains of the coffee and rinsed the cup and set it upside-down on the draining board. He was remembering how she had cut her thumb that day on the broken glass, and how the blood had run over her wet wrist, so swiftly, when she lifted it out of the dishwater.

'I didn't expect to see you,' she said. 'I didn't expect you'd be back.'

'I'm sorry,' he said again. 'I'm not good at this sort of thing.'

She glanced at him over a black-clad shoulder. 'What sort of thing?' she asked. 'Sympathising with the bereaved widow? Or are you thinking of earlier things? Sex, maybe? Love?'

This he could only ignore.

'I came,' he began, 'I came to say . . .' and stopped.

She had turned to him, and was drying her hands on a tea-towel. She gave him a smile, faint and sardonic. 'Yes?'

He walked to the table and laid down his hat and studied it for a moment. It looked incongruous, the black hat on the white plastic surface.

'I came to ask,' he said, 'what you were doing at Deirdre Hunt's house on the day she died.' She inclined her head to one side, the faint smile still there but forgotten now. 'You were seen. A woman opposite. Every street has its busybody.'

Now she frowned, as faintly as she had smiled. 'How did she know who I was, this woman opposite?'

'She didn't. She described you to someone else, who

described you to me. "Tall, good-looking, with black hair cut short." I recognised you.'

'That was clever of you.'

'I knew who it was. Who it had to be.'

She suddenly laughed, briefly and without warmth. 'And now you've come to confront me,' she said. 'Who are you being? Sherlock Holmes? Dick Barton?'

He said nothing, only stood there, in his dark suit wrinkled from the mist, his head sunk into his shoulders, lugubrious, bull-like, intractable. Outside, the mist had become rain, and in the silence it made a sound against the window-panes like a confused muttering heard from far off. Kate walked to the table and took up the newspaper and turned it back to the front page and folded it and set it down again.

'I never met him, you know,' she said, 'this Hunt person—what's his name again?'

'Billy.'

'That's it. Billy. I had never met either of them.' She was touching the newspaper still with her fingertips, pressing down on it gently. 'It was hardly the sort of situation in which we would socialise, the four of us, Laura Swan with her hubby and me with mine. Can you see the four of us, here, sharing a casual salad and a bottle of Blue Nun? No, it's not likely, is it. It doesn't quite *fit.*'

There was a pause, and then he asked again: 'Why did you go to see her? You told me the first time I came here that you'd telephoned her. But you didn't telephone, you went in person, didn't you? Why?'

She lifted her head and looked at him squarely. 'Why? To tell her to her face what a dirty little bitch she was. I'd found the photographs, remember, and that filth that she wrote, to amuse Leslie.' She paused and took in a deep breath, flaring her nostrils. 'I wanted to see what she looked like.'

'And she?'

'And she what?'

'What did she say?'

'Not much. She was drunk when I arrived—she'd had the best part of a bottle of whiskey. Everything had come unstuck, it seems. Leslie had been fiddling the money, as usual, and the bank was about to shut down that place they ran together. She was all of a quiver, the poor idiot. I could only laugh. She had trusted him—she had trusted Leslie! I almost felt sorry for her. And I suppose I'm sorry now, a little, that she killed herself.'

'She didn't.'

He had said it so softly that for a moment she thought she might have misheard. She frowned, and gave her head a tiny shake, like a swimmer who has just surfaced. 'What do you mean?'

'She died of an overdose of morphine. She had been drinking, too, as you say—there was alcohol in her blood. I imagine that made it easier to give her the injection.'

Kate's frown had deepened; she had the look of a person lost in a dark place and groping to find a way forward. 'She didn't give herself the morphine, is that what you're saying? I thought she drowned.'

'With so much drink and dope in her she would have been practically in a coma,' he said. 'She couldn't have lifted a finger, let alone driven a car.'

'What? Driven what car?'

'Her car was found in Sandycove. Her clothes were there too, neatly folded, the way a woman would fold them.' He was watching her so closely it seemed he might be seeing unhindered past her eyes and into her very skull. 'She didn't drown herself, she was already dead. Someone drove her out there—drove her body out there—and put it into the sea, and left her clothes and the car to make it look like suicide.'

'Someone,' she said, so softly it might have been a sigh.

'Now will you tell me what you were doing at her house that afternoon?'

They had been standing for so long that suddenly and simultaneously they both became aware of an aching stiffness in their legs. Kate sat down abruptly on one of the steel chairs at the table and set her elbows on the Formica top, while Quirke, dry-mouthed, walked to the sink and took the coffee cup and filled it from the cold tap and drank deeply.

'I've told you what I was doing,' she said dully. 'I went to see her because I was angry. But she was such a mess, such a hopeless, sodden mess, that I couldn't say any of the things I'd come to say.' She turned and looked at him where he stood by the sink with the cup in his hand. Behind him the window was suffused by a watery, mud-blue light. 'Who killed her?' she demanded.

'You tell me.'

'How can I tell you?'

'You were the second-last person to see her alive. Unless . . .'

'Unless what?' He would not reply, and looked aside. 'Unless,' she said, 'I was the *last*? My God, Quirke. My God.' In a strange movement, like a participant in a ritual, she folded her arms before her on the table and laid her forehead down on them, and rolled her head from side to side slowly, her body swaying. Despite everything, he had an urge to walk forward and place his hand on the nape of her neck, so pale, so vulnerable. When, after a time, she raised her head again he saw that she was weeping, though she seemed unaware of it, and brushed the tears from her cheeks with a distracted gesture. 'Tell me what happened,' she said, in a new, hollow voice.

Quirke, his thirst raging on, filled the cup again, drank again. 'What happened when?'

'With Leslie. With Billy Hunt.'

'He was in my daughter's flat—'

'Who was?'

'Leslie.'

'What was he doing in your daughter's flat?'

'I suspect it was the only place he could think to go.'

'Why? What was the matter?'

'A man he knew was murdered.'

She swivelled on the seat to stare at him. Her tears had stopped. 'What man?'

'Kreutz. Leslie's pal. He called himself a spiritual healer. He also took compromising pictures of his women clients, though mostly, it seems, with their consent, or more than consent.'

'They were the photographs I found?'

'I imagine so. When Leslie happened on them, he began to blackmail Kreutz.'

'What would Leslie have wanted from him?'

'Money, of course.' He paused. 'Drugs. You knew of Leslie's drug habit, didn't you? His morphine habit? You knew he was an addict.'

'An addict? I knew he took stuff, anything he could get his hands on. He had'—she smiled, sadly, bitterly—'he had a craving for experience. That's what he used to say, "I have a craving for experience, Kate, that can't be satisfied." Is that what it means, being an addict?'

'Did *you* take morphine?'

She seemed to have known the question was coming. 'And did I use up my supply on Laura Swan, is that what you mean?' She turned from him, and leaned back on the chair, squaring her shoulders as if they had grown suddenly stiff. 'You have quite a mind, Quirke,' she said, almost admiringly. 'Quite a mind.' She rose and went to the stove and took the kettle and carried it to the sink, forcing him to move to the side. She filled the kettle and carried it back and set it on the stove and lit the gas flame. She took down the coffee tin and found a spoon in a drawer and spooned the coffee into the lid of the percolator. 'This is *my* addiction,' she said. 'Coffee.' She turned to him. 'You were telling me what happened, between Leslie and Billy Hunt.'

'He thought Leslie was going to harm my daughter. He tackled him. Leslie fell through the window. It was an accident.'

'And what was *he* doing in your daughter's flat? Billy Hunt, I mean. She must be a hospitable girl, with all these men coming and going.'

'He had been watching the flat,' Quirke said. 'He had seen Leslie go in. My daughter didn't know who he was. She attacked him, tried to stab him.'

'To *stab* him?'

'In the shoulder. With a pencil. A metal propelling

pencil. Mine, as it happens. She had it in her bag.' He put the cup down on the draining-board. 'It's possible he saved her life.'

'Saved her from who—from Leslie?' He did not answer. Suddenly she saw it. 'You think Leslie and I killed them, don't you? Laura Swan and this doctor fellow. *Don't* you?'

'Your husband was on morphine. He didn't know what he was doing.'

She gave a shout of laughter, a derisive hoot. 'Leslie *always* knew what he was doing, especially if he was doing something wrong.'

The air in the room seemed to Quirke suddenly heavy and thick, and he realised how weary he was. 'You lied to me,' he said.

Kate was pouring water from the kettle into the coffee pot, measuring the level carefully with her eye. 'Did I?' she said distractedly. 'What did I lie about?'

'You lied about everything.'

She glanced at him and then turned her attention back to the coffee pot and the gas ring on which she had set it. She struck a match, drawing the head slowly along the emery paper, the sound of it setting his teeth on edge. 'I don't know what you mean,' she said.

He caught hold of her wrist, making her drop the match. She looked at his hand where it held her as if she did not know what it was, this hooked thing of meat and bone and blood. 'You know very well what I mean,' he said. 'You pretended to be broken-hearted that your husband had gone, that he'd taken up with another woman, all that. But it was all pretence.'

'Why?'

'Why what?'

'Why would I pretend?'

'Because . . .' He did not know. He had thought he knew, but he did not. His anger was turning to confusion. What had he come here to say to her? What did she mean to him, this tough, injured, desirable woman? He let go his grip on her. She held up her wrist and examined, the white furrows his fingers had left there to which the blood was rapidly returning. Everything rushes back, everything replaces itself. 'I'm sorry,' he said, and turned away.

'Yes,' Kate said, 'I'm sorry, too.'

At the front door she stood and watched him walk away hurriedly into the rain, with his hat pulled low and holding the lapels of his jacket closed against the chill sea-air. There were gulls somewhere above her, in the grey murk, cawing and crying. She shut the door. When she turned back to the hall the emptiness of the house rushed at her, as if she were a vacuum into which everything was pouring, unstoppably.

It was the closest he had come in the past six months to flinging himself off the wagon. At the seafront he even turned and set off in the direction of the Sheds at the bottom of Vernon Avenue, but made himself turn back. His throat ached for a drink. Despite the rain and the chill in the air he seemed to be smouldering all over, like a tree that has been hit by lightning. He stood waiting on the corner at the seafront for almost half an hour, but there were no taxis to be had, and in the end he was forced to get on a bus. He stood on the running board, holding on to the metal pole. The sad, wet stretch of seafront swayed past, the stunted palm trees glistening in the rain. Dublin, city of palms. Quirke grinned joylessly.

In Marlborough Street a cart horse had fallen between the shafts of a Post-Office dray, and there were lines of held-up buses and motor cars in both directions. The horse, a big grey, lay with its legs splayed, looking oddly calm and unconcerned. No one seemed to know what to do. A Guard had his notebook and pencil out. A cluster of schoolboys, idle at lunchtime, stood by and gazed in awe upon the fallen animal. Quirke got off the bus and walked along to the river, and then up the quay and crossed the bridge and into D'Olier Street and then crossed again and went into the Garda station. At the desk in the dayroom he asked for Inspector Hackett, and was told to wait.

He thought of the horse, fallen between the shafts, its great black eyes glistening.

Hackett as always seemed pleased to see him, delighted, almost. They shook hands. At the inspector's suggestion they went to Bewley's, hurrying head-down through the rain past the side entrance of the *Irish Times* offices into Westmoreland Street, and dodged among the swishing traffic and gained the café's curlicued doorway. They took a table at the back, from which Quirke found, to his vague dismay, that he had a direct view of the banquette where he and Billy Hunt had sat when they had met that day for the first time in twenty years and Billy had poured out his damp litany of sorrows and beseechings.

'Well, Mr Quirke,' the inspector said, when he had ordered his tea from a frumpy girl in a less than spotless apron, 'this is a right old confusion, what?'

Quirke had taken out his cigarette case and his lighter. 'Yes,' he said, 'that's a way of putting it, I suppose.'

Through the miasma of blue smoke above the table the Inspector was watching him with a hooded gaze. 'I'll tell you now, Mr Quirke, but I have the suspicion that you know a good deal more about this sorrowful business than I do. Would I be right, would you say?' Quirke looked down, to where his fingers were fiddling with the lighter. 'There is, for instance,' the inspector went on, 'the fact of Miss Griffin, your niece's, curious involvement in certain recent, tragic events of which we are both all too well aware. What was this Leslie White fellow doing in her flat, and what, for that matter, was Billy Hunt doing there, either?'

Quirke turned the lighter over and over in his fingers; he thought of Phoebe doing the same thing—where had that been, and when?

'My niece—' he said, and almost stumbled on the word, 'my niece knew White by chance. They met one day outside the Silver Swan, after Deirdre Hunt died. She felt sorry for him, I imagine.' He looked up and met the policeman's slitted stare. 'She's young. She has a sympathetic way. He brought her to the Grafton Café for afternoon tea. They struck up an acquaintance. Then when Kreutz sent those fellows to beat him up—'

'Why, by the way, did he do that?' the inspector asked, in his mildest of enquiring tones.

'White was extorting money from him. Kreutz was at the end of his tether. He wanted to give White a warning.'

The inspector stabbed his cigarette in the direction of

the ashtray, but missed, and the ash fell on the table, and with a schoolboy's guilty haste he brushed it away with the side of his hand. 'You know all this for a fact, do you?'

'Of course not. I'm guessing, but it's an informed guess.'

'And it was your niece who informed this guess of yours, was it?'

Quirke hesitated. 'She doesn't know why Leslie White was in her flat. She's not sure. She assumed he needed help, money, something—Kreutz had been murdered, after all, and Kreutz had been connected with White, she knew that much.'

'How?' Again that bland tone, again the gimlet gaze.

'How did she know? White told her. He liked to tell stories about the amusing people he knew, he was good at it. He made her laugh. He had that gift.'

The frowsty girl brought a tray with teapot and cups and set it down rattlingly. The inspector waited for her to be gone, and said: 'So Kreutz puts the heavy gang on to White, at which White is mightily annoyed, so much so, in fact, that as soon as he gets his strength back he goes up to Kreutz's place and gives him a beating and leaves him bleeding to death on the living-room mat. Then what?'

'Then in a panic he goes to Phoebe's flat—she'd given him a key—aiming, I suppose, to hide out there.'

The inspector dropped four lumps of sugar into his tea and stirred it slowly. He splashed in milk, but it was still too hot and he poured a measure into the saucer and lifted the saucer with tremulous care to his mouth and drank deep. 'And Billy Hunt?' he asked, wiping his lips. 'Where does he come in? And *how* does he come in—which is to say, how did he get into the house where Miss Griffin's flat is?'

'He convinced the mad old biddy who lives on the ground floor that he was Phoebe's uncle. He had seen White going in, and—'

'By chance, again?'

Quirke held out the open cigarette case but this time the inspector declined the offer with a curt shake of his head. His eyes to Quirke seemed as sharp as flints.

'The fact is,' Quirke said, and cleared his throat, 'the fact is, he'd been watching the house for a long time. He was convinced by now that Leslie White had murdered his wife. He knew my niece had taken him in once already, after the beating he got from Kreutz's people. He didn't know who Phoebe was. When he saw White going in he followed him. Then Phoebe arrived, Billy waited until she had opened the door, and . . .'

'. . . and ran in and pushed the bugger out the window.'

'He lost his head.'

'What?'

Quirke had to clear his throat again. 'He says he lost his head.'

'Aye. That's what he told me, too.'

'He doesn't know what he meant to do to Leslie White, but he didn't mean to kill him.'

'Do you believe it?'

'Yes,' Quirke answered stoutly, and stoutly held the other's gaze.

At last the policeman sat back on his chair, and smiled. 'I admire your benevolence,' he said. The tea had cooled and he drank it direct from the cup now; each time he lifted the cup, Quirke noticed, with idle fascination, a drop fell from the bottom of it back into the saucer, making a crown shape in the little pool of khaki liquid that was left there and sending a random spray of splashes on to the table-top. 'Well, then, Mr Quirke,' the policeman said, 'what do you want me to do?'

'I want you to do nothing.'

Hackett nodded, as if this were the answer he had been expecting. He mused for a moment, sighing. Then he laughed softly. 'Lord God, Mr Quirke,' he said, 'but you're an unpredictable man. Do nothing, you say. But two years ago you came to me with information about all manner of skulduggery in this town and wanted me to do all sorts of things, arrest people, destroy reputations, haul in respectable people—some of them in your own family—and show them up for the villains you said they were.'

'Yes,' Quirke said calmly, 'I remember.'

'We both do. We both remember well.'

'But you were taken off the case.'

Hackett chuckled. 'The fact is, as you and I know, the case was taken off me, and put neatly and safely away in a file marked *Don't touch*. It's a bad world, Mr Quirke, with bad people in it. And there's no justice, not that I can see.'

'Justice has been done here.'

'A rough class of justice, if you ask me.'

'But justice, all the same. Leslie White is no loss to the world. He poisoned a woman and beat a man to death. Billy Hunt saved the State the job of meting out due punishment for those crimes.'

The inspector gave a doubtful shrug. 'Billy Hunt,' he

said. 'Billy Hunt appointed himself judge, jury and executioner. Are we to let him off with that?'

'Look, Inspector,' Quirke said. 'I don't care a tinker's curse about Billy Hunt. My only concern is the girl.'

'Your niece?'

Quirke looked across the room to the table to where he and Billy Hunt had sat. 'She's not,' he said, 'my niece. She's my daughter.' The policeman, sitting slumped with his chin on his chest, did not look at him. 'It's a complicated story, going back a long way. I'll tell it to you some day. But you see my interest. She's had a hard time. Bad things have happened to her, some of them my fault—many of them, maybe. I have to protect her, now. What she saw last night, the things that happened ... You have sons, haven't you? You'd want to protect them, if they had gone through what my daughter has gone through. If she had to appear in a witness box I don't know what the consequences might be.'

Hackett shifted his bulk, pulling himself half upright, and reached out and took a cigarette from Quirke's case where it lay on the table. Quirke flicked his lighter.

'You're asking me,' the policeman said slowly, 'to hush this thing up, so this girl, your daughter, as you say, won't have to give evidence in court?'

Quirke hesitated, but then said only: 'Yes.'

The policeman let his head sink on his chest again, his double chins swelling, fat wads of flesh as pallid as the belly of a fish. 'You're asking a lot of me, Mr Quirke.'

'I believe you owe it to me. Or if not to me, then to my daughter.' He saw himself two years ago standing in a squalid kitchen where a woman's bloodied corpse lay on the floor, bound to a chair with lengths of braided electric flex and her own nylon stockings. What justice had there been for her?

The policeman was patting his pockets in search of money, but Quirke dropped a florin on the table, where it spun for a moment on its edge and then fell flat. Hackett nodded towards the coin. 'Aye,' he said, 'we owe each other, I suppose.' Now he gave Quirke a long, considering look, seeming to weigh something in his head. Then he decided. 'I think you're telling me the truth, Mr Quirke,' he said. 'I mean, the truth as you see it. I didn't think so at first. To be honest, I thought you were trying to hoodwink me.' Quirke was very still, his eyes fixed on the table, one fist resting beside his untouched teacup. The inspector went on. 'But you really don't see it, do you? I thought you were less gullible. I also thought you had a less rosy view of human beings and their doings.'

'What do you mean?' Quirke asked, still without looking up.

The policeman rose abruptly and took up his hat. He waited, and Quirke after a moment rose also, and together they walked through the crowded dining room and across the coffee shop to the doorway, where they paused.

'I'm sorry,' Hackett said. 'I can't do what you ask—I mean, I can't do nothing. What happened is not what you think happened. It's all much simpler, and much worse, in a way. There's a certain gentleman who thinks he's fooled us all.' He turned, smiling his toad's smile, and looked at Quirke, and winked. 'But he hasn't fooled me, Mr Quirke. No, he hasn't fooled me.'

'Who is it?' Quirke asked. 'Who are you talking about?'

The policeman peered out from the doorway squintingly into the morning's greyness. 'Do you know what it is,' he said, 'but the weather in this country would give you the pip.'

4

BILLY HUNT WAS well aware that people thought him a bit of a fool, but he knew better. Not that he had any great illusions about his brain-power. At school he had been slow, or so they had told him, but it was only because he was no good at reading and therefore sometimes he could not keep up with the rest of the class. That was why he had ducked out of doing medicine, all those years ago—he had not expected there would be so many books to be read. Quirke and that gang had looked down on him, of course. Quirke. He was not sure what he thought about him, what he felt about him. But talk about being a bit of a fool! The great Mr Quirke, who imagined he was so clever, had missed the whole thing. In any other circumstances it would have been funny, how wrong they had all been, without even knowing it.

No, Billy Hunt was no fool. He knew what was what, he knew his way round the world. For years he had been handling the big shots on his visits over at Head Office in Switzerland—those boys would make short work of the likes of Quirke—not to mention the fancy whores hanging around the city of Geneva's hotel lobbies. And he could sell anything; he could have sold suntan lotion to niggers. Not that he got any respect for it. Most people when he told them what he did immediately saw him as some poor joe shuffling from door to door trying to fool housewives into buying vacuum-cleaners. They had no idea what a real salesman did, how much thought went into it, how much psychology. That was the point of selling: you needed to know people's minds, to see into the way they were thinking. Not that they did much thinking. People, customers, clients—they were all fools.

He had not expected to fall so hard for Deirdre Ward. At his age, he had thought he was past that kind of thing. The Geneva whores had been sufficient to keep that old itch scratched. That was until he met Deirdre. He knew he was too old for her. He could hardly believe it when she agreed to go with him. What a dolt he had made of himself, boasting about his job, the big deals he was always clinching, and the trips to Switzerland, all that stuff. He had supposed she really expected he would do as he had promised and take her with him over there, introduce her to his bosses, Herr This and Monsieur That—*Call me Fritz*, gnädige Frau! *Call me Maurice*, chère Madame!—and treat her to grand dinners and put her up in deluxe hotels, show her the Matterhorn, take her skiing. What a shock it was for him when she turned out to be the one with ambitions, and a business head to realise them. And what a pity it was that she, unlike him, was such a poor judge of people. From the start he had spotted Leslie White for what he was. But, of course, there was no talking to her. Stubborn, she was, stubborn as a stone.

In a way, though, it had been a relief that it was White she chose to take up with. Billy's real fear, from the start, was that she would get tired of him because of his age and find herself some young fellow. He did not want to be like the old fools in the old songs who were a laughing stock because they could not satisfy their young wives. What was that one they used to sing?

> *Oh, eggs and eggs and marrowbones*
> *Will make your old man blind . . .*

Yes, that he would not have been able to bear, having people nudging each other and laughing at him behind his back. Anything was preferable to that, or almost anything.

As it turned out he was just as blind as any fond fool in a ballad. The evidence was there before him, if he had only allowed himself to see it. The change in her moods, the laughter and the tears for no reason, the flare-ups of irritation out of nowhere, the dreamy, almost sorrowful look in her eye, all these things should have told him something was up. The clincher was the way she suddenly became all lovey-dovey towards him, cooking him special dinners, the ones he was supposed to be so fond of, and sitting at the table with him while he ate, her chin on her hand and her shining eyes fixed on him, pretending to be fascinated by some story he was telling her about a tricky sale he had made, a crafty deal he had pulled off. She had not wanted him to touch her, either—she had allowed him to, but she had not wanted it, not as she had wanted it when they were together first, all over him like a cheap suit, then, not able to get out of her knickers quick enough. Twice he had noticed marks on her, red weals high up on the backs of her legs, as if she had been whipped, and another time scratches down her shoulder blades which anyone but him would have known were nail-marks. Oh, yes, it was all there, plain as plain, but he had not seen it because he had not wanted to see it, he knew that now. He had wanted it not to be true.

How long would it have gone on, he wondered, his blindness, his willed stupidity, if White had not sent him the photograph? And why had White sent it? Just for a joke? When it arrived that morning it had made him sick, literally sick: he had to go up to the lavatory and throw up the bacon and eggs and fried bread she had cooked him for his breakfast. He was like an animal that had been poisoned. Nothing like this had ever happened to him before; he had never experienced this kind of thing, this awful jumble of pain and anguish and fury, and something else, too, when he looked at the photo, something worse, a throb, a dull spasm in the gut, lower than the gut, a hot bone-ache at the fork of his thighs, the same that he had felt as a boy in school when he leaned over the shoulders of a ring of fellows in the senior lav and saw what they were crouching over, a picture torn from a smutty magazine of a tart lying back on a bed with her knees up showing off all she had. But this thing that had arrived in the post, this was no tart but his wife, sprawled there with her skirt round her hips and everything on view.

The moment he saw it he knew who had taken it. He had never met Kreutz, had never even seen him, but from the way Deirdre had talked about him and, more significantly, the way she had suddenly *stopped* talking about him, had been enough to alert him to the fact that this Kreutz was a wrong one. But why would Kreutz, having taken the picture of Deirdre, then send it to her husband? For at this stage he had thought it must have been Kreutz who had sent it. At first Billy assumed that Kreutz was going to try to get money out of him. He had seen it often enough in gangster pictures, fellows getting women drunk or drugged and taking compromising snaps of them—you never saw the snaps on screen, of course—and sending them to the women's husbands to blackmail them and force them to pay up. They always ended in gunplay, these plots, with bodies, much too neat and unrumpled, lying all over the place in pools of black blood.

He could not think why it had not occurred to him that it might have been Leslie White and not Kreutz who had sent him the photo, except that there had been no reason why White would have had the photo in the first place. Nor was it clear to him why, after Deirdre was dead, he did not go looking for Kreutz straight away, but instead concentrated on Leslie White. He had been following him for a long time, tracking him, monitoring him. He had seen him with the girl. He did not know she was Quirke's daughter. He did not know anything about her. But he liked the look of her. Or maybe 'liked' was not the word. He felt, even across the distance that he always made sure to keep between them, a sympathy for her, or with her; they were, he felt, somehow alike, himself and her. She was a loner, like him—and he *was* a loner, he had no doubt of that. He began to look out for the girl, to look out for her welfare, though it was true he had no idea what he could do to help her. He even used to phone her up now and again, just to check she was all right, though of course he never said anything, only listened to her voice, until in the end she, too, started to say nothing, and there they would be, the two of them, at either end of the line, silent, listening, somehow together.

Maybe it was for her sake, for the girl's sake, and not for Deirdre's, that he had sent the three lads to give White a hiding. They were good lads, Joe Etchingham and Eugene Timmins and his brother Alf; Joe was on the football team with him, a handy full-back, while the other two were hurlers; the three of them were in the Movement, and had done a few jobs on the border; they would keep their mouths shut, he could count on that. Yes, maybe it was—what was her name?—maybe it was Phoebe he was trying to protect by arranging for the lads to go after White with hurley sticks and give him a good going-over.

And it was them, Joe Etchingham and the Timmins brothers, that he should have sent to deal with Kreutz, instead of going himself. He had not meant to hit him as hard or as many times as he did; he had not meant to kill him. Kreutz was no hero, and had told him all he wanted to know within five minutes of his coming in the door, about Leslie White sending on the photo, and taking money from him and out of the salon, all of it, all the whole, dirty saga—he had even shown him where the morphine was hidden, in a meatsafe in the kitchen, of all places—so why had he gone on hitting him? There was something in Kreutz that had cried out for a beating, for a real doing, with fists, elbows, toecaps, heels, the lot. It was not just that he was a fuzzy-wuzzy. He had a weak, a womanish way about him, and once Billy had started hitting him it had seemed impossible to stop. He had got into a kind of trance. Each dull thud of his fist on the fellow's skin-and-bone frame had demanded another one, and that one in turn had demanded yet another. It was just as well that he had thought to bring a good thick pair of leather gloves, or his knuckles would have been in bits. And then there was blood everywhere.

Poor Deirdre. He would have forgiven her, he was sure he would have forgiven her, if only she had been able to ask him, to beg him. Strange, that she should have been the first to go. In his mind now he sometimes got confused, got it all out of sequence, so that it seemed to him that Kreutz had been the first, or even Leslie White, and then Deirdre, afterwards. But no. He had come home exhausted that night, the night of the day the photo arrived. He had been supposed to go to the west, to Galway and Sligo, to talk to them over there about the new arthritis drug that had come out—a miracle cure, yet another one—but instead he had spent the whole day wandering the city, hardly knowing where he was going, just walking, walking and walking, trudging the streets, trying to get the image out of his head, the image of Deirdre lying on that sofa with her legs open, displaying herself to the world, like she would never consent to display herself to him, her husband.

In the end there had been nothing for it but to go home—where else would he have gone, after all? He had smelled the whiskey as soon as he came in the door, the sour, hot stink of it. Her clothes were on the floor in the bathroom, her skirt, her slip, her drawers. The sight disgusted him, actually made his stomach heave again. It was mad to think it, he knew, but he was convinced that if it had not been for those clothes on the floor what happened afterwards might not have happened. He would have called a doctor, maybe, an ambulance, even. He would have made her drink hot tea, would have massaged her temples; he would have held her hand; he would have revived her. But those clothes, those dirty clothes, strewn there, they were another part of the great, hot, suffocating weight of filth that the photograph had made fall on to his world. It was the clothes that did it.

He had never given anyone an injection before. He had seen it done, he knew how to do it, more or less, but this was his first time. He had not expected her skin to be so rubbery, so resistant. He had to pinch the vein between his fingers and force the needle in at a slant. And then the strangest thing, the great, slow surge of calmness that had flowed back from his hand, the hand with the needle in it, and up along his arm and into his chest, slowing his heartbeat, a balm for his blood, as if what he was injecting, this clear, cool elixir, was going not into her but back into him. When he withdrew the needle Deirdre gave a long, shivery sort of sigh, and that was all. He watched her for a while in the light of the bedside lamp. He searched in himself for some feeling of guilt, sorrow, even only regret, but there was nothing: he was at peace. It had been necessary for her to go: he would not have been able to live, otherwise. She had become a poison suddenly in his life, not the Deirdre he knew, or thought he had known, but the creature in the photograph, that monster. Yes, there had been no choice for him. Poison for poison.

He put the needle and the empty phials into his samples case and snapped it shut; he would have to remember to get rid of them. What should he do next? She had a bath towel under her on the bed, still damp, and he wrapped her in that. There was an unpleasant smell. He would have to change the bedclothes and get rid of the towel. That would be easy. Everything would be easy. If there was one thing he had learned on the football field it was never to hesitate, but keep going, whoever was in your way or however hard the ref was blowing on his whistle. Put the head down, and bull on.

He went and stood by the window with his hands in his pockets, looking out at the big moon hanging there. Behind him, on the bed, there was no sound, no movement, nothing, only a broad, swelling absence. Low down in the sky a bank of cloud lay humped, blue as a whale with a fringe along its upper edge as bright as molten metal. The thing to do was to bring the car, her car, round to the lane at the back and carry her down the garden and out through the door beside the disused privy. It was late enough, no one would see. It was very bright, though, in the moonlight. The back shed was throwing a sharp black shadow diagonally across the grey grass. He would take her to Sandycove, where they used to go for walks sometimes in the weeks before they were married. It would be lovely out there, on a fine night like this, the moon on the water and the lights of Howth twinkling across the bay. Their last journey together, his and hers. All these last things. He had a strong sense that all that had happened had been fated, and inevitable. Maybe if you looked at anything, any event, closely enough you would see the future packed into it, folded tight, like the tight-folded elastic filling of a golf ball. That moment when he first saw her in Plunkett's pharmacy had contained this moment, too, with him standing at the window, looking at the moon, and Deirdre on the bed, or what remained of Deirdre. Fate. That was it.

He was a long time finding her car key. It was not in her handbag. He searched through her clothes, with no luck. He felt a flicker of anxiety, like the first lick of a flame that would soon be raging through the house, but then he walked into the kitchen and there was the bunch of keys, in the ashtray on the table, where she always left them—why had he not looked there first? Maybe he was more upset than he realised. He would have to go carefully: this was not the time to make a mistake. He turned off the light in the hall before opening the front door, and stood in the shadow of the doorway, watching the street. A few upstairs windows were lit, but all was quiet. Clontarf folk went to bed early. He scrutinised in particular the house directly opposite, where the ex-nun and the renegade priest lived. The Reverend Mother, as he called her, was a nosy bitch. He watched the upstairs curtains to see if one of them might twitch, but nothing stirred. He stepped out into the dark— the moon was throwing a shadow here, too—and used the key in the lock of the door behind him so he could turn the latch and keep it from clicking when he shut the door. Not a sound. The garden gate, too, he managed to open and shut silently. He did not care about the noise the Austin would make when he started it up—no one, not even the Reverend Mother, would be able to make out, in the dark, that it was him behind the wheel.

In the car the lingering smell of her perfume hit him like a soft blow to the heart.

Head down, keep going. Keep going!

What a weight she was. The last time he had carried her like this, draped over his arms, was the day they had come back from their honeymoon and he had insisted on carrying her over the threshold. She had tried to resist, laughing, and telling him not be such an eejit, but he had leaned down sideways and swept her up, and she had seemed no heavier than a stook of wheat. But that was a long time ago, in another life. In the laneway he opened the back door of the car and put her lying on the back seat, and just as he was shutting the door on her the big dark-blue cloud, which had been rising steadily without his noticing, deftly pocketed the moon's tarnished silver coin. He got in behind the wheel and took a slow, deep breath. Her clothes, the clothes she had left on the bathroom floor, were folded in a neat stack on the passenger seat. He thought of the coast road again, dark now, with the moon gone, and the sea dark, too, and that bank of cloud climbing higher and higher in the sky, spreading its shadow steadily over the world.

Then he started up the engine, and drove away.

Epilogue

QUIRKE WOKE INTO a grey dawn. He was in the open, under trees. He was cold, and his face was damp with dew. He felt vague pain, vague distress. He wondered if he had been involved in an accident, if he had fallen, or been knocked down. A large dark figure was looming over him, speaking. He could not make out the words. His brain was fogged. He was slumped on some kind of seat, an iron bench, it seemed to be. Yes, it was a bench, and he was by the canal, he recognised the place, for there was Huband Bridge, humped in the greyness. The dark figure put out a great pale hand and grasped him by the shoulder and shook him, and immediately his head began to pound, as if something heavy had been shaken loose in it and was rolling uncontrollably from side to side. 'Are you all right?' the figure was saying. It was a Guard, huge and hulking, with a round bloodless face, standard issue, not unlike Inspector Hackett's. Quirke hauled himself upright on the bench, and the Guard took his hand from his shoulder and stepped back. 'Are you all right?' he demanded again. Quirke's mouth was dry, dry and burning, and he had to work his jaws for a moment to get some saliva under his tongue before he could reply. He said yes, he was fine, and that he must have fallen asleep. 'You had a few too many,' the Guard said gruffly, 'by the cut of you.' How was it, Quirke found himself wondering, that Guards always seemed aggrieved? Even if you asked one the way to somewhere the fellow would look at you in that grimly startled way, furrowing his brow, as if the simple fact of being addressed constituted a personal affront. To be rid of him, Quirke closed his eyes, and sure enough, when he opened them again, a moment later, so he thought, there was no one there. The light was changed, too, it was stronger now. He was still sprawled on the bench. He must have fallen asleep again briefly, or passed out.

He sat up, and searched in his pockets for his cigarettes, but could find none. It was coming back to him, gradually, all that had happened. Yesterday had been Tuesday and last night he should have had his weekly dinner with Phoebe, but Phoebe was at Mal's, and he had not dared to call her. Instead he had gone, alone, to the Russell, and eaten dinner alone, and drunk a bottle of wine, and then had gone on to McGonagle's, and downed glasses of whiskey, he could not remember how many. What had followed after that, how he had come to be here on this canal bench, all that was a blank. He rose to his feet, swayingly, that weight still rolling about in his head like an iron ball. There was something urgent he had to do. What was it? Phoebe, yes—he had to do something about Phoebe. He did not know what it was but he knew he must do it. Save her. She was his daughter. He must find a way to bring her back to life. That was how he thought of it, those were the words that formed them-selves in his head: *I must bring her back, bring her back, to life.* He looked both ways along the canal. There was not a soul to be seen. He thought of the long, ashen day ahead of him. He tried to make himself move, to walk, to get away, but in vain: his body would not obey him. He stood there, paralysed. He did not know where to go. He did not know what to do.

If you enjoyed *The Silver Swan* you'll love

ELEGY FOR APRIL

the third Quirke Dublin mystery from Benjamin Black

1950s Ireland. As a deep, bewildering fog cloaks Dublin, a young woman is found to have vanished.

When Phoebe Griffin, still haunted by the horrors of her past, is unable to discover news of her friend, Quirke, fresh from drying out in an institution, responds to his daughter's request for help.

But as Phoebe, Quirke and Inspector Hackett speak with those who knew April, they begin to realise that there may have been more behind the young woman's discretion and secrecy than they could have imagined. Why was April so estranged from her family? What is her close-knit circle of friends hiding? And who is the shadowy figure who seems to be watching Phoebe's flat at night, through the frozen mists?

As Quirke finds himself distracted from his sobriety by a beautiful young actress, Phoebe watches helplessly as April's family hush up her disappearance, and all possible leads seem to dry up, bar one she cannot bear to contemplate. But when Quirke makes a disturbing discovery, he is finally able to begin unravelling the great, complex web of love, lies, jealousy and dark secrets that April spun her life from . . .

The first chapter follows here . . .

1

IT WAS THE WORST of winter weather, and April Latimer was missing.

For days a February fog had been down and showed no sign of lifting. In the muffled silence the city seemed bewildered, like a man whose sight has suddenly failed. People vague as invalids groped their way through the murk, keeping close to the house-fronts and the railings and stopping tentatively at street corners to feel with a wary foot for the pavement's edge. Motor cars with their headlights on loomed like giant insects, trailing milky dribbles of exhaust smoke from their rear ends. The evening paper listed each day's toll of mishaps. There had been a serious collision at the canal end of the Rathgar Road involving three cars and an Army motorcyclist. A small boy was run over by a coal lorry at the Five Lamps, but did not die—his mother swore to the reporter sent to interview her that it was the miraculous medal of the Virgin Mary she made the child wear round his neck that had saved him. In Clanbrassil Street an old moneylender was waylaid and robbed in broad daylight by what he claimed was a gang of housewives; the Guards were following a definite line of inquiry. A shawlie in Moore Street was knocked down by a van that did not stop, and now the woman was in a coma in St James's. And all day long the fog horns boomed out in the bay.

Phoebe Griffin considered herself April's best friend, but she had heard nothing from her in a week and she was convinced something had happened. She did not know what to do. Of course, April might just have gone off, without telling anyone—that was how April was, unconventional, some would say wild—but Phoebe was sure that was not the case.

The windows of April's first-floor flat on Herbert Place had a blank, withholding aspect, not just because of the fog: windows look like that when the rooms behind them are empty; Phoebe could not say how, but they do. She crossed to the other side of the road and stood at the railings with the canal at her back and looked up at the terrace of tall houses, their louring, dark brick exteriors shining wetly in the shrouded air. She was not sure what she was hoping to see—a curtain twitching, a face at a window?—but there was nothing, and no one. The damp was seeping through her clothes and she drew in her shoulders against the cold. She heard footsteps on the tow-path behind her but when she turned to look she could not see anyone through the impenetrable, hanging greyness. The bare trees with their black limbs upflung appeared almost human. The unseen walker coughed once; it sounded like a fox barking.

She went back and climbed the stone steps to the door again, and again pressed the bell above the little card with April's name on it, though she knew there would be no answer. Grains of mica glittered in the granite of the steps; strange, these little secret gleamings, under the fog. A ripping whine started up in the sawmill on the other side of the canal and she realised that what she had been smelling without knowing it was the scent of freshly cut timber.

She walked up to Baggot Street and turned right, away from the canal. The heels of her flat shoes made a deadened tapping on the pavement. It was lunchtime on a weekday but it felt more like a Sunday twilight. The city seemed almost deserted, and the few people she met flickered past sinisterly, like phantoms. She was reasoning with herself. The fact that she had not seen or heard from April since the middle of the previous week did not mean April had been gone for that long—it did not mean she was gone at all. And yet not a word in all that length of time, not even a phone call? With someone else a week's silence might not be remarked, but April was the kind of person people worried about, not because she was unable to look after herself but because she was altogether too sure she could.

The lamps were lit on either side of the door of the Shelbourne Hotel, they glowed eerily, like giant dandelion clocks. The caped and frock-coated porter, idling at the door, lifted his grey top hat and saluted her. She would have asked Jimmy Minor to meet her in the hotel but Jimmy disdained such a swank place and would not set foot in it unless he was following up on a story or interviewing some visiting notable. She passed on, crossing Kildare Street, and went down the area steps to the Country Shop. Even through her glove she could feel how cold and greasily wet the stair-rail was. Inside, though, the little café was warm and bright, with a comforting fug of tea and baked bread and cakes. She took a table by the window. There were a few other customers, all of them women, in hats, with shopping bags and parcels. Phoebe asked for a pot of tea and an egg sandwich. She might have waited to order until Jimmy came but she knew he would be late, as he always was—deliberately, she suspected, for he liked to have it thought that he was so much busier than everyone else. The waitress was a large pink girl with a double chin and a sweet smile. There was a wen wedged in the groove beside her left nostril that Phoebe tried not to stare at. The tea that she brought was almost black, and bitter with tannin. The sandwich, cut in neat triangles, was slightly curled at the corners.

Where was April now, at this moment, and what was she doing? For she must be somewhere, even if not here. Any other possibility was not to be entertained.

A half-hour passed before Jimmy arrived. She saw him through the window skipping down the steps and she was struck as always by how slight he was, a miniature person, more like a wizened schoolboy than a man. He wore a transparent plastic raincoat the colour of watery ink. He had thin red hair and a narrow, freckled face, and was always dishevelled, as if he had been sleeping in his clothes and had just jumped out of bed. He was putting a match to a cigarette as he came through the door. He saw her and crossed to her table and sat down quickly, crushing his raincoat into a ball and stowing it under his chair. Jimmy did everything in a hurry, as if each moment were a deadline he was afraid he was about to miss. 'Well, Pheeb,' he said, 'what's up?' There were sparkles of moisture in his otherwise lifeless hair. The collar of his brown corduroy jacket bore a light snowfall of dandruff, and when he leaned forward she caught a whiff of his tobacco-staled breath. Yet he had the sweetest smile, it was always a surprise, lighting up that pinched, sharp little face. It was one of his amusements to pretend that he was in love with Phoebe, and he would complain theatrically to anyone prepared to listen of her cruelty and hard-heartedness in refusing to entertain his advances. He was a crime reporter on the *Evening Mail*, though surely there were not enough crimes committed in this sleepy city to keep him as busy as he claimed to be.

She told him about April and how long it was since she had heard from her. 'Only a week?' Jimmy said. 'She's probably gone off with some guy. She is slightly notorious, you know.' Jimmy affected an accent from the movies; it had started as a joke at his own expense—'Jimmy Minor, ace reporter, at your service, lady!'—but it had become a habit and now he seemed not to notice how it grated on those around him who had to put up with it.

'If she was going somewhere,' Phoebe said, 'she would have let me know, I'm sure she would.'

The waitress came and Jimmy ordered a glass of ginger beer and a beef sandwich—'Plenty of horseradish, baby, slather it on, I like it hot.' He pronounced it *hat*. The girl tittered. When she had gone he whistled softly and said, 'That's some wart.'

'Wen,' Phoebe said.

'What?'

'It's a wen, not a wart.'

Jimmy had finished his cigarette and now he lit a new one. No one smoked as much as Jimmy did; he had once told Phoebe that he often found himself wishing he could have a smoke while he was already smoking, and that indeed on more than one occasion he had caught himself lighting a cigarette even though the one he had going was there in the ash-tray in front of him. He leaned back on the chair and crossed one of his stick-like little legs on the other and blew a bugle-shaped stream of smoke at the ceiling. 'So what do you think?' he said.

Phoebe was stirring a spoon round and round in the cold dregs in her cup. 'I think something has happened to her,' she said quietly.

He gave her a quick, sideways glance. 'Are you really worried? I mean, really?'

She shrugged, not wanting to seem melodramatic, not giving him cause to laugh at her. He was still watching her sidelong, frowning. At a party one night in her flat he had told her he thought her friendship with April Latimer was funny, and added: 'Funny peculiar, that's to say, not funny ha ha.' He had been a little drunk and afterwards they had tacitly agreed to pretend to have forgotten this exchange, but the fact of what he had implied lingered between them uncomfortably. And laugh it off though she might, it had made Phoebe brood, and the memory of it still troubled her, a little.

'You're probably right, of course,' she said now. 'Probably it's just April being April, skipping off and forgetting to tell anyone.'

But no, she did not believe it; she could not. Whatever else April might be she was not thoughtless like that, not where her friends were concerned.

The waitress came with Jimmy's order. He bit a half-moon from his sandwich and, chewing, took a deep draw of his cigarette. 'What about the Prince of Bongo-Bongoland?' he asked thickly. He swallowed hard, blinking from the effort. '—Have you made enquiries of His Majesty?' He was smiling now but there was a glitter to his smile and the sharp tip of an eye-tooth showed for a second at the side. He was jealous of Patrick Ojukwu; all the men in their circle were jealous of Patrick, nicknamed the Prince. She often wondered, in a troubled and troubling way, about Patrick and April—had they, or had they not? It had all the makings of a juicy scandal, the wild white girl and the polished black man.

'More to the point,' Phoebe said, 'what about Mrs Latimer?'

Jimmy made a show of starting back as if in terror, throwing up a hand. 'Hold up!' he cried. 'The blackamoor is one thing but Morgan Le Fay is another altogether.' April's mother had a fearsome reputation among April's friends.

'I should telephone her, though. She must know where April is.'

Jimmy arched an eyebrow sceptically. 'You think so?'

He was right to doubt it, she knew. April had long ago stopped confiding in her mother; in fact, the two were barely on speaking terms.

'What about her brother, then?' she said.

Jimmy laughed at that. 'The Grand Gynie of Fitzwilliam Square, plumber to the quality, no pipe too small to probe?'

'Don't be disgusting, Jimmy.' She took a drink of her tea but it was cold. 'Although I know April doesn't like him.'

'Doesn't like? Try loathes.'

'Then what should I do?' she asked.

He sipped his ginger beer and grimaced and said plaintively: 'Why you can't meet in a pub like any normal person I don't know.' He seemed already to have lost interest in the topic of April's whereabouts. They spoke desultorily of other things for a while, then he took up his cigarettes and matches and fished his raincoat from under his chair and said he had to go. Phoebe signalled to the waitress to bring the bill—she knew she would have to pay, Jimmy was always broke—and presently they were climbing to the street up the damp, slimed steps. At the top, Jimmy put a hand on her arm. 'Don't worry,' he said. '—About April, I mean. She'll turn up.'

A faint, warmish smell of dung came to them from across the street, where by the railings of the Green there was a line of horse-drawn jaunting-cars that offered tours of the city. In the fog they had a spectral air, the horses standing unnaturally still with heads lowered dejectedly and the caped and top-hatted drivers perched in attitudes of motionless expectancy on their high seats, as if awaiting imminent word to set off for the Borgo Pass or Dr Jekyll's rooms.

'You going back to work?' Jimmy asked. He was glancing about with eyes narrowed; clearly in his mind he was already somewhere else.

'No,' Phoebe said. 'It's my half-day off.' She took a breath and felt the wet air swarm down coldly into her chest. 'I'm going to see someone. My—my father, actually. I suppose you wouldn't care to come along?'

He did not meet her eye, and busied himself lighting another cigarette, turning aside and crouching over his cupped hands. 'Sorry,' he said, straightening. 'Crimes to expose, stories to concoct, reputations to besmirch—no rest for the busy newshound.' He was a good half-head shorter than she was; his plastic coat gave off a chemical odour. 'See you around, kid.' He set off in the direction of Grafton Street, but stopped and turned and came back again. 'By the way,' he said, 'what's the difference between a wen and a wart?'

When he had gone she stood for a while, irresolute, slowly pulling on her calfskin gloves. She had that heart-sinking feeling she had at this time every Thursday when the weekly visit to her father was in prospect. Today, however, there was an added sense of unease. She could not think why she had asked Jimmy to meet her—what had she imagined he would say or do that would assuage her fears? There had been something odd in his manner, she had felt it the moment she mentioned April's long silence; an evasiveness, a shiftiness, almost. She was well aware of the simmering antipathy between her two so dissimilar friends. In some way Jimmy seemed jealous of April, as he was of Patrick Ojukwu. Or was it more resentment than jealousy? But if so, what was it in April that he found to resent? The Latimers of Dun Laoghaire were gentry, of course, but Jimmy would think she was, too, and he did not seem to hold it against her. She gazed across the street at the coaches and their intently biding jarveys. She was surer than ever that something bad, something very bad, perhaps the very worst of all, had befallen her friend.

Then a new thought struck her, one that made her more uneasy still. What if Jimmy were to see in April's disappearance the possibility of a story, a 'great yarn', as he would say? What if he had only pretended to be indifferent, and had rushed off now to tell his editor that April Latimer, a junior doctor at the Hospital of the Holy Family, the 'slightly notorious' daughter of the late and much lamented Conor Latimer and niece of the present Minister of Health, had not been heard from in over a week? Oh, Lord, she thought in dismay, what have I done?

picador.com

blog
videos
interviews
extracts